GW00870741

For Tobias and Jess

You'll never know what you
can do until you do it

Love
Dad

An Escaping Angel and Other Matters of National
Importance

By Stephen Hall

ISBN-13:978-1511828543

2015

PREFACE

The imposition of the extremes of 'Political Correctness' is not a sound basis on which to tamper with the foundations of the conduct of humanity; be it our own personal environment through to global interaction depending on your position and view. Many are outspoken in the cause of freedom of speech and democracy. I am one of the many. Political correctness characterized by respect for our fellow man and bereft of prejudice is fine, but if and when it frightens us into self-conscious silence, it robs our lives of their colour. Justice is escaping control and taking up residence in the ether. For Cesare Beccaria read the Worldwide Web Social Media.

In my own country, which I am devoted to just as anyone would be, to wherever they began their life, our politicians come straight from school. I love my country; its glorious and blighted past, its diversity of geography and culture; its apron of rolling ocean and sea and its seams of national borders. If I were a bird I would need my right wing and my left wing in order to function as a bird. I am a bird. In my country politics has either a right wing or a left, and as such the school leavers fly round in circles. These circles are ever decreasing, but they are politically correcting us in accordance with the demands of www.socialmedia.com.

The English language is also something that I enjoy the richness and subtlety of. This is the first of a series of continuous stories using, I hope, the colours and rhythms of the language to bring to life characters and their experiences embroidered with details, found and imagined. These are stories without the political correctness that mires our lives. In them taboos are unmasked and the world in which we live is celebrated. I hope that you will be patient with the detail and enjoy the heart of these stories.

CONTENTS

PROLOGUE

At the centre of this story is the Walpole family, Thomas and Veronica and their children Terrence, Rosemary and Winston. This story is about the twelfth birthday of Winston, a late addition to the family and the series of events that unfolded throughout the day. As this is the first in a series of stories about the Walpole family it introduces several characters who will bring depth and breadth to the narrative. These characters include a Chieftain from Burkina Faso, an old Polish man who survived Auschwitz, a dwarf and a barber; with a special mention for the local television stations roving reporter.

Thomas is an English man married to a wife of Irish descent, they share a normal life together. Veronica keeps home and binds the family. Thomas manages the ironmonger's store. Terrence is a young policeman and Rosemary works in the Haberdashery. Winston is a dearly loved boy and the apple of his Auntie Gloria and Uncle Frank's eye.

It is Uncle Frank's birthday 'treat' for his nephew that lays at the heart of this first story. What begins as an innocent flight in a balloon, ends up as an international incident, due in the main to meteorological influences. Regional television news punctuates the day telling its own story. Life carries on throughout, oblivious of the growing danger to the young Winston and the Anglo-French relations.

THE BIRTHDAY BOY(S)

The telephone rang in number thirteen Captain Scott Terrace at precisely seven twenty three ante meridian. Thomas Walpole, the half shaved man of the house, laid his five blade gossamer glide safety razor in the moulded soap tray of the stressed glaze Victorian style bathroom sink, and headed across the landing and down the stairs, pulling, retying and tightening his pyjama cord as he went, two steps at a time.

"Thomas, can you get that please." his wife Veronica called from their bedroom, just as he picked up the telephone receiver in the hallway.

Thomas put the receiver to the unshaved, lathered side of his face. He emitted a phlegm gargled growl in clearing his throat which sprayed a mist of shaving soap onto the hall mirror above the telephone table. He could hear a distant voice calling as he swapped the foam flecked receiver over to the shaved side of his reflection and pressed it to his ear.

"Hello." said a voice.

"Yes." replied Thomas Walpole.

"Oh good. Is that Mister Thomas Walpole?" a voice asked in an accent imbued with the lilt of Gujarati.

"Yes it is." replied Thomas.

"Of number thirteen Captain Scott Terrace?"

"Yes it is." Thomas interrupted his interrogator.

"Ah that is good. My name is Aadesh and I have a very important piece of information for you from the Sarasvati Communication Company. SCC for short."

"Who is it?" called Veronica.

"One of Prateep's relatives I shouldn't wonder." said Thomas "Wrong blasted number no doubt."

Prateep Talati is the shopkeeper who runs the 'Five Thirty/Eleven

6

Thirty' shop at the end of George Street, in which Captain Scott Terrace and several other turn of the twentieth century, terraced or otherwise houses stand. Prateep's shop was formerly known as the 'Bunny's Store' (it was previously owned by Bertram and Bernice Bernard, a brother and sister partnership who ran it for a mild mannered lifetime of bachelor/spinsterhood). The shop is situated at the corner of the street that includes Captain Scott Terrace in its long opposite rows of Victorian dwellings. Prateep had renamed the shop using the 'Seven/Eleven' principle celebrated in the land of the free. 'God Bless America'. Prateep however, clearly had not grasped the rhythm of poetry in the same way that he had understood the rhyme and reason of commerce, extending the opening hours to maximize his income from the human traffic to and fro the three shift work pattern at Blenkinsopp's; the town's major employer...

"Not everyone from India has a relative called Prateep." Veronica answered.

"My brother is Prateep. Do you know him?" continued Aadesh the caller from the Sarasvati Communication Company "and I am pleased to tell you that you are entitled to a new complimentary mobile telephone Mr Thomas Walpole."

"I don't want a complimentary mobile telephone" said Thomas "and I would like to know where you are calling from and how you obtained my name and my telephone number?"

Thomas Walpole did not possess a mobile telephone. In fact, the possession of a mobile telephone was a very sensitive subject for Mr and Mrs Walpole because Thomas had made a stand on the subject and refused to own one, on the basis that it was an 'invasion of his privacy'. Despite the fact that Veronica had coyly suggested, as only a loving wife could that when the 'mood' took her, he might *like* her to invade *his* privacy. He had smiled, thought for a moment and replied;

"That is a completely different invasion of an utterly unique privacy. Nice try beautiful, but I will not be the owner of a mobile phone this side of the grave and I suspect that the good Lord has already invoked the thirteenth commandment; 'thou shalt not bring with you into heaven thy mobile phone, nor any such device that relies upon licensed banditry, as it interferes with the intricate function of the soul."

Thomas had remained firm on the subject of the non-ownership of a mobile phone.

"It is the number one UK business call centre of the Sarasvati Communication Company." said Aadesh "She is a very important Goddess and I can tell you are a religious man Mr Thomas Walpole."

"Is she? Very good. And what is the time in your UK call centre?" Thomas asked.

"It is seven minutes to one in the afternoon, no less."

"Well you're not exactly calling from Newcastle then are you?"

"Not exactly no."

"Neither are you calling to curry my favour from the extremis of Cape Wrath, The Lizard, Ardnamurchan, Lowestoft, or any point within this sceptered isle." There was a pause. "More like ruddy Delhi then?"

"You are a very clever man Mr Thomas Walpole. 'Curry.' Very good." said Aadesh 'employee of that particular week' of the Sarasvati Communication Company, Delhi branch.

"Indeed I Am." said Mr Walpole "And yet my cleverness does not protect me from the retribution served upon me by the history of the old empire"

"Pardon Mr Walpole" said Aadesh, but Thomas ploughed on.

"*I* have a question for *you*" Veronica sat up in the bed anticipating the worst "What are you like on the subject of human anatomy as opposed to the art of hard selling to the unsuspecting defenceless descendants of the once imperious architects of that forgotten empire eh?!"

"I am not sure if I follow you."

"Do you know where your Aristotle is?"

"I know that Aristotle knew some things about anatomy because that is what I am studying at university" said Aadesh "I am going to be a doctor very soon.

"Well I want you to take my complimentary mobile telephone and…"

"Thomas!" shouted Veronica rushing out onto the landing too late.

"…your Aristotle."

Thomas Walpole concluded the conversation, replacing the telephone receiver with celerity.

"Who was that unfortunate soul?" called his wife from the landing of number thirteen Captain Scott Terrace as she approached the bedroom door of their youngest son Winston.

"Another one of those bewildering sales people working from a call centre we have transplanted from the proud North East to the far reaches of the British Commonwealth."

"Oh well, at least you were able to understand them then." his wife replied as she burst into her young son's bedroom after three faint knocks on his door.

"True" replied Thomas after pondering his wife's remark "I hadn't thought of that. He will probably end up over here as our doctor Praline Chipolata or whatever his name is. I can just imagine with the way the National Health Service is going he'll be texting his 'grumpy old men' patients about their prostrates and their piles on mobile phones he sold to them as a student."

"Thomas, go and finish your shave it's your son's big day" said Veronica "he doesn't need to hear you preaching."

"I'm not preaching I am expressing an inevitable conclusion."

"Happy Birthday Winston." shouted Veronica Walpole as she whipped a pile of eiderdown off the bed to expose her younger son to the dawn of his twelfth birthday.

"Mum." shouted Winston

"Goodness gracious Winston where are your pyjamas?!" she cried, trying to look everywhere but at her naked offspring, who was trying to flick his outstretched foot free from a twist of taut linen bed sheet that his mother still held, in order to get up from the bed.

"Under my pillow." he said, curling up into a foetal ball.

"Why?" she exclaimed.

"Because you never come in to wake me" said Winston, which was absolutely true. Veronica had been quietly wondering to herself in recent days how her son managed not to crease his Winceyette pyjamas, or sully them with the suffused odour of summer sleep. Winston would not give up his Winceyette pyjamas in preference to cotton the year round, because he loved the softness of them even when he wasn't wearing them.

(I need to invent a word for adolescent sensuality that can be understood as describing an emotional experience of the spirit in the context of total innocence. I could have used it at this point).

"But it's your birthday." continued his mother.

"I know. I've got my birthday suit on." said Winston.

Veronica turned away and placed a parcel on Winston's bedroom chair. It was wrapped in shiny, stiff brown paper and tied with a piece of sinewy sisal.

"This is a present from your Granny O'Flannagan" she said "I think it is something she has made especially for you to wear on this auspicious day. I do think the needlework classes at St Audry's are quite helping your Gran; she can remember her purl stitch and cable needle even though she forgets what day it is two minutes after I tell her."

Winston stared through the arch of his armpit as he remained tightly curled against exposure to his poor parent and pondered the hidden contents with some trepidation. "Come on open it Winsey" said his mother "I wish Granny O'Flannagan could be here to see you."

"Okay" said Winston "but don't look."

His mother drew the bedroom curtains apart and opened the window. A breath of cool air chilled Winston's skin. He pulled at the bed sheet to protect himself. The sheet was anchored in folds under his buttocks, his grip slipped and his hand involuntarily slapped a rather tender part; the trouser fly of his birthday suit. Winston let out a pained cry.

"Stop complaining." said his mother looking out of the window, oblivious of his having hit himself "Your Gran always makes you a lovely present you, know she does."

Winston had curled into an even tighter ball, his eyes watering as he clutched the emergent jewels of pubescence.

"It's no good trying to cover yourself now Winsey the damage is done, we are, you and I, both embarrassed" said his mother "pretending to hurt yourself carries no weight with me."

Winston was twelve years old and celebrating his birthday on a Saturday. This was great because it meant a whole day of birthday without the punctuation of school, and the inevitable gang of class mates tossing him in the air; stirred up and spurred on by their mixed motives; the observation of someone else's suffering and the participation of inflicting it. They would count out his age and take him to the point of skeletal dislocation in all his main joints. Their juvenile strength unable to control his descent through the tension in his stretched limbs, so dropping him, on the post-ultimate birthday bump with the joyous proclamation 'and one for luck' as they bruise the cheeks of his bum (gluteus maximus and medius) and crack the back of his head (calvarium). Hooray for Saturday birthdays, they are the best closely followed by Sunday's, only because there are still a few more things to do on a Saturday.

It is one of life's disturbing rites of passage to lay, coccyx throbbing, painfully stunned and in tears beneath a shroud of so called 'friends' all grinning down at you and wishing you a 'Happy Birthday'. The violence of such friendship once brought me to the precipice of an emotional trauma twenty fathoms under the sea of inexpressible human experience. Perhaps my need to drag out this lost root to some of my disproportionate, misunderstood responses to life will be met by telling you about this very rite of passage that I once so stoically endured.

It was the custom on your birthday in my primary school class to have bestowed upon you the honorary appointment of milk monitor for the day, irrespective of who had been appointed the class monitor for the week. Our school milkman was Dudley 'Dud' Duddington who delivered milk from the Co-op dairy. Dudley had 'lardy' hands with fingers like sausages, his head was attached directly to his shoulders which meant the collar of his uniform tucked neatly under the lobes of his ears and his chin hid the knot of his tie, his voice came out through his nose and I am sure was filtered through bogeys, producing a unique musicality akin to nasal flatulence. He would drive up in his Cooperative Wholesale Society Float with its electric engine and leave a tower of seven steel crates of milk by the cycle sheds. In the winter birds would perforate and peel back the foil lids on the glass bottles and pilfer the cream.

I remember my tenth birthday. I had distributed the glass bottles with a third of a pint of classroom curdled milk to all my 'friends' and those, who could, had taken theirs into the cloakroom and poured it down the stone sink. Then teacher, who had not taken her beady eyes off me declared 'bumps'. The class surged forward sweeping me out into the playground at the bidding of the teacher, Miss Thickness. As I oscillated between the stormy sky and Gods firm earth, piloted by a mixture of weak nine and ten year olds, I could feel the slap of regulation issue school milk in my bladder.

Reginald Botwright, who normally sat next to me at our double desk, and lived next door to me on our street, had been absent with a bout of diarrhoea and Miss Thickness had insisted that I drink Reginald's one third of a pint of free school milk on top, quite literally, of my own, as it was my birthday and I 'deserved' it. I hated the taste of free school milk. I hated trying to remove the impenetrable leaden foil cap. I hated putting my lips to the sour cream around the top of the glass bottle and I hated the thought of swallowing any of the congealing clots. Having to drink the milk including the birthday extra, whilst feigning appreciation of the considerable honour bestowed upon me in front of Miss Thickness, and the waiting birthday bumps press gang, fully strained my ability to stifle a retch. I let go, and the cartwheeling projectile follow through smacked against the classroom boiler and hissed as it coursed sizzling down the piping hot cast iron. 'Hooray' they had shouted (Hooray?! I remember thinking).

At the top of each 'birthday bump' a tidal wave of milk crashed against the pre-pubescent sluice gate of my bladder. Each time it repelled the gathering swell. Each time I hit the pinnacle of my ascent letting out a heaving bark that burned in my throat as I involuntarily gargled clots of curdled cream. 'Six, seven, eight,' my so called 'friends' screamed. On the count of eight I felt that awful feeling, that single inordinate droplet of 'wee' escape into the soft white blotting cotton of my 'Co-operative Wholesale Society' underpants. On the count of nine I was concentrating all the clenching power of my *Gluteus medius* and *Maximus* muscle on locking that sluice gate but right at the top of the 'birthday bump' I experienced a millisecond of weightlessness, a cosmonaut moment when all tension was uncontrollably released, and with it probably about one third of the 'extra' one third of a pint of bladder warm, viscose, free school milk. If only I had then, the gnarled, knurled and nobbled prostate that I have now, it would not have happened. On the count of ten the other two thirds of the one third of the imperial pint issued forth. On the principle of last to enter first to leave combined with warm rises above cold, it was definitely Reginald Botwright's one third of a pint not mine; a gross injustice. I felt the shiver that my Grandma always said was 'someone just walking over my grave', I wretched mightily. Everyone screamed "And one for luck" except Elizabeth Solomon who screamed her disgust because she was supporting my left buttock through my warming, coarse, wet 'Co-operative Wholesale Society' grey flannel shorts, while bladder warm, fresh, kidney filtered, free school urinary milk trickled down her feminine forearm and dribbled from her funny bone.

Salvation was a puddle into which the children on my right side had walked backwards due to the strength of the group of children throwing me from the left being reinforced by Elizabeth Solomon screaming 'Miss he is weeing himself'. As I hit the ground for the last time, I rolled theatrically into the puddle obliterating my shame. Elizabeth Solomon was administered a humiliating reprimand by Miss Thickness for claiming that I had wet myself, a reprimand made worse by Elizabeth offering up her arm and telling Miss Thickness to smell it.

'Make a wish' shouted Rory Aylett. I wished Reginald Botwright all the diarrhoea in the world.

For Winston this would be a celebration free from the anxiety that accompanies the prospect of the birthday bumps. Saturday is the day named after the majestic Roman god Saturn, the Holy Sabbath day of the Jewish nation and 'Löverdag' to our pillaging Viking ancestors. Saturday was also the bath-day of the Vikings, a tradition upheld in the home of my own childhood.

Saturday night was always 'tin' bath night in front of the stove. On the other six days of the week, I received the rasp of course flannel followed by the burn of poor quality towelling up and down my delicate skin, whilst trying to breathe through the *pungent balsam of coal tar soap as I stood in a shallow bowl of tepid water on the kitchen floor beside the 'coke stove'. Being the oldest child I always got the scummy water that my siblings had already been scrubbed in. Maybe that's why the congealing clots of school milk scum generated such emotions in me.*

GILBERT HERRING

Becoming twelve years of age gave Winston mixed emotions, very different from the emotions he felt on his tenth birthday when he was overjoyed to be in double figures. Becoming twelve would, according to the half whispered scaremongering of his older brother, mark the eruption of puberty a subject that was beginning to arouse the emotional hinterland of Winston and his two great friends Ezra and Osborne, as the nascent, hormonal swirl of manhood began to transmogrify their child bodies. According to a legend peddled by his brother Terry, the growing of 'the manly wool' was paramount. It had to be 'grown' in time for the first cross country run of the winter term at secondary school, otherwise the winter could be long, and washing off the rigours of sport humiliating. Each torturous race ended with the regulatory communal shower into which every boy would be thrust shivering at the command of the PE master. Failure to 'sport the Brillo' led to deeply damaging derision. The pubic euphemism Brillo referred to a coarse pad of wire wool impregnated with soap and used for scouring saucepans. Terry terrified Winston, Ezra and Osborne with tales combining a rubbery glue that smelt of fish and various hilarious hairstyles that were the result of attempts to hide latent puberty beneath hastily applied 'wigs' made from lumps of hair cut indiscriminately from the heads of their wearers and pasted into their groin with Copydex, the product of one Jim Bean Sherwood. The rumour was of course the pure invention of a brother with a wicked sense of humour.

However, I have to admit that I knew a boy in my class at school who was very serious about science, quite an intense soul really. One afternoon we had returned to the changing rooms following a game of football played out on the school playing field in which we had stumbled about in a driving blizzard that branded flakes of freezing snow to our cotton shorts, short sleeved shirts and every square inch of our exposed and smarting skin. As we tried to untie thick wet pyjama cord laces with frozen fingers to which blood was hurriedly and horribly painfully returning, this boy suddenly announced that he had to date fifty seven puberty hairs because he had counted them. From that point until he disappeared off to university he was known as 'Heinz' after the beans and the other fifty six canned varieties. The very serious boy was recently knighted for his contribution to the world of cosmetic surgery.

What really happened to generations of young boys was much simpler and yet profound. Each boy exposed to this communal slippery scrum developed coping mechanisms that would range from sheer bravura to emotional breakdown somewhere on the road through life. Polite society has a serpent's underbelly of scarring rituals ignoring humanity while the ideals of the political and irresponsible populace desire for human rights ravage morality like maggots inside road kill.

Birthdays are special occasions. Celebrated or not they mark the inexorable march of time unappeased, pleasing many and pitying few. Winston had, a couple of years previous, witnessed but not understood the torture that passing into another decade of life had, uncharacteristically, caused his father some anguish. One Saturday morning, having returned from his regular visit to the hairdresser Thomas Walpole had been challenged by his wife over a change in his hairstyle. His only hairstyle. It had been longer in his younger days and thicker. The colour was beginning to lighten, 'salt and pepper' Veronica called it but colour is not style. The local barber is Mr Gilbert Herring, the second of three generations of hairdressing Herrings, the heir of Horace Herring and Pater of Perry Herring. Gilbert was barber to four generations of the town's men folk but always of the 'anything for the weekend sir?' school of hairdresser. Gilbert's craft was classic in style and timeless in execution knowingly in and out of fashion with the younger generation and the male menopause but thoroughly reliable, an absolute constant. The local tobacconist had been hounded out of business by the health guerrilla's unrelenting campaign for pure air. Ironically a political blitzkrieg had been directed from within the anti-smoking crusade bus that toured the area during local elections belching black clouds of noxious diesel fumes from an ancient engine that drank fossil fuel at a rate of gallons to the mile. Two butcher's, three bakers and a greengrocer had been bullied into retirement by painted yellow lines outside their establishments and the offer from the 'out of town' supermarkets of free car-parking, cheap alcohol and imported meats from dubious sources. Now everyone who smokes also has to drive to collect their cigarettes. Only the hairdressers, haberdashers and the hardware of the ironmonger, remains sacrosanct in the high street.

On the subject of the town's barber it is worth spending a moment, to acquaint you with Gilbert because his life is an interesting chronicle. The shop front advertises 'Herring's Parlour of Tonsorial Excellence' in bold lettering and retains a red and white spiral stripe barber's pole which he inserts into a socket on the facade of his barbershop, at an angle of about thirty degrees to the door post, every day from Tuesday to Saturday. By tradition Gilbert Herring is closed Mondays and attends St Edmunds the local Church and afterwards, across the road, the public house the Goat and Compasses on Sundays. On the first Monday of every month he visits the old people's home in the town to cut the hair of the doddering old men and one rather severe old lady. She is the scion of once landed gentry. As a young woman she had driven a tipping lorry for the local gravel works during the war delivering ballast for building runways to launch Spitfires and Hurricanes, Wellington's and Lancaster's. In her prime she was considered a somewhat androgynous soul who spent a great deal of her time dressed in baggy khaki exploring remote sites of antiquity including potholes and pyramids, deserts and dense jungles. She was rumoured to have married and buried a Bedouin, breeder of Camels, whilst abroad on one of her many expeditions.

Gilbert employs a historically significant, pneumatically elevated, leather upholstered barber's chair. The chair is one of a pair his father Horace bought at auction in 1936. It had been salvaged from the barbershop of the White Star liner the RMS Olympic. The ship was nicknamed the 'Old Reliable' because she had served as a troop ship in the First World War. RMS Olympic was the older sister ship to the RMS Titanic and HMHS Britannic, she was built in the Belfast shipyard of Harland and Wolff. There is framed certificate, rumoured to be a fake, hanging in the shop claiming that the ill-fated Captain E J Smith of Titanic notoriety was the first customer to grace the pneumatic chair as the then, newly appointed, commanding officer of the RMS Olympic. The other chair of the pair was retired when Gilbert's son and heir Perry Herring turned his back on the family business to seek his fortune plying his trade as a photographer of 'glamorous' ladies, in the capital. Some of Gilbert's clientele would occasionally try to tease him with examples of his son's photographic 'genius' that they had found in the pile of dog eared magazines Gilbert retained for their entertainment while they waited on a row of hard wooden chairs. The other barber's chair of the pair was bought for posterity by Frank O'Flannagan the brother of Veronica Walpole. Gilbert Herring 'pumps' the historic chair with what he refers to as his 'good' leg. His other ('bad' *I suppose*) leg was injured during active service in World War two. Gilbert served King and country as the regimental barber to the First Battalion Suffolk regiment. During service and as part of the 3rd Division of the British Expeditionary Force that fought in France and Belgium in 1940 he was evacuated from Dunkirk on one of the treasured 'little ships'. He had managed to climb aboard the auxiliary gaff cutter the 'Providence' a carvel construction of pitch-pine on grown oaks hewn from the banks of the Helford River and built by Gilbert & Pascoe. Gilbert Herring had the salt sea seared into his soul by the suffering of the long night of June 2nd 1940, the night Gilbert was evacuated as part of the 'miraculous delivery' that had been prayed for by the nation and provided when God's angels held back the enemy on the French banks of the English Channel. Perhaps there will time for more of Gilbert later, it suffices to say his other leg had originally been his 'pumping' leg and though being tone deaf he was enrolled into the choir of St Edmunds at the ripe old age of thirteen appointed to relieve Arthur Harrison of the duty of pumping the Church organ whenever Arthur's gout got the better of him. The church organ at the time had a wooden lever for pumping, by hand, the bellows that supplied the pressurized air to the organ pipes. Arthur Harrison had fought for Queen and Country in the second Boer war and had been injured at the battle of Spoin Kop in January 1900 so when he returned home from war to his voluntary duty as the 'second' organ pump man at St Edmunds the lever was adapted for pumping by leg through the attachment of a stirrup. When Arthur was asked to train a young Gilbert Herring as part of St Edmunds succession planning, he instinctively trained Gilbert to pump with his, later to be injured, leg rather than with the strength of his arms. This is a fine example of irony.

Gilbert Herring supplements the height of the barber's chair with the addition of an upturned wooden crate. This is for little boys to sit on to experience their first few haircuts or until they reach a stature measured between their bottom and the nape of their neck that is sufficient to prevent Gilbert having to stoop to clip away at his art. The wooden crate had once brought avocado pears (*Persea Americana*) all the way from Surinam to Sackville's the delicatessen next door in 1954. The bottom of the crate is reinforced with wire stapled over every join and covered with a remnant of Wilton carpet as padding. The carpet is a deep rich hue the colour of the wine of the Syrah and sprinkled with a pattern of gold fleur-de-lis. Mr Herring keeps a leather strop with which he sharpens his cut throat razors and he uses steaming hot towels as a pre-shave ripener. His price list includes the following options a wash and cut, a dry cut (at half price for boys up to the age of 14), a beard trim for the full face and a half face with a moustache and sideburns at a correspondingly reduced rate and a full wet shave. He also trims the hair from the lobe and orifice of older men's ears as well as the wiry hairs that spring from their eyebrows. He offers a complimentary nasal singeing for the stoic amongst his congregation. It is complimentary simply because anyone undignified enough to have their nasal hairs singed involuntarily entertains Gilbert and his waiting customers, Gilbert then passes round an old bowler hat in the manner of a street performer and any contributions are sent to the local orphanage.

I once sniffed a lighted match on the advice of a so called friend to try to rid myself of burgeoning nasal hairs at a time when I was also suffering from a prolonged bout of hay fever. The inescapable smell of barbequed bogeys is unpleasant and words cannot describe the days of pain I suffered as I continuously expelled the fine grains of pollen, like a sandstorm scouring the delicate domed pustules of my blistered snout, with uncontrollable sneezing. The torturer's rack would be a picnic in comparison. Today my nasal hair grows in sheaves which I scythe weekly in front of my magnifying shaving mirror in despair.

Winston will never forget his first time in Gilbert Herring's chair. The coarse tufts of carpet irritated the backs of his legs and he felt very silly as, with each pump of Mr Gilbert's 'good' leg, his head began to grow from the bottom of the vast gilt framed mirror that hung over the old vitreous clay sink in front of him. The cold steel of Gilbert Herring's scissors made him squirm and the cascading fine hair of his shortening fringe made him squint so much that his mother kept up simultaneous streams of humiliating apology to the bewildered barber and scolding for the wriggling Winston who finally burst into tears at the scrape of Gilbert Herring's cut throat razor on the soft skin of his infant neck. The Barber had congratulated Winston on his first trim as he held a silver flask of cold water in one hand and pumped a rubber lung with the other spraying a fine mist onto Winston's new mown hair. The chilling caress of Gilberts vapour acted as a balm and the salt tears dried on his quivering lip.

I apologize for wandering off down this little diversion but Gilbert Herring and others like him have lived lives that are such a rich source of interesting facts that to not tell you a little about them is to deny you of some of the more unusual colours of life's rich tapestry. I must however return the reader to number thirteen Captain Scott Terrace and the day, around the time of Thomas Walpole's fiftieth birthday that Winston witnessed a rare but mild spat between his parents. As Veronica Walpole considered her husbands 'new' hairstyle she said,

"I hadn't heard that Gilbert Herring had died or retired for that matter" as if it was better to die than to retire, "has he retired Thomas?"

"Gilbert didn't cut my hair this morning thank you my dear." Winston's father replied.

"He *hasn't* died has he?" Winston's mother continued a little shamefully.

"No" answered Winston's father "he was in the Goat and Compasses last Sunday lunch time."

Veronica changed tack and enquired "Has that perverse and prodigal son of his finally given up the seedy photography down in London and returned to the respectability of the family business?"

"Not as far as I know and anyway your brother Frank has the other chair so he cannot return now can he."

"Disgraceful way to make a living photographing them girls," Veronica pondered "has Gilbert sold the business then?"

"I don't think so."

Veronica waited for the explanation she was clearly fishing for, Thomas in turn waited for his wife's patience to give way. Winston looked at his father and saw mischief.

"Then who cut your hair?" Veronica asked.

"Are we playing twenty questions?"

Winston tried to remember how many questions his mother had used already.

"Oh come on Tom who cut your hair?" There followed quite a long silence filled with an exchange of looks between Winston's mother and father that ranged from her earnestly coaxing, to him contemplating his wife winsomely.

"Cassandra if you must know." said Thomas Walpole after a long pause.

"Cassandra" exclaimed Veronica "Cassandra of Cassandrablanca the Unisex hair salon in the high street next to that Leticia's Luxury Lingerie?"

"For the discerning lady" said Winston's father with a shameless flourish "correct."

"Ooooh Thomas how could you go anywhere near there?" she asked "it's for girls and men who probably should have been girls."

"I pass it every day on the way to the store, and unisex is a phrase that has long since passed into everyday language because it means suitable for both sexes."

Winston was hearing both his parents benignly using the word sex but to him as to many a twelve year old boy it was evocative, a grenade tossed between the two most important adults in his life. Veronica approached her husband with the cup of tea that she had been pouring for him during his interrogation. She put it down purposefully on the table in front of him.

"There's no milk in my tea." he said.

"The milk, George Clooney" she replied "is in the fridge."

Winston's mother stood back and stared at the 'new look' Thomas Walpole. She walked over to the kitchen sink and stood staring out of the window for a few moments then she turned and said.

"You have the hairstyle of the man whose head has gone missing from my home shopping catalogue."

"What man is that?"

"The headless man from the swimwear pages."

"Why do you need to look at men in swimming trunks?" Thomas chided his wife, she ignored his taunt.

"You owe Winston an apology because he did not play football on the green on Tuesday evening as a punishment for mutilating my catalogue which he had strenuously denied and now I can see why poor boy."

Winston had vainly pleaded his innocence at the time over the headless man in the shopping catalogue which had so infuriated his mother who, with only a sensible husband and two adult children one of which is a woman in a happy relationship, had no one to suspect but her twelve year old son. Maternal justice had been swift and absolute, there was no football.

"I thought it would be easier than trying to describe what I wanted" Winston's father protested "and anyway you only buy an ironing board cover every few years from the catalogue oh and those horrible stocking sock things, I don't know why you have it."

"I like to read the whole catalogue and I do not expect you to carry out wanton decapitations." Winston's mother said finishing the conversation with emphasis on the 'read' as if reading distinguished her from those who only look. "You owe your son an apology".

"Winston" his father began "it is written in the family bible that 'A continual dripping in a very rainy day and a contentious woman are alike' I am sorry you carried the can for the headless man but my son learn to be wary of the fairer sex for as you can see they're worse than Sherlock blooming Holmes."

That word again thought Winston what was wrong with his parents. 'Get...no don't get a room'.

A selection of Dictionary definitions of hair read; 'any of the numerous fine, usually cylindrical, keratinous filaments growing from the skin of humans and animals; a pilus' (a hair or hair-like structure), 'an aggregate of such filaments, as that covering the human head or forming the coat of most mammals', 'a similar fine filamentous outgrowth from the body of insects, spiders etc.' However we define hair, for many men (and possibly ladies) our hair defines *us*, sometimes to a dangerous degree. For centuries the mutable commandments of fashion have retained the periwig within its canon. The sexes have worn the hair of other humans (including at some considerable risk, those dying from the plague), for the sake of fashion, the hair of horses, goats and buffalo's, sheep's wool and even feathers, all to shade bald heads from the sun, to portray a thespian character, to fulfil some vain desire and almost always to indulge human vanity. In more recent times wigs have been in the diametric employ of human dignity to disguise the ravages of aggressive cancer therapies, the term side-effect seems infelicitous when used to describe the varying degrees of change to a sufferer's appearance. What we look like is not just a matter of vanity it is profound, it weighs upon us and demands we think. For vanity alone an ocean of viscid products is manufactured every year to ensure that our hair is our crowning glory. Whether natural or dyed (and here I would like to make it clear to anyone, of the carotene ($C_{40}H_{56}$) hue reading this, that it never entered my head to associate hair dye with salvation most especially for you as you hide from the baying throng who seem to think that being a 'ginger' makes you an alien in this universe). Whether real or synthetic, someone somewhere is making a fortune out of the power that the cylindrical keratinous filament has over us all except for the brazen, incurably bald.

Hair does not just grow on our heads and, passing over, for the sake of time, the obvious substratum of substantial hair growth on the human body I want to raise a point of personal suffering. When I was young and downy I longed to become pubescent amongst my pubic peers, to raise my arms proudly above my head and, simultaneously, realize my potential as the shortest basketball player in the school's history whilst letting my underarm forests compete in the masculine arena. I understood masculine simply to mean hirsute and dropped octaves. Postponed puberty is very painful and life changing especially when it finally arrives with an obvious conscience as if to make up for having got distracted along the way. I have been for more years now than I care to count covered in hair from my toes through the lush Pampas that is my back (my children call me the 'Silver Backed Gorilla') to my neck, nose, ears and mutant eyebrows. I like to wear smart shirts but they have to be of such a dense weave because with the 'extra' hair insulating me beneath a fine cotton shirt I end up looking like I am smuggling two peanuts vainly disguised under a dark corset of wet horse hair. I dry myself, after ablutions, with a towel that without fail painlessly drags enough hair from my myriad follicles to carpet a doll's house. I have to hose the bath or the shower pan depending on where I am living, for the benefit of whoever follows me in turn or cleans my hotel room (my day job involves a lot of travelling). I have, as already mentioned, to trim nasal hair and strim the lobes and deep dark wax-ways of my ear holes. Even if I had a reasonable body I

*couldn't possibly show it off on the beach because there must be
public performance laws against wild animal impersonators plying
their trade in the open air and I, at the very least, am sensitive to
the sensibilities of the very young. For me hair is not a matter of
vanity more a curse really. I felt cursed without it and I feel cursed
with it.*

Winston had noticed a few days after the incident
involving the decapitation in the shopping catalogue, that his
father had applied a dull greasy 'substance' to his hair in an
experimental phase of his evolution, the creation of a new 'style'.
Thomas Walpole had purchased a tub of Walter Winterbottom's
Silky Smooth Grooming Gel for the 'MetSex' (Metro-sexual) Male
from an internet site and had it delivered to the ironmonger's
shop, where he worked, in order to avoid further domestic
inquisition.

In a drawer in the sideboard of the sitting room at number
thirteen Captain Scott Terrace there was a collection of somewhat
tatty photograph albums containing old black and white
photographs of Thomas as a boy his hair combed flat and stuck
tight to his disproportionate childhood head with brilliantine.
Winston had heard his father proclaim on occasions 'you can be
grateful that never will I subject myself and any son of mine to such
humiliation as befell me at the slimy hands of my late father
especially on Sundays'. Winston's brother, Terrence, had laughed
at the slicked back and parted style of their father in those early
snap shots. And now here he was recanting and humiliating
himself with Walter Winterbottom's proprietary gel.

"What on earth is that kulsh in your hair?" Veronica had asked her
husband.

"It is not kulsh it is a special hair gel for styling, I am experimenting
because we are living in an enlightened time and we men can be
just as liberated as our women." said Thomas.

"The nearest you ever got to style was the stile you used to help
me over when you were trying to enlighten me."

"Veronica! That's too much information." said Thomas cocking a
wink in the general direction of their young son Winston who was
listening intently and then the two of them laughed together at
her risqué reminiscence. Was he, Winston Walpole, being given
access to the adult world by this edgy playfulness between his

parents?

Like many a young man Thomas Walpole had, in the first flush of his passion for Veronica, certainly fallen in love with her and with the idea of marriage and the opening chapters of their life together had met all his desires and needs but marriage, he had found, was much more than an idea, a concept; marriage had demanded that he discover what was in his soul. Veronica was a free spirit who wanted only to belong, solely to him. His beautiful wife and then his children as they grew were at times like mirrors reflecting back someone he did not want to recognize but someone he knew intimately yet shrouded in a dense emotional fog. Such reflection was most honest when Veronica expressed it, she loved him deeply with a woman's love despite his mild caprice and she was open, safe and her love drew him down ever deeper into the truth that lay in his own heart. They continued to grow together something that, at this time in his life, began to make Thomas feel good about himself. The change in hair style seemed to Veronica disconnected from their life, an unwelcome intrusion and yet it was somehow born of the confidence her love gave him.

Just after the episode of the 'hairstyle' renaissance, in a moment when life can hang in sobering suspension prompted out of the blue by a feeling that bubbles up from the deep darkness of the human heart and breaks the surface of the soul, Thomas Walpole found himself sitting at his wife's dressing table staring into the mirror. He looked at his head framed slightly off-centre against the bed they had shared for twenty seven years, a bed in which he had experienced the height and the depth of the intimate relationship, hid from the world, that he shared with Veronica, the exhilaration of becoming one in body, in mind and soul and the despair of conflict when they had fallen out of step. Whatever they took from that bed into the day was what the world would think and feel of them and whatever they took to that bed the world had made them think and feel and determined the quality of their sleep.

Veronica had spread a fresh cover upon the bed on the morning of that particular day its colours warm, inviting, it smelled of freshly aired, ironed cotton. Thomas focused on his face and began to look into his own eyes. Inwardly he asked himself 'who I am I looking at' and for a while he could not answer. He saw the passing years in the greying creased skin beneath his eyes, his forehead sculpted like beach sand left by a receding tide and the slackness in his jowls. After a time he replied inwardly 'I see a man who is scared, afraid that he has largely failed to live, to realize his true potential, his dreams, that it is too late because his time is gone, a man not sure of the things that really matter, a man who has shied away from what he fears is in his own heart without ever really discovering it'. It was a profound moment. Thomas wanted to capture the essence of it, to remember it, he tried to keep on looking at himself but his imagination dragged him away to the bed behind him to the very first summit of his passion for Veronica and her for him. A tremor of sensuality ran through him he closed his eyes again and saw her as she was, ripe, perfectly contoured her skin so smooth and warm, poised at that threshold once crossed forever, it overwhelmed him. Thomas became aware of his shallow breathing and pumping heart, he opened his eyes the bed was there still and now suddenly the bed reminded him of the most recent depth of emotional conflict between them. He had feigned not understanding what Veronica had tried to say on some matter between them simply because he did not want to hear. In his mind she had not heard him on some previous instance which now seemed trivial. Thomas questioned himself again 'how can I be so selfish'. As he stared at his own face his expression distilled in his heart he was staring at what Veronica reflects back to him. He placated himself 'you do not let her in, you have never ever completely let her in' and then 'you don't go there yourself'. He sat motionless wrapped at once in the gossamer and gorse of the unique emotion of twenty seven years of marriage. 'Oh God' he said, he shuddered because he knew that he meant it, he felt everything and all at once.

Veronica had walked silently into the bedroom and come and sat down gently on the bed behind him rustling the clean cotton. He smelled her but he did not turn from the mirror. Of all the things she might have said, she said;

"I love you Thomas."

His eyes moistened with tears that broke glistening the grey creased skin beneath them, he sighed a deep cathartic sigh that let her into his heart deeper than ever before.

"I love you" he said "I love you so very much."

"I know." she said.

"Do you?" he replied "do you really know it?"

"I know your heart Thomas."

There was a long silence and then she said, "It's not your age I think about it's the time you have loved me, I liked your hair the way it was."

Just after the episode of the 'hairstyle' Winston awoke to the happiness between his parents, it had always been there in measure but a temporary unconscious bewilderment had overcome him in regard to his father's struggles with the advent of his fiftieth birthday. Winston's older brother Terry had simply proclaimed a period of Jubilee Jubilation and begun referring to his father as 'Bro' a derivative of brother and 'Jubi Jubi' much to his father's annoyance and his mother's sense of harmless fun. Veronica would in time refer to this phase as Thomas's 'wobble'. Thomas had not quite broken the illusion that sustained his younger son in their relationship whereas Terry was 'well over' the 'father becomes just another dad' phase of their familial journey together.

Maybe boys need there to be something mysterious about their father, an honourable unknown, a secret act of courage, a hidden depth of morality. This organic need passes through a unique morphology from childhood to into manhood. Men, remembering the mythology of their childhood imaginings, try to create a mystery about themselves to embellish reality and nurture a respect in those around them, perhaps especially their sons and daughters. This mystery, this otherness was a natural and inherent anointing for every generation that ever went to war. My father, his brothers and father before him, the same with the men of my mother's family, served their monarch and their country and returned home or became a legend swallowed by the high seas or a corner of some foreign field. My father had campaign medals that he wore every poppy red, tear wet, Armistice Day parade. His mystery was assured, sealed in a knowing brotherhood of men who have served and remember together under the swirl of the regimental flag. My history has not included voluntary or conscripted service of my beloved country in peacetime or war. My mystery is shrouded in social changes that evolved in the wake of increasing liberty hard won by the generations who had gone to war. I am not a part of some heroic act in defence of the realm, I have no regimental lineage that traces the Somme, Blenheim,

27

Waterloo none of the saline of Trafalgar, Nile and Jutland coursing my veins. There have been many who continue to volunteer who have exercised choice and served, I deeply respect them. I am, as part of my generation, a benign spectator at the trampling of its soul. My generation holds no mystery for its sons it is just lost, sandwiched between those who served and those who have not been served by the self-serving generation that begat them.

Finally came the day marking the summation of his fiftieth year. Winston's father had clearly insisted that he didn't want any special surprises or any fuss made of him. His wish was duly granted. He received three cards, one from his wife one also bought written on and tucked into the envelope by his wife but from his loving sons Terrence and Winston and one from his daughter Rosemary and her man 'Herb'. He got a 'Grow your own' Bonsai tree pack from his good lady, a paisley matching tie and shirt set from his sons to remind him of his youth and a treat of a half-litre tub of his favourite rum and raisin ice cream. Rosemary bought him a book about the history of Kew Gardens and a bottle of his favourite single malt. Winston's father had sunk into a long fiftieth birthday sulk, days passed until he was eventually salvaged by his loving wife to the relief of everyone.

"You need something to wake you from your despair" said Veronica "have you smelt the drain under our kitchen window, clearing it would be cathartic."

She had looked knowingly at Winston as she spoke. She paused briefly.

"Did you hear what I...?"

"I am going" Thomas had interrupted "you may all laugh but you will be fifty one day and then we'll see how you cope with the ageing processes of life."

"I have already bought a bottle of peroxide I'm going blonde not grey" said Veronica thinking she was having the last word on her husband.

"Ah!" he said "could you spare me some for the drain."

Thomas Walpole had fathered Terrence and Rosemary while he was in his twenties then when he was at the age of forty Veronica Walpole produced baby Winston whose joyous arrival

28

lifted the gloom that had shrouded his father's fortieth birthday. Winston in his infancy was often introduced by his proud father as the 'celebrated issue of mature loins'. Winston's older brother Terrence spun one of his many mythologies interpreting his father's cavalier utterance by telling anyone who would listen that his baby brother Winston had been adopted from a dilapidated safari park where he had been fostered by a pride of geriatric lions. Terrence as we will see has a head that is filled with an exaggerated imagination.

THERE ARE PRESENTS AND THERE ARE PRESENTS

'Twelve years old' thought Winston as he pulled his pants on, flexed his biceps in the pose of Atlas the mythical Titan and clenched his buttocks sideways on in front of the wardrobe door mirror.

"Two...welve." he shouted shadow boxing in his vest and then somersaulting onto the eiderdown and grinding the bed springs down through the octaves.

"Winston" his mother shouted up the stairs "your bed is not a trampoline and you will crack the ceiling you are now twelve years old and I will make sure that your father holds you responsible for all future damages starting from just then."

Winston finished dressing and made his way down stairs two steps at a time with the brown paper parcel from his Gran under his arm. His sister Rosemary had called in on her way to her job at Ribbons the haberdashers in the high street.

"Another year and then responsibility Wincey." his sister said as he entered the room to the sound of Terrence with his head thrown back, trumpeting a vocal fanfare through the circle of his left thumb and forefinger pressed against pursed lips while the fingers of his right hand fluttered over imaginary valves.

"I started a paper round *before* I was thirteen" said Terrence "to supplement my meagre pocket money" he added looking towards his father "I used to be chased by a Rottweiler, threatened by an old tramp, rained on, snowed on and burnt by the sun, blown along by the wind in a race with the leaves the postman and the milkman all before breakfast and I had the oldest paper bike in the western world built by Baron Karl von Drais no less."

"Terry" said Rosemary "shut up, you thought you were the pony express you used to wear a toy cowboy gun and holster."

"You used to think you were Elizabeth Taylor in National Velvet whenever you got on your bike" replied Terrence.

"Boys and Girls" said Thomas "please."

"Oh Rosemary" said Veronica admiring her daughters handy work in the wrapping of her present for Winston "what a lovely ribbon."

"I love wrapping presents mum its raw silk it was in the remnants box at work."

"Pinch it from the hab-er-dash-ery?" chided Terrence.

"Hold your tongue Terry" said Veronica "or you'll be working in the garden with your father while I visit your Auntie Gloria this afternoon."

"I've got a game this afternoon" replied Terry "we're playing the Coppersmiths and Gasfitters apprentices in the cup."

"And I am working today not gardening" added Thomas.

"What is dad growing at the moment?" asked Rosemary "what are you growing Dad?"

"The ingredients of the gods Ambrosia." Veronica said dryly.

"Still not enjoying your fifties then Dad?" Rosemary joked with her father as he sat ignoring Terry's pulled face and sipping his cup of hot tea.

"Rosie my lovely I cannot escape the primordial principles of our universe but I would love a little familial harmony." said Thomas between silent sips.

Winston unwrapped his present from his Gran. She had knitted him a woollen singlet vest and a pair of pants. They were striped red, white and blue and the vest had a large black number 12 portentously embroidered into two separate squares of white worn cotton bed sheet sewn onto the vest. Terry and Rosemary laughed with Winston at the outfit.

"All you need is a great big handlebar moustache a rubber ring and bathing machine Wincey and you could travel back in time to the seaside." said Rosemary.

"You could take dad with you." added Terry "then he would be younger."

"Your father doesn't like a pebble beach he always looks like a lame flamingo walking on embers." said Winston's mother

"Winston let's see you with them on then."

"Come on Wincey." Rosemary pushed her young brother towards the downstairs toilet "you can change in here."

"There isn't a mirror." Winston protested.

With the toilet door shut on Winston, Rosemary returned to the kitchen to make an announcement that she had struggled to contain within her bursting heart from the moment she had walked into the kitchen.

"Mum, Dad I know its Wincey's birthday but I have something that I want to tell you." There was a moment of silence and then the sound of Winston pulling the chain in the toilet, the cistern emptying a single wave that crashed against vitreous enamel and gargled in the throat of the 'Nessie'.

"I knew it" her mother responded "as soon as you walked in, I knew it I could it see your bloom."

"Let her tell us then." said Thomas.

"Winston" Veronica called "Winston hurry up your sister has some news, go on Rosemary, Winston…have you fallen in the Nessie?"

"First of all Colin has got a new job assignment and it could air on a national network television. He is going to be the soundman on the new 'Bellwether Swap' reality show. The new town mayor is swapping lifestyles with an African chieftain or something and the families of both men are moving to the other one's home in their countries and swapping their entire lives and everything and Colin is recording the African family everyday right here in town. They have already made the move and filming starts in two weeks."

"And?" said an expectant Veronica Walpole.

"Well that's pretty fantastic" said Terry "she's not going to top that is she, Herb on the national network."

"I never read anything about it in the local rag." said Thomas.

"I am going to have a baby." Rosemary announced.

"The mayor eh! Who'd have thought." continued Thomas

"Oh what did I say, congratulations" said Veronica scurrying over and embracing her daughter.

"Herb whey hey!" said Terry "good one Herb...who's the Daddy oh! Oh! Who's the Daddy?"

"Terrence Walpole how dare you suggest." began Veronica.

"It's a saying mum" Terry interrupted his mother "who's the Daddy...it's a kind of slap on the back."

"It sounded like a slap in the face to me." said his mother.

"Well done my girl and well done Herb." said Thomas.

'Herb' was the name by which Rosemary's 'life partner' was known. His real name was Colin Sage but right from primary school he had been called Herb because that had been the nickname of his great-grandfather, grandfather and father who were all named Arthur. Colin was his father's fourth son his oldest brother Arthur carried the uncut Gordian knot of family tradition but all four boys were known as 'Herb'. Their father however affectionately called them, in order of their age, Biferous, Bivore, Baceous and Robert to distinguish them despite their difference in age, height, breadth and hair colour.

Etymology, which is the study of the sources and development of words, states that the term 'nickname' is derived from a Middle English word 'ekename' from the verb to eke, "enlarge"; it compares to the Swedish word öknamn which is interesting because in Viking societies many people had nicknames which were used in addition to, or instead of a family name. Names have meaning and it was the meaning that was attributed to the child more than the name. So presumably there was a time when 'Assassin', 'Ransack' and 'Pillage' were popular boy's names in parts of what is now Scandinavia.

It is possible Arthur is a Celtic name which means 'noble follower of Thor'. It may be true that great-grandfather Arthur 'Herb' Sage was born on Thursday which is named after Thor or more likely that he was simply born with red hair. Colin Sage has red hair. It is an unfortunate coincidence that a specific hair colour has come up again as this could leave you thinking there is some underlying motive being woven into this story, which there clearly is not. It is however a rather sad irony that Thor, unlike his father Odin, did not require human sacrifice which was the unfortunate and rather tragic demise of Herb's forebear.

Colin's grandfather's cousin also Arthur had his name writ large into the gray granite obelisk that is the local war memorial. Arthur Thomas Henry (also allegedly, though most probably, known as 'Herb') Sage, Corporal in the 16th/5th the Queen's Royal Lancers gave his life for King and Country in Foundouk, North Africa on April the 9th 1943. Rumour had it that Herb also had a distant forebear Thomas Henry who was awarded the Victoria Cross in the Great War. Following an attack on an enemy strong point East of Ypres, at the Tower Hamlets Spur, on the 4th October 1917, he was one of nine men huddled together in a shell-hole. One of his compatriots stood up to lob a bomb towards the enemy. The gallant bomber's tin helmet could not withstand the force of the bullet that whistled, from the perfectly puckered 7.92 millimetre lips of a German sniper's Mauser Gewehr 98 courtesy of Kaiser Wilhelm II, across no-man's land and violently deposited in the Occipital lobe via the Frontal lobe of the brain of the bomb lobbing unfortunate, having been considerably slowed down by the steel of the 'Brodie' tin hat. The slain soldier fell back into the overcrowded shell hole and with him the 'un-lobbed' bomb. Acting quickly, and with great presence of mind Thomas Henry Sage courageously threw himself onto the bomb, thus saving the lives of several of his comrades, although he himself was fatally wounded. There can be no doubt that Arthur Thomas Henry 'Herb' Sage the Royal Lancer had died a hero's death. There can also be little doubt that 'no-man's' land in this particular instance could have been no wider than a decent throw of the 'pin and pineapple' Mills bomb which would explain the penetrating bullet.

Rosemary stood for an abiding moment quietly glowing at the very centre of her family, exuding a pure joy and wafting one of the warmth's that distinguish humanity from the inhumanity that demands sacrifice.

"Herb wanted to be here with me to tell you but he had to leave in the middle of the night he's working on an outside news item broadcast throughout today and he's going to France on the ferry with Ranjit."

"What about the African chieftain?" Terry asked.

"There's nothing in the mayoral diary for today for Ranjit to report,

Colin has a copy of the mayor's diary so he knows what is coming up, what has to be filmed and the actual programme series doesn't start for two weeks."

Colin worked for the regional television news as part of a three man team. He is known amongst his colleagues by a second larger nickname 'Sonic Herb', his actual job description is sound engineer. He is the one you see wearing large headphones, carrying a back-pack and dangling an over inflated rodent on a long stick between two people whenever the camera operator gets the zoom in and zoom out instructions the wrong way round.

Veronica chided her husband;

"Just think Thomas you will soon be a *grand*...father."

Thomas shuddered, his good lady had had the last word on the march of Father Time through his life, fifty two years of age became somehow meaningless now that he was going to be a Grandfather and he knew that further defence of his vanity would be in vain.

"This must mean you will be getting married now" Veronica Walpole said to her 'modern' minded daughter.

"Mum" Rosemary replied "you know what we both think."

"I do" she said "and I know what I think to as a child who discovered that her parents were decidedly unmarried and that only after they were both dead and resting in the churchyard."

"Uncle Frank thought it was funny." said Terry.

"Uncle Frank is Uncle Frank, 'funny' and Uncle Frank is not the same as 'funny' and normal people" replied Veronica of her older brother "and your Auntie Gloria is a saint for putting up with him."

Veronica Walpole *née* O'Flannagan had remained close to her older brother Frank because she was very fond of her sister-in-law Gloria and tolerant of her inimitable sibling.

Winston emerged a little coyly from the toilet. He was dressed in his red, white, and blue striped, knitted woollen vest and pants. The number 12 emblazoned across his chest and his back. The coarse wool pressed his tender skin. Nobody noticed him. His

35

mother was overjoyed for his sister. His father sat uncomfortable behind what Winston would call a faint smince. *(In Winston's mind a 'smince' is a cross between a wince and a smile)*. Terry had gone through into the sitting room and brought back a bottle of Oloroso sherry with three matching dessert wine glasses and a six inch high schooner. He held the glasses in one hand their flat feet overlapped in his upturned palm the stems threaded through his fingers and the glasses hung like empty clapper-less crystal bells.

"This calls for a celebration." he said.

"Really Terry?" said Veronica Walpole "a sherry at this time of day I'll be no more use for the rest of it and I've your Auntie Gloria and your Gran to see."

Winston hoped as a mark of his having become twelve years old that he was about to be granted membership of that somewhat elitist club known as the 'grown ups' that drinks sherry or port or even ginger wine in the home at Christmas and special occasions usually only celebrated on Sundays.

"You've only got four glasses Terry" Winston said.

"There are only four grown-ups" replied his brother adding a teasing "Uncle Wincey" for good measure without even looking at him.

Once Terry had poured the sherry and raised his glass, which happened to be the six inch schooner, to Rosemary, her 'ever present bun in the oven' and her absent Herb in a toast to the coming generation of the 'perennial Sage genus' he noticed the sartorial dilemma of his little brother.

"Whey hey Wincey" Terry continued in the commentary style of a 'Dimbleby' "Master Winston Walpole emerges from the English Channel rewriting history as the youngest British Bulldog ever to complete the crossing through sewage and salt water dodging the maritime traffic, duodenal debris, and hungry seagulls along the way. Welcome ashore young Winston issue of those ancient lions."

Terry drank a deep draft from the schooner and shifting linguistics to a faux French accent began

"On behalf of my Gallic brothers...."

"Shut up Terry. Ooooh Winston they're lovely, how thoughtful of your Gran" said Veronica "you must wear the striped socks your Gran knitted for you last year with that outfit they go together a treat."

"But." began Winston

"Mother?" said Rosemary.

"You must wear them for your birthday trip with your uncle Frank, you must."

"But they itch."

"Then I will rub some calamine lotion on you first." said his mother

"Only the vest itches." interrupted Winston aware of the threat the application of cold calamine was to his dignity.

"You can take the lotion up to your room to do the area of your pants yourself, you are twelve now."

Terry was about to swallow a mouthful of sherry when Veronica Walpole mentioned the 'area of your pants' to Winston. Terry's face exploded and gullet warm Oloroso erupted from every orifice of his head in a volcanic rupture. He turned away coughed, choked, laughed, and splattered his father's broadsheet newspaper which Thomas Walpole was holding up spread between his outstretched arms having settled into an armchair behind Terry.

"Thank you Terrence" said Thomas sarcastically from behind the broadsheet "there is a swimming race today across the channel between the French and the English it is to celebrate the launch of an Anglo-French cultural collaboration and to celebrate the 'Entente Cordiale' I had not finished reading about it and you have just *papier-mâchéd* it with Spanish sherry how very European of you."

"Oh Winston an Anglo-French race on your twelfth birthday" said Winston's mother "we must keep the paper for posterity."

"That's where Herb is today covering that race with Ranjit" added Rosemary "keep the paper, Herb likes to put things like that in his scrap book."

The Oloroso drenched newspaper Thomas had been reading was slowly falling into his lap of as it absorbed Terry's sweet cream sherry lava.

"Sacra bleu" Thomas mumbled "then you had better make something with it to mark the occasion, how about a papier-mâché microphone."

"So what have you got Winston the boy wonder?" Terry asked his parents as he tried to suppress the magma and recover some dignity.

"Winston is having a surprise day out with your uncle Frank." said Veronica.

"Uncle Frank!" exclaimed Terry and Rosemary in harmony.

"I have tried to say" interrupted Winston's father "but your mother believes her brother will be alright without the calming influence of your Auntie Gloria."

"Dad Auntie Gloria is at this very minute a guest of the local mental health authority at St Audrey's" said Terry "she's hardly a calming influence."

"Terry your Aunt is having a break and taking some convalescence for her troubled soul and Frank has always been good to you children more than can be said for *your* brother." Said Veronica referring to Thomas's sibling.

"My brother just never got on with children even when he was one."

"He is headmaster of the primary school for heaven's sake Thomas. He has a dimple in his chin and you know what they say in my country?"

"Yes Veronica my love I do." said Thomas.

"A dimple in the chin, a devil within."

"There you said it anyway."

"It was not his first choice for a career you know that." Winston's father took up the challenge "he was denied his birth right by two flat feet."

"Oh! Those immortal words of your snob of a mother." Veronica continued "your father must have run over his feet when he tried to steamroller him into the county constabulary."

"He would have followed my father into the world of criminology I am sure if he had not been cursed with flat feet. Many sons followed their fathers into work the times change quicker than the generations now."

"He is a curmudgeonly old schoolmaster flat feet or no flat feet and he has always frightened our children especially at birthday parties."

"Well" said Thomas "is your brother Frank picking Winston up or do you want me to take him over there?"

"Frank will be calling." she replied.

"I think I will be making my way to work now then." said Thomas scraping the remains of the sweet papier-mâché from his cardigan and trousers as he rose from the armchair and deposited his matching dessert wine glass on the draining board.

"Don't forget that you promised to give me a hand with the party this afternoon" Veronica reminded her husband "he has got his friends coming round at teatime so we will need to start setting things out and getting the games ready, you do have the games sorted don't you?"

"Yes I will be home at tea time" he replied "I do have the games sorted thank you and I warn you now I expect my brother will arrive wanting to play Scoop as usual."

"He'd probably get a fortune for that old game on the internet." said Terry.

Winston has two great friends Ezra Shilling and Osborne Troughton. The three boys had started school on the same day and remained in the same class of pupils as each year passed. Ezra and Winston are in the blue team known as Trafalgar and Osborne is the red team known as Bosworth. Apart from this they are inseparable as friends. Ezra is spastic. That is to say Ezra suffers a disorder of his body's motor system called spasticity in which some of his muscles are continuously contracted causing stiffness or tightness which interferes with his gait, his movement, and

39

sometimes with his speech. Because Ezra has hereditary spastic paraplegia (HSP), which some people in the medical profession call familial spastic Para paresis, he is deaf. Winston and Archie have learnt to sign even though Ezra is fitted with hearing aids, because Ezra sometimes gets angry and takes them out and hides them. HSP is a genetic disorder it is progressive and Ezra has to have motion exercise therapy every day. Winston and Osborne are accomplished therapists, they each take turns in helping Ezra to stretch his muscles while the other one counts to ten. Both boys learned to swim because Ezra goes to the local pool three times a week to do aquatic exercises which provide the optimal exercise conditions. Water creates a kind of weightless environment in which the effects of gravity are removed. This liberates Ezra's, water supported, stress less body and lets his weakened limbs enjoy a greater range of motion. Osborne and Winston are the schools swimming champions in the 'two man' long distance relay in which they swam a half mile, each taking turns to do two lengths at a time. The 'race' so to speak, is a sponsored event in which pupils are encouraged to take an interest in social responsibility and raise money for a registered charity that is active in the local community. Ezra chose the charity SCOPE which was originally founded as the National Spastics Society in 1951. It changed its name in 1994 because the word spastic had become a term of insult over a number of years. As the school champions of this event the two boys were awarded a shield to be held for a year by the victors. Osborne has had the shield on the sideboard in his parent's sitting room for nearly six months. He is planning to bring it round to Winston soon because it's his turn to 'hold' it.

Osborne is a twin. He was, according to his father, thirteen minutes and thirteen seconds older than his sister Geraldine. Their father will tell anyone who listens that thirteen is a very lucky number indeed and he will 'never ever suffer from triskaidekaphobia' as he has 'no fear of thirteen whatsoever'. Osborne and Geraldine are fraternal twins, which mean they are non-identical. They came from two fertilized eggs which formed two zygotes from which the name dizygotic is derived. Miss Grace taught the boy's class about this during a biology lesson one day. Ezra listens to Miss Grace through his classroom induction loop system which isn't always as clear as it should be and from the end of that biology lesson onwards he took to calling Geraldine a dizzy gothic because she can be silly and his favourite subject is history which the four of them act out sometimes when they play together. Obviously, Geraldine started school at the same time as the boys and coincidently, is in the same class. She is also in Bosworth which levels up the partisan team spirit in their group friendship. Recently Winston has been noticing Geraldine in a different sort of way. Different to how he had noticed her before and secretly he had begun hoping that she might notice him.

I know a little earlier I introduced the idea that I needed to invent a word for adolescent sensuality to describe emotional experience in the context of total innocence. Well I also need a kind of desire 'lite' at this juncture that indicates the first stirrings of that 'more than anatomical differences' realization a young boy begins to half consciously encounter at a certain point in his development. The sudden awareness of your heart beating in your throat and then a sensation in the skin of your face that becomes familiar in the older man after a shave.

Winston hoped that she might accept his invitation to her to come to his birthday party with her brother and that this might just be a legitimate excuse for a kiss.

Thomas Walpole pulled his light mackintosh on walked over to his wife and kissed her on the cheek.

"I have some good games planned he will have a nice party" he said "and I will control my brother, lighten him up a bit, trust me."

"I know and Winston will be fine with Frank on his outing treat, Gloria's not going to be there with them this year but they'll have a good time whatever Frank does with him. I'm going to the hospital to see Gloria and mother this afternoon, I will thank her for Winston's present."

Thomas and Veronica Walpole's marriage was in their pearl anniversary year. Thomas Walpole and Veronica O'Flannagan had met through their work. He was apprenticed to the local ironmongery, PA & RA Fin in the High Street. It was next door to the Temperance Bar being run by Winston's Grandmother Mrs. O'Flannagan who had come to England from Ireland as a widow to work for her great uncle Zechariah Fitzgerald. The Temperance Bar was as popular with everyone who, back then, had signed the pledge and every nine who hadn't. It was popular with children with its rich sweet syrups. Thomas Walpole developed a simultaneous liking for Veronica and for sarsaparilla until he could not bear to have one without the other. He became the envy of many a young man when he wed the handsome counter girl from Zechariah Fitzgerald's Temperance Bar. It was almost thirty years ago in the early spring time of their lives that they had 'tied the knot' the strength of their promise was holding, bound and fastened with a strong rope whose knot had seemingly got tighter with every fresh strain until it was loosened by a mystery that remains to them unsolved. Loosened between them because we can only look in from the outside on a marriage we cannot know for sure what years of intimacy reveal to the intimate, how much is laid bare to the knowing of the other and what is really being tolerated beneath appearance. The mystery occurred shortly after the birth of Winston.

Thomas Walpole possessed a rather imposing brass encased antique barometer which had been ritually handed down through family tradition to the first son of the first son upon his coming of age at twenty one. Mr Walpole had had the inherited instrument remounted upon a polished Yew (Taxus Baccata) plaque by a local cabinet maker. It was his favourite tree the origin of its name traces back to one of the given names of God, Jehovah, The Immortal, borne out by the discoveries of palaeontologists, Celtic folklore and the Yew's own propensity for reproducing itself from within its original root bole. The ancient yew dictated where the Saxons and the Normans laid the foundations of their new Christian churches. Thomas admired the same tight grained wood that has been honed in singular craft into the extremes of the fearsome English longbow that loosed death upon the French at Agincourt and the melodious soul soothing harp synonymous with life eternal. He appreciated its high polish patina and took great delight in knowing the axiomatic irony of his choice that the Yew had more successfully than any other species survived the great climatic changes that mark the Ages of history. The Yew had the measure of the weather. Thomas believed there was no other wood more appropriate for mounting the mercurial barometer, the invention of one Evangelista Torricelli, Galileo's secretary and professorial successor at Florence. In a fleeting moment Thomas's barometer had disappeared, suddenly, more than ten years previous. He had always suspected his wife who, without his even accusing her, had categorically denied interfering with the precious artefact. On several occasions since, she had jokingly confessed that she would have 'happily broken it over his head at times' but would never have made it disappear even if it were within her power because it was a part of him. Years before, after a short honeymoon by the seaside and on the day that he had carried his handsome young bride over the threshold of their new home, Thomas hung the instrument on the wall of the narrow passage they would call 'the hallway'. At precisely 08:20 and again at 18:10 Greenwich Mean Time every day since, except on the occasions of the birth of Rosemary and Terrence, Thomas Walpole would tap the glass and observe the direction of the needle as it moved one way or the other. At first Veronica admired her husband for what she saw as his winsome 'little habit', his 'husbandly thing'. He would forecast what 'outer garment' to wear and whether to 'gird up with umbrella'. Over time she discovered more of his 'winsome little habits' the barometer began to create an altogether different atmospheric pressure in their happy home. You see Thomas insists on hanging his own shirts in his own single wardrobe on his collection of wooden clothes hangers bearing identifying motifs from exotic hotels like the Plaza Athénée Paris, Langham London, Bristol Beirut and the Djalan Gadjah Mada Jakarta 'borrowed' from famous hotels by anonymous people who then donated them to the Oxfam shop in the High Street. His shirts were hung with the top, second, third and fifth buttons done up and the shirts not squashed together on the rail but hanging loosely. He ensures that his handkerchiefs are pressed diagonally. Anything to the contrary would brew storm clouds. If cutlery is returned to the wrong compartment in the cutlery drawer a deep depression descends in the kitchen. He has a particular knife, fork and spoon that he uses that are engraved with his father's second world war NAAFI number and a blue and white vertical wide striped clay mug from which he drinks his tea or coffee. His obsessions often brought a cold front that divided the normally consummate map of their life together. He was always adjusting the width of the un-drawn curtains and realigning mats and stepping over cracks and watering the cactus with the same old eye drop pipette. It was this and the effect on his mother that indirectly drove Terry to do what he did when, as a young lad, he stole the barometer away from the hallway. On that day mystery descended on Thirteen Captain Scott Terrace.

When Terry was 12 years old he witnessed an extraordinary moment between his parents. It was just turning 18:11 one evening and his father had tapped the glass the needle had dropped back a little and he was about to say something about low pressure when his heavily pregnant wife exploded verbally.

"For once I would like to be surprised by the weather and what is more I would like to be surprised by you!"

"How" Thomas had replied, himself somewhat taken aback.

"By you not having to tap your stupid instrument every day at exactly whatever time it is in order to maintain your consistent whatever they ares, I only wish you took as much interest in me or even looked at me as many times a day because if you did I would get myself ready on time and at the precise moment so that my hair would not be out of place and my face covered in whatever I am washing, polishing or cooking for your tea, just for once I would like you to want to know which way my needle has gone because of what sort pressure I have had in my day because you wouldn't know would you how could you, you haven't asked me."

"What?" he asked, sheepishly.

"That I have had poor Gloria round today and she is beside herself and my heart is breaking for her, that poor little mite of a child what is it doing to her mind with the stigma of it all, people do not understand unless it happens to them and I would not wish it on anyone and yet it is the only way they could understand what it's like and I feel so helpless and all and she is sure the boy will be taken prematurely and I fear it is a premonition and Father Costello comes out with absolutely unbelievable stuff about having faith and......"

Veronica Walpole began weeping and as her husband took her in his arms and let her hot breath and warm tears seep into his soft cotton covered shoulder and as he soothed her in the late stages of her straining pregnancy and stroked her tired tousled hair and wiped her tears with the bare knuckles of his hand, Terry determined to rid their happy home of the barometer, of obsession. The barometer was the only thing he had ever seen them argue over in otherwise happy years, the barometer that had caused such sudden pressure. Two days later sometime between 08:20 and 18:10 he managed to take the instrument down from its brass picture hook, wrap it in yesterday's broadsheet newspaper and carry it into town to the pawnbrokers, the first shop he came to with a barometer in the window. Terry stared up at the pawnbrokers sign of trade the distinctively symbolic three polished brass balls hanging from a wrought iron arch that are taken from the coat of arms of the Medici family of 15th century Florence. Europe's most powerful pawnbrokers.

44

The pawnbroker was an old man by the name of Gideon Posner. He looked at Terry through spectacle lenses reminiscent of lead latticed wrapped casements of Tudor glass that magnified his eyes. He studied the boy and then the artefact.

"Very old and very young" he said "what can I do for you master Terry?"

"I want to sell this." Terry said.

"Sell?" he queried.

"Sell." repeated a young Terrence Walpole.

"I am a pawnbroker young man not an antique dealer I cannot really accept this wonderful antique from one so young."

"I am nearly thirteen and I already have a paper round and it's mine" Terry said "it was left over from our scout jumble sale and our patrol six was going to burn it on our camp fire so I saved it and I am going to put the money in the troupe funds and it was Simba who sent me."

"Simba?" said Gideon "who is Simba?"

"The scoutmaster Mr Pembroke he works for the brush and carpet factory."

"Ah" said Gideon "then you are a member of the First Sun Rise Road Scouts who meet in the old corset factory no less. The locals call it the Imps hut though heaven knows why."

Terry realized that the old man was acquainted with Mr Pembroke and that he needed to revise his story a little to protect himself "Please don't tell Simba I" he paused reaching deep into his 'imagchinery' (it's what Auntie Gloria and Winston call the engine of the imagination) I was going to tell Simba but he had left I haven't done anything wrong he would have sent me if he had been there when I asked."

"Well even if I don't tell Mr Pembroke and I can assure you that I won't" continued Gideon Posner "it is worth more than twenty five pounds and that means I will have to get a Commissioner for Oaths a Justice of the Peace or a Notary Public to witness you signing a statement with your pawn-receipt young man it is our

45

law."

"I don't need twenty five pounds" said Terry "I just need to get rid of the weather clock."

Gideon Posner gripped his chin with his right hand and thought and then he shifted a little leaning backwards and then he pushed his glasses up onto his forehead and his eyes shrunk to a normal size and his soul danced behind their twinkle. He frowned, his glasses dropped back onto his nose and his eyes magnified

There was mystery to Gideon Posner, local legend spoke of his having arrived in the town after surviving religious persecution and certain execution at the hands of Adolf Hitler's henchmen in Poland the country of his birth, many years ago. He had come to the town having married a local girl Isabel Quadling; they had met in London after the war where Gideon, a refugee, had been taken in by a Polish émigré, a childhood friend of Gideon's father who had worked in the glassworks in Gideon's home town and who as a salesman had been stranded in London at the outbreak of the Second World War.

Isabel the daughter of Pastor Isaac Quadling had originally gone to London to help nurse the victims of the Blitz and then stayed to care for seriously wounded British servicemen. Isabel Quadling had become Isabel Posnerowa upon her marriage to Gideon such is the tradition that the woman's marital status acquires a suffix to the surname her husband gives her and Gideon had followed this tradition in memory of his father and mother who did not survive the Holocaust. Gideon Posner slowly removed his spectacles and after taking a handkerchief from a pocket in his waistcoat he breathed warm breath onto the glass, steaming the lenses. He polished the glass steadily and looked at Terry.

"I'll give you twenty four pounds then and I will waive the redemption time limit."

"What's that?" asked Terry.

"It means that I will keep the barometer until you come back to collect it, as I am sure you will once you realize the value of the instrument and give me the money in return."

"Okay" said Terry wondering if it would ever be safe to return the barometer now that he had taken it "you won't put it in your window will you?"

"No I won't." said Gideon Posner "and I will see you I am sure, when you have become a man, now, are you going to tell me the truth about all of this?"

There are those who can know the truth. The sense of their soul where truth must find its throne in this world, has been sharpened by the temporary loss of the possession of the senses. Senses by which they lived their daily existence. Temporary because liberty has been cruelly denied or loss and sorrow has overwhelmed. They cannot return anymore to where they came from but they journey on in a clearer light than those around them. They live by the primary paradigm of life.

Gideon Posner knows the truth because he had taken from him, in a few interminable years that followed the invasion of his country on September 1st 1939, the possession of everything that makes up life. Gideon spent the formative years of his childhood in the town of Wolomin in central Masovia about twenty kilometres from Warsaw. Wolomin thrived after the advent of the railway from Warsaw to Bialystok. A railroad that one day would run right through to Auschwitz. Gideon's father worked in a lumber yard run by Mendel Rozenblit. Gideon was the same age as Mendel's son Avraham. Avraham had a half-sister Torvah, Gideon experienced his first flush of adolescent love in the thrall of Torvah. In the autumn of 1940 Gideon and his entire family were sent to the Warsaw ghetto to an area known as Sienna close to the one of the gates that closed on the ghetto and opened up to railroad cattle carriages commissioned to carry the tribes of Israel to the land of the rope, gas and bullet, the land of the final solution. The mixture of her love for Gideon and the faith of Isabel had restored to him some possession of life, a very different life, a better life? Who knows? Of Avraham Rozenblit? Gideon's boyhood friends Avraham and Torvah were eventually gassed by the Nazis in Auschwitz. Gideon was liberated by Russian soldiers on January 27th 1945. He had been shown quiet, discreet kindness by a German guard in the factory where he was put to work, that was part of the Buna Werkes of I. G. Faben at Monowice. In the universe of absolute darkness that was Auschwitz Gideon saw a handful of stars. The brightest of these was the kindness of the guard. Gideon had determined at his liberation to take this star with him from that darkness. Through Isabel's kind heart her Jesus had become Gideon's Yeshua as he let her deep love for him enter his tortured soul. Kindness rekindled him and justice and righteousness showed him that war does not change God, war changes people.

Terry looked at the old man, at the magnified eyes that looked back at him. Terry was uncomfortable but enveloped in the aura of kindliness that pervaded the pawnbrokers shop.

"I've told you the truth" Terry said.

"You have told me what you think is easier for me to believe I just don't think you need to carry the truth all on your own young man there will be time enough for that in life."

"But I want you to keep the thing that's all until I can come back and get it perhaps."

"Why don't you let me buy this off you so that you can have the money for the First Sun Rise Scout funds I would give you more than twenty five pounds?"

"If I sell it now then I won't have it to sell later will I?" said Terry thinking on his feet.

"Understood" said Gideon "but you can tell me I am an old man with a door on my memory that I can lock, that means you can leave the barometer and the truth with me and I will look after both of them for you."

"It's my mum and dad" Terry paused and watched the magnified eyes of the old Polish, Messianic Jew in transition from enquiry to empathy "the weather clock thing makes them argue so I thought if I just took it away for a little while it ..." Terry did not really know what he thought it would do he had acted spontaneously.

"Well" said Gideon "what you want for your parents is very commendable but you will have to know if the empty space on the wall at home is better than what is worrying you won't you?"

"Yes" said Terry.

"I will pray for your parents" Gideon said "you could do that to if you really want them to be happy"

"Okay" said Terry.

"I will pray for you to young man" Gideon added.

Terry knew what prayer was because he had once secretly and quite accidentally watched his Auntie Gloria work the beads of her rosary with her fingers quietly exhorting the 'Queen of the Holy rosary' enunciating each heart felt 'Our Father' and praying in sequence through 'Hail Mary' Glory be' 'Oh my Jesus' to the last 'Oh God whose only begotten Son' ending with a lachrymatory Amen. Every prayer was for 'my dear child Michael' and Terry felt a deep unnecessary guilt at having wandered into that innermost sanctuary.

I remember things like that, moments when I traversed the invisible barrier between a child and the adult world not at all meaning to. The feelings are vivid even now. I was the one who was wrong I was the one who should not have been there. A feeling became permanently planted and every innocent indiscretion clung to it as it grew. Stupid things that adults do, now when I look back at them, walking into a store cupboard that my father had sent me to fetch a wad of cotton from and seeing that travelling salesman with dirty shoes doing grown up things with Margaret who had always made me feel special, running round the corner into the squadron leader urinating in the manor house hedge after he had opened the fete to great respect, being early to choir practice and finding the sweat smelly verger in the vestry drinking sacramental wine from an ancient gold chalice. I can still see the look on their faces, except Margaret who didn't see me which kind of made it worse. There are loads of things and it just always feels too late, too far to travel emotionally, to put them right. Guilt is the coat I am left to wear, inside out. Guilt for not changing the things that I witnessed, for not fixing the broken. Just thinking about it is exhausting.

Terry left the pawnbrokers with his pawn-receipt and twenty four pounds in a plain brown envelope like the one his father used to open every Friday evening before giving his mother her 'housekeeping'. He was twelve years old and determined to hide the money until the right time for him to redeem the barometer a time when he knew for sure that it would not come between his father and mother. Over the years the principle of the barometer gave way to the ripening pressures of temptation and Terry occasionally 'dipped' into his secret fund, failing miserably to honour his intention to repay himself his own IOU's, as he saw it. Terry knew that Gideon Posner was praying for him and at times that was all that mattered. Veronica Walpole regretted the position she had taken over the barometer or more particularly the compulsive activity of her dear husband. What he did habitually tapping out and reporting the veracity of his heirloom was somehow for all its annoyance a virtue of family life akin to eating together around the kitchen table, baking fresh bread or being in on the 'bundle'. The 'bundle' was the energy sapping wrestling match between Thomas Walpole and his children on the hearth rug or the sofa or the lawn in summer. The 'bundle' which had left him at various times with a bloody nose, a blinking eye, a wrung thumb or a throbbing gonad was wonderful. It burned the children's energy gave them confidence and let them celebrate small victories while all the time they were safe because they knew their father's strength. Such virtues remain what to Veronica Walpole, make up their family life.

UNCLE FRANK O'FLANNAGAN

"What hare-brained scheme is Uncle Frank currently pursuing?" Terry asked his mother after Thomas had left for the store.

"It is your father's opinion that my brother has hare-brained schemes" Veronica said "your father is not fair to your uncle. Frank is a well-meaning man."

"Well you know what I mean, dad is always saying"…

"I know what your father is always saying" interrupted Winston's mother "if anyone pursues hare-brained schemes it is your father. As a matter of fact your Uncle Frank is building your Auntie Gloria a pergola for when she starts her visiting soon."

"Visiting?" asked Terry "are they letting her out?"

"They are letting her visit home on Saturdays to begin with."

"Well I must be getting down to the shop myself I suppose I'm opening up today, the Misses Ribbons nephew has a surprise birthday treat for them." said Rosemary.

"That's nice" said Veronica "now you must be careful my love you'll be looking after that little one on your bicycle."

"Of course mum" said Rosemary. "I'm cooking Colin a special meal tonight to celebrate."

"What are you baking? A cake shaped like a microphone!" Terry chided his sister.

Winston laughed at his brother's joke.

"You two" Veronica scolded her sons "now hurry along Rosemary if you're in charge to today you must not be late with such responsibility." she added looking directly at her mischievous sons.

Winston turned on the breakfast television news broadcast

with the banner headline 'The News from your Region'. The news studio anchor man was questioning a reporter making an outside broadcast link to the studio.

"Listen mum" said Winston "it's that race the channel thing and its Ranjit the reporter Herb will be pointing the microphone boom at him."

"So it is" said his mother "I will never forget you standing behind him in the middle of all that steam Winston your little face was a picture."

The studio anchor man at the news desk announced "And now courtesy of 'Rubblers Sand and Gravel, Goose Quarry for all your sand and gravel requirements' the sponsors of this report we are going live to Ranjit Livingstone on the beach where there are many stones but only one Livingstone…Hello Ranjit."

"Hello Dan" replied the outside broadcast reporter "good joke there. Dan I am standing on the platform cut by waves looking down onto Shakespeare beach and its deep pools' full of tidal water where earlier today several intrepid English and flamboyant French men began the race. I am not looking forward to the long climb back up the staircase I can tell you."

"The French have the advantage being naturally part buoyant then?" chided the anchor man.

"There are over a hundred steps to climb" continued Ranjit enigmatically failing to take the bait.

"Tell me Ranjit, when was it that the competing swimmers entered the sea?" asked the anchor man.

"At the start of the race." replied Ranjit Livingstone.

"Ah yes" said the anchor man "and was it at the break of day perhaps after a hearty Full English or the sharp retort of the starter's pistol?"

"Neither" said the reporter "it was just after the top of the tide."

"Did you start your day with a full English Ranjit?" asked the anchor man "or do you have curried cornflakes?"

"Actually I am not your stereophonic typecast I have prunes, fresh orange juice and cinnamon pancakes."

Ranjit the reporter was wearing an imposing sheepskin three quarter length coat and staring into the camera through his distinctively heavy rimmed spectacles. He was trying to maintain an authoritative air as he addressed his invisible audience hidden deep inside the camera. Ranjit Livingstone was more familiar to Winston as a man with a full noddle of shiny, coal black hair, today he had hair but mainly on one side of his head in a long flapping ponytail of straggly hair at right angles to the top of his right ear.

"Look at roving Ranjit ace reporter mum" shouted a laughing Terry "he's Mr Comb-over."

"Shut up Terry" said Winston "it's interesting, Herb is there somewhere."

"Tell me Ranjit" continued the studio anchor man "what are the conditions like down there."

"Quite windy I think you will agree." he said trying to pin down his errant tresses.

"Toupee or not toupee" shouted Terry "he needs a syrup."

"And this race, can you tell us about it?" continued the anchor man.

"The race is from right here under the white cliffs across the Strait of Dover or as the French would have it after half way, the Pas de Calais to the Cap Gris Nez. The earliest man to make the swim was Merchant Navy captain Matthew Webb."

The studio anchor man interrupted the reporter "Ranjit I thought that as this was a race the entrants would all be starting in a line together?"

"That is correct Dan; Captain Webb swam in 1875 a total of 38 miles in 21 hours and 45 minutes".

"But Ranjit my research tells me that the distance between these two points is only 21 miles" said the anchor man.

"That is correct Dan one and three quarters of a mile shorter than Loch Ness as a matter of fact."

"So why did captain Webb swim 38 miles it's nearly there and back?"

"No Dan, Antonio Abertondo an Argentine was the first man known to have swum there and back in 1961". Ranjit was having trouble keeping his ear piece connecting him to the studio anchor man, in his ear because it was being platted with strands of his hair...

"Tell me Ranjit how long is the race expected to be?"

"Twenty one miles Dan." replied Ranjit Livingstone.

The studio anchor man smiled insincerely into the studio camera.

"Expected time of arrival, lunchtime, afternoon tea, how long in the water Ranjit?"

"The first swimmers are expected onto French soil sometime early this evening."

"Don't you mean sand and shingle or is the French beach all dirty?"

"No I don't think it will over by four-thirty." replied Ranjit as his ear piece and hair undulated in the breeze like the tentacles of the sea anemone in its symbiotic relationship with a breakfast of marine algae, gobbets of wind whipped salt sea foam spattered Ranjit's smart sheepskin and then jumped onto his face.

"He looks like Ranjit the rabid reporter." said Terry.

"Those are awful conditions I hope Colin is alright." added Veronica.

"Okay Ranjit we'll let you go and let you top up with the prunes."

As the live broadcast from the blustery beach descended into farce in the face of the fearsome wind, Dan the anchor man ran an interview that Ranjit and his outside crew had recorded at dawn on the beach. Ranjit was standing in the glare of arc lights and speaking to an English contestant by the name of Winston Fotheringay-Hepplethwaite who was wearing the number 12 on the front of a vividly striped one piece bathing suit. Ranjit Livingstone standing in the stillness of the emerging day with his coal black shiny hair neatly straddling the saddle of his bald head and secured with the aid of a modicum of styling substance and the stirrup support of his right ear began his earlier report in the changing light.

"I am standing here on the beach at the start of this historic race between the English and the French to celebrate the anniversary of the 'Entente Cordiale' which was agreed in nineteen hundred and four and which means that these two great nations remain intent upon a cordial understanding. With me is Lieutenant Winston Fotheringay-Hepplethwaite of the Royal Hussars who is taking part today. Winston is a swimmer and an Olympiad. Tell me are you really in the Royal Hussars?"

"I most certainly am" replied the Lieutenant "The Queens Royal Hussars, actually the Queens own and Royal Irish to be precise."

"Is it more of a challenge for a man who is the height of a boy to swim in such a grown up race?"

Lieutenant Winston Fotheringay-Hepplethwaite who clearly had not expected this opening question paused. The first moan of a developing breeze could be heard through Herb's microphone.

"I think that swimming is for all ages and physical appearances, my regiment accepts the shortest men in the British army if they have the right credentials after all we are all of a similar height when mounted on a horse and I think that my record speaks for itself. Anyway my brother Isambard is a quarter of an inch shorter than me and he is a squadron leader in the Royal Air force flying fighter bombers."

Ranjit continued merrily "Have the doctors passed you fit despite your problems?"

"What problems are you referring to?" asked the Lieutenant

"Your exceptionally greasy skin" replied Ranjit "isn't that a sign of puberty?"

Lieutenant Winston Fotheringay-Hepplethwaite laughed a charitable laugh but Ranjit remained seriously quizzical. A few strands of Ranjit's hair were lifted by the breeze and unfurled windward.

"Very funny" said the Lieutenant "I may be a slippery customer but

I think that I am a warm one under this lot" he continued indicating his extremely greasy skin "I am wearing three and half tins of the best Army issue the Quartermaster could find."

"You smell a bit" said Ranjit "like a duck pond."

"It is goose grease." the Lieutenant responded.

"Geese have been slaughtered so that you can swim the channel?" Ranjit challenged.

"No of course not I mean yes they have been slaughtered, I think killed in the cause of feeding humankind is probably a better understanding and I have to say very much in keeping with the spirit of the event today because the geese were all French reared for the production of Foie Gras that wonderful harmony of goose liver forced by gavage and blended with cognac and truffles served as a mousse".

"I agree that it is most savage and were these innocent geese murdered in France or England?"

"France of course" the Lieutenant responded before correcting himself "they were not murdered they were killed for human consumption like every other meat and I said gavage."

"The French eat the parfait and the English get covered in the grease" Ranjit finished the culinary exposé.

"Well yes so to speak I suppose." Winston Fotheringay-Hepplethwaite said limply.

"Is it organic?" asked Ranjit

"Would that make it more acceptable?" the Lieutenant countered.

"There is a lot of history between us and the French." began Ranjit following a new angle.

"Between we" interrupted the Lieutenant. "I think you must be mistaken."

"Between us, the King Harold, the Duke of Wellington and the Lord Vice-Admiral Horatio Viscount Nelson" insisted Ranjit with some pride "and the French. You must feel the burden of enormous national responsibility upon your skinny shoulders."

"Until now" replied Lieutenant Winston Fotheringay-Hepplethwaite "I had not really…"

"Your costume isn't it in breach of the competition rules?" Ranjit interrupted changing tack. Enough strands of his hair were now oscillating away from the top of his right ear to reveal the emerging dome of pale sun starved skin that is Ranjit's not so hidden secret.

"Certainly not, rule B clearly states that no person in a Standard attempt to swim the Channel and today we are abiding by the Standard swim rules, shall use or be assisted by an artificial aid of any kind, but is permitted to grease the body before a swim, use goggles, wear one cap and one costume. The word costume and cap shall mean a garment, not made of neoprene or rubber or any other material considered by the Federation to give a similar type of advantage, and not in any way designed to contain body heat, and/or aid buoyancy. We are competing in Edwardian style costumes that mark the anniversary and my observer has validated my costume."

"Very good" said Ranjit "very good I wish you all the best swimming La Manche."

"The Channel thanking you to be British." corrected the Lieutenant.

Ranjit turned to look along the beach and pointed at a Victorian bathing machine. His hair wrapped around his glasses and he ducked beneath the camera's roving eye and frantically adjusted his crowning glory, sweeping it from ear to ear. The cameraman panned round collimating his lens to the object of Ranjit's interest creating a blurred vision of 'Sonic Herb' the soundman and budding branch of this particular television audience, swinging his microphone boom in parallel pursuit of Ranjit's randomly roving attention.

"Hey" shouted Terry followed by "Ooooh Herb not to professional."

"Quiet Terry." said Veronica.

Rosemary threw a frosty glance towards her brother.

"What" continued Ranjit "is that?"

"A Victorian bathing machine" said the Lieutenant.

"A bathing machine!?"

"Yes a machine. Someone had the rather bright idea of being totally faithful to the Edwardian theme and have us to all emerge from Victorian bathing machines except that we could only find one that was not in trust to some museum or other and then of course it would have broken the rule."

"What rule?" asked Ranjit.

"Rule C" said Lieutenant Winston Fotheringay-Hepplethwaite "for a swim to be officially recognized, the swimmer must walk into the sea from the shore of departure, swim across the English Channel one to finish on dry land, or two to touch steep cliffs of the opposite coast with no sea-water beyond. Swimmers may finish in harbour water provided they land as in one on dry land. You see to use a bathing machine properly one has to enter it by mounting steps at the back and after using the machine to change into ones costume to enter the sea from the front so you see one would break the rule."

"Of course" effused Ranjit imperiously "that would be a blasphemous crime?"

"Yes it" Lieutenant Winston Fotheringay-Hepplethwaite corrected himself "not blasphemous heinous just........"

The local church tower clock struck the hour and chimes sounded through Herb's microphone drowning the last syllables of the Lieutenant's response.

Winston's mother turned the television off.

"Oi" said his brother Terry "I was watching roving Ranjit."

"Less of the 'Oi' it's time for Winston to get ready for his Uncle Frank. You never know when Uncle Frank will turn up to collect you Winston and your football boots need cleaning."

"You never know *if* Uncle Frank is going to turn up." said Terry.

"Uncle Frank is a reliable man. I'll have you now that when we were all children growing up in our family it was our eldest brother Frank who would bring home a bird for mother to cook. Frank made sure that there were always fresh vegetables for us."

"Until he got caught stealing them." laughed Terry.

"Your uncle Frank got caught stealing only once" said Winston's mother as if it were a virtue to only get caught the once. "He was unfortunate he went to the borstal. He served his sentence."

"You don't get two years in a borstal for two cabbages six carrots and a bantam" said Terry " Aunty Kitty says that you stopped moving from town to town and nearly starved after Uncle Frank was put away."

"Your Aunt Kitty is bitter and cannot see the good things in your late grandfather."

"She says that Uncle Frank stole because Granddad was lazy and irresponsible and always late home from the bars." added Terry.

"I will remind you young man that your Grandfather served this blessed country and it's King and died on active service."

"Dad says he was something to do with the battalion's hygiene." Terry continued "and he died of dysentery."

"Do not dishonour the dead." Veronica said forcefully.

"Why" interrupted Winston trying to lighten things a little "do you have eleven brothers and sisters and Dad just has one?"

"I come from a family that had to drag itself up into the world around it whereas your father comes from a dynasty that the world has slowly dragged down into itself. Now did I hear your Uncle Frank's van?"

Winston hurried up to his room to get ready.

"Don't you think that Uncle Frank is out of his depth" said Terry after Winston could be heard through the kitchen ceiling using his bed as a trampoline confirming that he was safely out of ear shot.

"Out of his depth?" replied his mother.

"Taking Winston out without Auntie Gloria to keep an eye on

proceedings I mean it's only a couple of years ago since the railway bridge and all."

"Your Auntie Gloria was with them then."

"Yes but." began Terry.

"Frank O'Flannagan has never been out of his depth in anything that he does" Veronica interrupted before shouting "Winston stop using your bed as a trampoline you will crack the ceiling you are twelve years old get yourself ready.

There were two loud 'parps' out in the street and an engine shuddered to silence. Frank O'Flannagan stepped down from the cab of his van and shut the door. He walked around the van and paused at the curb stone to allow a woman and her two children to pass by on the pavement courteously touching his cap in acknowledgement as the woman walked by. Frank made his way to the house.

"So Frank are we to know the nature of the birthday treat you have in store for our Winston?" Veronica enquired of her eldest brother as he entered the kitchen

"Only if you promise not to tell the young man when he comes down I assume it was Winston bouncing up and down past the bedroom window." replied Frank O'Flannagan smiling whilst clenching his right fist in his left hand and looking directly at Winston's brother, Terry.

"It's a secret Uncle Frank" said Terry submissively

"Good" said Frank "it's a secret then. Now where is the hare-brained iron-mongering horticulturist you call your father?"

"He thinks you..." began Terry who was interrupted immediately by his mother.

"He's gone to the store already."

"Okay so he's working today, right" said Frank "I'm taking young Winston ballooning."

"Oh what a lovely idea" said Winston's mother "ballooning. He'll enjoy ballooning."

"I have always wanted to fly in a balloon myself" continued Frank "in a simple fashion after our own great uncle Frank."

"Did he have a balloon then?" asked Terry.

"Sopwith Pup" said Frank "it had a 9 cylinder, Gnome Monosoupape, air cooled rotary, 100 horse powered engine."

"Gunner Frank O'Flannagan and Captain Pilkington-Frobisher" said Winston's mother "The stories our father used to tell us about their exploits in the bi-plane."

"Were they true?" continued Terry.

"Do not think of your late great-great uncle in such a way" his mother remonstrated.

"Or your Grandfather, God rest his tortured soul. Sopwith versus the Fokker's, dog fights over enemy lines." continued her brother Frank.

"The Red Baron no doubt." added Terry.

"It was another world son" said Veronica "your great forebear and his adventures."

"The captain took up archaeology after the war and great uncle Frank always said he'd swapped his Browning for a Brownie photographing the ancient sites of Middle Eastern civilizations from the clouds" added Frank O'Flannagan proudly "except it should have been a Vickers point three 'o' three."

"I know what a Brownie is because Rosemary was one but what is a Browning?" Terry quizzed.

"It's the 'peacemaker' a machine gun designed for the Spanish-American war by John Moses Browning which he later adapted for aerial combat in the First World War. Great-uncle Frank loved that old gun". Frank paused thoughtfully "their work was often in the National Geographical towards the end."

"The end of what?" asked Terry

"Well it is a mystery that may never been solved, they vanished into history" Frank sighed "quite literally disappeared...still I have our Great-uncle's medals. Now, where is that boy?"

COLLECTIONS MADE DELIVERIES ACCOMPLISHED

Before Rosemary and Terry were born when Winston's father and their Uncle Frank had been young, newly wed and unavoidably related, the world was their oyster and they combined their 'hare-brained' talents in the construction of the O'Flannagan Pantechnivan Mk1. This was the name they gave to Frank O'Flannagan's van which he commissioned for the purposes of commerce. Frank constructed the vehicle utilizing a retired American 1942 Dodge WC-54 three quarter ton military ambulance that had seen service during the Second World War. It had a much stronger chassis than its half-ton predecessor, a heavier frame, leaf spring suspension and axles. Frank had retained the Masonite interior side panelling and the honeycomb insulation that was fitted between the panels. He had however dispensed with the front mounted winch and the stretcher brackets. The four stretchers, one of which had what looked like blood stains on its frayed, faded canvass, were stored in an old pigsty at the bottom of Frank's yard. The stretchers were for carrying patients known, euphemistically, as litter in the lexicon of militarism. There was a small dog tag metal plate on the glove compartment door that was stamped with a serial number identifying the vehicle that had once rolled off the production line at the Dodge Division of the Chrysler Corporation in Mound Park Michigan, USA, and into the theatre of war sometime between 1942 and 1945. Frank O'Flannagan had occasionally exhibited his vehicle at local fetes to raise money for the Michael O'Flannagan Memorial Trust that he and his wife Gloria had established in memory of their son. It was always one of the most popular attractions at 'Pirates day' an annual event which Gloria organized to celebrate Michael's life.

Frank once exhibited at the county show in a parade procession to mark another ten years farther on as the world progressed away from the end of world war two. I the main parade ring Frank stalled the Dodge T214 six-cylinder, four cycle cast iron block engine, with its cylinder head trimmed with a Zenith carburettor, whilst trying a slow movement gear change. The action caused a loud grating of the wonderfully titled 'banjo hypoid gear differential' which echoed around the grand parade ring and sent a rippling tremor through the surrounding ground.

The result was an exodus of earth worms from their labyrinth in the damp summer warmed soil up and out through silt casts to squirm in the sunlit grass. Ladies in their seasonal sandals were not amused. The gear change sounded like a bucket full of spanners being thrown down an iron stairwell inside a galvanized helter-skelter tower. Gloria and Winston, along for the ride in the cortege of veteran vehicles, and the day at the show, had laughed together enjoying the moment as a retired Brigadier, commentating through a terribly tinny tannoy system, had tormented Frank in finest received English 'I do believe the rouge red repainted American Army Ambulance has blown its disguise by conking out on us, another Yankee late making it late on parade'. The Brigadier received an encouraging cheer from the parochial partisans participating but was later and in private, strongly advised by the bowler hatted stewards from the county set to affect an apology of praise for Uncle Sam when Frank finally stroked compression through his charge, seeing as how the American Ambassador had opened the show on behalf of his President. This was an uncharacteristic departure from the 'traditional' opening ceremony which had previously, always been conducted by a 'royal'. Political pressure had broken tradition due to their Majesty's incumbent government being at a delicate juncture in negotiating terms on some important issue with the land of the free.

Various spare parts for the Pantechnivan Mk1 were supplied by Thomas Walpole to augment the vehicle at the time of construction and had been collected through a part exchange initiative at the ironmongery. These spare parts included a creation that Frank called the wardrobe which had been made by Winston's father and stored in the recessed panel behind the drivers' door on the outside of the body. Hidden behind an additional door, also included among the spare parts, were more of Thomas Walpole's family heirlooms cleared out from his own father's workshop following his untimely death. These included a leather pail reputed to have survived the great fire of London and a complete copper pipe arterial greasing system from a 1930's Bentley.

Winston loved the pages in the family photograph album that recorded this era in the lives of his parents and his beloved uncle and aunt. The corners of the small prints tucked into symmetrical slits in the stiff unbending dark brown card of each page or held in place by neat little fret-worked card corner brackets stuck down with strong glue. Their colourful lives were frozen in black and white and grey. They were young but looked old fashioned to Winston, standing still together, the scenery shifting through social seasons, seasides and Sundays. Even his mother and Auntie Gloria held their cigarettes like ladies though he had never ever actually seen either of them smoking in real life. Every picture captured happiness. Winston would look at the pages mounted with photographs that recorded Rosemary and Terry and his cousin Michael growing up, family holidays, school sports days, religious family celebrations and the perpetual flux of fairs and fetes, sandwiches and sandcastles. He did not understand what was it was draining from the photographs as he turned the pages, as his parents became older but increasingly modern. Their black and white lives for some time evading the eventual capture of technicolour. Michael vanished, his image gone. Michael died. Uncle Frank and Auntie Gloria to, slowly dissolved from this chronicle of Walpole family life. Winston was, on his birthday, missing his Auntie Gloria. Recently she had begun spending time convalescing, living at the same 'Home' as his woolly, birthday present knitting Gran. Winston was not sure what it meant except that it meant no Auntie Gloria. His mother visited every Tuesday, Thursday and Saturday afternoons. Veronica fretted over her brother Frank's Gloria. She loved her as a sister and tried to bear her deep loss with her but some sorrow can be impenetrable even to the strongest love.

When Michael was born he was a beautiful child with a shock of dark hair and deep chestnut grained eyes. He smiled sweetly through his infancy. As a weaned child he seemed to hit a patch of unusual behaviour. Frank and Gloria took him to the doctor. The doctor sent them to see a 'specialist' who confirmed through a number of 'tests' that Michael had a handicap. Only his childhood development would reveal the degree of his handicap and it did. Michael's spatial awareness was fine it was the development of his cognitive functions such as attention, memory his thought process and perceptions that were leading to the conclusion that he had a deficiency of intelligence due to brain 'damage'. No authoritative diagnosis was ever forthcoming just assumptions of frustrating and hurtful opacity. Michael suddenly, one day, became epileptic as a small child. Epilepsy then, was a cause of social exorcism to protect the innocent and uninitiated. Frank and Gloria were warned that the pathology of this condition could lead to a deterioration of Michael's cognitive functions, of his physical life. Frank and Gloria continually asked questions of the 'experts' all of which were answered except the question 'Why?'. Michael was their angel, their purpose. Gloria never fell for another child, a sister or brother for Michael, he was to be the one act of procreation for Frank and his Gloria whom he called 'my girl' just as he had proudly announced Michael as 'my boy'.

Wherever we were, wherever we are, somewhere in our world there probably is one, maybe more, handicapped child, handicapped adult. Physical handicap I could cope with. I can cope with. I went to school with a girl who was disfigured by having some fingers that were normal and some that were tumid. She had a humpback. At birth she was consigned by midwives and doctors to the shadows and expected to expire. Her poor mother did see her for the first three months of her life. Her grandmother and great aunt visited every day at the end of a fifty mile round trip by steam train and omnibus. These two older ladies protecting her young mother from the perceived 'horror' of her physical condition whilst she busied herself with her other children. How times change. Over the years the skill of surgeons lessened the impact of her appearance and made her life more comfortable for her and for us bystanders. No one could add anything to her beautiful soul and handicap could take nothing from it. She lived her life naturally. She had no time for pretension, for people who strained to maintain their 'normal expression', to pretend that she was 'normal.' She was normal. She made with her ill-made hands the most beautiful inventions of a seamstress. She nursed, professionally, premature babies, holding them, changing their nappies and their intravenous lifelines with her challenging hands. I know that she loved with a wonderful capacity way beyond her children, her extended family and into the classrooms full of friends at the infant school she attended. A generation later, all over again she went back to that school as a teachers' assistant touching children hearts and children's hands with her peculiar hands. Teaching from life's curriculum a generation with fewer prejudices than her own. She died a daughter, sister, wife, mother and friend being taken too soon by the cruelty of cancer. Her very essence remains at the depth of those who still mourn her passing.

Mental handicap is different. It is beyond the skill of the surgeon. It is strangely manifest, obtuse. Searching to touch the soul of someone with mental handicap demands an absolute love that takes hold and does not let go.

Gloria loved Michael so clearly she let him be himself always. It was her blessed gift to him. Frank marvelled at his wife who never tried to make their dear child conform to the world that would stigmatize Michael and Gloria. Winston's parents tried honourably to understand. Michael living and dead became the marrow of Frank and Gloria's marriage.

Winston loved riding with his uncle Frank because his van was the only one of its kind on the road. Uncle Frank would sound a brass bugle horn clamped to the wing mirror on the driver's door as a salutation to all and everyone would stare at it passing by on journeys to the regular market to set up his stall or a farm sale to buy geese or a runt pig or sometimes just a picnic. This was before Auntie Gloria began her convalescence. Winston always sat in the back seat on bum tempered brown leather and watched the world go by through a porthole in the side of the van. On the inside of the van the porthole had a polished brass casement that was secured by a big sprung clip that snapped when it was opened or closed. The first time that Winston had closed the porthole he had got a blood blister on his pointing finger. He remained scared of this particular type of clip. Last Christmas one of his presents had been a set of paints and coloured pencils in a flat wooden box it had two of the same clips on it although they were smaller than the polished brass clip in the van. Being fearful of the porthole contraption he had not yet done any painting or drawing with his new set.

On the outside of the van the porthole had a white capital 'O' painted as its border. This was the 'O' of 'Frank O'Flannagan Master Wagoner Collections Made and Deliveries Accomplished' the script that ran in two gentle, parallel arched banderols from front to back on both sides of the body of the O'Flannagan Pantechnivan Mk1. The script was the creation of one Pierce Herbert the illegitimate son of Mr Fairfax Herbert a sign writer and painter decorator. I make no apologies here because like Gilbert Herring the barber, Fairfax Herbert has an interesting biography himself and who knows where he might 'pop up' in this narrative. Fairfax was one of two orphan boys adopted from the care of a Dr Barnardo home for boys once known as a 'ragged school'. The boys became the adopted sons of the local fishmonger and his wife Mr and Mrs. Herbert. These two local, popular, portly figures were, in appearance, practically identical whether in their 'Harris' tweed suits of the subtle coloured weave of brilliant and mellow yarns or white working coats and gaily striped aprons topped off with navy blue felt Chester trilby hats with sweat mapped Petersham bands. It was impossible to tell the fishmonger and his wife apart. They were the epitome of androgyny, phlegmatic to their core and determinedly homogenous with a subtle glint of affectation. Their brilliantine coated short back and side's hair styles, their portly gait, the smell of their trade and, in the course of their twilight years, their downy moustaches made them two peas from the same pod. Mrs Herbert was the only child of one Billy Eastoe late of trawler skippering and fish mongering. She inherited the family business following the unfortunate death of her father who was crushed beneath a rusting, redundant World War Two German naval contact mine that had bounced onto the deck of his trawler, the 'Fair Dotty', as his trawler-men hauled in the nets. The barnacle encrusted sphere rolled right over Billy gruesomely tenderizing him with its solid, unyielding brass fingers. Many treasured their knowledge of Mr Fairfax Herbert in accordance with local legend. It is purported that on the day the King, George VI, declared war on Germany through the wireless, Fairfax Herbert had begun sign-writing in Stempel-Garamond script over a wood grain finish he had previously worked onto the front of the tobacconists shop in the high street. The tobacconist was about, proudly, to take a son into the business. Mr Herbert had got as far as 'Lewis Dobbin &'. The following day only the emblems of his trade, ladder, trestles and boards, pots of paint, white spirit, apron and brushes remained. Mr Herbert did not return to his craft to accomplish his task. He had ventured to the capital to enlist in the service of his king and country as a soldier. It was a fresh task from which he never returned to the town. Unbeknown to Fairfax he left his fiancée Gladys Purbright 'with child'. Gladys bore the social disgrace with great dignity and the child with stoic resolve. She christened him Pierce and gave him his father's surname although she remained a Purbright and became an early feminist. Pierce was the painter of 'Frank O'Flannagan Master Wagoner Collections Made and Deliveries Accomplished'. Gladys raised Pierce in widowhood and with the loving support of his fishmonger family. It was said as a mark of the character of Mr and Mrs. Herbert that 'never have two orphans and a bastard child been so completely loved'. Mr Herbert was another enigma in Winston's world after Great Uncle Gunner Frank. After four years of the war Lewis Dobbin sadly sanded the '&' away. The Dobbins only son had made the ultimate sacrifice the freedom of his king and country could demand of him. He died a 'POW' in a German prison camp from septicaemia as a result of a burst appendix. His named etched forever in the town's achromatic war memorial between 'Day' and 'Dunn' and exactly opposite 'Arthur Thomas Henry 'Herb' Sage Corporal 16th/5th The Queen's Royal Lancers', who, 'gave his life for King and Country (Foundouk) North Africa April 9th 1943' in the other continuing column of the town's war dead that are a still slowly dying memory, with those they left behind.

The lettering of the script on the O'Flannagan Pantechnivan Mk1 was creamy white in colour with a black shadow cast from the left onto a maroon background (The Brigadier of the Grand ring commentary was a little colour-blind). Over the rear wheel arches was a further script in a straight line which ran Telephone: 3134 (Rest day Sunday). This also appeared in an arch across the double doors at the back of the van above the polished brass handle for securing them before journeys. The back doors opened up what Frank called the hold. They could be pinned back to the sides of the van and the original folding step of the Dodge let down to enable someone to climb 'aboard'. It was the empty storage space for cargo. There was an ornate hook, just behind the dome light and roof ventilator that protruded from a socket on the roof of the hold, it resembled the hook of Captain Hook the story book pirate. The hook had one purpose it was for hanging Mr Birtwhistle. Mr Birtwhistle was Auntie Gloria's budgerigar he was pied with a cummerbund of white feathers across his otherwise blue chest. He was a boisterous bright blue budgerigar and he lived in a deep domed cage with pristine, polished brass bars. Mr Birtwhistle could say his name minus his nomenclature so everyone except Auntie Gloria called him Birtwhistle. He could whistle and recite poems that Auntie Gloria had written and taught him except that he dropped his 'aitches' due to a glottal impediment which was also the reason that he could impersonate coughing but not sneezing. Winston's father had given Birtwhistle to Gloria a decent time after they had lost Michael. He had found the cage restored it to its antiquated glory and filled it with Birtwhistle. Auntie Gloria loved her Mr Birtwhistle whom she had respectfully named after her bank manager, a local man who graduated through the banking ranks after leaving the Grammar School in Sun Rise road, respected for his sensitivity, discretion and an impeccable manner, he was a bastion of local society. Mr Birtwhistle went everywhere when the absence of cargo meant there was room for him to hang and swing, at corners, on journeys in the hold.

The van was augmented with two enormous brass headlights at the very front which were mounted on a shining chromium plated bumper of flat steel that was scroll rolled inwards at the ends. In the middle of the bumper was a small hole shaped like a lemon. Uncle Frank had told Winston a long time ago that this was the hole for the crank handle which was no longer used to start the engine because his clever father had fitted an electric ignition soon after they built the O'Flannagan Pantechnivan Mk1. Winston's father had also built the unique steering wheel of the O'Flannagan Pantechnivan Mk1. Unique because it converted when occasion required from a steering wheel designed for an adult of average build for the singular purpose of steering the van, into the multi-purpose requirement of a dwarf needing the steering wheel to control not just the steering but the gears, brakes and acceleration in fact the entire motion of the O'Flannagan Pantechnivan Mk 1. Unique because it was a composite of components culled from the ironmongery managed by Mr Walpole.

The dwarf for whom this modification was made was Clement Longfellow. Everyone apart from his mother and father and Gloria O'Flannagan called him by his nickname 'Long Clem'. His mother usually made first time introductions thus; 'This is my Clement, he wouldn't stop a pig in an alley' on account of his bandy gait which gave him a rolling walk which she was more conscious of than the fact that he barely came up to his father's belt buckle, hence her 'ice breaker' for people who generally found it hard to hide their first reflex on encountering Long Clem. Winston's Auntie Gloria often chided Clement that he had the same rhythmic movement as the pendulum of her clockwork metronome, which had been crafted a century before in Paris by Maelzel. Gloria had given Clement piano lessons as a kind of therapy since he was a young boy. To Clement the pendulum was kin that emerged from the polished mahogany case when he removed the door, having wound the mechanism up with its old brass key. The pendulum had a range from grave at 40 up to a frantic 208 beats by which to keep time. From a gentle walk, to the annual village fete obstacle race for 'all comers', Clements' roll remained within the range of the metronome. As a small boy he liked to take the case door and press the gilded metal 'makers' plate hard into his stubby forearm giving himself a fading and embossed tattoo that read, Maelzel of Paris- France, Belgique, Angleterre, Amerique & Hollande. As he got older Long Clem was casually employed to carry out occasional jobs for Frank and

Gloria O'Flannagan. It is said that by wearing a 24 carat gold earring and having a face as big as a ham and in it a glass eye (he lost his eye in an accident running with a kaleidoscope and using it as a telescope when he was a boy) over which he usually wore a black patch may have inspired his nickname. However it arose, Clement Longfellow the dwarf was always known to almost everyone who knew him as 'Long Clem' and the unique steering wheel made him feel very special. The O'Flannagan Pantechnivan Mk1 was the only vehicle Long Clem could drive and gradually it became the only vehicle he would drive after one or two slight accidents in vehicles belonging to visitors to his parent's business premises that he had pirated in the spirit of an inquisitive child. The wearing of the patch always got him off with a sympathetic reprimand although I do not understand why.

Eye patches should not prejudice the very necessary developmental importance of discipline and the security it gives a child.

The engine sat behind an impressive brass radiator and beneath two maroon coloured 'L' shaped covers that shared a single hinge that ran the length of the bonnet from the windscreen to the radiator cap which was also made of brass. The radiator cap was topped off with a globe that spun on an axis held in a crescent mount. The globe was embossed with the map of the world and wrapped in the lattice-work of latitude and longitude. The two engine covers where fastened by two short leather fetters threaded through brackets on the chassis. When the engine covers were released they rose and spread above the engine like the wings of a huge eagle preparing to launch off from its eerie. The windscreen was an absolutely flat pane of thick glass set in a chromium frame which could be folded down onto the bonnet. On summer days Uncle Frank would fold the screen down and pin the back doors round against the sides of the van. He would drive along at speed the breeze and everything on it would pass right through the O'Flannagan Pantechnivan Mk1. Uncle Frank, Aunty Gloria and Winston would sing songs and laugh as insects splattered on their faces and they breathed in the tiny florets of the dandelion or the cotton seeds of the crack willow, making them cough or sneeze. A green woodpecker once flew in its undulating flight right through the van clipping the brass hook from which swung Mr Birtwhistle, startling him with its hysterical laugh.

And so at last the day had come and Winston waited

patiently on the pavement outside number thirteen Captain Scott Terrace for his uncle Frank to give his assurances to Veronica that Winston was perfectly safe in the very capable hands of his favourite uncle. Frank then walked towards Winston with a look of satisfaction and a bounce in his step.

"Today Winston" declared Uncle Frank "you are my co-pilot not only of this shrunken pantechnicon but of its wonderful cargo to." with this Frank O'Flannagan flung open the back doors of the van.

"What is it?" Winston asked.

"A basket." replied Frank O'Flannagan.

"How do we pilot a basket Uncle Frank?" Winston asked.

"Suspended from my enormous balloon young man that's how" continued Frank pointing to a pile of faded membrane on the floor beyond the basket "your present on this auspicious occasion from your Auntie Gloria and me is a flight in a balloon." Frank's eyes opened as wide as was physically possible until all the tiny veins were visible and his whole face travelled through a slow metamorphosis from a smile to a grimace waiting upon Winston's carefully considered response.

"Is Auntie Gloria coming then?" asked Winston after a few ponderous moments.

"Well no" said Frank O'Flannagan "you know how it is for your Auntie Gloria at the present time eh Winston I mean your Gran she needs the company you know."

"Does Auntie Gloria know about the balloon?" continued Winston.

"Not exactly Winston no" said Winston's Uncle Frank "you see your Auntie knows all about me so in one sense she would know about the possibility of the balloon but not exactly so to speak because at this time she is a little delicate as you know."

"Does mum know where you are taking me?"

"Oh yes" Frank said turning and waving to his sister Veronica who was standing on the raised step at the front door ready to wave them off on their adventure "your mother knows you are coming on an outing with me and she knows that I recently purchased a hot air balloon."

"How much does she know Uncle Frank?"

"Enough Winston enough we don't want to concern her now, do we?"

"Hold on Winston" called is mother suddenly stepping down and hurrying towards him from her red tiled polished pedestal at which Frank quickly closed the van doors "have you got a handkerchief for your nose."

Winston looked at her blankly.

"Oh here you are you could do with three pennyworth of memory powder you could."

Veronica Walpole stuffed a neatly pressed and folded red and white polka dot handkerchief into Winston's trouser pocket pressing the coarse wool of his 'birthday' pants into his thigh triggering an itch which he scratched intently until she told him to stop. Then she kissed him on his cheek and he felt the soft tissue paper skin of her face delicately touching his, a zephyr of her 'Oloroso' breath mixed with the scent of her talc wafted right under his nose and he felt safe and warmed on the inside.

"Be a good boy" she said "and enjoy yourself and Frank, Winston has to be back by five thirty because he is having a little party with Ezra, Osborne and Geraldine."

Winston coloured a little at the mention of Geraldine he remonstrated weakly that it was 'mainly' Ezra and Osborne and then climbed into the seat beside his uncle and fastened his seat belt. He wound down the window and waved farewell to his mother and his brother Terry who had joined her at the curb side. Frank O'Flannagan squeezed the black rubber lung of his brass bugle horn in his large hand twice, sending loud 'parps' echoing through the houses in the street. The O'Flannagan Pantechnivan Mk1 pulled slowly away from the curb bumped across a street drain, ground through two more gear changes and set off for the launch site.

Winston loved journeys. The beginning of a journey is exciting and he felt the excitement concentrated in the mysterious rumblings of his stomach and his, all of a sudden, quite floppy limbs. He would look back holding up one bidding hand until the curve of the street left everything and his waving mother behind and then he would stiffen and watch strangers and people that he recognized walking the pavements, waiting at the curb, talking silently, greeting, or saluting across the street. Shop assistants and their customers distorted through window glass stared out at the O'Flannagan Pantechnivan Mk1 as it passed will-o'-the -wisp across them. The engine was like a fairground organ rolling along the highway broadcasting a steady timbre of percussive rhythm under the gurgle and spit of blown brass and the bowed hum and plucked twang of tuned gut, breaking into and enriching the soundtrack of life. Today on birthday number twelve it sounded no different except that there was no Auntie Gloria.

Winston felt the absence of his Aunt. He did not know how much she really meant to him because measuring did not matter. He missed her. He missed what he felt when he was with her. Gloria was, according to Winston's mother 'taking a break' it was 'a bit like a rest'. Gloria had 'a sensitive soul which sometimes tired of everyday things'. Gloria was actually spending time in the local psychiatric hospital recovering from a diagnosis of severe depression brought on by the 'irrepressible effects of an earlier trauma'. Frank and Gloria O'Flannagan had had their son Michael. He was born a while after Terry and Rosemary Walpole. He was a beautiful little baby and a great joy to his parents because they had despaired of ever conceiving. In fact Frank had taken Gloria to America for a holiday, a second honeymoon on the advice of their local GP Dr Woodhead who had been treating Gloria for a case of mild depression brought on, he surmised, from their childlessness. Dr Woodhead had suggested to Frank that a second honeymoon might create the right 'emotional' atmosphere for Gloria to relax enough for his wooing to bear fruit. In fact as it later turned out the very promise of a holiday in the Hamptons on Long Island New York in the glorious fall had had the required effect. Gloria had conceived before they set out for their second honeymoon unbeknown to them both. Morning sickness had been diagnosed as travel sickness and missing a menstrual cycle as the stress of flying for the first time in her life. Michael was born into a harmonious and deeply loving world. He gave them such joy as any, longed for child would. His first smile borne of his soul and not of his wind, his first gurgled laugh, the explosions of food as he was given independence in his high chair at meal times and the emergence of two pearly white teeth in the middle of his bottom gum were all treasured by Frank and Gloria. The path

73

through life for another O'Flannagan seemed set and the early journey well under way. But there were other signs in Michael of a life less natural, little instances, slight nuances that left Frank and Gloria, at different times, unsure as to whether they had really seen or felt 'something' not quite as they expected it. Gradually it became apparent that he had 'problems'. The doctors had, eventually agreed that Michael was mentally handicapped. He began to suffer those epileptic fits from the age of two. Gloria was sure in her own troubled mind that she 'understood' why Michael was so beset.

While Frank and Gloria had been enjoying their second honeymoon on Long Island a hurricane had developed further south. It was the hurricane season. To Frank's dismay the hurricane was named Gloria and it was to be one of the costliest and most intense hurricanes to hit US land in the twentieth century. Hurricane Gloria first passed over Cape Hatteras, North Carolina on September 27 rated as a category 3 Storm and moving at more than 30 mph. It made landfall again over southern Long Island, New York as a category 2 storm. Economic losses were estimated at $900 million. Frank had tried to persuade Gloria that hurricanes were named by the same ilk of people who compose horoscopes in newspapers but he could not convince her. Gloria was certain that hurricanes were always named by someone seeking to exact some sort of revenge. She wondered who the real Gloria was whose name was being taken in vain and how she would feel being powerless to stop neither this act of retribution nor the force of nature bearing her name. She feared for what it might do to all the other Gloria's in the world. Michael had borne the brunt of her inner turmoil in the secret place of her womb. Her name was given to destruction she was cursed by some meteorologist's spell casting. Her delicate spirit, her profound sensitivity were crushed, turned inward. She could be troubled in an instant even in the normal warp and woof of life. She had carried a horrible personal secret from early childhood. As a little girl she had been given a hamster as a pet. Gloria did not want a pet hamster she was afraid of them. Gloria was afraid of pet mice and rats and guinea pigs. Her father christened it with the name Fawkes because he had bought it home in a little cardboard box on the evening of November the fifth. Fawkes the pet hamster was an imposition to cure her musophobia *(the fear of rodents)* that her father in his wisdom regarded the appropriate remedy. The next evening after school Gloria, in trepidation, went to get Fawkes out of his new cage which her father had placed on the wooden lid of the old brick boiler in the washhouse. In her anxiety she had squeezed Fawkes a little too firmly and he reacted by sinking his rapier rodent incisors into one of Gloria's delicate fingers. Gloria shook her painful hand involuntarily sending Fawkes into orbit around the washhouse hitting and cracking a glass pane with a muted thud and then disappearing behind a tool cupboard. Instead of telling the more explainable truth Gloria erred into a criminality that would haunt her for years. She created a scene around the new cage on top of the brick boiler that pointed to a great escape by Fawkes. Gloria feigned sorrow at her loss but her tears were real if somewhat misleading. She believed that it was Fawkes' fault and that it exacted a cruelty upon her she did not deserve and it seared a sombre secret into her sensitive soul. It marked the first step on the long path she was to take through her inner life. It had been her fathers' proscription of fear. It was a prescription for insidious guilt. She blamed her wounded finger on herself for getting it jammed in drawer she should not have been opening anyway.

My father grew prize cabbages and in one particular year he was after the hat-trick of winning the (late) Gertrude Blanchflower perpetual trophy. It was awarded annually at the local horticultural society exhibition to the gardener growing the best Savoy cabbage, in memory of her husband (yet the cup bore her name?). He had worked at the Savoy Hotel in London during the years that Dame Nellie Melba had lived there. As a matter of interest I know that various types of Savoy cabbage enable the Savoy to be in season nine months of the year from June to February. I know this because my father used to tell me every little detail he had learned about the ubiquitous cabbage and then he would question me in front local dignitaries, usually after the Remembrance Day parade. My father was the standard bearer for the British Legion branch. There was always a 'cuppa' and the relaxation of social etiquette in the melee around the local cenotaph. It was at such events that my father, being renowned as a champion grower of the Savoy, would be questioned by an old admiral or retired schoolmaster and once by a minor royal in the company of vicar who was a former chaplain to the monarch. Such folk uncomfortably searching for a subject of conversation, had stored in their vast memory banks, the newspaper picture of my jubilant Dad winning the Gertrude, as he called it. Thus the subject, the only subject, anyone of consequence raised in my experience of being with my father was the incorrigible cabbage. He in turn would turn to me and ask the most obscure question and I would duly oblige with a clear and precise answer, impressing that my father had clearly spawned a prodigy. Did you know for instance that this cruciferous vegetable is a vital ingredient of Minestrone soup, it takes its name from the Italian Duchy of Savoy that borders France and Switzerland and that it has properties proven in the fight against cancer? Anyway I digress. Near to the time of the annual horticultural society exhibition my father's hat-trick crop was attacked by caterpillars. I remember my father using a word to describe the epidemic caterpillars that I found to my shame and pain, when I proudly repeated it to my great aunt at a family christening tea a few weeks later, was not their actual moniker but an expletive and I felt the full force of my mother's embarrassment around my ear-hole at the only time in my life she used violence to correct me. (It was a profound moment from which I have never fully recovered) To add to this my father expressed the full force of his deep frustration the sight of bored and shredded prized brassica gave him on my tender backside. He did this through the violence of his leather belt for the very minor offence of my scrumping of a single pear from his tree full of the Clapps Favourite variety. The pinched pear was so hard and unripe that it bruised my gums and had white pips in the middle. You can imagine the antagonism that built up in me towards caterpillars. I hated them not through fear but by association with raw buttock pain. One day I was playing hopscotch on the pavement with some of my friends who lived in the same street. I had thrown my pebble into the single square of the number seven and was about to start hopping through the chalked pattern of squares on the pavement, one foot to two feet to one foot to two feet to one foot landing on the square with the number seven when, ironically, my next door neighbour Reginald Botwright, joined us. Reginald had in his hand an enormous Privet Hawk-moth caterpillar (Sphinx Lugustri) and we persuaded him to let the caterpillar join in our game on the basis, not understood by any of us at the time that the caterpillar would be playing Russian roulette not hopscotch like the rest of us. The caterpillar was free to roam over our chalked hopscotch grid while we adapted a slight variation on the game by hopping with our eyes shut. I took my turn and two more and then temptation seized me. The swollen juicy Sphinx Lugustri was motionless in the square beyond where my pebble had landed. My eyelids quivered as I tried to make them appear shut tight by screwing my cheeks up as high as possible but I could discern the green grub with its vivid side stripes and from the apex of a giant hop I descended on the innocent *representative of a species that had denied my father his hat-trick and left me with a swollen ear, raw buttocks and an uncomfortable rite of passage in my relationship with my mother. I experienced the briefest moment of sensual pleasure (I need that word) that revenge brings before the scourging effect of guilt which has lasted a lifetime. I recently took my wife out to lunch at a reputable restaurant. We ordered a salad. I was commenting on the flavours that can be enjoyed when a salad has been gently warmed when my wife bit through a warm caterpillar secreted in the bed of mixed lettuce leaves of her salad. I am not one to complain. In fact I suffer deeply when I do, much more than the person I am complaining to. It was the worst moment because I perversely compounded it by suggesting that as she was my wife perhaps we should just avoid any confrontation. She confronted my favouring a bitter sickly caterpillar over her dignity. I cannot see or think of the caterpillar, any caterpillar without my mind filling with that expletive my father used and my souls' cruel wrench from my mother and the months of enforced celibacy I have recently endured. Yet I adore butterflies.*

Collecting Long Clem

Winston found the steady vibration of the Pantechnivan Mk1 engine that permeated his entire being somehow comforting, reassuring. It was like feeling sound through a sixth sense. When he spoke he felt his voice tremor.

"Why don't mum and dad ever come for a ride in your van? Winston asked his Uncle Frank.

"When we had Rosemary, Terry and Michael all together we used to go out into the country on Sundays after the Mass. Your Aunt Gloria would never ever miss Mass. I would go back and collect your mother, brother and sister from number thirteen and your father either from his garden or the Goat and Compasses, depending on the length of father Costello's sermon. We travelled the lanes and even the odd bridleway" Frank chuckled "we used to roll up into dead end farm yards or a copse or out on the common watching the golfers. Your father made this contraption which I always called the wardrobe because it looked like a wardrobe that had been perfectly compressed condensing everything inside it. When he flicked a single spring clip it erupted into a table with seven ladder-backed unfolding chairs. Each chair was in correct proportion to the person whose name was carved into the top stave of it and Winston, your father is actually quite a thoughtful fellow you know, he occasionally adjusted the capacity of the chairs as the children and particularly their mothers grew completely unbeknown to any of them." Frank chuckled to himself "Inside the wardrobe there was crockery, cutlery and condiments, a small chilled churn and a caddy of tea. Your mother and your Aunt brought the rest in baskets. What feasts we had under the sky. We owned the world you know, we did."

"I have only been on picnics with you and Auntie Gloria." said Winston.

Frank pondered Winston's enquiring and then said after a short while.

"I think it was after Michael yes it was definitely after Michael, things changed, the picnics were fewer, more infrequent I suppose" Frank O'Flannagan changed the subject. "So Ezra is coming to your party then?"

"Yes" said Winston."

"He's a plucky young steer that boy, you know."

"He's as mad as a box of frogs sometimes" said Winston "even with those callipers wrapped around his legs to help him walk. He took an inch of skin off Archie's shin the last time we played football. Archie's only just rubbed the rove off."

"Where was Archie's shin pad?" Frank asked.

"Round the back of his sock" replied Winston.

"A fat lot of good that is."

Frank O'Flannagan drew the O'Flannagan Pantechnivan Mk1 up stopping in the yard beside the windmill and squeezed the rubber lung on the brass horn 'par-parp-p-par-parp.........parp-parp' he leant out of the cab and shouted.

"All hands on deck Long Clem the Millers boy, ballooning calls."

The sails of the windmill were turning gently and the muted sounds of greased wooden cogs rolling, their teeth biting and millstones cracking and crushing coarse grains, drifted out over the half door in the roundhouse below the Buck of the old Post Mill. Winston spied the thinning crown of his head as Long Clem called up a storey through the stair well to his father Mr Roy Cobb the miller who was standing on the flour sack polished elm wood bagging platform. Winston and his Auntie Gloria always thought it was funny because his wife Mrs. Cobb, in her rich dialect, pronounced her husband's name as 'Rye'. Mr Cobb ground the flour that was used by Baxter's the local bakery founded in 1837 the year of the coronation of our sovereign Queen Victoria. The bakery's most popular bread roll was the Rye Cobb made using rye flour ground by Roy. One day when Winston had visited the windmill with his Uncle and Aunt to tell Long Clem about a 'collection to be made and a delivery to be accomplished' the following day, Mrs. Cobb greeted them with what sounded like the most alarming news. She told them that Long Clem had crushed 'Rye' in the morning. Gloria O'Flannagan had all but fainted as her 'imagchinery' ran through the gore of Roy's wise old head being crushed into the pepper of cracked grain between the millstones and his torso broken and bent into a hundred peaks and troughs by the wooden cog wheels. Frank O'Flannagan had chided Mrs. Cobb, asking her if she had called the St Johns Ambulance Brigade to which Mrs. Cobb replied 'you are a funny one you are Frank O'Flannagan St Johns Ambulance indeed, you know old Baxter always collects his own flour in that jalopy of his not an ambulance for goodness sake, yours is the ambulance'. Roy Cobb and his son Long Clem then appeared like an apparition, flour dusted from head to foot, standing on the retractable wooden balcony they used to carry out maintenance on the base of the sails. Frank called up to them to reassure his wife and nephew 'rye today Roy?' and Roy shouted down 'Rye all day today Frank' so everything became clear.

Mr and Mrs. Cobb had adopted Clement Christmas Longfellow from an Orphan Home in Scotland. The home had been started by one William Quarrier back in the early 1870's. Roy's family had supported the Homes ever since a great uncle, suffering from tuberculosis, had spent some time being cared for in the sanatorium at Bridge of Weir the location of the home. Once a year the Cobb's would make a pilgrimage to the village in Renfrewshire to spend a few days amongst the orphan's children and those who cared for them acknowledging a commitment way beyond their generous bankers' draft. They were dear souls who enjoyed such a tender matrimony despite the torment of their own childlessness. On the day that they had become Mr and Mrs. Cobb, in the spring time of their lives they drew down deep into their hearts the words of Parson Baggot on the occasion of their marriage when he recited;

'And in the fear of God; duly considering the causes for which matrimony was ordained. First, it was ordained for the procreation of children, to be brought up in the fear and nurture of the Lord, and to the praise of his name.'

It set a longing within them, a purpose beyond the threshold of their singular bond. They both dreamed as Parson Baggot continued;

'Secondly, it was ordained for a remedy against sin, and to avoid fornication' a word they did not understand anyway. Life their one life has hung for several, child barren years on the fact of the Parson's third and final ordination 'it was ordained for the mutual society, help and comfort that the one ought to have of the other both in prosperity and in adversity.'

Roy Cobb treasured the knowledge that, in the upholding of human dignity, his father had cradled him in his infancy and as life had run its meandering course so Roy, in turn, had cradled his father in the twilight of his life until the last simmering ember had extinguished. The lineage of such mutual society as Parson Baggot had spoken of, had been broken by their childlessness, no thought of who would cradle Roy at his calling home to the heaven he would look toward all his life in communion with Mrs. Cobb. And then along came Clement Christmas Longfellow Cobb. The child Mr and Mrs. Cobb had fallen in love with above all the children at Bridge of Weir. Long Clem was not really an orphan he was just abandoned, wrapped in a woollen cardigan and newspaper and snug in a strong, steel stapled, waxed-cardboard box which had Clementine Christmas's Chantenay Carrot and Wild Coriander Soup advertised in bold print on its sides and tucked in leaves. The box had been left outside a police station and was discovered by one Sergeant Horace Longfellow who had christened the abandoned baby boy Clement Christmas before he handed him over to the Matron of a Cottage Hospital. The Matron, in honour of the Sergeant gave the little boy the surname of Longfellow when she entered it into the hospital register. The rendering of the solemnization of matrimony by Parson Baggot had had one more deep effect that was to bless the nurture the little boy enjoyed as he grew up in the joy of the millers life when he recited;

'I require and charge you both, as ye will answer at the dreadful day of judgement, when the secrets of all hearts shall be disclosed'

Mr and Mrs. Cobb held only the very intimacy of their union secret from the little boy. They opened their whole world to him and he became a huge part of it. Clement Christmas Longfellow Cobb grew, loved by hearts that knew no secrets, no bounds and when he did not grow as you would expect, well, a child to grow, hale hearty tall and strong, he was safe with them. The little boy, their little boy, had skeletal dysphasia. And it was in the form of spondyloepiphyseal which meant that his condition went undetected until he was almost seven years old. He had always been slightly barrel-chested but no-one seemed bothered by this. The spontaneous mutation of a single gene inherited from his father who had abandoned his mother who in turn abandoned

Clement now marked the little boy out. Mr and Mrs Cobb ensured that the word dwarf became a word like any other word, ordinary, properly used and stamped with love by his true parents before Clement Christmas ever heard it uttered by people who do not know what to say in describing someone like him.

My Grandma used to explain things brilliantly with descriptions like' you know the woman, she wears a blue coat and limps' about someone whose name she had forgotten, or an observation like 'I would rather kiss a toad than buy my candles from him', the him in question being Mr Larter the local ironmonger, on account of his rather smarmy demeanour and the fact that he used eyebrow pencil to 'fill in' his thin moustache. We all use description to help us communicate, to fill the gaps were memory fails or prejudice creeps in. But we also have a store of labels, our default, bone fide descriptions that we do well to update as convention dictates. At the present moment in time I am 'white', my skin colour. That is my description plain and simple but am I 'white' and is that why the other skin colour is 'black' because the other person is of African origin and what about the person who is of Asian origin what colour do I use then. Well I don't think we have a colour for Asian so I had better use 'Caucasian' rather than 'white' and African instead of 'black' except that there are 'black' people everywhere just as there are 'white people and Asian people. Perhaps I am 'English' yes I am English but then I have black and Asian friends who are English…yes but are they as English as me? They are the same as age as me and were born in England which is where I was born so if they are not as English as me, then it has nothing to do with being born or birthdays. The Americans have got it right, haven't they? Everyone in America is American, Afro-American, Asian-American, Hispanic-American, Chinese-American etc. I get it, I am English-English or is it Anglo-English which means I am originally a Johnny Foreigner. Now there's another description that is outside convention. Anyway in this story I am telling, I believe Clement Christmas Longfellow Cobb is a 'little person' hence forth but I will still describe him as a dwarf, if I have to.

"Be right with you Frank." Long Clem called out from below the half door as the 'parps' echoed off the round red brick tower around the mill yard. Mrs Cobb stepped out of the round house onto the cobbles. She slipped slightly sideways suddenly emitting flatulence that sounded like an anxious bumble bee on steroids flying the inverted wall of death around the inside of a large church steeple bell.

"A phartin 'orse never tyers." she announced with dignity and some authority.

Long Clem looked at Winston and winked his good eye which looked more like a grimace on account of his eye patch. Frank was employing Long Clem to drive the O'Flannagan Pantechnivan Mk 1 on balloon reconnaissance during and for, balloon recovery at the end of the proposed flight. This was a new role for the dwarf and an adventure that he relished. He appeared from behind the half door beating himself all over with his short stout arms as he walked towards the van. Flour dust swirled around and wafted away from him revealing someone looking like an extra from a Charlie Chaplin film.

"Hello Winston Happy Birthday." he said.

"Thank you Long Clem." replied Winston.

"I will be changed a jiffy." Long Clem said as he made his way to his 'house'.

Long Clem lived in a converted railway carriage which had been parked in an ancient orchard of hazel trees just off the mill yard. His adoptive parents had acquired the carriage on his coming of age to give him some independence. They would have built him a small self-contained little cottage in keeping with the historic windmill, mill house, outbuildings and cobbled yard but the local planning committee at County Hall had refused their application to build. This was based on an EU planning directive that said that the internal utility features of the home should be doubled up in terms of height. A toilet for Long Clem and a toilet for everyone else, a sink for Long Clem and a sink for everyone else, windows for Long Clem and windows for everyone else. I think you get the picture. Roy had argued that like all children growing up in the majority of family homes throughout the country, Clement Christmas Longfellow Cobb had used a 'step up' contraption. His had been fashioned and built by Roy, it was of polished walnut salvaged from and old piano that had fallen off a cart in the mill yard years ago. A farmer had been heading home from the market, where he had bought the piano as a gift for his new young wife. He had called in to 'make up' his load with sacks of flour that Roy's father had milled for him. The horse in harness of the cart was a young Suffolk Punch Colt on his first outing. The horse was called Colony Boxer, he was spirited and a little nervous. The farmer had purchased, along with the piano, 8 young Norfolk Black turkey stags which were in two wooden crates and an English Buff Back gander which was tethered in sack, with his head sticking out of the neck which had been tied loosely. During their journey from the market the birds had all been subdued by the trundling of the cart wheels and the rhythm of Colony Boxer's shod feet on the road. After a few moments of stillness in the mill yard the sack trussed gander let out a hearty honk, this in turn disturbed the turkey stags who erupted in a chorus of high pitched gobbles and Colony Boxer reared and tipped the cart. The weight and motion of the piano broke the tail gate of the cart and it fell out onto the unforgiving cobbles. The badly damaged piano was consigned to an outbuilding known as the Nettice until Roy commandeered some of its forgotten parts for the construction of the 'step up' for Long Clem. The County Hall planning committee had to uphold the EU directive which did not recognize the innovation that was the 'step up'. Roy did not have the sort of money required by the European Union to build two homes inside one and so he purchased the carriage.

The carriage that became the young dwarf's home was built around 1890 for the Manchester South Junction and Altrincham Railway. It was originally a four compartment second class carriage that had been re-trimmed into two first class compartments with a third class compartment at either end. The carriages were taken out of service between the two world wars and Roy bought it from a sculptor who once claimed to be on the periphery of the famously artistic Bloomsbury group and lived in the coach house next door to the Cobb's property. In truth he had spent two terms in the same school class as Burgo Partridge and had once been invited to tea at Ham Spray. Roy would say of the sculptor 'cultured fellow, knows a lot about nothing though', Mrs Cobb would retort, 'Rye that en't very sweet of you'. The carriage was 'planted' on a length of old railway track supported by wooden sleepers these were kept dry by the fact that they were laid upon the remnant of a flag stone floor that had once been part of an old cottage that had long since gone even though the Hazel orchard remained

Long Clem emerged from his home in the ancient orchard in freshly restored technicolour and as he boarded the van he dug his strong hand into his pocket and brought out a crumpled white paper bag. He flicked at the neck of the bag to open it and he proffered the contents.

"Pomfret cake?" he said to Winston.

"Yes please." Winston replied as the O'Flannagan Pantechnivan Mk 1 pulled away from the mill yard gate and set off along the road continuing the birthday adventure.

Long Clem shook the bag up separating the black liquorice Pomfret cakes that had become clung together in the warmth of his pocket. Frank O'Flannagan drove along in quiet reverie. Winston and Long Clem chewed the liquorice into a crude oil, smiled at each other with blackened teeth and liquor juiced lips, and then laughed out loud. Long Clem closed his seeing eye and lifted the patch over his green glass eye.

"Let's play I spy me hearty." he said to Winston mischievously.

"Hold tight everyone." shouted Frank O'Flannagan.

Uncle Frank pushed his foot down hard on the brakes as the O'Flannagan Pantechnivan Mk1 rounded a bend in the lane and came upon the tail end of a herd of freshly milked cows swinging their slack udders in pendulous rhythm to the awkward gait of their back legs whilst making their way along the long lane towards a tasty pasture. The herdsman walking behind them called 'Goowarn goowarn hup' repeatedly and stung the backside of any straggling cow with a switch of peeled ash. The smarting cow retaliated with the swish of a tail loaded at the end with clinkers of moist green dung variously slapping the herdsman on his arm, his chest, or his face. Twice his flat cap was knocked to the ground and once before he could pick it up the herd bull stamped it into a fresh cowpat. The herdsman slapped the cap against his rubber, milking parlour apron a couple of times and then pulled it back onto his sweating head.

"Goowarn goowarn hup you old beggar." he called as he stung the bull across his broad haunches. Long Clem laughed.

"He's a character now isn't he Winston?" said Frank letting the van roll gently forward behind the herd by 'feathering' the clutch pedal "salt of the earth he is I'll wager and worth his weight in carat gold. Most people have no idea how milk gets from a cow to a cup of tea or a bowl of cornflakes, I mean how many people have a milk man leaving bottles of the stuff on their step in the early hours but you and me Winston now we have seen the mysterious cowman."

Winston was far enough into the biology curriculum at school to distinguish the cows from the herd bull even though he and his uncle Frank had only the rear view but the term 'cowman' confused him "Which one do you mean is the cowman?" he asked.

"He'll be the cowman the one without the horns or a ring in his nose" replied Frank O'Flannagan "or in his ear like Long Clem here."

Just then the herdsman turned and looked at Winston and his Uncle Frank sitting in the O'Flannagan Pantechnivan Mk1 he signalled a grateful acknowledgement of their patience and smiled. Winston could see that there was no ring in his nose he did not appear to have many teeth either in a mouth loosely hemmed by a bottom lip that was stuck with the remains of a hand-rolled cigarette, still smouldering.

"The one in the cap?" said Winston.

"He's the cowman." said Frank O'Flannagan laughing.

Miss Powell, who was Winston's history teacher, had recently begun taking the class through the subject of Greek mythology in the new government's 'ground-breaking' education curriculum with accompanying 'targets'. Miss Powell herself was the subject of local mythology. She had taught Winston's father and his schoolmaster uncle with the flat feet. She had been in the same class at school as Winston's paternal grandfather. Miss Powell was omnipresent in the younger branches of Winston's father's family tree. Local myth had it that her fortune was hidden behind some lose bricks in a secret tunnel that joined her Gothic style house to the imposing, square towered, Norman church that commanded the flint stone walled grave yard sitting on the high point of the town. There is a capstone on the wall that has deep parallel grooves like glacial striations that are believed to be where Oliver Cromwell's army sharpened the heads of their pikestaffs before beheading the stone angels and saints that decorated the Norman temple. Miss Powell attended church three times every Sunday. She was a re-galer at every religious feast, blessed every baptism, celebrated every confirmation and forlornly frequented every funeral. Myth would have it that she kept her lose change in a pocket stitched into the left leg of her knee length drawers. Her knee length linen drawers were themselves legendary because she would lift her calf length skirts and petticoats to fetch a pretty lace handkerchief from under the gathered frill above her knee whenever she needed to blow her nose or beside the insouciant grave to 'dab' a funereal eye. Miss Powell lived for the lives of her pupils, generation upon generation. She championed the left-handed child using her position to exorcise a Victorian demon. She had for company in her large house only the companionship of two ginger cats one old and one young, one a neutered Tom (male) and the other a spayed Betty (female). She had these two cats for more than fifty years. Not the same two cats of course just one old and one young cat in a timeless rotation of feline friendship provided to her by the cat protection league for a regular charitable consideration given under no declared obligation, just emotional blackmail. Miss Powell made Greek mythology come alive when she taught it and Winston was sure that she had mentioned something quite recently about a 'cowman' when she had spoken of the anatomical combination of the body of a man and the head of a bull locked away deep in the labyrinth at Knossos on the island of Crete and fed human flesh.

"What do cows eat?" asked Winston.

"Ah" said Frank O'Flannagan "I am not falling for that old nutmeg Winston you young clever clogs. Cows eat green grass but they produce white milk and if you want to know where the colour goes when it is filtered out from the milk look at what is pouring out of that old girl." He continued pointing at a cow that was walking just in front of the herdsman with her tail raised and an arch of gratuitous green gravy gushing from her backside, hitting the road and splashing the rubber apron of the herdsman and the tall dry grass on the bank pulling it down into submissive arcs dripping droplets of fresh rejectamenta.

"Do they eat anything else?" asked Winston.

"They eat rolled oats, cotton cake, kale, chopped mangel-wurzel, silage and hay, that sort of thing."

"Is a mangel-wurzel somebody who lives in the countryside?" Winston continued to question his Uncle with the faint recollection of a bedtime story his Aunt Gloria used to read to him when he was younger from one of Michael's old books.

"Good grief no it's a kind of beet."

The last cow followed by the herd bull and finally the herdsman turned out of the lane and into a lush pasture. The herdsman dragged the rusting gate to with one hand and signalled his gratitude by raising his cow-pat coated cap to Long Clem, Winston and his Uncle Frank. Frank O'Flannagan returned the salutation by squeezing the rubber lung of the brass horn three times in quick succession, parp...parp...Parrrrp. Winston watched as the exploding 'parps' possessed the hitherto languid cows and their squire causing them to stampede away from the herdsman across the field bellowing and coughing, their tails erect with the overwhelming rush of fear and a borborygmus accompaniment to the spraying of dung flack and divots of turf everywhere. A cloud of startled starlings rose in Murmuration like thick smoke before the vanguard of bovine panic and a charm of goldfinches scattered thistle down in the wake of their escape as cows crushed the banquet nature had set before the ember coloured birds. The herdsman's hostile gesticulations and language that pursued the O'Flannagan Pantechnivan Mk1 as it sped away down the lane was a marked contrast to his appreciative wave moments before.

"I am sorry that you had to hear his French Winston." said Frank.

"French?" said Winston "that's not French Geraldine's mother calls it Anglo Saxon profanity."

"Saxon, French it's all the same to me anyway I don't think hooting was a good idea on reflection." Frank O'Flannagan said as he grated the gears propelling roosting pheasants from a hornbeam tree in the hedge into a frantic flight over the crazy cattle. After a few minutes and a couple of miles of country lanes the three passengers of the O'Flannagan Pantechnivan Mk1 sat in the tranquillity that often follows a storm, not needing to speak but each just observing the world, ponderously as it sped past on the road to adventure

THE ARRIVALS

The launch site for the balloon flight was through a wagon wheel gouged, gully grained gateway and into a small field surrounded by tall trees at the end of long narrow lane. Frank O'Flannagan pulled to a stop just in front of the gate. Wood pigeons up in the surrounding trees chorused their repetitive yet unique, softly cooed ditty 'take two cows Taffy, take two cows'.

"Right Winston you open the gate and I'll drive through you can leave it opened as I am expecting the rest of my passengers shortly."

"Passengers." said Winston.

"Passengers." replied Frank O'Flannagan "we are doing a bit of business today, company for you and me, ballooning is expensive but passengers balance the books so to speak."

The gate was a wooden five bar gate made of ash. Many seasons had eroded its grain. Black and green detritus stained Winston's hands as he and Long Clem wrestled the gate open, its one remaining cast iron hinge pushing a fractured bottom bar against the lank autumn grass. Frank drove the van past them both, squirting flumes of muddy water as his wheels spun through the ruts, out into the middle of the field, as they strained at their task. With a great deal of effort, some frustration expressed in quiet Saxon-French and the occasional passing of a peal of wind by Frank, they began to unload the van;

"Too much organic cabbage" said Frank. This was followed with giggling from Long Clem and Winston as the van was disencumbered of its load. There was the basket, an enormous mechanical fan in a cage, a small portable generator, torpedo shaped steel bottles of gas, assorted ropes and the faded membrane envelope that comprise the main ingredients of ballooning along with the paraphernalia of piloting. The final ingredient of ballooning, the passengers, began to arrive all through the opened gateway except for one man who emerged from behind a tall tree dusting the lichen powders of the hedgerow from his tweed suit and adjusting the fly buttons on his trousers. He had a large cigar protruding from his florid lips slightly sunken between two Braeburn apple cheeks topped off by small sparkling eyes. Winston recognized the man as a local market stall trader who sold clothing from camel coats to cashmere pashmina's and footwear for anything from dancing to deep sea diving.

"Well Frank" he said "this is going to be a bit of fun reckon that thing will take my weight?"

"You'll be weightless the moment we take off" said Frank "and you'll not be smoking that Churchill anywhere near my gas Billy."

"Is that balloon going to fly on your old cabbage gas Frank?" the man replied.

Long Clem threw Winston a cheeky glance. The two men knew each other well having spent many Wednesdays side by side trading, through all seasons, from their respective stalls on market day in the town. Billy Butterworth was the market trader's name although most folks called him Billy Butterball on account of his shape being largely sculptured by pork pies, pork sausages, pork chops, especially pork belly, pork brawn, chips and ale. In fact it was often said to him 'Billy Butterball the pig will kill you' his answer was always 'my Churchill strains the fat and keeps me slim' goodness knows what mystical qualities the tobacco leaf must have to distil pure fat but Billy Butterworth clearly believed in it. Frank had several business interests including his regular market stall 'O'Flannagan's Hog Fare, Hen Fruit and Fresh Produce from the Garden of Epicurus' selling 'Organic' fruit and vegetables, free range eggs from his prize Buff Orpington hens and meat from his Berkshire pigs. He ran the stall every Wednesday in the town and Gloria would be at his side when she was not otherwise engaged. Billy Butterworth was probably his best customer for the Berkshire pig pork. Wednesday was market day except when it fell on December the 25th or 26th, half-day closing was Tuesday.

Now here's a thing. In what historians call pre-literate society a week could be anything from 4 to 10 days long and was based on the gap in days between one market day and the next giving farmers time enough to produce and transport their organic and free range offerings from the barn, the yard or the sty, from orchard store and henhouse, the milking parlour and the beehive, presented fresh, cured, dried, salted down, bottled up or wrapped in muslin. Farmers markets are not new they are from the dawn of civilization, the source of Adam and Eve's first income. So how did we get to a 7 day week which had originally been considered unlucky? It depends on what you choose to believe. It is most widely held, even by those of alternative faiths to the Judeo-Christian that it originated with the creator God of the Bible, making or working and resting. Others believe that it was adopted by Roman fans of Persian astrology and involved the five known planets plus the sun and the moon. Either way farmer's market day gave us the week just as the farmer's markets immemorial gave us our staple diet. The current day organic nonsense bewilders me. I mean organic and free range what is all that about? The logical term for 'organic' and free range is unadulterated. Chickens allowed to wander about in fields to be eaten by foxes and intimidated by disease carrying seagulls that's what free range amounts to. To the urban 'enlightened' this adds value to the egg eating experience and I assume poultry adrenalin adds to the flavour. The true power of 'organic' and 'free range' is psychological. Successful psychology gets into your head and if you can get into somebody's head you can get into their wallet. The terms 'organic' and 'free range' are in the same category as a 'stealth tax'. The big supermarkets love it because they can operate a lucrative system of licensed banditry off the back off it, simultaneously robbing farmers and horticulturists of their living and customers of their hard earned wages.

Frank O'Flannagan's local 'farmer's' market stall was a healthy earner because the wealthy, well-heeled customers bought the 'organic' label believing that he was selling them healthier food than even the local supermarket and local people bought from Frank and Gloria because they knew them. The real value in the transaction was integrity and a shared experience of humanity.

A loud bang startled Winston it was followed by some chugging and then another loud bang and more chugging that faded away with a last loud reverberating bang that provoked a shivering shudder in Winston similar to the spontaneous sensation someone gets when, with bladder close to bursting, a descending chill passes through every nerve. A motorcycle and sidecar had arrived in the launch meadow. A man dismounted exposing a tiny pink passenger on the pillion. The dismounting man wore a helmet the shape of a basin covered with white leather which sat on his head. The brim was just above his ears on the equator of his head that runs through the eyebrows across the temples over the helix of the auricle (ear) to the occipital fontanel (back of the skull). His ears were covered by matching soft calf skin flaps that had tiny listening gills stitched onto them. The flaps tapered into straps and buckled under his chin. Incongruously mounted on top of the helmet was a chauffeurs' cap. He wore a double breasted jacket with a high, chafing, mandarin collar and semi-spherical silver buttons embossed with a coat of arms. His trousers were tailored with elephant ear thighs, each calf clad in a leather gaiter over burnished black boots and more calf skin in the form of motorcycle gauntlets that wrapped his long forearms. He was attired entirely uniformly in black. He had a large white moustache that seemed to gush from under the centre his goggles and freeze with perfect symmetry over his mouth. He did not speak as if gagged by the magnificent moustache but every chivalrous movement he made had meaning and function to each of his pink passengers the one already visible, alighting down from the pillion and two more up from under the Perspex cockpit canopy of the sidecar that had been opened and tipped on its hinge towards the motorcycle and out through the wing half-door on the 'outside' side of the sidecar. These three pink passengers were identical triplets, sisters celebrating their eightieth birthdays. The sisters were dressed in one style, in hats and scarves, gloves and coats and stocking legs and shoes in a variety of shades of pink. Winston smiled at them and the ladies smiled back sweetly revealing the patina of the stain of long lives on their teeth. They will have names thought Winston and then he wondered if the man in the black outfit could actually tell them apart or was his silence in addressing them really the trick. An elegant gesture carries such import and can disguise a failure of memory or an ignorance of convention.

"Thank you Gustav" said each of the sisters in turn. The tall man touched the peak of his helmet mounted chauffeurs cap in acknowledgement. Long Clem prepared himself for the enrolling of each new arrival into the O'Flannagan 'adventure of a lifetime' register of passengers for inaugural O'Flannagan flight number zero, zero one. The dwarf was as tall as the octogenarian triplets, which pleased him no end.

Frank O'Flannagan handed Long Clem the passenger list fastened to a dog eared clip board that had a pencil swinging on the piece of parcel string attached to it. Frank began issuing instructions.

"Check in starts in ten minutes Long Clem and make sure that everyone goes under the metal detector." (This was in Frank's mind a sort of substitute passport cum border control even though they would not be leaving the country as such). The metal detector 'gateway' was a hastily constructed galvanized wire arch normally used to support roses in an English country garden and held in place with some electric cable and unusual knots. Each passenger was meant to walk under the arch. Each passenger would duly oblige and Long Clem waved the detector paddle at them.

Winston we need to unfurl the balloon" said Frank "can you give me a hand and mind you don't stand on it."

"Okay Uncle Frank." Winston was pleased to be a part of the crew.

Long Clem began firing up the metal detector by switching on the battery supply which he carried on his back in the bottom of an olive green canvass day sack that was Norwegian army issue. It made the sound of a Geiger counter as he swung it round in an arc beside the van as he tried to position the padded shoulder strap comfortably across the back of his neck.

"Hi ho Hi ho it's off to work I go" he sang as he removed a long handled trowel from the webbing pouch on the side of the sack "I won't be needing this today." he said as he tossed it into the back of the truck.

Winston turned to look at his uncle for instructions. Frank O'Flannagan was standing very still leaning against the basket with one hand and clutching his chest with the other.

"Indigestion" he said as he tried to breathe against the pain "I'll be alright in a moment or two."

Just before Gloria had volunteered to 'convalesce' at St Audrey's she had been cajoling Frank to 'get himself checked out' with Doctor Woodhead. The frequency and strength of his indigestion pains had worried her especially as it would stop him in his tracks for long moments, he had recently dropped a pail of pig swill on her foot when another pain struck as they walked together across the yard to feed a suckling sow. Frank had promised that he would indeed get checked out and was due to attend the surgery the following week however a problem with the Muscovy ducks had distracted him and he forgot.

Long Clem eyed the passenger list for any suspicious sounding names and awkward special requests. Frank was very particular about passengers being 'indigenous' although Gloria often reminded Frank on this subject that the only truly indigenous people in the whole world are the citizens of Iraq - Mesopotamia and by divine proxy the Jews of Israel. Even as a royalist Gloria faced the truth of the Saxe-Coburg and Gotha lineage of her dear Queen Elizabeth II, the surname 'Windsor' being a taken only in the light of the provocation of the First World War Teutons. The metal detector was in fact a decommissioned mine detector last used in the disposal of ordnance from a playground of a Balkan primary school planted in the fiercely fractured lands of the late Marshall Josip Broz Tito. Frank had adapted it by secreting a small battery powered alarm with an LCD screen that flashed the words 'Danger' and 'Search before proceeding'. The alarm was activated manually and at the discretion of Long Clem to frighten suspicious looking listed passengers as he worked off a directory of Frank's guidelines that included instructions to search 'interloping' wearers of what Frank considered to be the signature of the cabal, the Hijab or Burka, the Fez, traditional fur trimmed Tibetan hats, the dreadlock disguising headwear of Rastafarians and the turban wrapped kesh of the Sikh Kahlsa. They had successfully practiced the search routine on a Berkshire sow, a Nubian nanny goat and some runner ducks, It went without saying, although Frank had listed it, that pregnant ladies were verboten and all ladies should have been required to present a doctors certificate to the effect they were not 'with child' except that Frank had forgotten that he had ever thought of it when he printed the definitive directory. Smoking, eating and drinking was forbidden during the flight and passengers were to be asked the time of their last visit to the bathroom. A few days earlier Frank and Long Clem had constructed a 'Ladies Latrine' in one corner of the field using a world war two army field kitchen with extra poles and divided by dense camouflage webbing, and two separate galvanized steel latrine drums with worm holed wooden seats. The acrid smell of the greeny-blue chemical 'additive' combined with the prospect of having to use Izal the 'fine strong toilet tissue for hygienic cleansing which helps to kill bacteria and germs' would probably cause total retention in the most stoic. Men were directed towards the hedge.

Frank O'Flannagan and his young nephew worked

together to roll the balloon envelope out a task that wasn't altogether straightforward on account of its irregular construction.

"It's very long isn't it?" said Frank.

"Is it long or should you say high?" countered Winston.

"I suppose it depends on where you are standing."

"Or lying" interrupted Winston "when you are standing you are a tall person and when you are lying down you are long person" he continued.

"Unless" said Uncle Frank inclining an affectionate nod in the direction of Long Clem "you are one of these people who towers over us in a different way." Winston liked that, he was fond of Long Clem.

They continued to work in silence until Winston spoke again.

"Except perhaps when it's a story then lying is a tall story even if it takes a long while to tell."

"You've got your fathers' brains and your mothers' mind you have." concluded Frank O'Flannagan with a gentle laugh.

They walked back towards the basket. A large red London Routemaster double-decker bus poked its bonnet into the launch meadow. It was displaying a '00' number and the words 'Not in Service' in the bulkhead window above the driver on hand wound canvass rolls of route numbers and destinations. It edged gingerly into the meadow through the rutted gateway. The driver appeared fraught and Winston could see many inquisitive black faces staring out from the windows in the top deck. In fact the driver was alone on his deck except for a large black man dressed in tribal costume standing at the back on the unique Routemaster platform hanging onto the polished conductor's chrome pole and punctuating his shouts of navigation with the ringing 'pings' of the stop start bell. The bus was balanced precariously by its heavily populated upper deck and it began to turn in the meadow. Frank O'Flannagan ran towards the bus.

"What are you trying to do?" he called to the bus driver.

"What does it look like?" he answered.

"Do you intend trying to park in this launch meadow?" Frank asked.

"Do you think there's room for a double-decker bus a hot air balloon and half an African tribe on this piddling little pitch?" said the driver "I am turning around to park back in that lane, I should never have listened to the tribal fella and come through that gate."

"Couldn't you have turned round in the lane or better still reversed down it?" continued Frank.

"Couldn't you have found a bigger field with a car park instead of this dead end 'Timbuktu' goat paddock?"

"Well you'd be best to drive around the outside of the field on the headland where it's firmer only meadows can have pockets of sand beneath them that sink you out of sight. And then you'll come back up to the gate now wouldn't you?" said Frank trying to remain restrained.

The large black man in tribal dress disembarked in a stationary moment between gear changes as the bus driver set off on the circumnavigation of the launch pad pasture on the advice of Frank O'Flannagan hoping for all the world there were no hidden sand pockets waiting to swallow the bus and its wondrous voyagers..

The large black man was by appearance, to all intents and purposes an African chieftain. He had come to England at the invitation of the local television station's newly appointed 'Millennium 3' director of cultural programming. Originally he was here to participate in a reality TV show called 'Bellwether Swap' which had been commissioned to celebrate the practice of twinning towns in Europe. The show is sponsored by the Burridge Burdizzo Clamp Company and the Taylor John Bell-foundry. The practice of twinning towns was created by a movement that arose in Europe after the end of World War II in an effort to draw municipalities together in a spirit of shared understanding and experience, letting bygones be bygones. And to try to ensure that centuries of nationalism didn't break out again across the map of federal infancy being drawn by the realpolitik of mature civilization in the second millennium anno dominie. The local town council had recently voted, in chamber, to extend this town twinning malarkey to a global reach as no-one from the major political parties could agree to another European neighbour that anyone of them wanted to be twinned with. The local socialist councillors had nearly persuaded the sole representative of the 'Monster Raving Looney' party to form a majority coalition in exchange for a place on two health and safety sub-committees and subsidized travel. The 'raving looney' had declined their greasy allure on the grounds that he considered submarine travel however safe to be injurious to his mental health even if the tickets were half price. The failure to raise an executive legislative quorum doomed the socialist desire to twin the town with Vaduz in Liechtenstein was further dented by the fact that on the evening of voting the Raving Looney monster councillor and two of his socialist colleagues had double booked themselves and were retained by the local constabulary at an unlicensed Naturists Moonlight Tennis Tournament for inebriation, voyeurism and improper dress under the bylaws of naturism, as none of them were in fact participating in the nature bit of the evening.

The remit of the reality television show was to get a local municipal mayor to agree to exchange their whole position in life with an equivalent opposite number in another part of the global village. The town had previously been twinned with a French town in the Limousine region near the Vienne River simply because a previous mayor, a farmer, had been, in fact still remains, a leading breeder of Limousine Cattle. These magnificent French creatures are bred to produce 'British Beef' and were first introduced to Britain through the Leith Docks in Edinburgh in 1971 and are thought to be descendants of the cattle depicted in the drawings discovered in the caves of Lascaux, drawn twenty thousand years ago that today are the largest numerical breed of beef cattle in the British Isles.

Like every living detail of creation these magnificent beasts along with grain and grape, and all things quaffable, digestible and quenching were once in the minds of the God fearing folk indigenous to Iraq/Mesopotamia. But now they have become British beef, French Bordeaux and German Bockwurst, Knackwurst and Pinkel and exist simply as humankind's purchase of an expired divine patent. Unlike the bourbon masterfully distilled by Augustus Bulleit. This from rye, yeasts and water coursing through limestone, into flame charred, white oak barrels and nurtured until mature russet nectar. Not found in Eden. Like the murals of Rothko, this captured essence of a man's creative soul was briefly in the custody of the Seagram Company many years ago. It is a favourite tipple of Gilbert Herring around Christmastime and the long evenings of winter.

The town was also twinned with a town in Germany that was proud of its sausage factory that had specialities like the 'Blutwurst' or blood sausage and the 'Gehirnwurst' a sausage comprising of a pigs brain, its fat and a bit of its flesh, incorporated for good measure, stuffed into its own intestines, boiled, cooled and then fried in butter. Billy Butterworth (Independent Party) who also served an influential term as mayor of the town used to visit the German sausage factory bringing back fare for his market stall and supplies to local delicatessens. Gideon Posner did not serve as mayor but he did serve the town from a depth of such gratitude that the town itself chose to be twinned with the Polish town of Wolomin a few years ago. The list grew to three twins and then, as I have already stated, very recently the local councillors agreed to a fourth twinning with a large village elsewhere other than Europe in, in fact, Western Burkina Faso. They were influenced by the fact that the current local Mayor's son, an anthropologist, was working amongst the Bobo (tribe) there and writing regular bulletins for the local paper. These bulletins had been gaining an ever increasing readership because of his mixture of interesting experiences amongst the Bobo interspersed with his reveries as the son of the Mayor. It was this twinning that had fascinated the television programme makers and promised a guaranteed fillip to the viewer ratings. The exchange was made with assurances from the anthropologist son to his hitherto (apparently) dominant father that everything would be alright. For the record his father had recently divorced his mother after nearly thirty years of 'blissful' marriage. Amidst emerging rumours of his having for several of those years been philandering, he decided to marry a young, ambitious and quite flirtatious filly from within the corridors of local power. She having designs upon a career in television. The anthropologist son had initially, innocently introduced them at a family barbeque to which he had originally invited her himself having designs upon romance. The Mayor and the 'filly' had exchanged wedding vows in a 'documentary' filmed to introduce the new series in which the latter-day lascivious louche and one time lion of the people had promised to make her his star. The pre-nuptial agreement, which viewers witnessed, had put a limit on the duration of the marriage directly relative to her media success. Many were predicting fireworks in Burkina Faso. The mayor's son was secretly conjuring retribution as he had mischievously coerced his closest friend the African chieftain into his dastardly scheme.

This was going to run and run. And run.

This was the first successful bus trip that the tribal chieftain had taken in his newly adopted country with his extended family. This was due to the fact that in Burkina Faso catching a bus is an altogether more relaxed affair than it is in England. In Burkina Faso you find the bus that is going to where you want to go and you get on and then you wait until it fills up before the driver decides to set off with a full complement of patient, paying passengers. Waiting in Burkina Faso is an integral part of a life of meeting, greeting and getting to know by catching up, of discussing purpose and hopes and of looking forward. Since their arrival and up until the day of Winston's birthday and the balloon flight the chieftain and his family had never actually managed to all, be on the same bus at the same time going to the same place such was the number in his entourage, the number of local buses and the limited time a bus actually 'stops' at a bus stop due to there always being passengers already on board.

The chieftain addressed Frank O'Flannagan speaking with authority.

"Good morning sir I am pleased to be accompanying you on this flight it is my first in a balloon though I am acquainted with the exploits of the Montgolfier brothers of course being myself of the Upper Volta and a French citizen to boot."

"Pleased to make your acquaintance sir" replied Frank "I didn't think golf was a game the French enjoyed much of."

The man from Burkina Faso looked at Frank a little bewildered and then continued.

"If this goes well today I think the television people will be keen to film a second run."

"That would be great we could get Ranjit with Herb in the basket to fly with us" said Winston.

"That almost sounds like something I could sell from the market stall" said Frank "Ranjit with Herbs."

"You have a stall?" queried the Chieftain "what do you sell?"

"The best pork this side of heaven" said Billy Butterworth joining the conversation.

"I am not sure about pork in heaven" said the chieftain.

"Ah" said Billy "you must be one of those Muslims then."

"I am a Christian actually and I think you must be referring to the Jewish tradition" replied the Chieftain" I come from two minorities in my country, Bobo and then Christian and irrespective of this I do not believe that I would want to share heaven with an animal that lives on offal and uses its own excrement for sun screen it is both morally unacceptable and an offence to my sensibilities however in this life it is delicious but in eternity there will just be fruit I suspect."

"And recycling" added Billy "will there be recycling in eternity?"

"Well" said Frank "much as I would like to stand and talk I have a flight to prepare for so if you don't mind I am going to have to leave you to your theological, environmental and gastronomic debate about the heavenly sun screen business." Winston was mightily impressed with the range of his uncle's vocabulary.

"Before you carry on with your procedures do you have three ladies by the name of Ribbons?" asked man from Burkina Faso "I was at Haberdashers' Aske's with Lawrence Ribbons when I was younger, do you know Lawrence, he is local. In his last postcard he told me that he had booked the same flight as a birthday treat for his aunts who I must say were legendary at school with so many of those exploits in the French resistance, Spitfires and all."

"Funny that because my niece Rosemary works for Lawrence Ribbon's aunts they passed the shop to Lawrence a good few years ago" Frank replied "but I'd rather you didn't say anything to them as they may get me confused with someone else and I wouldn't want them to worry and spoil their flight."

"Wonderful" said the chieftain "Laurie said that I would meet them here today."

"Well I do believe you will find them over there by that motorcycle and sidecar."

"Thank you." The chieftain sidled off to meet the pink octogenarians.

"That bellwether swap show's going to be an absolute disaster or a raving success with him in it" Billy Butterworth concluded "Mayor today and who knows Prime Minister tomorrow".

The red Routemaster completed a circuit of the launch site its tired AEC motor running quietly. The bus driver spoke above the sound of the idling engine.

"How did this tribe book a flight in your balloon anyway it's like a journey from the back of one beyond to the back of another beyond if you ask me?" said the bus driver through the half glass window in his isolated cab.

"I am not taking the tribe just the chieftain as I understand it." said Frank.

"Indeed I am the only one booked to fly." said the large chieftain turning around after over hearing the conversation as he walked away to join the Ribbons sisters "and these women and children are not a tribe they are my family. My tribe did not come with me because it is the time of planting in my village and the television company only wanted my closest family."

"So you're that chieftain chap from Borneo we're being twinned with." the bus driver exclaimed.

"Burkina Faso." Frank corrected.

"Burkina Faso." Said the chieftain.

"My older brother fought for the British army in Borneo he was a member of the SAS, ruddy fit fella he was" said the bus driver "now where have I got to collect this Borneo chap from when the flight is over?" he asked.

"He's from Burkina Faso and you will be able to collect him from the end of the flight" Frank O'Flannagan replied.

"Obviously but where is that likely to be, Borneo?"

"Burkina Faso he's fr…" replied Frank and before he could add anything the bus driver exclaimed.

"You must be joking do you know where Borneo is?

"You can collect us some when at the end of this breeze where the gas runs out" said Frank "I expect you to follow the flight we will be in the air for approximately one hour."

"So not Borneo then?" said the bus driver.

"Not Borneo, not Burkina Faso, Timbuktu or Narnia just somewhere up the road." said Frank.

"Oh so you follow the roads from up there do you?" continued the bus driver "I wondered how it all worked."

"Not quite" Frank O'Flannagan answered "we go with the wind and you follow."

"Follow the wind?" you can see from this goat paddock that my bus is not equipped for 'off road' manoeuvring."

"It's not hard to follow the flight of the balloon" said Frank trying to reassure the bus driver "the roads are good away from here you just follow the little fellow Long Clem over there in the van after we take off we are further from the roads up there than ever we are when we land".

"Roads good! Not if that lane is anything to go by" he replied tilting his head in the direction of the gateway as he climbed out of his cab. The bus driver continued to mumble about having to ask the man from Burkina Faso to tell his wives and children to come downstairs otherwise the bus was in danger of toppling over the next time they all rushed to one side of it to stare at another Tandoori takeaway queue, tanning parlour or Rolls Royce. At the bus depot earlier in the day when the large man from Burkina Faso and his entourage boarded the Route-master he had informed the driver that he had expressly chartered the tall bus for his family to 'see your country beyond the high hedges and traffic jams to experience the culture and what the British had done with God's creation, the avenues of trees, patchwork of hedge hemmed meadows and complex coordination of canals.'

"Right" said Frank just as another passenger arrived "let's be getting ready then we can begin the flight briefing."

        The large man with the entourage made his way towards the pink octogenarian triplets and their uniformed chauffeur

Gustav. The tall Teuton stepped forward to intercept the African, protecting his delicate pink clad charges. The African thrust out his large right hand and grasped Gustav's hand shaking him vigorously.

"I am Tertius Napoleon Sawadogo" he said through a wide pearl white toothy grin "at your humble service it is an honour to finally meet the intrepid aunts of my good school friend Lawrence Ribbons."

"You are Tertius *the* Tertius from Haberdashers' Aske's Boys School" exclaimed the first of the sisters to speak.

"Indeed" replied the man "I am he."

"From Burkina Faso" squealed the second sister excitedly.

"And to think" added the third "you both fagged for the Prime Minister."

"Yes" said Tertius Napoleon Sawadogo "it was an honour to black his boots, braise his kidneys and warm his toilet seat in winter."

The sisters surrounded the African reassuring Gustav with what they knew of their nephews' good friend from the tales Lawrence had regaled them with on his holidays. They took turns to formally introduce themselves as Hermione, Hester and Henrietta and, curiously observed by Gustav, the redoubtable octogenarian triplets and the African fell into deep conversation sharing the 'skinny' on Lawrence.

An ice cream van tinkled its jingle slowly down the lane and parked in the dead end just beyond the gate. A man climbed out of the serving hatch on the side of the ice cream van and walked into the field carrying a bunch of carrots and a large silver cup, the sort you win at school sports days. In fact it looked similar to the swimming trophy that Winston was sharing with Osborne.

"That's thoughtful of you Frank" said Billy Butterworth "organizing refreshments while we wait, is he going to follow the flight behind the bus because I reckon I'll need a cornet at regular intervals."

"I haven't organized anything" said Frank "he is a punter."

"The doors broken" began the ice cream man walking up to the ground crew of Frank O'Flannagan, Winston and Long Clem, explaining his use of the serving hatch.

 "So I used the emergency exit I'm sorry about the van but I have come straight from a village fete. I completely sold out of ice lollies today and my carrots won 'the freakiest bunch' award in the produce show so I had to wait to collect my trophy what do you think?" he asked the assembled group holding up a bunch of carrots (Daucas Carota) that included an effigy of Abraham Lincoln, and likenesses of a Shish Kebab, assorted body parts, an eagle's talon and the head of a Malayan Tapir *(Tapirus indicus)* with its prehensile snout and curious proboscis. "And I got a highly commended rosette for me Savoy cabbages."

"Do you have any ice cream left?" asked the chieftain from Burkina Faso who had returned from introducing himself to Gustav and the Ribbons sisters.

"As a matter of fact I do" replied the ice cream man "but as I said to our pilot no ice lollies".

"Then I would like twenty seven large cornets please."

"But I am about to give the flight briefing" said Frank.

"Not to worry" said the chieftain wrapping one of his strong arms around the neck of the bus driver "my friend here will help to distribute the ice cream for me as part of the service, do you know, my favourite bus driver back home Sunday Wahab Sawadogo gives a wonderful service for a man of eighty three, for a start off he sells the most wonderful eggs from chickens that have been especially vaccinated against the Newcastle disease."

"Newcastle disease?" said the ice cream man.

"It is the common cold of the chicken world and if you arrive early for your journey he often cooks up their gizzards in oil and vinegar seasoned with onions and garlic and served with rice" the French African drifted off into the sensual nirvana induced by his soothing reverie of the culinary excellence of his colonial conquerors.

"What about some boiled carrots?" asked the ice-cream man.

"And pork brawn." added Billy Butterball.

"Okay" said the ice-cream man then turning to the bus driver "two scoops to a cornet and stick a chocolate flake in it that'll do nicely."

"And I will try one of your carrots yes." the Chieftain added "raw."

"You can eat the Shish Kebab it's the least convincing the rest I want to get photographed for the Friday Gazette and Bugle."

      Long Clem was checking the last of the passengers in before joining Frank and Winston in the task of unfurling the balloon membrane. Joining the triplets, the chieftain and the ice-cream man on the voyage manifest and of course in the balloon basket was a young married couple. These two lovebirds were on their honeymoon no less spending much of their waiting time canoodling. There was also a tattooed man in cap sleeved tee shirt, he was as tall as the large black man and he had the muscular form of one Charles Atlas *(born Angelo Siciliano) the most celebrated pioneer of* body building. Long Clem ran the metal detector over each of the passengers. He used his frightener option early on the honeymooners triggering a 'bleep' in the hope others would just confess without the fuss of being scanned.

"Maybe it's a sign that I should not go up." said the new bride as Long Clem insisted on searching her handbag and asked her new husband to check her pockets etcetera after a single bleep.

"Not at all" said Clement Longfellow "its routine I am sure it's nothing important."

"What could it be?" she asked.

"Well it's definitely metal do you have any jewellery or a pen or comb or money concealed on your person?"

"No none" she said "I read the literature and I took the precautions."

"Oh dear" said Long Clem turning to the other passengers "then what could it be?"

There was a long pause and then one of the octogenarian triplets offered a possible explanation.

"Do you wear a girdle?" she asked.

There was another pause during which the young woman, who was really not sure about the flight, coloured up before making a whispered admission to the triplets.

"That's it" she confessed "it's only so that I could wear this dress for my husband he loves me in this dress and we are on our honeymoon."

"Before you scan me we might as well admit it we both have a piercing that you can't see" the honeymooning young man said loudly trying to protect his brand new wife from further embarrassment "it's sort of body art…everyone is having it done you know it's the latest."

The octogenarian pink sisters looked at each other with a mischievous twinkle.

"We don't need to see them" said Long Clem, acting check-in clerk "it's just standard procedure."

"I meant that you can't see them" began the honeymooning young man again "they're…"

Frank O'Flannagan intervened swiftly as the check-in procedure began to unravel in the hands of Long Clem.

"Let's introduce ourselves shall we and then we can get on with the all-important briefing."

"Do hearing aids make the machine bleep?" asked one of the octogenarian triplets.

Long Clem was about to answer her when one of her sisters asked "will my hearing aid set that machine off?"

"I am going to appear regularly on your television screens after this" the chieftain said between munches on the ice cream man's shish kebab carrot effigy "I am visiting your country with my family although I have lived here before" he continued, pointing at the bus with its crowded top deck of black faces all licking ice cream and staring wide-eyed back at them "we are over here doing reality television and I am teaching my ladies and their children about your peculiar lives and I am joining you all on this flight I am quite exhilarated."

"Where'd you book up then if it's not being rude?" ventured the tattooed muscle man.

"On the internet before I came over here to your delightful island." replied the French African as if coming over from Burkina Faso was like crossing to the middle of the road.

"Its' very good the internet" said one of the octogenarian triplet sisters "I download music that we used to dance to during the war we had seventy eights then and today we are eighty." Her sisters tittered in agreement "why I downloaded one of my favourites only last week it's by Danny Kaye and it is called Civilization Bongo, Bongo, Bongo and it goes" and here Hermione Ribbons began to sing this popular song from 1947 by the Andrews Sisters;

"Each morning, a missionary advertises missionary sign

He tells the native population that civilization is fine

And three educated savages holler from a bamboo tree

That civilization is a thing for me to see." Henrietta and Hester then joined in the chorus.

"So bongo, bongo, bongo, I don't wanna leave the Congo, oh no no no no no

Bingo, Bangle, Bungle, I'm so happy in the jungle, I refuse to go

Don't want no bright lights, false teeth, doorbells, landlords, I make it clear

That no matter how they coax him, I'll stay right here."

"Thank you ladies." shouted Frank conscious that a possible political incorrectness may break some health and safety rule.

The song was conceived as a statement about a happy native fellow who has no desire to embrace the advantages of modern life.

"The internet?" said the tattooed man, picking up the conversation after the impromptu musical interlude.

"We use satellite not cable in case you are wondering." the French African chieftain replied.

"But the advert was in the Friday Gazette and Bugle." the tattooed man continued.

"Yes it is but it's also on the World Wide Web www.fridaygazettebugle.co.uk" said one of the sisters "that's where we read it now in order to save the world."

"Save the world!?" questioned the tattooed man.

"Rain forests" added another of the pink sisters "we read about global warming in newspapers made from the disappearing rain forests, we should be more concerned about our waste."

"And our carbon footprints" added the third triplet.

"Anyway" continued the chieftain "that is where I found the advertisement 'OFF into the Blue Yonder' a very clever piece of copy I have to say."

"The OFF is an acronym." said Frank

"It means O'Flannagan's Flights into the blue yonder" said Long Clem proudly "me and Frank thought it up."

"You could have had Frank's full name" said Billy Butterworth "then it would have been 'ef' off into the blue yonder, you'd have been guaranteed a long passenger list from amongst the disenfranchised then for sure."

"Now there's a thought" said the ice-cream man "a basket full of folk all obsessive, compulsive and blowing on the wind."

"No" said the chieftain "it couldn't work they wouldn't stand on the wickerwork, too may cracks."

"You're not one of them African princes who keeps emailing me about using my bank account to help them get their money out of the country are you?" asked the tattooed man.

"Goodness me no" replied Tertius Napoleon Sawadogo "I can only apologize for the deceptive and despicable behaviour of a minutiae of my brother Africans if African they are."

"Good" said the tattooed man "we don't want no criminals on our telly especially foreign ones, I mean since we joined that common market well, don't get me started..."

"No, right, well okay then, back to the briefing?" said Frank O'Flannagan "only proceedings are getting a little bit behind here with all this conversation perhaps we could continue it when we are up there" he added pointing into the blue yonder.

The gathering of passengers, their sponsors and the ground crew, Long Clem, spontaneously looked up. Everyone on the top deck of the bus looked down and waved. All the passengers began waving back. Every black face was smiling through a ring of white ice creamed lips. They resembled the chorus of the Black and White Minstrel show.

As a child I used to watch the Black and White Minstrel Show on television. It had begun to be screened by the British Broadcasting Corporation on Saturday the 14th of June 1958. The show was based on the 'Nigger Minstrel Shows' that began in New York around 1843 the form of which the author Mark Twain said 'the genuine nigger show, the extravagant nigger show' was 'the show which to me had no peer' and [was] 'a thoroughly delightful thing.' As early as 1967 the Campaign against Racial Discrimination in Great Britain petitioned the British Broadcasting Corporation on the basis of the show's racial implications and eleven years later the show was taken off.

Eleven years!

The origins of minstrelsy began in the early 19th century in the mansions of the slave owners as the more musical slaves entertained their masters. Thomas Dartmouth T.D. (Daddy) Rice, a white comedian, 'blacked up' painted exaggerated white lips on his face and sang in broken English purporting to reprise the negro dialect. This damaged the advancement of the abolition of slavery. T.D. 'Daddy' Rice had an acolyte Asa 'Al Jolson' Yoelson the son of Moshe Rueben an immigrant Lithuanian Rabbi of the Talmud Torah Synagogue in Washington DC. Al Jolson, who, as an émigré Lithuanian Jew escaping from the anti-Semitic Tsarists, 'blacked up' with burnt cork as a Negro slave in Burlesque, appeared in one of the first Hollywood 'talkie' movies, singing 'My Mammy'. A 'Mammy' is the most enduring racial caricature of the African daughter shipped slave.

It is uncomfortable for me to look back as an adult and see the tightening of a birds nest knot of contradictions in the mind of myself as a growing child but my world presented me with mammy 'golliwogs' and black dandy 'golliwogs' on jam jars, in books and more frighteningly in my cot. As a small three year old sitting on steps above the candy striped awnings of the market stalls in Norwich with my mother, throwing bread crumbs to strutting pigeons I saw my first real live, ordinarily dressed black man. I shouted out gleefully 'Look Mummy a golliwog'. I cannot remember my mother's hideous embarrassment or the nature of my correction I was too young. The gravitas never softened over the years that my poor mother repeatedly recounted the episode as if to confess the unforgivable sin. She always finished by saying that the man whom I had clearly insulted responded as a gentleman. I may have been too young and now I am, naturally, considered too old by my children but I do not really understand what I am to do with the ever changing history of my life and the shifting morality regarding my brother and sister human beings. When I think of the Burkina Faso family enjoying their ice creams on top that iconic bus it stirs something but I am not sure what it is. Maybe it's the same confused feeling I had as a child when watching a plain looking white man dressed in extravagant couture and bouffant coiffure impersonating a beautiful white woman singing as a star of the Black and White Minstrel Show on a Saturday night, on an electric box at the centre piece of the family living room and life.

Now we have the internet so all bets are off.

THE BRIEFING

Frank O'Flannagan coughed loudly and cleared his throat and fixed everyone simultaneously with a Captains hypnotic stare gathering his passengers round and preparing to address them on all issues relating to flying in the hot air balloon.

"How many of you expected a basket for two" Frank O'Flannagan asked his passengers. Everyone raised an arm except Winston who had not really expected a basket at all at the start of his birthday.

"Well this is economy class. Now safety is the most important thing you will need to know about ballooning. I need to ask your forgiveness before we begin this wonderful journey because I am sure I will drive you to madness with the number of times that I talk about safety. Safety and trust" said Frank O'Flannagan breezily "I will need you to trust me as your pilot when we are up there" he said pointing only with his eyebrows as if afraid to look up himself "and" he added with some gravity "so it is a good job that I have read a book about it hey?"

"What was the title of the book?" asked one of the old ladies' who is herself widely read but Frank O'Flannagan did not hear her and launched straight into his safety talk.

"You will see that there are canisters of gas in the basket of the balloon enough gas to heat your house for a month in very cold weather, when it's cold enough to cook a penguin and snap the tail off a brass monkey, so there is a no smoking ban in operation at this launch site".

"Why is that?" asked the tattooed man.

"Here, here" said Billy Butterworth.

"Because there is enough gas to blow your house up in one second whatever the weather" said Frank curtly "If you need to smoke go and stand outside the gate to the launch site".

"Thank you captain" said the tattooed man as he set off towards the gate.

"Where are you going?" asked Frank

"I need a smoke".

"Not now you don't" said Frank O'Flannagan "Right now you need to listen. You only need to smoke when my talk on landing in a balloon has turned your bowels to water…"

A smell drifted through Winston's mind stimulating a 'smellemory' his own simple word for smells that evoke a memory. It was his Uncle Frank's annunciation of bowels that did it. He was back in time walking across the landing at home when his Gran was staying with them for recuperation from her operation for the 'stones'. Winston had walked straight into an invisible wall of gas hanging outside her bedroom door. Of course it bore no relation to the deadly phosgene gas of the trenches at Ypres in 1915 in terms of the suffering it caused humanity but Winston was gradually overcome in the stinking envelope that was beginning to drift further afield in number 13 Captain Scoot terrace. He had staggered down the stairs trying not to breathe anymore as his heart began to pound against his ribcage and his brain whistled out through his ears. As he leant against the cold water butt by the back door gasping huge mouthfuls of fresh air he heard his father upstairs.

"Where's Winston?"

"Why?" called his mother from the kitchen.

"He's been playing with that blooming chemistry set again."

"I don't think so" she said "that's more likely to be mother for sure her bowels are working again which will please Doctor Woodhead no end."

Winston continued gasping and gulping, his snorts unable to dislodge tiny clouds of the gas lingering in his nose.

"……..Behind the rope barrier for safety" said Frank O'Flannagan as Winston drifted back into present consciousness. "Now we are going to practice embarkation there will be some of you in each corner of the basket I will read out the names of each grouping starting with those in this corner."

The balloon basket was four feet tall and oblong in shape. It was divided up into five compartments four equally square compartments one at each corner that met at the mid-point of either the port or starboard side of the basket and a single oblong compartment through the middle which was equal to two of the squares. The middle compartment housed the gas canisters and all other paraphernalia relating to the work of the balloon pilot Mr Frank O'Flannagan and the man himself, occasionally seated on an old bar stool during flights.

"As you will see there are steps woven into the basket one at the bottom one a third of the way up and one two thirds of the way up the middle each step being offset to allow you to climb comfortably into the basket"?

Winston thought about this, about how holes could be woven into something. Certainly the top and bottom edges of the hole were a weave of the basket work ending and then beginning again to form the hole. There was even a thoughtful addition of green canvass padding on the bottom edge but the hole itself, is a hole with nothing there, you cannot weave nothing. You can make a hole in something by slicing, ripping, digging, puncturing, breaking but you can't paint or draw or weave the hole not a real, actual, hole you can't.

"I can see the holes" said one of the old ladies "I think we shall need more holes don't you?" she continued, addressing her identical sisters "to climb in there?"

"You will have to embark quickly when I give the order" Frank continued "the rim of the basket is well padded so you shouldn't go injuring yourselves on any broken basket weave as I once did years ago when my Uncle stuffed me into the basket on the front of my mother's bicycle to ride alongside the Salvation Army band. I bled like a stuck pig it took the whole of 'Onward Christian Soldiers' to stem the flow" he paused "to coagulate so to speak."

That ancient bicycle Frank spoke of is actually still in use. Thomas Walpole had taken the tyre and the tube off the back wheel and raised the bicycle fixed on a stand so that when it was peddled the back wheel flew round but the bicycle stayed in the same place. A narrow canvas belt was fitted into the open wheel rim crossed over once and then fitted onto the flywheel of a small generator. It had been Terry's and more recently had become

Winston's punishment for often the slightest misdemeanour, depending on the time of year and/or the weather, to peddle the generator to charge the bank of old car batteries that supply power to the heating system of the Walpole family greenhouse. Thomas Walpole believed that punishment was no good unless it served a purpose. The bicycle was so old it was probably worth a small fortune to a museum because it still had a good bit of its original livery clearly showing that it was a Humber model made by Raleigh Industries with a logo that depicts Sir Walter Raleigh's gallant act of sacrificing his cape to save the lustre of his sovereign's silk slippers. It also has a chain-wheel with fine fretwork of five little human figures, their heads joining at the middle and their feet running round the inside of the heavily greased circumference of worn down cog teeth.

Frank read out the names in the respective groupings and everyone said hello to their immediate fellow passengers with whom they would share one of the four communal corner berths. Winston was to share his berth with the honeymooners. Two of the pink octogenarian triplets and the Tattooed man were the next to be assigned to share their small corner. Billy Butterworth and the ice cream man were then paired in the opposing corner to the African Chieftain and the remaining Ribbons sister. Frank engaged the African.

"Sir, do we have a name?" said Frank directing his focus towards the man from Burkina Faso.

"Is that a royal we?" the man asked.

"If you are a prince in your country then I suppose it is although we haven't exactly swapped you with a prince have we."

"My name is Tertius Napoleon Sawadogo I am not a prince but I am an important man in my own country just as your mayor is here."

"Are you related to that bus driver with the Newcastle disease trouble?" asked Billy Butterworth.

"No relation" replied Tertius Napoleon Sawadogo my family calls me Djembe because as a child I was always playing the drums.

"What do we call you?" asked Billy Butterball.

114

"Is that a rhetorical question?" asked Tertius.

"He wouldn't know I doubt." said the ice-cream man.

"You can call me Tertius."

With the list confirmed as 'all present and correct' and the name of Tertius Napoleon Sawadogo pencilled in Frank continued with procedure.

"When I call you to embark you must climb in quickly because I call you just before the balloon is ready to be released we must not delay embarkation or we could crash land before we take off if the wind decides to do funny things."

He must mean God, thought Winston because wind cannot decide what to do. Wind only does what God decides in terms of when it blows. In terms of what it does, well men decide to build the things that the wind blows away, that is apart from leaves and trees and sandstorms and cows that get sucked up into tornados and stuff like that.

"Right I am going to call you to embark." said Frank who then waited a mute meandering moment.

"Embark" he shouted suddenly.

"But there's no balloon" said one of the old ladies "it's just an empty basket and my nephew Lawrence paid a lot of money for this balloon flight I am sure he expected us to go up there?" Her two sisters nodded in agreement as the little pink lady gesticulated towards the firmament.

"Oh" said Frank O'Flannagan as the honeymooning man vaulted into his corner "thank you madam for pointing that out but I can assure you there will be a balloon" and without hesitation continued, "Now if we could all practice the embarkation only when I say."

The honeymooning man tried hurriedly to abandon the basket and re-join the stalled practice unfortunately he hesitated whilst travelling through the airborne element of his gymnastic vault from the willow wicker work to lank dank grass. He landed firmly with the bearing of an accomplished horseman, straddling the narrow padded rim of the basket and resting upon the delicacy at the apex of his groin. He gallantly stifled what should have been a pain relieving; scream, and then passing out in unrelieved pain, he continued his journey to the ground. As he lay stunned on the grass beside the basket his new young bride gasped in horror.

"I wanted to have babies one day!"

"Okay everybody" said Frank O'Flannagan "stand back give him room let him have some air I'm sure this will not stop you having babies young lady."

Winston stood in the open field with the basket, the huddle of passengers, the distant gathering of well-meaning family, and so called friends who were largely responsible for booking as advertised in the Gazette and Bugle the 'experience of a lifetime' for their unsuspecting relatives, and his Uncle Frank. All of the assembled were letting the newly wedded man have the room for more air and consoling his new bride with promises of an immaculate conception. Winston watched as Frank climbed into the basket and retrieved a square maroon coloured tin with the words Oxo Beef Stock Cubes printed in creamy white embossed letters. Frank knelt down opened the tin and took out a small brown glass bottle. He shook the bottle vigorously opened it waved the bottle under his nose.

"Smelling salts" he said to the inquisitive group of passengers who had crept gingerly into full view of the stricken man "I think he will have to make a booking for another time don't you?" but no one answered.

The man began to regain his equilibrium sucking down deep drafts of pollen spiked meadow air, snapping his eyelids and trying to focus his vision.

"I think I've must have lost my contact lenses." he said.

"I was right" said Frank "definitely another booking there's no way he will enjoy this flight if he can't see anything."

"It's alright" said the young bride "their disposables and I always carry his glasses in my bag."

Frank then encountered an awkward enquiry from one of the pink sisters.

"I saw a rather strong gust of wind pass through that plantation of Poplars over there while we were all being concerned for the young gentleman" she paused thoughtfully "will that affect our chances of a safe take off."

"I wouldn't think so" Frank O'Flannagan reassured her "the weather forecast is good."

'Is that the local or national forecast' thought Winston. His father was always complaining about the differences between the two and how the 'glass' had always supported the national forecast when the barometer had been hanging in the hallway before its mysterious disappearance. Winston remembered the channel race report on the breakfast news; the wind had been quite strong by the coast especially around Ranjit Livingstone's head and it seemed to be getting stronger.

"Now we will stay as we are in the groups" continued Frank O'Flannagan "and we will go on my word" he paused.

"What word is that" asked Billy Butterworth as Frank shouted

"Embark... but not yet." he shouted as the tattooed man put his foot into one of the woven holes.

EMBARKATION PART I

Winston clambered into the creaking basket as the passengers boarded from all angles. He watched as the visiting African, Tertius Napoleon Sawadogo, bent down to pick up the tiny pink octogenarian sister assigned to his corner in order to help her into the basket except that he picked up the wrong identical triplet. The little old lady became a little confused, remonstrating with him shrilly as the deep resonate tones of the Bobo dialect drifted down her auditory canal percussively piercing her tympanic membrane to pass mallus, incus, stapes and beyond to cochlea and the organ of Corti; addling her brain in the process. The visiting African grinned hugely until the little old lady grasped his Burkina sun bleached bone earrings to steady herself. As the Chieftain straightened up in some pain from his stretching ear lobes, the woven fibre threads adorned with masks of the rainmaking Bobo elephant deity Dwo and vintage Colobus monkey skulls, lassoed the tiny pink octogenarian and lashed her to his considerable torso. The mask of Dwo came to life on the back of the triplet's head the deity nodding wildly atop a tiny pink clad body that dangled the wrong way round as she struggled frantically to free herself. Her legs became entwined in the visiting Chieftain's voluminous leaf kilt and she kicked out, accidentally connecting with the delicate region of his groin. His legs buckled and the two of them fell against the basket and onto the ground. The ice-cream man who was trained in first aid took control of the problem and with two fingers strategically and firmly placed at the nape of the neck of the tiny pink sister he helped her to relax from her terror into a deep sleep. She stopped squealing and released her grip of the African's bone earrings releasing him to grip his groin and call for smelling salts. The tattooed man then took hold of the tiny ankles of the pink triplet and with one pull ripped her out from between the Chieftain's rippling stomach and his cultural jewellery. A necklace of Colobus monkey skulls broke loose scattering skulls into the air above the basket. The tattooed man then placed two fingers gently upon her forehead, she revived, and everyone had a little laugh at what had happened. All except the gasping man from Burkina Faso who was being administered the smelling salts by Frank O'Flannagan as the nerves in his groin registered the Ribbons sister's kick.

Frank read out the names in the respective groupings and everyone said hello to their immediate fellow passengers with whom they would share one of the four communal corner berths. Winston was to share his berth with the honeymooners. Two of the pink octogenarian triplets and the Tattooed man were the next to be assigned to share their small corner. Billy Butterworth and the ice cream man were then paired in the opposing corner to the African Chieftain and the remaining Ribbons sister.

EMBARKATION PART II (WITH BRACING)

"Okay" said Frank after a period of adjustment for the passengers "let us try another practice embarkation" he put a little emphasis on the 'practice' and looked at the three octogenarian sisters hoping to spook the one he thought had interrupted him before.

"Okay" repeated Frank O'Flannagan "are we ready to try embarkation" this time applying a little emphases on the 'try' and 'embarkation' and looking out into the distant blue yonder. "Embark."

Winston clambered up and over the padded rim of the creaking basket and then offered a supporting hand to the young bride whose buttocks were nestling evenly in the supportive palms of her straining husband as he shoved her up into the slip stream of Winston before pushing his spectacles firmly into the bridge of his nose and gingerly attempting a revised mode of embarkation himself. Simultaneously, Billy Butterworth and the ice cream man appeared to be trying to foxtrot themselves aboard while Tertius Napoleon Sawadogo (divested of much of the tribal accoutrement he had applied for reality television) deftly lifted his eighty year old pink companion over the baize padding and into their corner of the basket cheered on by the excited audience on the omnibus. Gustav declined the help of the tattooed man as he unfolded a solid mahogany Regency library step chair that was stowed in the nose cone of the motorcycle sidecar and placed it against the basket, he dusted and then steadied it and requested that the tattooed man enter the basket ahead of the two remaining Ribbons sisters in order to help them down into their eerie, one after the other, guided by the steadying hand of the tall, attentive chauffeur. The passengers boarded in the requisite time amid congratulatory chatter.

"Now" said Frank "you have to learn the brace position because the landing of a balloon, though perfectly safe, is a little unpredictable. You will see a number of rope loops near the top of the basket. There are two for each of you to grasp. To assume the brace position stand with your back to the direction we will be travelling, during landing grip the ropes lean back and bend your knees. I suggest that for the pairing of the threes the biggest or strongest person is at the bottom of each section with the other two slightly to the side and on top and for the pair of the pairs of you take the position of that the two that are in the threes."

"Bottom" said the tattooed man trying to unravel Frank's instructions "we can't be at the side and the bottom as well."

"That's the trick" said Frank O'Flannagan "perhaps I should have said behind, nine times out of ten one of the sides becomes the bottom on landing we bounce along on our side until the balloon has totally deflated and as long as it doesn't turn from a deflating balloon into a billowing sail we come to a stop in a few seconds although it can feel like an eternity to those of a nervous disposition."

The three pink sisters began a rather intense though indecipherable discussion involving the rapid activity of eyes, ears, noses and lips with a simultaneous kaleidoscope of pink gloved hands resembling a flush of rubicund spiders. Gustav counselled calm.

"Thank you. Now statistics" said Frank O'Flannagan as he looked towards the convenient visual aid "clearly show that there is more danger of you being run over by a large red municipal double-decker bus whilst sitting on the toilet in the comfort of your own home than there is being injured during landing in a balloon in fact ninety nine percent of balloon accidents never happen."

The large family of the visiting African Chieftain again waved to the bewildered passengers from the upper deck smiling dried ice cream ringed smiles and wobbling the bus on the soft meadow earth foundation.

"Never happen?" queried Tertius Napoleon Sawadogo.

"Never happen." said Frank.

"How can an accident never happen?" continued the Chieftain.

"Because ballooning has an immaculate safety record" replied Frank continuing his instruction "when I call brace I usually sound the alarm as a secondary precaution of course."

Without warning Frank shouted "brace" and squeezed the rubber lung of the brass bugle hooter that he had requisitioned from the O'Flannagan Pantechnivan Mk1. A loud 'Parp' rent the air of the meadow startling small birds hiding in the hedgerow, shaking wood pigeons from the trees and striking fear into distant, shrieking pheasants, and the huddled passengers. There was a silence and then the sound of some dogs barking a way off in the scattered distance. Everyone eventually relaxed from the tense posture of bracing and then disembarked cautiously, instinctively reassembling in their groupings outside the basket.

INFLATING THE ENVELOPE

"Now I need four volunteers" said Frank O'Flannagan "to help me with the inflation of the balloon envelope. My nephew will assist me here by the aperture and my ground and recovery crewman Long Clem will take you over to the mooring control ropes."

The Tattooed man, the ice cream man and the newlyweds stepped forward. Frank O'Flannagan looked appealingly at the visiting African Chieftain and Billy Butterball but without persuasion, their weight would have served his purpose better. Frank separated the newlyweds putting the young woman with the ice cream man to ensure maximum concentration.

"Right" said Frank "we have to push the basket over onto its side." which was duly done by the volunteers.

Frank O'Flannagan then fastened ropes from the basket to the front bumper on the O'Flannagan Pantechnivan Mk1. This would serve as an anchor for the fully inflated balloon prior to take off.

"Now I want each pair of you to walk with Long Clem beyond the end, or the top if you see what I mean, of this balloon envelope laid out before us maintaining a firm grip on these ropes. These ropes will help us to control the balloon while Winston and I inflate the envelope into an upright position using this encased fan which is driven by the generator. My crewman Long Clem will ensure that you are holding the ropes correctly. We don't want anyone getting constricted or burned do we now."

Frank turned and looked particularly at the pink sisters as he addressed the remaining passengers.

"Do not be surprised by the noise of the generator" he said loudly "it will prepare you for the noise of the burners, which reminds me" he added looking at the ice cream man "have you got a hat to cover your bald head because you will get a very large blister if you don't the burners give off quite a bit of heat up there."

"I have my ice cream cap." said the ice cream man pulling a white captains cap stripped of the gold cord and nautical badge and its peak smeared with a powdery crust of stale ice cream.

Billy Butterworth took a grubby handkerchief from his trouser pocket he tied a knot at each corner and then inverted the faintly green flaked side and pulled it onto his head giving him the facial appearance of the Minotaur as a boy-calf with horn buds. Long Clem marched the two pairs of human anchors out to where he had laid the controlling ropes that steady the balloon envelope as it begins to rise up through inflation as the release of the lighter hot air into the cool air begins to lift the envelope. A cubic foot of the ambient air weighs about an ounce when Frank heats the air blown into the envelope by 100 degrees Fahrenheit it loses about 7 grams so each cubic foot can lift 7 grams. Frank's balloon envelope had a capacity of 140000 cubic feet lifting around a ton. With the combined cargo of Tertius and the tattooed man added to the overall passenger load Frank would be sailing close to the wind, in more ways than one.

"Pick up the rope with your leading hand run it up your arm across your shoulders and down your trailing arm and through your trailing hand then grip. Do not wrap the rope around your limbs" said Long Clem in a well-rehearsed patter.

"Why not?" asked the newlywed wife.

"Because you could be constricted or burned" replied Long Clem. Her husband looked across to her reassuringly silently mouthing 'it will be fine my love.'

Frank O'Flannagan pulled the starting cord on the generator and the fan wound up its mesmerizing revolutions to full speed making the envelope billow out from the aperture that Winston was holding open. It took a while for the balloon to inflate horizontally and as it began to fill out Winston's Uncle Frank fired up the burners lying on their side in the upended basket. The air in the envelope shimmered like a mirage and between blasts of hot air the envelope began to rise. The faded taffeta membrane began to swell gradually into the heavenly body of a giant angel standing with its distal feathered pinions half elevated as if hovering more upright than in the tilt of full flight. As the angel stood up it reminded Winston of those films that are sometimes run in reverse to show a demolished chimney or a grand felled tree returning to magnificence. Here though was quite the most unique resurrection.

"I recognize that" said one of the pink sisters her siblings joining in with her recognition of the balloon envelope agreed "it's from that travelling show years ago where the showman died in an elephant."

"Yes" added another "it was awful, that poor man."

"That poor elephant" added the third sister "he landed right in its bum and it never really recovered."

As it rose a gust of wind caught the inflated angel and the basket skewed a little on the ground tugging at the O'Flannagan Pantechnivan Mk1. It dragged the two pairs of human anchors commissioned by Frank to steady its gradual ascent across the grass like tug-o-war contestants teetering at the brink of defeat. They tried to hold on and control the balloons ascent but they stumbled and fell into the lank grass reluctantly letting go. Long Clem eventually overtook them as he ran towards the basket encouraging them to get up and run with him which they did. The balloon envelope was upright. Frank called to the tattooed man to hand the dangling ends of the mooring control ropes to him for securing on the outside of the basket simultaneously pulling on the valve chain that released a blast of hot air up into the envelope.

The group of paying passengers stood looking up in awed disbelief at this emblem of Gods visitation which Frank O'Flannagan had bought off the internet as part of a job lot left over from the chattels of an old travelling showman. The previous owner of the angel had died many years ago at the conclusion of a high dive that was part of his regular performance at fairs, country and urban, the length and breadth of the British Isles. A high dive that should have been, indeed was intended to be, had hitherto always been into a shallow tank of cold, refreshing water siphoned from a natural spring belonging to his family who farm a large estate set amongst rolling hills and verdant pastures, and governed from a medieval castle. The water was delivered every week throughout the year enough to fill one shallow tank and hydrate the show's elephant known as Betty and assistant to the showman on show days. This son of an historic dynasty that had served King and Queen and country for generations. Once he had been formed in Eton's hallowed environs, matured in the cellars of Oxbridge, apprenticed to an uncle, a distinguished brigadier in the British army and had served his time, he ran away and joined a circus. Upholding the tradition of his lineage he became the eccentric member of his generation and continued to receive the support of his family. Amongst his forebears had been variously, pirates, minstrels, actors and a Guinness book of records adjudicator.

A second cousin was in the crowd watching on this fatal day. For the first time in more than a hundred and twenty performances he did not plunge eighty feet from his flimsy diving board attached to the salvaged main topgallant mast of the barque 'Champion', built in Whitehaven by Lumley Kennedy & Co, directly down into three feet four and quarter inches of water being constantly shimmered by his assistant, the gentle elephant Betty. A freak gust of wind blew him off course halfway through his descent. The slight diversion became more exaggerated as he plummeted towards the earth and he plunged into a fatal collision with the rear end of his high dive assisting elephant. Betty performed breath taking handstands on a gaily coloured conical trapezoid podium beside the shallow tank whilst wearing an expansive pink, elephant sized, tutu and blowing air from her trunk to make guiding sun kissed glinting ripples on the awaiting water for the showman to aim at and hopefully, 'hit'. Instead he hit the bulls-eye of the slack and uncontrollably ajar, age-old anal flap of the acrobatic elephant and was asphyxiated in a bolus of bound faecal matter (normally the staple diet of birds and dung beetles in her native Africa) deep in Betty's rectum. Before he could be rescued from the tragically toppled *Elephas Maximus*.

Betty the elephant survived her owner and was retired and pensioned by a family trust. In recent times the second cousin who witnessed the showman's dramatic demise had, as his next of kin, inherited via the rules of intestacy, from the depths of a dark disused dusty hanger, the dry remains of 'A Most Spectacular Show'. Making a quick buck on the internet these artefacts vanished back into the oblivion that feeds upon the information highway. The headline in the local Daily Chronicle on the 4th of July of that fateful year read 'Freaks Accident'. The creation of such a damning, low-down epitaph proved equally fateful for the ink stained cynical soak who set it as it was the last headline ever produced by the newspapers senior typesetter. He was well known locally as a drunkard and yet captain of the Goat and Compasses domino team. The bitter irony is that the balloon effigy was of 'Our Lady of Loreto' the patron saint of aviators, a cast iron guarantee to fairground punters of a safe flight, a banner headline used by the travelling showman on all his fly posters. However the idea of balloon flights in the company of a daredevil never really took off. The showman's takings were always far higher for his singular daring in diving than for daring his customers to fly high with him in the basket of 'Our Lady of Loreto'. This narrative will return to the tragic death of the showman, we are not finished with that fateful day.

Frank's passengers stared on in utter amazement at the angel as it reached a voluptuous fullness of hot air and began a gentle, standing waltz with the wind.

"Embark." Frank shouted as the balloon caught another gust.

Everyone approached the basket. Winston was first up and over the rim of the willow wickerwork weave his feet hit the bottom of the basket with a loud creak. Yet another strong gust of wind hit the top of the balloon envelope spinning it, 'Our Lady of Loreto' leaned. The basket was hovering about 18 inches above the ground and began dragging the O'Flannagan Bull Mk1 across the grass in its wake as it responded to the force of another gust.

"Stand away" cried Frank O'Flannagan to the eager passengers "stand away" not a term he had used in his briefing it must be said. Another gust hit the balloon and the O'Flannagan Pantechnivan Mk1 reared up onto its back wheels as it cantered across the field between dangling and anchoring as the balloon pulled, slackened and pulled again. Long Clem tried to guide the passengers to safety behind the rearing, bucking O'Flannagan Pantechnivan Mk1 but to his horror the tattooed man was attached to the errant basket because he had been partially successful in his embarkation only to shake loose on unexpected take off and now he was clinging on desperately. Tertius Napoleon Sawadogo was running and jumping up flailing his arms beneath the tattooed man trying to rescue him.

"Emergency" shouted Winston's Uncle Frank drawing a vicious looking machete from its sheath and wielding it above his head. The tattooed man had grasped the rim of the basket with one hand, a mooring rope with the other and had one foot in a woven hole in his attempt to embark. Unfortunately he and the mooring rope became entangled. He let out a hideous scream as Frank O'Flannagan brought the machete down onto the taught rope between the tattooed man's hands as he gripped the basket and the rope. He let go of the rope which he had accidentally straddled on his attempt at boarding and which was now scorching him from his crotch to his chin as it strained between the bucking van and the ascending basket. The rope snapped no longer anchoring the balloon to the O'Flannagan Pantechnivan Mk1. The tattooed man's fall was broken by the gallant Tertius Napoleon Sawadogo. The basket passed right over the terrified passengers as it lifted the O'Flannagan Pantechnivan Mk1 up into a sitting position resting on its back doors.

"Oh my poor van" sighed Frank as he looked down on the carnage below and the gaggle of paying passengers wondering if the consequences of a sudden gust create a storm of claims against an act of God which could constitute a non-refundable conclusion succinctly put by the ice cream man.

"I'll be wanting my money back."

The tattooed man lay face up on top of the prostrate chieftain. His vest had been pulled up over his head by the taut rope masking his face and as he gasped air he rhythmically sucked a grubby white cotton sinkhole and blew a mushroom just below the hillock of his nose. On his chest he had, tattooed, a large bulldog wearing a waistcoat made from the union flag of the United Kingdom. The rope burn had given the bulldog a nose bleed. The middle two letters of his name, I assume it was his name and not the name of the bulldog with the bleeding nose, which he had tattooed across his belly had been obscured by a brown skid mark of rope burn leaving the word Goon.

ASCENSION

Winston clung to the 'bracing rope loops inside the basket as it floated away from the ground and the other abandoned passengers. He felt that everything in his body and his head had stopped working. He somehow sensed trees passing, going down silently as he was going up like he was in a transparent lift. He opened his mouth to let a peculiar taste escape but it didn't. He heard his heart beating in his ears. His stomach was pleading to go to the toilet and his brain was shouting no. Then his brain screamed jump out before it gets too high but his stomach pinned him down.

"Scared Winston?" asked his Uncle Frank still wielding the large machete and staggering around in his middle station in the basket trying to get his bearings and control of the liberated craft

"No Uncle Frank" Winston replied weakly "it's fun."

Dogs were barking, many dogs and the wind whispered loudly.

"That was a bit unfortunate" continued Frank O'Flannagan "it's never happened before I have never had an unexpected gust at take-off there'll be some unhappy customers down there and the van will need some repairs again it must have been force seven on the Beaufort scale."

"Is that Auntie Gloria's Beaufort?" asked Winston.

"Certainly is" replied Uncle Frank.

"Ezra has a Blow-forth scale." said Winston.

"It's the measure of wind." said Frank.

"I know, Ezra's force one is a silent but deadly one that people do in the classroom or on a bus or in a shop, I think his force seven is when it is quite loud, lasts for at least seven seconds continuous and has a smell and everybody giggles."

"I'd hate to think what his force twelve is Winston! It's not that kind of wind I am referring to" continued Frank "this scale is the work of Admiral Sir Francis Beaufort and it is for helping sailors to estimate wind speeds, force seven is whole trees in motion and inconvenience felt when walking against the wind."

"I understand them walking on the deck but where would sailors see trees at sea?"

"Ah well you see Winston there's a scale for land and a scale for the sea force seven at sea is something like the sea heaping up and that white foam you get on the crest of waves getting blown along in the wind." said Frank.

There was quite a silence after the lesson in wind scales which had arisen out of the confusion and then Frank said quietly "my poor old van."

The van had been repaired three summers previous following an accident involving a bi-plane, a steam locomotive from a bygone era and a crumbling railway bridge encased in scaffolding. The accident had been somewhat fortuitous as first it had resulted in Winston's photograph appearing on the front page the local broadsheet the Friday Gazette and Bugle incorporating the Traders Bugle an incorporation which had revived an ailing circulation for both and saved the old 'local rag' publication which was held in some affection. Terry called it the 'bungling gazelle'. Secondly, Winston also appeared on television standing behind Ranjit Livingstone the outside broadcast reporter for the regional television news programme 'News in Your Region'. Winston's mother had made a video tape of this precious moment of fame which she played to everyone who came to Sunday tea until Winston's father used the tape to record a documentary about a famous robbery that his father, Winston's grandfather, had been involved in when he was a young man. Winston's mother and father did not actually speak to each other for several days following the incident and after his mother had said all that she needed to say on the subject of what was certainly likely to be Winston's only appearance on television ever. This appearance however led to the first meeting between Winston's sister Rosemary and Colin 'Herb' Sage who as a young sound man had found out where Winston lived and paid him a visit on behalf of the news team to make sure that he was alright following the dramatic incident. Auntie Gloria always said, wishfully, that the 'Uncle Frank's unfortunate accident with that old bridge' was meant to happen because of the 'happy consequence of Rosemary's eventual matrimony, one day'.

On this occasion Winston his Uncle Frank and his Auntie Gloria had been returning from Winston's ninth birthday outing, a visit to the local otter sanctuary, flamingo and dinosaur park and, a picnic in the countryside. They had the windscreen folded down and the rear doors pinned back. They were enjoying the warmth of the breeze and singing one of Auntie Gloria and Winston's favourite songs 'The alphabet duet' which Auntie Gloria had written for her son Michael to teach him about all sorts of people using the alphabet. One singer (Auntie Gloria) sings the first line and the other singer (Michael and more latterly Winston) sings the next line and then the two singers continue to alternate between the lines. On these occasions Winston and his Uncle Frank were usually two quarters of the other half of the duet singing the alternate line. Auntie Gloria always sung the first line.

"Adam ate the forbidden apple, digesting all our rights

Beaufort and his gale force wind blows out all our lights

Nicolaus Copernicus found planetary motion

Charles Dickens wrote to us with Victorian emotion

Edward Elgar's England was a land of hope and glory

Freud and his myth Oedipus well that's another story

Garrick down Drury Lane breathed life into old Willy

Hieronymus Bosch was thought by some as being rather silly

Isaiah of the Old Testament wrote wondrous prophesies

James Joyce wrote of Dublin in the novel Ulysses"

Uncle Frank suddenly stopped singing interrupted by the sound of an aeroplane flying low above the van it flew past them on Frank's side and then looped the loop in front of them before ascending vertically into the heavenly vault.

"Could it really be?" cried Frank O'Flannagan.

"Could it really be what?" asked Auntie Gloria

"Gunner Frank O'Flannagan and Captain Pilkington-Frobisher, it looks like a Sopwith Pup it could be them and an end to the eternal mystery of the history of my redoubtable forebear."

"That's remarkable." said Gloria.

"Isn't it." replied Frank.

"For two men." continued Gloria "who are both more than one hundred and twenty years old to be flying that aeroplane why that surpasses the fabulous mystery of their disappearance in the first place". Gloria turned and smiled at Winston. Frank's elation dulled to a hurt silence.

"Oh I do love you Frank O'Flannagan." Gloria said and she leaned across to kiss him on the cheek to restore his dignity. He leaned towards her.

"I know you do." he said.

They were cheek to cheek blocking Winston's view of the road when suddenly the bi-plane re-appeared dropping out of nowhere and flying straight at them above the road. Instinctively the kissing couple ducked below the dash board, the bi-plane swooped up and over the van and Winston suddenly got a full view of a fork in the road marked by a black and white striped signpost which was protruding from the overgrown verge at the apex of a small copse.

"Uncle Frank." Winston yelled. Frank sat up and responded by swerving the van around the signpost taking the right fork which was very narrow and shrouded by the overhanging edge of the copse. Frank turned to look at Winston to make sure that he was okay as Auntie Gloria sat bolt upright and a little shaken.

Winston glimpsed a road sign as the O'Flannagan Pantechnivan Mk1 veered to the right it was cast iron with a black foreground and white background and vertically oblong. In the top two thirds of the sign there was a black right angled triangle with the hypotenuse running top left to bottom right and in the bottom third the word HILL and beneath this 1 IN 7. The O'Flannagan Pantechnivan Mk1 seemed to plummet.

"Uncle Frank" yelled Winston again "a bridge".

"Hold tight everyone." shouted Uncle Frank as he steered the van into the middle of the narrow road towards the bridge. There was another sign cast iron black foreground and white background and vertically oblong. In the top third of the sign was a silhouette of a bridge. The bottom two thirds contained text in capitals first 'LOW BRIDGE' and then beneath in a slightly smaller font size 'HEADROOM' and beneath that 8'-6".

It was a quaint little bridge built in the pioneering years of rather pedestrian steam travel which had multiplied the flush of rural line capillaries that travelled through the surrounding country villages. Steam trains would fetch and carry passengers and freight to the coast or the towns and the provincial capitals. Cattle, sheep and pigs, grain, vegetables and wood would depart to become the fuel of the urban industrial communities of the revolution. Lives would be changed forever at the end of a journey. Tar macadam had long since replaced steel rail and wooden sleepers and the quaint bridge had been swallowed by the juvenile copse. Until recently that is, when various 'steam enthusiasts' had joined together to restore an engine and then reclaim a derelict station, fell trees, re-lay a length of standard gauge track, strangle the habitats of wildlife, erect a couple of signals and start shunting their precious steam engine back and forth transporting tourists over the quaint bridge and into recent history. The latest voluntary effort of the steam enthusiasts was the strengthening of the arched aesthetic brickwork of the bridge that was becoming unbound as the sandwiched porridge of ancient mortar between them became a crumble. This involved a substantially braced structure of spars and shafts, joists and joints of galvanized steel encasing the bridge. Unfortunately, although the O'Flannagan Pantechnivan Mk1 standing at seven feet and six inches in height could go under the bridge if it stayed in the middle of the narrow road, which Frank O'Flannagan was trying to achieve, it was taller than the scaffolding which it hit as it passed under the bridge. The top of the van was sliced cleanly away from the supporting sides by a robust length of galvanized steel scaffold pole like taut cheese wire through a ripe Stilton. It continued its missile momentum, guided between the severing pole and the pole above it and struck the weakened arched brickwork which showed no resistance as the keystone and its attendant voussoir and extrados were rudely loosened and the parapet scattered its rubble onto the railway line. Equally unfortunate was the untimely arrival of the precious steam engine on its shunt forth, laden with passengers re-living some history.

The volunteer engine driver was a full-time undertaker by

the name of Mr Tom Sorrow. He has an interesting business card which he presents to the recently bereaved which is embossed with the message 'At this time of sadness let Tom Sorrow do tomorrows work'. Tom Sorrow yanked the brass chain and sounded a warning whistle forthwith and his stoker, his only son and heir, Tom (who was named after his Grandfather) and whom he employed as a grave digger and trainee funeral director, slackened his swing and thrust of a loaded shovel of coal towards the open fire doors in the boiler. Braking gear on the King Arthur class locomotive locked the polished steel wheels against the power of the steam pistons. The engine and its trailing carriages slid from a forward speed of five miles an hour to a screeching halt crumbling a few bricks into a red mist that powdered the wooden sleepers and the spiteful nettles on the embankment. The passengers were considerably inconvenienced. Cups of warm tea and glasses of cream soda were spilled in laps and half masticated bites of sandwich spat forth, little children cried and old people awakened as the locomotive slowed from its imposed travelling speed over the bridge. The smell of fear mingled with the gaseous humidity of the gasping engine. There was steam and restrained pandemonium everywhere until the police arrived to take statements from the engineer and the guard, the 'bungling gazelle' had taken a photograph and Ranjit Livingstone, with Winston standing just to the side and slightly behind him, had wrapped his exclusive report 'live' from the scene to be broadcast on 'News in your Region sponsored by 'Roman C Menter Finest Decorative Plaster Craftsman because everyone's stuccoed on Roman' in the tea time slot. Just as Ranjit 'wrapped' an attending fireman noticed a critically chancy crack in a spandrel between the extrados and the perpendicular of the brick arched bridge. All movement was temporarily suspended until hydraulic support jacks could be brought in to take the weight of the train and its' passengers and a rescue procedure contrived and executed. Ranjit rolled the camera for take two. In the Friday Gazette and Bugle there was a four page 'centre spread' of the averted local catastrophe. The local vicar was quoted as saying it was a miracle and the bridge became a site of pilgrimage for a while for 'snouty locals' who hadn't witnessed the event first hand and needed to 'believe'.

From that day on Auntie Gloria always made Uncle Frank go round the long way whenever she saw a sign for a bridge with its height restriction marked in feet and inches. On more recent 'post 1963' signs, the contentious metric measure, rather than risk passing under it and having the wonderful van decapitated again.

RETURN TO THE ASCENSION

"We're climbing fast into the flight because we're travelling light look how high we are already Winston" Frank O'Flannagan shouted.

Winston looked straight ahead at blue sky and white clouds and then gradually he looked down to the dark brown horizon and then further into the emerging pattern of fields, woodland and villages joined by weaving seams of hedge and road then trimmed with piping of a river and a railway line.

"Look below Winston if you dare" said his uncle.

Winston took the challenge and dared to look to where directly below could be found.

"Can you see the fairies Winston going about their business" Uncle Frank asked "in their fairy cars and buses and living in their fairy houses?"

Ponds winked at him, rooftops and roads punctuated the endless mosaic of every colour of green, and the fairies waved from the gardens of their fairy houses. Dogs continued to bark.

"It is another world is it not?" Frank continued.

"How high are we Uncle Frank?" Winston asked

"Six hundred feet, shout down to the fairies" said Winston's Uncle

Winston called down and waved to a little girl, her mum, and Gran in their garden. He could hear them calling up to him with faint sounds but dogs wherever they were barked louder.

Frank O'Flannagan released more gas, the burner ignited it sending an explosion of heat up into the envelope of the balloon, and it rose quickly.

"How do you know how high we are Uncle Frank?" Winston asked.

"I am reliably informed by my instrumentation" Frank replied "this is an altimeter" he said pointing to chromium encased dial crudely fastened to a bracket on the willow wicker work partition separating him from his nephew "I rely upon my altimeter and its aneroid barometer you see we measure our rising altitude against the falling air pressure."

"So what is the air pressure for 100 metres?" asked Winston.

"Well" said Frank "one hundred millibars equals eight hundred metres so its eight metres to a millibar and eights into a hundred is...... ten in eighty so eights into twenty is two and then eights into four goes......a half......ten...two and a half twelve and a half" Frank exclaimed jubilantly.

"What is a millibar?" asked Winston. Frank strained his myriad brain.

"It's something to with centimetres, seconds and grams and I do know that one thousand dynes per square centimetre is a bar."

"Does Auntie Gloria know that you know all this stuff?" Winston continued his questioning "only you could be in her quiz team you know she is always asking you to be in her quiz team Uncle Frank."

"It's not the same thing Winston" said Frank "quiz teams are for quizzers not for me."

"What's a quizzer" Winston asked.

"A quizzer is someone who is able to store a lot of useless unconnected information that they can access at the drop of a question in a competitive environment...Now let's look at our direction shall we" he said as he slipped the machete back into its sheath hanging. Frank pulled a long silver chain from his trouser pocket one end of which was attached to a braces button inside his trouser waist band by a leather tab with a crafted slit and the other a round rather bruised leather case with large brass button holding a flap of the stitched leather over the face of a compass. Frank unbuttoned the flap and read the compass "not so good" he observed "we must hope that we are relying upon a faulty compass here Winston or this is going to be an exceptionally long birthday".

"Why?" asked Winston.

"Because it says that north is to the port side"

"But we are not near the coast" said Winston misunderstanding the meaning of port.

"Nor should we be if north was to starboard the sea would be aft. I am afraid we could eventually be making the acquaintance of the sea shortly if we don't descend in good time".

The balloon continued to rise quickly. Dogs continued to bark from everywhere. Frank O'Flannagan began to pull on a rope that hung from the balloon into his pilot's station in the middle of the basket. Winston looked up into the envelope of the balloon as Frank tugged on the rope a small aperture opened in the material.

"There is a tear in the balloon" said Winston.

"That's not a tear Winston I am letting some hot air out to help us to descend" said Frank.

"We are still going up" Winston added.

"It's a hot day" replied Frank "the balloon stays up better the warmer the air".

It certainly was hot. Winston's birthday present from his Gran was beginning to make him itch. The calamine lotion had dried and powdered into a sticky rim under the elastic of his pants. There was a deepening film of pinkie-white powder that had drifted down his legs, building up on his shoes.

"Do you think wool makes sheep itch?" Winston asked his Uncle "especially privately".

"I know your Auntie Gloria won't eat lamb on principle, because Michael loved the little lambs you know, but she will boil a bit of ugly mutton" his Uncle replied "Privately; I don't know about the personal itching of a ram Winston but I do know you never see a strawberry with a rash."

THE GRAPPLING HOOK

The balloon began to descend very slowly as Frank O'Flannagan tried to maintain the fine balance between an inflated and a flaccid angel envelope and the consequences of too rapid a descent.

"The ground is moving very quickly underneath us" said Winston "I can't feel the wind though".

"We are travelling at the same speed as the wind and with the wind so the air is still for us" said Frank.

"The wind must be going fast then" Winston continued.

It was, the gusts that ripped them from their mooring earlier had not abated indeed the lulling that divides wind into gusts had disappeared. The continuous wind was blowing Frank O'Flannagan's balloon towards the changing horizon which was fading from brown to a deepening blue-grey, the distant continent called. The coast loomed clear ahead from the elevated perspective of the basket. The balloon was travelling down the hypotenuse between its vertical ascent and a rendezvous possibly angled beyond the safety of land. Winston opened his sandwich tin in the hope that eating something might take his mind off the itching under his vest and pants.

"Would you like a piece of mum's square pie?" he asked Uncle Frank.

"No thank you I am going to give my attention to landing just now"

"Do you want me to brace then" said Winston closing the tin.

"Brace?" said Frank momentarily forgetting the procedure he had outlined to the passengers, in his distraction "Ah brace yes, no, not yet anyway".

Winston tucked into the pie.

"My calculations lead me to conclude that I need to take a more urgent action" said Frank O'Flannagan producing a four pronged grappling hook from the bowels of his station in the basket.

"Is that an anchor" asked Winston.

"It's a four clawed Grapnel and these sharp bits at the end of the claws they are flukes. It's more of an emergency brake really" replied his Uncle throwing it overboard "it's attached to four hundred feet of the best jute rope Winston and it will find a crevice in which to lodge and grasp".

The grappling hook dropped like a stone trailing the jute rope that snaked out over the side of the basket. Winston wondered if his uncle had thought about the nature of the crevice the 'emergency brake' would find. Finding a policeman or the finer point of an historic building might get them into trouble. The trailing rope hummed out over the rim of the basket at an increasing rate of knots and suddenly stopped; reverberating like the plucked 'C' string of a cello.

"The rope is fully extended" shouted Frank "prepare for heaving to and don't be frightened when we are moored because you will suddenly feel the wind".

Unfortunately when four hundred feet of the best jute rope threaded and secured with an 'Anchor Bend' knot perfect for making fast, rope to an anchor, spar or a buoy *(note: thread the rope through the eye of the shaft taking two turns follow this by making an underhand loop then thread the bitter end through the two loops that were formed by passing the rope through the eye and pull tight finally give the bitter end of the rope an extra hitch around the working rope for greater strength)*. When with the addition of the twelve inch shaft of a four pronged grappling hook the rope becomes fully extended approximately seven and a half feet above the ground, it is only dangling. It is extremely menacing when it is dangling in the main street of a provincial town in the early afternoon on a busy Saturday. It is unexpected, unusual, uncontrollable, and useless until it serves its intended purpose, to anchor its claws and their flukes into a strong resistant crevice.

The Coppersmiths and Gasfitters team bus had broken down twenty miles away with a blown gasket and so Terry's football match had been postponed. He decided to stay in town and emboldened or more accurately influenced by a crafty second and then a secretive third schooner of the celebration

Oloroso, had made his way into the main street in order to turn back the clock or more precisely to return the barometer back to its home on the hallway wall. The subject of the Walpole family heirloom had become a vapour in the years that ensued following its mysterious disappearance. Various rites of passage had matured young Terry and recent considerations had stirred him. Now as a fledgling detective constable in the local constabulary, following in the footsteps of his paternal grandfather, he knew this final expression of remorse, the return of the barometer, would purge his secret act of criminality and redemption would free him to sit his police sergeant's exam with an untroubled conscience. Terry decided the event of his young brother's birthday presented him with a perfect foil for replacing the antique and fading memory. His father was at work and his mother was visiting his Auntie Gloria and Gran. Terry intended putting it back and then not returning until the party was well under way, when everyone had gathered for the party they would be too busy to notice that the barometer had come home. And by the time the party was over well who knows.

Before the story takes us through the door of the pawnbrokers did you know the origin of the nursery rhyme 'Pop goes the Weasel'? It is the oldest financial institution known to mankind Pawning. Pawning is based upon the Bibles teaching on usury where the Church in medieval times prohibited the charging of interest so capital was raised from lenders by surrendering to their safe keeping, possessions with the equivalent value subject to lawful conditions. There were no sub-prime mortgages and short selling of shares in those days. Anyway it is clear from 'Pop goes the Weasel' as you will see.

The monkey chased the weasel,

The monkey thought 'twas all in fun

Pop goes the weasel.

A penny for a spool of thread,

A penny for a needle,

That's the way the money goes,

Pop goes the weasel.

A half a pound of tupenny rice,

A half a pound of treacle,

Mix it up and make it nice,

Pop goes the weasel.

Up and down the London road,

In and out the Eagle,

That's the way the money goes,

Pop goes the weasel.

I've no time to plead and pine,

I've no time to wheedle,

Kiss me quick and then I'm gone

Pop goes the weasel.

Columbus's voyage to America was financed by Queen Isabella of Spain pawning the crown jewels. The land of the free opened up by an interest free loan. This is the same land that harboured, nurtured and feted the Lehman Brothers, the crown jewellers of Banking depending on how much money you lost when it came crashing down

The pawnshop doorbell pinged as Terry entered the shop and the opening hours' notice swung to and fro against the security glass. Gideon Posner, beckoned from his back parlour, appeared behind the counter.

"Hello young man" he said greeting Terry "It has been some time but I told you I would pray for you and for the conundrum of your meteorological instrument." Terry had forgotten about Mr Posner's prayers.

"I have come to redeem the barometer" said Terry.

"I am very pleased to see you at last. Every day we have to make a choice, how much do we want our today to be about our yesterdays and how much do we want it to be about our tomorrows."

Gideon Posner knows all about making each day more about tomorrow because of the torment of his childhood yesterdays as a passenger of the chartered death trains of the German Reichsbahn.

"I've got the redemption slip and the money" said Terry.

"And I've got the old barometer" Gideon replied "it's still working as well as the day you brought it in it is moving towards a fairly windy day today I believe. You know your father has inquired about it over the years but I have never let on that I know anything. I give an assurance of absolute confidentiality and discretion"

"My father, you know my father how does he know?" Terry asked more than a little worried that his secret was not at all a secret.

"We are fellow Rotarians and from time to time he just enquires as to whether I have seen his barometer in my line of business and I tell him that I have only seen one barometer in all these years, that it was it was left by its rightful heir and that it was placed on deposit with me until the customer returns from his journey to reclaim it and that is the truth private and confidential as God is my judge."

Terry was about to apologize for compromising Mr Posner's relationship with Judge God in order to protect him when there was a loud clanking sound right outside the shop followed by a wrenching crunch and the sight of Gideon Posner's three polished brass spheres flying past the shop door. A dust cloud of old mortar hung outside in its place.

"What on earth was that?" exclaimed the old pawnbroker.

143

"I don't know" replied Terry going to the door and out into the street.

As pedestrians scattered under the canvass canopies of colourful shop awnings the grappling hook had swung in threatening concentric circles rotating slowly until it grappled. Two prongs of the grappling hook swung under the iron arch of the pawn-brokers symbolic signature of trade, from which three polished brass balls hung rigid under the arch, ripping it from the bracket above the shop door. The pawnbrokers sign tore through the Rexene roll top of a maroon and black 1981 Citroen 2CV Charleston one of those iconic French cars beloved of drivers who are driven by infinite causes. The brokers' brass balls lodged beneath the dashboard between the pedals of the clutch, brake, and accelerator as the balloon continued to lose height down the high street. The resistance of the French car was of little consequence to the balloon of Frank O'Flannagan. As Frank and Winston stared down the four hundred feet of arbitrarily slow spinning best jute rope they listened to the sharp chiming of the French, political sticker plastered material symbol of the liberal left, as it clattered against assorted other vehicles, lampposts and litter bins in the English high street. Frank took the momentous decision to release a blast of hot air up into the angel above to prevent further damage to life and infrastructure below. He knew there would be consequences ahead but they had to climb above the carnage in the wake of the continental motorcar clapper being grappled. Gideon Posner and Terry ran out of the shop and stared up at the balloon and then down the high street at the maroon and black French wrecking ball as it ascended.

"Uncle Frank?" Terry whispered.

Further down the street his sister Rosemary ran out of Ribbons Haberdashery and Classic Gentleman's Outfitters at the sight of the car swinging past her shop window clouting a plane tree (Platanus x acerifolia 'Augustine Henry') one of several that adorned the expansive pavement and then knocking over the red, roadside Post Office pillar box with its historic VR royal cipher, scattering the royal mail through the high street. At the far end of the street Thomas Walpole was using a long pole to fetch down, for a customer who was standing behind him waiting to take possession of her purchase, a two gallon watering can with a polished copper rose nozzle, from the display hooks that ran along the bottom of the hardware stores sign board over the shop window. He looked up in amazement at the balloon as hot air gushed from its flame throwing gas burners up into the angel envelope and rose above the mayhem it was creating. Rosemary called to her father. Thomas looked back down the street first at the liberated letters fluttering towards him then his daughter and then beyond her to Terry standing beside his fellow Rotarian Gideon Posner.

"Terry?" he whispered and then before he could acknowledge his son a young woman stepped across his field of vision blotting Rosemary and Terry out.

"Tal locura" she said.

"Pardon" Thomas Walpole returned.

"Such madness" she smiled at him "people could get seriously hurt."

"Ah" he exclaimed "the young lady who was learning Spanish, yes we could indeed, how is your mother."

"Mummy is fine, she is visiting constituents with Daddy, could I come in to shelter from the flying car if I promise to buy something."

"What would you do with a mantle, keyhole cover or a bottom roller eh?" he asked.

"A bottom roller? She laughed.

"You ought to come into the shop out of harm's way" he continued above the commotion in the street as he tried to see where his son and daughter were and whether they had found safety.

"Thank you I will until this all passes."

"Could I have that watering can?" the customer asked dragging Thomas down off his cloud and pointing at a shiny snow-flaked zinc coated two gallon can with a double, threaded brass tipped, nozzle and a bottom stamped with the makers brand 'Cooper & Nephew Casks & Canisters since 1881'.

"Certainly madam" said Thomas Walpole "of course".

The dangling French car began rising away from the terrified shoppers, swinging like a fairground ride above them threatening at any moment to fall off. Rosemary cast her glance up the street to her father unhooking a watering can from a brass hook whilst engaging with a pretty young woman and a middle aged, middle class, middle England, wool and tweed, pearls and back bone of virtue, lady customer. Rosemary looked down the street for Terry but he had gone. She waved to her father and pretended that he had noticed her as she caught the eye of the lady standing inside the Haberdashery by the counter that she had been serving before the 'Angel of Loreto' had come calling. Back in the ironmongery her father was cashing his sale on an old, hand cranked, 'National' cash register, a distant offspring of the invention of James Ritty bought many years ago in an auction by Zechariah Fitzgerald for his Temperance Bar.

"Thank you madam" he said courteously to the lady with the watering can "now what can I get you?" he asked the young lady who had engaged him outside the shop.

"Well" she said "seeing as how you are asking I'll try a sarsaparilla soda please."

"Go through" said Thomas hesitating for a moment and pointing her to the Temperance Bar at the rear of the shop "I'll be with you in a moment".

Thomas then ran back out in the street to see Rosemary disappearing into the Haberdashery.

He returned to the Temperance Bar area of the shop. One of the shop assistants, Emmett ran past them.

"Is there an invasion going on Mr Walpole?" he shouted.

"No Emmett just some lefty protest I suspect that car is covered in those stickers."

"Those stickers?" the young lady queried.

"You know" replied Thomas "political stickers, legalize it, recycle it or slow down for horses stickers".

Just as he was about to start pouring her a drink he was interrupted by another assistant.

"I think your wife is on the telephone" she said.

"Right" he said "I'll be back in two ticks." It was actually Rosemary who had called to see if he was alright, she had to call someone after the incident with the car and the pillar box and all that. As Thomas walked towards his 'back office' a distressed Gilbert Herring the hairdresser hurried up.

"Thomas what on earth is going on out there?" he said "it's terrorists."

"Terrorists don't use those cars Gilbert" Thomas replied "it's too risky anyone driving one of those immediately raises suspicion, mind it looks like a balloon towing a car someone's going to have a rum insurance bill, it'll be the talk of the Goat and Compasses this evening."

"It'll be prison" said Gilbert "they've knocked over the letterbox outside the haberdashery there's private letters flying everywhere I believe you can be sent to the Tower for less."

"I think you'll find its some political extremist complaining about taxes or discrimination or another coffee shop being built in the main street."

"Well in my day they'd get hard labour Thomas just for dropping litter."

PASSENGERS TO THE RESCUE

While all this was happening the passengers who had enrolled or been enrolled by generous family or friends for the 'OFF into the blue yonder adventure of a life time' had stood and watched in horror as their adventure went off without them. Long Clem who had chased the O'Flannagan Pantechnivan Mk1 in a thoughtless attempt to climb aboard and 'do something' walked back from his upended charge to address his bewildered congregation. He looked with his natural honesty straight into the eyes of the octogenarian triplets the midriff's of everyone else except Gustav the chauffeur with whom he was at an eye to elephant eared trouser level.

"Well" he began "I have to admit we had not practiced for that particular eventuality but I am sure that when we catch up with Mr O'Flannagan you will be able to reschedule your flights with him."

"Catch up?" said the ice cream man "where and when are we going to catch up with him?"

"Well" continued Long Clem "if I could have some help to correct the position of the van I will be able to lead you in pursuit I do have some experience of this."

"I don't think we will be able to tip that van back onto its wheel base it's a bit mighty" said the tattooed man "I've recently recovered from a hernia operation or I would have given it a good go."

"My brother had one of those" said the bus driver "was it in your undercarriage his was he showed me it, it was like a small sack of seed potatoes."

"Yes well" interrupted Tertius Napoleon Sawadogo "I think we need to start organizing ourselves into a rescue party I think, is it Gustav?" he said looking at the pink sister's chauffeur.

"Yes" said one of them "it is Gustav."

"Gustav Eberhardt at your service" said the tall man.

"Strong as a boar" said another of the sisters, which was true (as any etymologist will tell you).

"Gustav you and I will lead the vanguard I am sure that I can fit into your sidecar. Clem you had better ride pillion as navigating officer and this happy young couple, you lovely young ladies" he said to the pink sisters "and the man with the skin art can be my guests on the chartered omnibus with my family and you sir" he said to Billy Butterball "you can hitch a lift in the ice cream van."

""You'll have to be careful in my van I don't want my cones crushed" said the ice cream man "and there's no smoking."

"If you don't mind I'll stand on the platform at the back of the bus and have a puff of my Churchill" replied the market trader.

"My wife and I would love to ride in the ice cream van" said the young newlywed man "we really don't mind."

"You'll have to stand in the back and, what's your name love?" said the ice cream man.

"Gwendolyn" said the young woman "and my husband is Billy."

"Gwendolyn and Billy you must watch my cones."

"Two Billy's you must be a William to save our confusion" said Tertius Napoleon Sawadogo to the young man.

"Actually I am a Billy it's what my parents christened me" he replied "I have never been a William."

"I am a William but I've been a Billy for many years now" said Billy Butterball "my parents christened me William Pepys Salisbury Butterworth no less. I have forgiven them and I am most comfortable being a Billy."

"Right" said the man from Burkina Faso "two Billy's it is then one in the bus, Billy bus and one in the ice cream van, ice cream Billy, shall we go?"

Gustav kick started the 1955 350cc Douglas Dragonfly motorcycle into life, Long Clem climbed up onto the pillion and Tertius Napoleon Sawadogo squeezed himself into the two-seater sidecar normally the reserve of Hester and Hermione Ribbons with Hester taking the slightly raised 'pilots' berth in the rear. Their sister

Henrietta always rode pillion behind Gustav. The Douglas Dragonfly registration RVF 157 was immaculate despite regular use its Celadon and Chromium, neatly polished by Gustav patiently filling his waiting time wherever the 'girls' excursions took them.

"You can move zee seat backvoords by pulling zis lever" Gustav instructed Tertius.

"Thank you" he replied.

"And eef you vaunt you can have zee cockpit canopy open."

"I will" said Tertius raising his left arm in signal to the convoy of ice cream van and Routemaster waiting in formation behind. The Ribbons sisters were settling into the front row seats on the top deck of the bus surrounded by inquisitive African children and their graceful mothers.

"This is just as exciting as a balloon ride" said Hester.

"I love making new friends" added Henrietta as she looked at the many faces smiling at her. Tertius Napoleon Sawadogo let his left arm drop into the sidecar of the Douglas Dragonfly in a sweeping arc gesturing a tally-ho. The ice cream man joined in by switching on the musical chimes of his hand tuned Swiss movement which was amplified through Grampian Horn speakers. The tune of Brahms lullaby 'Cradle song' *Wiegenlied* echoed against the trees surrounding the meadow. Gwendolyn began to sing.

"Lullaby and goodnight with roses be dight creep into thy bed there pillow thy head if God will thou shalt wake when the morning doth break."

"Where did you get that from?" ice cream Billy her new husband asked.

"It's an original Swiss job" said the ice cream man proudly.

"I meant my Gwendolyn actually."

"My Gran taught me when I had chickenpox once that's how she got me off to sleep to stop me scratching."

"What does dight mean for heaven's sake?" Billy continued.

"Gran said it meant to dress up or something and that it was old

150

like her."

"Hold tight" said the ice cream man "we're off."

The convoy began to move slowly across the dank grass and out of the meadow. The Douglas Dragonfly led the way. Gustav rode the machine bolt upright his long legs folded like a spider at rest. Long Clem perched behind Gustav dwarfed by his immense height clamping his stubby arms around the tall torso. He peered ahead through the gap between Gustav's upright flank and the slightly cricked bow of his right arm. Tertius Napoleon Sawadogo commanded from the comfort of the bullet shaped sidecar. The jingling ice cream van followed and the red Routemaster brought up the rear with its cargo of pink ladies, tattooed man and tribal harem with Billy Butterball keeping the flies away with clouds of cigar smoke.

"Poop-poop my fox" Hester squealed delightedly impersonating the Master of the local hunt in pursuit of the pack.

CRASHING CAR FLYING DOG

Winston and his Uncle Frank had drifted in silence for a while. Winston sat with his knees up under his chin in a corner of his station in the basket, his legs apart. He was etching the face of his favourite comic book super hero into the pinkie-white calamine dust that had built up on his shoes. As he began to illustrate the slimy script stamp of 'Slug Man' 'the ordinary bus conductor with the extraordinary powers' of 'sonicosmorphosis' he was distracted by the silent passage of a high speed train across the window framed by one the steps woven into the basket for the purpose of Uncle Franks orchestrated 'embarkation'. Winston stood up and peered over the side of the basket.

"Uncle Frank look there's a train we are following the railway line exactly."

"It's the Euro-star train to France" said Uncle Frank "we are approaching the coast" with this Frank opened the summit of the balloon envelope to let hot air out and force another descent.

"What about the car on the end of the rope?" Winston said.

"We are in open country now" Frank assured his nephew "at worst it will only hit a tree or a barn just as long as it finds an anchor point I'm just not sure that I am insured for all this activity I don't know what you'd call it I hope it's an act of God."

On the other hand, perhaps it could hit a quietly grazing bullock thought Winston as he began to contemplate a re-run of the railway catastrophe prematurely ending another birthday outing with his Uncle Frank. He only hoped that poor Auntie Gloria did not get the 'News in your Region' at teatime in the sanatorium just in case any of this was being reported by Ranjit. He could see it now, British beef sitting in a French car in the middle of field, being described by Ranjit Livingston. The balloon began another descent. Winston watched the pendulous French car below, between the more distant parallel silver rails, swinging back and forth through a contracting ladder of sleepers under the tracery of overhead electric cables. He looked ahead to where the rails and cables vanished into a large black hole framed in grey concrete and buried in a manmade mound of turfed mould. The balloon continued its descent.

"Uncle Frank" Winston shouted "there's the tunnel is it going to swallow us"

Winston watched the colour of his uncle's face change quicker than a chameleon in a discotheque but Frank's face was not blending with his surroundings. The French car began clattering and bouncing along the railway, earthing nuclear reactor fuelled locomotive power lines showering the embankments and a group of linesmen working there, with cascades of molten sparks. The linesmen scattered into the painful embrace of gorse and the stinking pods of the abundant broom that grew by the tracks, protesting loudly and drowning out the sound of dogs barking.

"We are going into the tunnel" shouted Winston.

Frank O'Flannagan once again pulled hard on the gas chain igniting a ball of flame up into the envelope of the balloon. He slackened and then pulled again and then again. Winston waited for the balloon to respond. The French car continued to clatter and the linesmen protest. Suddenly and silently the balloon rose right in front of the black maw of the channel tunnel with its dim and deep set fizzing constellations.

There was a collision, a loud crash followed by the catastrophic return to earth of a badly damaged French automobile. The grappling hook had lost its grip on the yoke of the pawn brokers' brass balls as the battered car collided with the coping stones in the concrete façade and was then dumped at the threshold of the tunnel. The balloon jarred momentarily then released to continue its journey upwards and onwards towards the open sea.

A solitary man was out walking his dog along the chalk white coastal pathway that ran close to the precipice of the white chalk cliffs rising above the beach, hem of the garden of England. He was a man who had been blind from birth. He was holding firmly to the harness handle of his trained guide dog taking trusting steps, speaking kindly to, and restraining his devoted dog in the strong gusts that buffeted them both as they walked. He was dressed for walking in proper boots, woollen socks and a Cagoule.

He was carrying a knapsack that stored his Braille compass, a tactile map based on the Ordnance Survey Route Planner map of 1946 with Braille labels. In his knapsack he had some 'Kendal' mint cake, a banana, a bottle of blackcurrant juice for refreshment and treats for his faithful guide dog. No-one walking the cliffs that day had a keener sense for creation than he, yet even he did not suspect the angel approaching or the consequences about to beset him.

I remember once when I was a boy scout having to call at the local school for blind children during a bob-a-job week. It was in the area my patrol six (leader) in collusion with Reginald Botwright who was at the time my patrol second allocated to me. I had recently passed my semaphore badge and Reginald hadn't which made my assignment at the school for the blind feel like a bit of retribution on his part. I was sure that Simba, our Troup leader, checked up on us making sure that we didn't avoid certain properties or establishments so as not to miss opportunities to earn maximum funds for the Baden-Powel legacy. I dare not refuse to venture up the long daunting driveway lined with lime trees. I usually got a bit of gardening in overgrown herbaceous borders or tidying up a fusty, spider traceried potting shed and once I had to hold by the hocks every screaming struggling terror-stricken boar pig in a litter of Wessex saddleback pigs upside down between my legs while the Vicars wife castrated them tossing their warm freshly liberated testicles to her hungry Labrador 'Montgomery'. For my bob-a-job at the school for the blind I was assigned as a 'sighted' companion for the day to a girl of my own age. Her eyes were almost black which she told me was because her blindness was caused by a condition called Aniridia. Her name was Caitlin. She had red in her dark hair and melting freckles scattered over her pretty face. It was the best shilling I ever earned but I paid dearly with my stupidity on my first day of meeting with blindness. I committed the cardinal sin of telling her to look when a squirrel ran across the lawn in front of us and then later making adolescent small talk I asked what her favourite colour was and later still if she would like to come to the pictures with me, obviously outside of my bob-a-job responsibilities. They say that accidents happen in threes. I felt so bad that I went back after I had eaten my tea and finished my bob-a-job day to see her I felt so sick inside. It was my most grown up moment. Caitlin was sitting in the old reading room of the rather stately house bequeathed to the blind charity, heavily curtained into almost total darkness. I sat beside her in the gloom wondering if I had depressed her with my thoughtless company. 'Shall I put the light on' I said by way of gently making my presence known to her and seeking redemption. She laughed out loud and said 'it is lovely to see you again'. I know now, that then I was touched by something so fleetingly deep within me that I have never since found again. Men, most of us who never quite stepped up despite our dreams, search out our first love in the wake of unfinished lives and through the open secrecy of the World Wide Web in the hope of finding what was fleetingly deep and claiming it. I often think about Caitlin and try to recapture that moment spent with her when her irrepressible joy touched something in me. I hope Caitlin met a man who knew that she did not need his eyes but that he desired her soul. I hope Caitlin found true happiness I really do. Every time I think of her I believe a little deeper in the wonder of life and the incredible power of hope.

"I am afraid Winston that there is nothing I can do to prevent us ditching in the sea now so we will have to get down as quick as we can to be as near to the shore as we can get for rescuing." Frank O'Flannagan said.

"Shall I brace now?" asked Winston.

"No not yet" replied his Uncle "in fact bracing might not be necessary."

"It's alright Uncle Frank I am a good swimmer, Osborne and I are both good swimmers."

"Swim?" said Frank O'Flannagan his colour changing again.

The Grappling hook was again swinging to and fro and rotating slowly barely inches above the ground. In the course of a 'swing to' the grappling hook rotated through an arc that swung so close to the blind man walking along the cliff path that it grappled the harness handle from his grip and dragged the guide dog over the cliff suspending it beneath the basket where a few minutes earlier the wreckage of a French car had dangled. The blind man felt the direction of the pull of the kidnapped dog and desperate and in a moment of panic thoughtlessly pursued it, over the cliff. He began a free fall that was abruptly, quickly and quite miraculously broken by his knapsack strap snagging a tent peg driven into the cliff face below the edge. A tent peg to secure a guy rope that was supporting one of two very tall poles between which was strung a huge canvass banner proclaiming the 'Anglo-

155

French Channel Race to Celebrate the Anniversary of the Entente Cordial'. The balloon descended rapidly. The precipice of the white cliffs passed beneath the basket which ripped the huge banner from between the two very tall poles as the blind man fell. Winston thought he glimpsed the poles falling over the cliffs and then he heard gulls screeching people shouting and the sound of a stampede over shingle and then some splashing. The banner squirmed upwards in the strong wind and wrapped around the ropes suspending the basket from the balloon like a small marquee shutting out the world. With the outside world cut off from him Frank O'Flannagan in a moment of disorientated panic released a long blast of ignited gas up into the envelope of the balloon aware that the basket was now just a few feet above the low tide of the English Channel and even more aware that he, not being able to swim, would be at a major disadvantage if he carried out his threat and ditched the balloon. There had been a loud thud and a slight jolt of the basket as it stopped momentarily in its flight followed by the wood of the poles splintering the vibrating timbre of strong wire being stretched to breaking point with a loud and final twang at the crescendo as it snapped. A whip crack sliced through the banner, Uncle Frank let out a cry of pain falling down against the gas canisters in his station.

"I've been shot" Frank shouted "somebody is shooting at us from the cliff top!" Winston curled up into the corner of the basket trembling.

"You fascist land owning gentry toff shot gun totting pheasant blasting idle rich I'll have you know I have a child up here in this basket and his life is threatened and my Gloria will kill me if any harm comes to him" Frank continued in pain induced irrationality.

People somewhere close below began swearing and shouting 'Terrorist' in two or three languages. A dog spluttered, whimpered and then began barking. Frank had aborted the idea of landing in the water now his only hope was a one hundred and eighty degree change in the direction of the wind and he began asking for it in a loud voice.

"Dear God forgive me I cannot let this darling boy down you must turn this wind as in the days of my dear wife's favourite man of God, Joshua, when you stopped the sun from going down at his beckoning in the heat of battle so Lord send me a wind that will blow me home amen." Frank paused from his praying and then continued in earnest "or Moses when he parted the Red sea, or Elijah the Jordan or Jesus feeding all those people with what amounted to a single meal deal in today's money…you can do it God I know you can amen."

Winston stood up and peered over the brim of his wicker-worked corner at his distressed and bleeding uncle.

"Uncle Frank" he said "we just have to wait now because Auntie Gloria says that God will always answer."

"Right enough" shouted Frank "you're right enough Winston."

Down below people began to piece together Franks desperate rant at what he thought was a gun being fired at him.

"Do you think he is a fascist?" said one "Europe is once again their lair."

"Maybe he is just anti the French and using today to vent his spleen" echoed another.

"He's definitely Irish so probably a paramilitary or something."

"And I think he's kidnapped somebody called Gloria and he is threatening to kill them."

"Well" added yet another "I think trailing that poor dog on the end of a rope is significant."

"Isn't that what the Mafia do to send a message to others?"

"That makes complete sense" said a more knowledgeable soul "although I don't think they would expect the Angel of Loreto to be dangling it" pointing to the balloon.

OUT TO SEA

Frank got up slowly, clutching his head. Blood was oozing from a wound that had lacerated his scalp and his right ear.

"We didn't ditch did we?" Winston said

"To be true Winston no we didn't because the truth is that I can't swim" his Uncle responded very loudly "I could not bring myself to ditch us and I am sorry because I am not sure where we are going to land now."

"Never mind Uncle Frank you're going to need some vinegar and brown paper on your head" said Winston.

Frank released hot air into the balloon and Winston could feel that they were again ascending flying above the bark of a dog and the swell of the sea.

"This is great fun Uncle Frank thank you" said Winston "we are going to be alright I know we are all we have to do is pray that's what Auntie Gloria always says 'before you get into a corner pray or when there's something you want', I prayed that I would have a great birthday".

"This is the fault of those blasted meteorologists" moaned Frank loudly as he fudged around in the bottom of the basket for the first aid tin.

Winston looked at the slash in the banner letting air and light into the shrouded world between the basket and the balloon. There was writing like characters in a shadow theatre circling round backwards. Anglo-French Channel Race...Entente Cordiale. Winston began pronouncing phonetically "race, that's easy chan, channel, fern, French dash, angel angle, Anglo En'tent'ee cordial. Isn't that a drink?" he asked.

"No its iodine" shouted Frank as he poured a thick green liquid from an old glass cordial bottle embossed with lime fruits and rambling roses, into a fist of cotton wool before swabbing the side of his injured head.

"Pooh what is that smell?" said Winston.

"Iodine" repeated Frank "now Winston can you hold this pad over my ear while I wrap a bandage around my head and then try using this safety pin to hold the bandage in place and don't for goodness sake go and stick the pin in my head".

"Okay Uncle" said a willing Winston "I have a first aid badge."

Frank pressed one end of the bandage to his forehead with the fingers that, to Winston, doubled as the barrel when his hand was used as a gun for shooting Ezra and Osborne. Frank began unrolling it in his other hand which was circling his injured head. One full circle brought his hands together and he pulled the bandage tight over the gun barrel fingers Winston wiggled them out and pressed them again on the next layer of bandage.

"Uncle Frank" said Winston.

Frank then repeated several more revolutions of bandage around his throbbing skull until he came to the end of the bandage over the ear on the opposite side to the injured ear.

"Uncle Frank" said Winston

"Right Winston stick the pin in here but be careful" shouted Frank O'Flannagan.

"Uncle Frank" repeated Winston.

Frank noticed his nephews' lips moving and he could hear a voice like it was speaking under the bed clothes or down stairs in the front room.

"Why are you mumbling Winston" he shouted

"Uncle Frank" Winston shouted back "you've bound my fingers to your head".

"Oh Winston why didn't you say" shouted Frank a little impatiently.

Winston was very careful and fixed the pin in the outer layers of the bandage leaving it a little loose around his Uncle's head. Frank O'Flannagan released a long blast of hot air up into the balloon to ensure the craft would continue to rise away from the danger of ditching in the briny below. A dog barked.

"Always the last sound to fade away" shouted Frank O'Flannagan with the sound of the pain ringing in his ears making the dog bark reverberate through his Cochlea like an echo faintly under an old railway bridge .

"It sounded quite close really" said Winston.

"Drifting on the wind." said Frank "it's an unusually strong wind caught me out a bit."

"But the wind can't overtake us can it you said about the wind and the same speed thing so how can it carry noises now?"

Frank drowned his nephew's question with another blast of ignited gas.

For a while the two souls drifted along quietly in the balloon. Frank was afflicted with the distracting high pitched hiss of pressure whistling from the pain of his lacerated lug in the starboard frontier of his brain. Winston breathed iodine vapour and listened to gulls gossiping about the ridiculous humans racing in the sea below. Frank adjusted the irritating hem of bandage above his eyebrows by rolling it under which tightened it a little. The overlap of the curtain of banner canvass was drawn on Winston's side of the balloon.

"Winston" shouted Frank after a while "can you grab an edge of that banner and pull on it?"

Winston responded and hauled on the banner. As he pulled the banner began to slip down the umbilical ropes harnessing the basket to the balloon envelope. One end of the banner drifted out dragging itself in an arc around the basket. Winston felt his arms stretch and tighten in his elbows and shoulders. His feet slid to the side of the basket stubbing his toes and he began to feel the deep impress of the 'knit one pearl one' woollen stitches of his 'birthday vest' across his chest as the creaking willow wickerwork weave of the rim of the basket threatened to break his ribs.

"Do you want a souvenir" shouted Uncle Frank "something to hang on your bedroom wall to make that brother of yours jealous?"

Winston wanted to say no but talking requires the aid of breathing which he could no longer achieve. He tried to shake his head but it was jammed between his outstretched arms.

"You'll have to let go of that banner Winston your bedroom isn't big enough." laughed Frank.

Winston let go just as his whole body had begun rising up the inside of the basket like mercury in a thermometer. Winston fell back into the basket dizzy. He got to his feet slowly and peering over the side watched the liberated banner floating away below convulsing like mayfly larvae in jam jar of the cow pat polluted freshwater that he would dredge up on fishing trips with Ezra and Osborne from the beck that flowed through Westbrook Green. Geraldine occasionally accompanied them. Winston, sunk to the basket floor, thought wistfully of Geraldine and imagined her at his birthday party this coming teatime at the end of his outing with Uncle Frank once they had landed safely.

INTO THE CHANNEL

"I wonder what mum is doing right now" said Winston because thinking of Geraldine had made him think of home and home made him think of his mother.

Frank looked at his watch.

"Well after she has finished her ironing she usually visits my mother and now your Aunt Gloria as well, she's a creature of habit your mother" he shouted.

Winston breathed long and deeply through his nose trying to savour the smell the vapours of warmed washed cotton airing under the hot press of the gliding iron in his mother's hand as she held the garment taut on the ironing board.

"Don't be rude Winston the only wind you can smell in this basket is your own" shouted Frank interpreting the deep long sniff Winston was taking as hinting that his nephew was taking pleasure in his own flatulence as boys are wont to do.

They are, trust me. Well at least some boys and I am ashamed to say that I was amongst them. As humans we are the sophisticated species in all creation or evolution depending on your conviction and it is peculiar that as adolescents we derive olfactory pleasure from inhaling our own methane expulsions. Our instinct of knowing our own unique percolation is extremely strong especially when we practice this tribally. In my limited experience with my fellow boy scouts in a tent or with team mates on the football bus or during the epilogue at the Methodist Youth Club where rattling the floor boards was a bonus effect that would start an uncontrollable riot for Reverend Scoggins. We each knew our own distinctive odour.

Winston stared at his uncle. "Actually my smellagination was my Mum ironing but it took me to another place". He said.

"And where would that be?" asked Frank.

"The care home where Gran is and Auntie Gloria it smells a bit like ironing and disinfectant and something else mixed up. Mum is there today, this afternoon she is visiting them like you said."

Frank O'Flannagan pondered.

"What" he shouted "is a smellagination for heaven's sake?"

Winston laughed, he was laughing at his Uncle's shouting. Winston thought that the bandage was making him deaf.

"It's how a smell reminds me of something and I close my eyes and I can see it and hear it in my brain."

"I think am going deaf" shouted Frank O'Flannagan "all I can hear is some infernal whistling in *my* brain".

Frank O'Flannagan pulled on the cord hanging from the burners above his head. Gas exploded into a pillar of flame that filled the canvass envelope lifting them upwards.

"Smellagination" Frank pondered the word "do you have any other words?"

"Wale" said Winston.

"Whale?" questioned Uncle Frank "but we all know what a whale is".

"A wale is a journey" said Winston.

"I don't think so" said Uncle Frank trying to be ahead of Winston "a whale is the transport that took Jonah on a journey but it was only the transport"

"I'm not talking about a creature it's the word, it means a long way and a long while a 'wale' of a journey."

"But all journeys that are a long way, take a long while" said Uncle Frank.

Winston sighed deeply and then began slowly educating his uncle in the rudiments of quantum jumping.

"How long would it take us to reach ten thousand feet in this balloon?"

"I don't know right away I would have to work it out."

"If I jumped out of here at ten thousand feet without a parachute how long would it take me to get back down?"

"Ah I see" said Uncle Frank "same journey different transport.....no transport in fact". Frank thought for a moment "that's very clever Winston.........but you do realize you'd immediately be starting another journey once you got to the bottom of down, out into the beyond, the moment you landed."

Winston looked at his Uncle Frank.

"Out into the blue yonder" Uncle Frank looked pleased with himself, a pioneer, an explorer of life; a man to whom an intelligent reply was his crown, especially with his lovely Gloria because she was really the one with the brains and the one who concluded most of their conversations.

"When did you think this word up then Winston?"

"When we went all the way to Wales for a holiday." replied Winston laughing.

      The bandage was slipping down over Frank O'Flannagan's eyes again, its frayed edge toothlessly sawing at his lashes making his eyes water.

"Why are you sad Uncle Frank?" asked Winston mistaking his watery eyes for tears.

"Does it show?" Frank shouted.

Winston wondered what his Uncle Frank was thinking, his mother had spoken of Auntie Gloria and how it was all turning out a 'right peculiar do' for her brother Frank having to search for his wife in the dead of night and listen to her confusion during the day. His mother always insisted that you wouldn't know it was happening because Frank never ever bothered anyone with it. Winston wondered how it was that his mother knew such detail of his Auntie's suffering. His father always shed a different light on family things, but Winston knew that they both cared.

"Do you think we should sing Michaels song it always makes us happy?" Winston asked and then began singing random couplets that Gloria had made up to stimulate Michael with rhythm and the poetic resonance of words.

"Edward Elgar's England was a land of hope and glory

Freud and his myth Oedipus well that's another story

Kennedy the president constrained by Castro's Cuba

Louie Armstrong shared his world on a trumpet not a tuba."

His singing reminded Frank of his wife's poetic gifts.

"Your Auntie Gloria likes poetry. She likes to read it out loud during the day and she writes poetry of her own at the dead of night when she ought to be sleeping."

"What sort of poetry does Auntie Gloria write is it like the Alphabet duet she wrote for Michael?"

"Sort of, its proper poetry the sort that rhymes, she likes to express herself in verse as she puts it"

"What does she say?" Winston asked.

Frank tucked the hem of the bandage up under itself above his brow and wiped his eyes.

"I don't understand it very well." he paused "I don't understand some of your Auntie Gloria she's a bit like her poetry really" he paused to think "enigmatic" he shouted that's the word enigmatic."

"I miss Auntie Gloria Uncle Frank."

"And so do I Winston, so do I." Frank drifted a little. "What do you miss Winston?"

"I miss" began Winston "when you do things for her and she always says oh I do love you Frank O'Flannagan and stuff like that. Singing the Alphabet duet and collecting the 'hen fruit' with her as well."

"Eggs she loves collecting the eggs" said Frank.

"What do you miss Uncle Frank?"

Frank thought deeply it took him some time to answer.

"Lots of things really" he paused "when I make a cup of tea in the mornings lately" he paused again "I've only been making one. Yesterday I forgot and I made two cups hers with and mine without."

"Auntie Gloria is coming home though isn't she?"

"I hope so." replied Frank "I do really hope so Winston I mean she did look much better this week".

"What were my mum and dad like when they were in love" asked Winston.

"They still love one another" replied Frank still shouting above the whistling in his head.

"Well" continued Winston a little unsure, "when they were still kissing and going for walks together and not disagreeing sometimes.........what were they like before me and Terry and Rosemary?".

"Well I've never heard them argue" said Frank very loudly "not agreeing is not necessarily arguing we all have different views on some things."

"Do you and Auntie Gloria have different views on things?"

"Not that I can recall your Aunt usually tells me what my view is" Frank laughed "that is her prerogative and I love her prerogative just as much as I love her." He laughed.

"Does my Auntie Gloria like ballooning?"

"She's never mentioned it" said Frank.

A dog barked.

"I am Sir Oracle and when I open my lips let no dog bark" shouted Frank "Merchant of Venice, Graziano scene one did it at school and never forgot it. I told you Winston it's the only sound you will hear up here" shouted Frank O'Flannagan. "I was Graziano and Sinead Costello was Nerissa I married her in the play and it was, until I met your Auntie Gloria, the happiest day of my life."

"We must be quite a way out to sea now" Winston said.

"It is overtaking us carried on the wind from England" Frank continued "and that is what we are going to have to do. I think that we have enough gas just to get us across the channel because the weight is so much less without the other passengers."

"And the channel is only twenty one miles across." said Winston.

"How do you know that?" asked his Uncle Frank.

"Ranjit Livingstone".

"Ranjit the Englastani newsman as your bug ugly brother calls him?" Frank shouted.

"He was on the beach with a Lieutenant from the Hussars."

"Twenty one miles, that should be okay then" Frank thought for a moment "we might have a little trouble with the French."

"Why Uncle Frank?" asked Winston.

"Well, have you brought your passport?"

"No." replied Winston "I didn't need a passport when I went to Wales for a holiday and that was further away than France".

"You are a chip of the old block you are Winston always working things out your father works things out thinks stuff through, likes his arts and all that."

"What do you mean chip off the old block Uncle Frank?" Winston asked.

"It means that you've got a bit of your father in you Winston."

Winston looked away into the distance, thought a while and then turned back to look at his Uncle.

"I wish that he had a bit of me in him." said Winston.

"What do mean by that then my boy?"

"Like Auntie Gloria."

Frank O'Flannagan looked at his nephew and wondered what he was trying to say.

"Auntie Gloria feels like the whole of Michael is a part of her" said

Winston.

"Your father wouldn't be without you or Terry and Rosemary or her Colin, he's a prospective son-in-law. Your father runs deep Winston he understands a part of my Gloria that's alien to your mother and I, he's a good man, it couldn't have been easy for him as a boy himself with that uncle of yours, the headmaster. I'm sure he eats little children when no-one is looking."

"What happens when we get to France how do we get home for my party?" Winston asked.

"There's always the ferry" replied Frank.

Passengers to the Temperance Bar

Tertius Napoleon Sawadogo ably chauffeured by Gustav Eberhardt under the shrill guidance of Long Clem had kept the Angel of Loreto in his sights. The convoy was falling further behind the errant balloon on two accounts, one the balloon was travelling at approximately 30 knots and in a straight line whereas the convoy although regularly clocking greater ground speeds was at times travelling in the opposite direction due to the historic meandering of the rural highways. And two, the balloon was travelling in open sky, the convoy was beset with road works. Not any old road works no; these were major excavations being carried out by the local authority.

During the Second World War in Britain there emerged an immortal line of defence against the invading Germanic horde that we affectionately call 'Dads Army'. The real title of these fighting elite was the Home Guard. It comprised of men over the age of 40 and boys under the age of 18. Undoubtedly the nation owes them a debt their conspicuous presence must have given the women and children of our absent servicemen a sense of security in troubled times. Their legacy gave the boys and girls of my generation somewhere to exercise our childish make believe and later explore our fascinating adolescence together. That legacy was the bastion of the Home Guard, the bunker known as the 'pillbox' which was constructed under the deepening cloud of invasion being threatened by Hitler in 1940. These tiny fortresses were 'dug in' concrete machine gun positions similar to those used in the Hindenburg Line. Where is this history lesson going? Well I'll tell you what happened to the mixture of corporals and privates, men and boys once Hitler had been consigned as a lesson of history. This subaltern stratum of the working population found post war employment as reward, for its heroism, with the local authority department of public works and for successive generations has plagued society with its cult ethic most keenly expressed through the plague better known as road works. Symptoms such as the illogical positioning of signs, bollards and traffic lights the trenching of newly surfaced paths and roads, the congregation of reflective clothing clad smoking clubs and hard hatted tea parties are easily detected. The disease is incurable it can only be treated with tolerance and it can break the most philosophical spirit. There is nothing worse in the world (at the time) than following a trail of diversion signs out into the middle of nowhere and then for the signs to evaporate. The mind takes over and instead of trying to find a way back to the interrupted route originally being followed a search automatically begins for the next diversion sign. You cannot remember driving the vehicle up into the bedroom and through the open wardrobe door or through the looking glass. I digress.

"I am sure" said Gustav as they waited patiently for a green light at an unmanned road work that consisted of three bollards marking a broken storm drain cover "zere is a loophole in zee law zat zez zat you can go if zere is noughzing coming in zee oppozeet direction". They were staring down a two mile stretch of old roman road with no other vehicle in sight and rabbits loping about as if vehicles never passed that way anyway.

"I've heard Frank say that" said Long Clem "but Gloria would never let him break a law she wasn't sure of."

"Well" said Tertius Napoleon Sawadogo "I am a visitor to your country with diplomatic immunity in these matters as far as I am concerned and I am concerned that the balloon is getting further away and it is a matter of urgency and public safety that we catch them I am also about to be sworn in as your new reality television Mayor so forward through the red light I say with the authority invested in me by the television."

The convoy eventually entered the high street in the wake of the havoc wreaked upon it. Gustav drew the procession up outside the Ribbons Haberdashery and Classic Gentleman's Outfitters. It was his habit six days a week to deliver Hester, Hermione and Henrietta to the shop at some point in the day. The omnibus shuddered to a stop behind the ice cream van which began doing a brisk trade with shocked shoppers the moment Brahms lullaby had stopped. The calming catering service being augmented by Gwendolyn and ice cream Billy who were thoroughly enjoying themselves. The Ribbons sisters invited their fellow passengers to disembark and join them for a sarsaparilla in the Temperance bar of the hardware store further down the street.

"I think I'll just pop for a drop of Napoleon's favourite in the Goat and Compasses if you don't mind" said Billy Butterworth "I'm not far from home here."

"Do they sell hot chocolate, coffee and lavender?" asked Henrietta Ribbons knowing it was an aphrodisiac concoction of Josephine Beauharnais Empress of France for her Napoleon, in which only English lavender would do.

"They don't use lavender in brewing do they?" Billy Butterball queried. Henrietta knew her French history, she knew her French. Henrietta knew Vera Atkins who had recruited and trained her in the aftermath of the Dunkirk evacuation in 1940 to work for the Special Operations Executive behind enemy lines in Nazi occupied Vichy France. Henrietta, Hester and Hermione had lived life. This much I will tell you now but the rest must wait for another time. Their lives became entwined with the Spanish Civil War, World War Two and post war social revolution. They delivered Spitfires, nursed at battle fronts, rode camels, danced as debutantes and marched to ban the bomb. They knew artists, musicians and writers, politicians and priests. They have played their parts in history and yet remain a mystery to all but themselves.

"Napoleon liked Josephine's hot chocolate just as much as he enjoyed the aging cognac Mr Butterworth the distillation of the 'waters of life' might well have aroused his ardour but Josephine's alchemy satisfied it of that I have no doubt" said Henrietta with a twinkle in her eyes at the discomfiture of Billy Butterball.

"Err yes Miss Henrietta I dare say" replied Billy colouring up.

"Is there a Mrs. Butterworth?" she asked mischievously.

"Indeed there is, she is quite partial to a hot chocolate."

"Well then, English lavender Mr Butterworth, English lavender." The sisters chorused.

"I'll be off now then." He replied a little shaken but not stirred.

"Goodbye Mr Butterworth."

SECRET HISTORIES

Billy Butterworth took leave of his fellow adventurers and headed across the high street in the direction of the Goat and Compasses Public House. Rosemary came out onto the pavement outside the haberdashery to greet her employers, their new found friends and especially Long Clem who she knew well as the occasional employee of her uncle and aunt.

"You have just missed the weirdest thing Ma'am" she said to Hester Ribbons who had picked up one of the letters blowing around in the street which incidentally was addressed to Sir Cecil Pitt MP House of Commons SW1AA 0AA and stamped second class.

"I shall have to pop this through his door on the journey home" said Hester "now, what has been happening, apart from this liberation of the letters?"

"Well ma'am" said Rosemary "a huge balloon flew over the town and it was using a car like a wrecking ball."

"We want to take all these lovely new people to you father's store for a sarsaparilla Rosemary can you organize them" interrupted Hermione. Then out onto the pavement stepped Rear Admiral Phillip 'Pip' Ribbons the baby brother of Hester, Hermione and Henrietta and father of Lawrence. Rear Admiral Ribbons was the chairman of 'Ribbons' a local family business institution that traced back beyond Victorian times in 1802 during the reign of George III and the English resistance of Napoleon. A resistance clearly innate in the intrepid triplet's genealogy.

"Before you all go for your sarsaparilla" he said in his slow commanding voice slightly slurred by the effect of years of loneliness and Plymouth Gin "does anyone need to pump ship?"

Everyone from Long Clem to the smallest of Tertius Napoleon Sawadogo's infants looked at the Rear Admiral in bewilderment for different reasons.

"This means do any of you vaunt zee toilet" said Gustav "zere is a toilet shrew at zee back off zee shop."

"Thank you Gustav" said Hester "well; does anyone need to pump ship?"

After everyone had taken a turn in the queue and another in the toilet at the back of the haberdashery. Everyone sitting upon or aiming at the elaborately embossed and decorated, late Victorian toilet took a few moments in contemplation of the extraordinary beauty of what functions purely as basic waste disposal. After an extended period of ablutions Rosemary led them through the afternoon's carnage in the high street to her father's ironmongery and the Temperance Bar deep within. Every spare seat in the shop was commandeered to accommodate the passengers and their accompanying sponsors on bar stools, deck chairs, one swinging veranda seat, assorted shooting sticks a ships hammock and supplemented by assorted seats commandeered from the haberdashery including an antique child's Kermode that had been in the nursery of the Ribbons siblings post Edwardian childhood. Refreshment was dished up in the form of drinks of sarsaparilla, dandelion and burdock, black beer and raisins, ginger beer all produced from the secret recipes of Zechariah Fitzgerald. Rosemary helped her father behind his dark mahogany counter where she had worked as a schoolgirl before embarking on life in the haberdashers. Her father busied himself, between snatches of conversation with the young woman who had spoken to him earlier, juggling ingredients that included cinnamon and clove, Wintergreen and cherry tree bark, liquorice and sarsaparilla roots, anise, nutmeg and molasses.

"What does your father do?" Thomas asked the young woman.

"He is a member of Parliament for the constituency" she replied "what is that" she added as Thomas poured molasses into a copper measure.

"Blackstrap molasses" he replied "it's very good for you full of minerals and vitamins."

"It looks pretty potent to me" she said.

"Drinks all round" Thomas Walpole called out as Rosemary lifted the hinged end of the mahogany counter to let him through with the first tray of Temperance beverages.

Rosemary spoke to the young woman when Thomas had gone out from behind the counter to serve drinks including black beer to

Tertius, Gustav and Long Clem who were sitting on a garden bench together.

"Do you know my father?" she asked.

"Your father?" the young woman replied.

"Yes" said Rosemary "my father, I saw you speaking with him just as the car came swinging down the street."

"Oh right, well no, no I don't know him, well I clearly know of him as the proprietor of this shop and I have been in before with my Mother, Lady Pitt."

"Lady Pitt" questioned Rosemary.

"Two more dandelion and burdocks please Rosemary" interrupted Thomas.

"Well" said the young woman "I suppose I had better get going on my way it was nice to meet you and to meet your daughter."

"Do you" said Thomas trying to sound matter of fact "want a drink?"

"That is very kind but I must get going."

"Very good" replied Thomas "has everyone got a drink?"

Gustav Eberhardt, Clement Christmas Longfellow Cobb and Tertius Napoleon Sawadogo sat, in that order, each enjoying his black beer, on the garden bench priced at forty five pounds and forty five pence. It had a blank brass plaque, with an embossed rope decorated border, screwed into the middle of the top rail at the back of the seat.

"If I bought you this seat little man what would you have engraved upon the brass?" Tertius asked Long Clem "just out of interest?"

"William Quarrier, Bridge of Weir Renfrewshire."

"Is he family?" Tertius asked.

"Yes" replied Long Clem "he was the start of my family really you see he was a kind man who lived by his shoe business and he saved so many children because that is what he chose to do with his time and money."

"Unusual" observed Tertius "so how do you know Mr Quarrier?"

"I don't know him" said Long Clem "I know that he saved me and hundreds like me through the work that he started."

"Hundreds like you?" said Tertius.

"Dwarves?" asked Gustav "I don't know vot else to say vot uzzar vird to use, did he save Dwarves?"

"No not Dwarves they are mythical freaks" replied Long Clem "Dwarfs is what we are"

"I apologize" said Gustav.

"It's alright" said Long Clem "I know that you would call me a zwerg in your native tongue and that dwarf is dwerg in Dutch, nain in French nano and enano in Italian and Spanish, törpe in Hungarian and pitic in Romanian. It is wonderful to look at in Russian Cyrillic, Chinese characters and Arabic script but I don't know how to pronounce it."

"So did he save hundreds like you?" asked Tertius again.

"Yes but not dwarfs he saved orphaned or abandoned children, children from impoverished backgrounds" said Long Clem "I was abandoned that's how I got my name."

"I voss abandoned, I vould engrave ziss seat like you viz tribute 'Hester, Hermione and Henrietta, Heaven zent zem' you see I vos one of the original designer babies of Adolf Hitler and his Zeosophy and I vos created by designated Aryan parents who ver mated, I voz a freak based upon a miss, destined to rule zee vorld as zee pinnacle of genetic perfection."

"Who gave you your name?" Long Clem asked.

"I don't know" replied Gustav "it is vot I have alvays been Gustav Eberhardt it vos not my farzer's name for sure."

"Why didn't they give you an English name" said Tertius.

"Because I am a German" said Gustav "zee sisters made sure zat I vos" he hesitated "zat I am alvays vot I am naturally, a German."

Gustav looked compassionately at Clement Christmas Longfellow Cobb a heart-warming human bundle of skeletal dysphasia.

"Isn't it funny" he said "vee zit here togezzer. I vos designed and you ver created and still vee live in a vorld that favours design over creation, perfect genetically modified children over you and me and vee have bows been rescued by zee love off people who had no original part in our existence it iss a miracle no?"

"It is a miracle" replied Long Clem.

"Do you ever wonder" asked Tertius "who your parents were what they were like, where they are now, do you ever wish you could meet them?"

Gustav looked down and Long Clem looked up at Tertius Napoleon Sawadogo with querying expressions.

"Well you see" he continued "I have some experience of these things because although I do remember my parents I was orphaned when I was quite young and some of my sisters they were babies and they cannot remember and; I was later adopted."

"Didn't the tribe just kind of swallow you up?" asked Long Clem.

"We don't really have tribes as such we are a people, the Bobo" he said proudly "after my parents died my people found me work as a house boy for a French couple in the town where we lived Monsieur Hervé and Madame Madeleine Rousseau it meant that I could provide for all of my sisters."

"Do you not have any bruzzers, Uncles vot about zee uzzar men of your people?" Gustav asked

"Hervé Rousseau became the main man in my life he was an interesting man, a business man with connections to the French colonial administration and Madeleine was from the English aristocracy she had a very posh voice you would say, like the sisters and the Rear admiral. They met during the Spanish civil war he was a wounded communist fighter and she was a fascist nurse caring for injured prisoners of war although she wasn't really a fascist herself, she was an aristocrat. They fell in love. They fell in love with me is what she would say I think that I answered the prayers of their childless marriage, they adopted me and provided

176

for my sisters when they sent me to England to be 'schooled' it was Madeleine's wish for me to attend the institutions that had 'schooled' her brothers with whom I stayed in the holidays.

"How did your parents die?" Long Clem asked.

"They were crushed by an elephant" Long Clem and Gustav looked amazed "it was carrying wealthy French tourists on a sightseeing trip when it got spooked and stampeded over the parapet of a bridge and crashed down on an open lorry full of Bobo that included my parents, they were going on an excursion to baptism's in the local river" concluded Tertius before continuing where he had left off "I eventually returned home to Burkina Faso with a first in history from Merton College Oxford and now here I am today showing my sisters and all their children around the country that I really grew up in, a country that is dear to my heart and dear I am sure to the hearts of many who would love to be considered English in some way."

"Did you wear that skirt at Cambridge and all those monkey skulls and things?" asked Long Clem.

"I wore tribal dress on certain occasions, parents insisted that my education was an enriching not an alternative experience."

"I consider myself to be sumzing of the English because of vot Hester, Hermione and Henrietta have done for me" said Gustav.

"I have a secret that I feel I can share with you both to salve my conscience" continued Tertius. The long and the short of the Temperance Bar listened in confidence. "This reality television what a fraudulent exercise it is for me but it is a wonderful opportunity!"

"But" said Gustav "America iss supposed to be the land of opportunity."

"Not for a Bobo" replied Tertius Napoleon Sawadogo.

The three men fell into a silence between them, a silence that maybe marked the forging of a lasting friendship, a friendship of souls.

"I like this black beer" said Tertius finally. Thomas Walpole was about to offer them a refill of their glasses.

"It's made using raisins nowadays" he said "it used to contain quinine years ago"

"Ah" said Tertius "you remind me of the mighty molecule that masters malaria."

"I think it would have cured anything" continued Thomas Walpole "probably would have kept the pharmaceutical giants from ruling the world I mean what, will they do, when we are all genetically perfect?"

"Sell us drugs for the maintenance of perfection I expect and capitalize on our vanity" said Long Clem dryly.

Gustav Eberhardt, Clement Christmas Longfellow Cobb and Tertius Napoleon Sawadogo sat on the garden bench in the middle of the busy Temperance Bar proffering their glasses for more of the black beer, and laughing heartedly at the strange world in which we all live.

THE PASSAGE TO FRANCE

"Do you think we will see angels playing harps up here Uncle Frank" Winston asked a little tongue in cheek "or signposts to France or the North Pole or the Milky way?"

"I'm looking out for the wreck of Great Uncle Frank's bi-plane resting in a cumulonimbus." Frank replied loudly.

"Do you think we will see heaven if we can get above the clouds I bet Auntie Gloria would have liked to have been here with us, do you think Michael can see us, I like it when Auntie Gloria waves to the sky and says 'I love Michael'."

"I know it's funny isn't but if we can't see it on a clear day then we are not going to see it however high we go" shouted Frank "and anyway she's not one for heights either, her God would not want to frighten her."

"He would hold her hand though Uncle Frank she often says that he holds our hands even when we cannot feel it."

Thin wisps of grey floss began to drift past the balloon as it crossed the bounds and into the parish of a cloud. The cloud became a silent place, cold, wet and sort of beyond, with no port or starboard, no fore or aft, simultaneously fathomless and stratospheric Winston looked carefully at Uncle Frank's face gauging whether or not he should be frightened.

"We are in a cloud" shouted Frank sensing the mood of his nephew "there is nothing to fear in a cloud because a cloud is not hiding anything".

"But a cloud can hide the Sun." said Winston.

"Yes" replied his Uncle Frank "but that is just a perspective obscuring your view. On my word Winston we are not about to collide with the sun you must stop thinking too clever thoughts."

"Clouds surround mountains Uncle Frank."

"There are no mountains between England and France."

"The Prime Minister said there was a mountain to climb between the English and the French on the news the other day."

"That was over beef Winston" said Frank "I can assure you that there is nothing this cloud can hide, on my life not even a mountain of beef."

A terrifying screech rent the drenched air heralding the sudden arrival of a miscalculating gull in the parish. Its bulging eyes stared in terror at Frank O'Flannagan from either side of a gaping beak and rigid spear of a tongue. The gull threw its wings out behind its petrified body with two webbed feet splaying either side of the clearly visible anatomical, feathered rimmed orifice that abruptly discharged viscose fear. A volley of organic waste matter, the product of digested raw fish and cold fatty chips hit Frank somewhere inside his involuntarily gaping mouth, sprung by surprise at the rending screech of the terrified gull. As Frank retched and spat and spat and retched and then repeatedly spat, the gull vanished down into the cloud and then a second terrifying screech rent the air setting off the hideous yelping of a dog that mingled, musically off key, with the screaming of the gull. Frank O'Flannagan continued spitting the seagulls business that had hit him full in his cakehole. His violent retching shook the bandage down over his eyes as he groped around for a bottle of water. Frank grasped a bottle unscrewed the top threw his head back and gargled the libation. Iodine seared his tongue, taste buds and tonsils. It made a mucous mouthwash of disinfectant and gannet defecation and once Frank had spat everything out the taste that remained seemed somehow to cohere with the sounds swirling around inside the rest of his head and he vomited a soup of seagull faeces and iodine.

"It was a natural reaction" he shouted as he wiped his lips with the back of his hand "fear does that to you, you lose control of your bodily functions in a moment of intense fear, that gull was afraid like those cows in the field when I parped the hooter."

"So it didn't have time to aim then?" asked Winston half chuckling at his Uncle's increasing yet comical misfortune

"No; it was fear." said his Uncle.

"Only Terry says he is sure that the gulls target certain people and are extremely accurate because from the whole of the sky they can always pick him out at will in a crowd at the seaside and if they don't dump gull guano on his chips then they dive bombed them, the greedy Gannets".

"You need sights to aim with any accuracy" said Frank "you need to be able to look down the barrel of your browning, they can look down their beak when they're stealing your fish and chips but they don't have sights fitted to their bomb doors."

"Do you think the seaside gulls prefer their fish deep fried in batter then Uncle Frank?" Winston asked.

"Which would you rather have in your beak young Winston a juicy worm trawled up from autumn stubble, a butchered head of a cod overboard in an icy sea or a warm fillet of Haddock bursting succulent through the crisp batter?"

"The seaside's gulls are a superior species aren't they." said Winston conscious that his brain was busily expanding with the virgin use of gathered language now that he was twelve.

"And ruthless" shouted Frank "they are the Mafiosi of the local skies, parks and alleyways."

Winston was quiet for a while. Frank O'Flannagan occasionally swilled his iodine green mouth out, having found the water bottle, slowly dissipating the antiseptic taste.

"There's no need to be worried about being in this cloud" said Uncle Frank loudly "we will be out the other side of it shortly".

"That gull wasn't afraid of the cloud was it" said Winston "it just didn't expect to find us here".

"It couldn't hear us" continued Frank "what else could you possibly find in a cloud as quiet as us".

"Another gull or an aeroplane that flies faster than the speed of sound" replied Winston.

The colour drained from Frank O'Flannagan's mottled green face as he realized the odds of that compared with the possibility of the mountain of beef and Winston moved quickly to reassure his uncle.

"I think their radar would see us first Uncle Frank."

The iodine had soaked into the loose, swelling bandage around Frank O'Flannagan's head.

"You look like a fungus is growing on your head Uncle Frank." said Winston.

"It's a blessing that your Auntie Gloria can't see me then." he shouted.

Winston knew that it was a blessing to that his Auntie couldn't see either her husband's bound head or her nephew suspended over the English Channel in a hot air balloon bound for either France or Davy Jones locker.

Somewhere down below them a dog barked and whimpered rather pathetically in the bowels of the cloud.

"That is strange" shouted Frank O'Flannagan "we must be well out to sea and yet the sound of a dog stills carries to the balloon".

"It sounds like the balloon is carrying a dog." Winston replied.

Suddenly the balloon escaped the shroud of the wet cloud and clear sky and other clouds surrounded them. Winston peered over the side down into the sea.

"The balloon *is* carrying a dog uncle Frank" exclaimed Winston "look it's hanging on the end of the rope."

The dog that was trained to guide the blind man who had been left hanging by his knapsack strap from a tent peg driven into the precipice of the cliffs, swung gently to and fro below the balloon at the end of four hundred feet of the best jute rope in a harness held by a grappling hook tied with an Anchor Bend knot.

"We will have to haul him aboard" said Frank "and he looks more like potatoes than feathers to me."

"Potatoes?" said Winston.

"Weight" replied Frank O'Flannagan "ballast to be precise, that dog is ballast and we don't need ballast Winston, not more ballast at this stage."

Frank pulled the machete out of its sheath.

"What are you going to do Uncle Frank?" asked Winston.

"We can't afford to carry ballast Winston and the dog is ballast, goodness knows how it got down there."

"You can't cut the rope Uncle Frank you just can't."

"But it will set it free and dogs can swim Winston."

"Not with all that rope and a great big hook" Winston remonstrated.

Frank mumbled something under his breath, loudly, his mind scrambling all the options and all the odds.

THE LONG HAUL

Frank made a 'hoik' sound, spat into his iodine green hands and rubbed them together.

"Viscosity" he shouted looking to Winston "more grip on the jute with a bit of spittle if you insist on saving the ballasted dog".

Frank O'Flannagan began to pull the rope in over the rim of the basket. He pulled with both hands together stepping backwards until his back was against the cage containing the torpedo shaped steel bottles of gas. He then stepped back to the edge of the basket gripping the jute rope hand over hand not letting an inch of gain slip. Winston watched him helplessly as he progressed back and forth retrieving about three feet of rope at a time. Occasionally the guide dog barked when the rope went slack, occasionally it whimpered as the harness compressed its rib cage on the taught pull. Winston counted every completed enormous effort of his uncle as he pulled the dog up towards the basket. After sixty seven pulls his Uncle Frank stopped against the gas bottle cage and pulled on the chain that released a blast of hot air up into the envelope. The dog barked, yelped and whimpered.

"I reckon we're about half way" Frank shouted.

"What the dog coming up or us crossing the sea?" asked Winston.

"Both" replied Frank "he's half way up and we're half way across best not to celebrate yet though."

Gloria O'Flannagan always looked for an excuse at every opportunity, to celebrate in life. Half way to anywhere was always cause to get the toffee bonbons or share a swig of fizzy drink. Finishing the alphabet song, arriving at a picnic spot or cleaning the O'Flannagan Pantechnivan Mk1 all these occasions presented Auntie Gloria with a good excuse to celebrate. There had been so much sadness, celebration was everything. The dog continued to bark occasionally and from the increasing volume Winston could tell that it was coming up nearer the basket and as it did the faint sound of a drum beat began to accompany it.

"What is that?" said Winston.

"It sounds like a bodrun I think it's hitting the dog which is not the right way round. It should be played with a bone" shouted Frank O'Flannagan "but a dog can't hold a bone and bark at the same time."

"A bodrun?" questioned Winston.

"A percussion instrument used in Celtic music it's like a tambourine without those jingly bits in the body. Your Auntie Gloria loves to hear the fiddle, the pipes, and the bodrun; she says that it stirs her heart. She would sing forever to the sounds of her own soul she would" Frank shouted wistfully before pulling the best jute rope again. The intermittent drum sound got louder and so did the dog's barking as it neared the zenith of its rescue.

The balloon basket had passed over the precipice of the cathedral congeneric chalk cliffs climbing up out from the Cenomanian foundation of Shakespeare beach. The grappling hook had stolen the guide dog away from the blind man and ripped the channel swimming race banner from between the tall poles. The balloon had drifted down towards the sea where an ocean going yacht had set sail behind the racing swimmers. The balloon basket had struck the mast of the yacht breaking it off and snaring the communication cable of the global positioning satellite receiver drum. The crew comprising a variety of tongues expressed their annoyance volubly. As the balloon ascended after the last minute, last ditch blast of hot air had been released by Frank O'Flannagan it pulled the cable disconnecting it from an expensive and sexy 'state of the art' technological satellite sextant system in the cabin and dragging it out through its protective conduit to its full length. The ruptured connector jammed in the angle of the willow wickerwork weave of the basket that had snared the cable. Momentarily the balloon stopped dead. The bracket holding the satellite drum to the broken mast, that had itself been felled and pulled overboard into the sea explosively puncturing the inflatable lifeboat hanging aft, in its tumbling trajectory, gave way releasing the drum (which did look like a percussion instrument used to accompany the playing of Celtic music). Until the bracket gave out, the cable was stretching with increasing torsion and cutting the wind with a note rising through myriad octaves to a crescendo beyond the reach of all but a dogs hearing. The cable snapped with the twang that Frank O'Flannagan heard less than a millisecond before the communication cable of the global positioning satellite receiver drum ripped through the hijacked banner, Frank O'Flannagan's right ear and scalp. The drum had then dangled somewhere between the basket and the grappled guide dog, spiralling around the best jute rope. The guide dog had got caught up with the 'bodrun' as it was being hauled on its staggered ascent to the safety of the basket the dog's limp tail beating a rhythm into the satellite receiver's skin.

Every time Frank rested between each appearance of another three feet of the jute, the dog dangled, slowly rotating clockwise. As the guide dog reached the underside of the basket its head and shoulders disappeared out of sight and the animal became wedged.

"Must be magnetic." shouted Frank "like the needle of a compass his head has swung north to south just at the moment I needed him to swing east to west."

Frank slackened the rope and waited for the guide dog to swing out from under the basket as soon as it did he pulled on the rope the willow wickerwork creaked as the dog scuffed at it trying to get a paw hold and scrabble aboard. A flailing back leg thrust through the woven hole in Winston's compartment and out again like a piston rod. Frank reached out and grabbed the dog by the scruff of its neck but he lost his grip of the dogs fur because it had been greased by further expulsions of viscose fear from the seagull's overworked bomb doors as it had encountered the dog in the depths of the cloud on its way down the hasty retreat from its bum bombing of Frank O'Flannagan in the balloon basket moments before. The dog tipped away from Frank who instinctively made a second grab and hauled the dog aboard by its tail dumping it into a birds' nest of randomly coiled best jute rope on the floor of the basket. The harness handle of the guide dog hit Frank, square in the forehead, followed by the eye of the grappling hook with the shaft rapping him across his knees. He dropped on top of the dog which barked and snapped at him defensively, grazing the exposed ear that wasn't bound to the side of his head by the fungus bandage. This unfortunate exchange was quickly followed by the global positioning satellite drum tumbling into the basket and hitting Frank on the back of his head with a deep resonate timbre reminiscent of the bodrun. A little blood began to ooze from the wound inflicted by the guide dog and after the simultaneous bark and bite of the dog Frank could not hear anything as he lay in the bottom of his station holding his throbbing knees as waves of pain from his forehead, back head and now both of his injured ears converged in the middle of his brain causing a tidal swirl that was sucking his pain down into a bodily vortex that expelled as reverberating flatulence. Winston suppressed a giggle. 'Was that fear?' he thought to himself. The dog wriggled out from under Frank and stood on the crown of his fungus bandaged head as it flopped its front paws over the willow wickerwork partition between Frank and Winston. The dog licked at Winston's face as he greeted it.

"Uncle Frank it's got a name" he yelled as he tried to read an engraved brass disc attached to its leather collar "he's called Betty, she's called Betty" the dogs back paws where screwing Frank's hair into his bandage.

"Get it off me Winston" Frank called feebly from the depths of the basket as he began to revive. The dog responded by springing off Frank O'Flannagan's sore head and hauling itself over the divide and tumbling down into Winston's corner of the basket. The dog was smeared in seagull excrement and its fur showed signs of beginning to dry out from a decent dipping in salt seawater.

"A passenger for us to carry Uncle Frank." said Winston "we've got a passenger."

Frank O'Flannagan was trying to get his bearings despite the excruciating scream of the pain inside his head. He clawed at the willow wickerwork weave that surrounded him and breathed the vapour of the salt sea juiced best jute rope through iodine lined nostrils. Once he was sitting upright propped against the steel cage containing the gas bottles he adjusted the green fungus of a bandage that bound his lacerated lughole to his splitting head. He felt his bitten ear, and inspected his fingers to gauge the blood loss. Satisfied that it could only be a scratch he began to get to his knees and as he did the pressure of his own weight aggravated the blow to his knee caps from the grappling hook and he was involuntarily sprung forward by the renewed pain. Frank reached up to grab the loops of rope that were for passengers and pilot to brace for a crash landing. He grasped the ropes but in mid ascent met the crudely fastened altimeter with the full force of his shoulder buckling the instrument back on itself puncturing the glass casing and mangling the calibration mechanism. He collapsed back down into the basket and lay still for a while. Pain can make a man selfish and Frank was no exception, wishing to see the gates of heaven and hear the Hallelujah. All he could see through a thin film of green tears was woven willow. All he could hear was the inside of his head. He eventually emerged to confront Winston and his new found friend Betty the guide dog staring back at him in awe.

"Uncle Frank" said Winston "you look like you've been through a combine harvester" it was Winston's favourite expression used by his Auntie Gloria whenever he had had a rough and tumble session with his Uncle Frank usually at the end of a picnic. Auntie Gloria would smooth his hair down vigorously dust the grass off his jumper and pretend to scold the pair of them.

Frank smiled a grimace, he was glad that his Gloria could not see him.

"Thank you Uncle Frank" continued Winston "this is the best birthday I have ever had".

"I hope that we will see land soon then we can make your birthday complete."

But Frank knew what he really meant was 'and then we will survive because if we drown your Auntie Gloria will kill the pair of us' but he did not say what he was thinking. Winston looked at his Uncle who was concentrating on somewhere on the horizon beyond his nephew. Winston watched his eyes to see his thoughts swimming across the black moons with their halos of deep green hanging in the bloodshot, curtained skies where the whites of eyes should have been.

"What are you thinking about Uncle Frank?" he asked.

"I don't know about the dog Winston" Frank shouted even louder than before making the dog bark defensively "the extra weight could mean the difference between getting to dry land and having to ditch in the sea."

"Extra weight" said Winston "what extra weight?"

"That dog there" replied Frank pointing at Betty.

"She still weighs the same" continued Winston.

"The same as when" shouted Frank O'Flannagan.

"The same as when she was dangling at the other end of the rope and we didn't know that she was there and it didn't matter then."

"Ah" shouted Frank "I am a little distracted at present what with my head and all I need to think" seeing the pained expression of his nephew who was befriending Betty with some of his birthday tuck that his mother had packed up for him.

"Uncle Frank" he said "why would Betty be wearing this harness with a handle that looks like those things on Ezra's legs."

"You mean Ezra's callipers" replied Frank.

"Yes" said Winston.

"Well now a harness like that one on a dog like Betty usually means that she is a blind dog"

"A blind dog?" said Winston.

"Well the dog's not blind Winston it's a guide dog for the blind."

"*The* blind, all of them?" exclaimed Winston.

Frank O'Flannagan had not really thought about this, his thoughts had been, in the main occupied by the shrill whistling sound of pain and the prospect of drowning. As he focused on Betty's presence in the balloon basket the possibilities began playing with his mind.

"How do you think Betty got hung up on the anchor hook?"

Frank thought; 'Perhaps the dog had been left in the car with which the grappling hook had originally become entangled. But surely the blind person who needed the dog would not need the car and if the driver of the car was the guide of the blind person then why bring the dog along for the ride and then leave her in a car. Maybe they were all still in the car when the grappling hook struck. Were they still in the car, then why didn't he hear them shouting at him as he swung them against anything that got in the way? They couldn't be in the car or was their shouting drowned out by the people in the street.' Frank had two aching knees as testament to a consequence of the fortuity of being struck by a grappling hook it made him think some more 'What had the grappling hook done to the blind person and their guide before dumping them on the main line from London to Paris or Paris to London, of course, depending on where you live. The cat would be in the direct path of the Eurostar. Oh God? But then if the dog had been left alone in the car which of course is possible then at least he had rescued it from being cooked alive airless, behind window glass and Rexene. These dog owners they should be more responsible. Or maybe he had just 'caught' the dog that had got lost at sea so actually he had saved it from drowning which might help his reputation back home if and when they got back home. To have been the rescuer of a drowning dog that had been neglected by its blind owner to the extent that it had wandered off unable to guide itself when bereft of its dependent charge who was after all the only purpose of the dog's existence. Didn't these blind people realize that they were responsible for the emotional stability of their guide dogs? Frank thought of all the silver milk bottle tops Michael had saved for the Blind Charity.' Was this 'his' dog inasmuch as he had paid for it with the foil from a thousand breakfasts and a million cups of tea. His case was getting stronger. He would be publicly redeemed whatever the outcome of the next couple of hours.

FRANK O'FLANNAGAN IS FADING

Frank leant back against the willow wickerwork partition of the basket and looked askew at France. A bank of dark clouds hung out to sea marking the foreboding border of the French sky. He turned and looked over his shoulder into the swell below, they were flying more slowly. Rain, if it was rain, in the clouds ahead would cool the air and the balloon would drop. He had to decide, did they have enough gas to take them up above any storm, and he questioned himself thinking would it be colder higher up and the air thinner? They could fall into unconsciousness and then freeze to death. Frank busied himself. He opened the Oxo Beef Stock Cubes tin containing the first aid kit as a bit of a distraction from the weighty problems facing him.

"Do you want me to help you with your bandage?" Winston asked.

"No its okay I am just adding an adjusting safety pin" his Uncle replied.

Frank took out his handkerchief and began buffing up the inside of the tin lid so that he could see himself reflected. He recognized himself only because he was expecting to and because he knew that it could not be anyone else staring back at him from the misty sheen of the Oxo tin lid but he did not recognize himself as the person he expected to see. The silhouette of his head was out of kilter, with one ear buried tight under the bandage and the other a swollen protrusion. The bandage, though functioning as a bandage, did look like a large fungus. His skin was a mottled mess of shaving shadow, dried blood, and caked iodine. He was a sorry sight to his own eyes thinking that a combine harvester might actually have shown more kindness than the combined assault of the satellite communications wire, the grappling hook, the bodrun and Betty the guide dog for the blind. Perhaps it was his shattered nerves, his shocking reflection, or just the dog Betty jumping up at Winston in play but Frank O'Flannagan did not really need to thread the adjusting safety pin through the furrows of forehead skin as he tried to re-tighten the bandage. But he did. The caked iodine absorbed Frank's fresh warm blood as it meandered down his face and dripped off his stubbly chin from the pinned pricked furrow of his tortured brow

"You're bleeding again Uncle Frank" said Winston.

"I am?" shouted his Uncle "try keeping Betty calm Winston we need to steady the basket"

Winston encouraged Betty to look through the woven embarkation step her back leg had shot through as she had scrabbled for a foot hold on her way up. He looked out over the rim of the basket. Frank O'Flannagan had maintained the balloon's height over the channel managing the gas sparingly. In his estimation the first steel torpedo had discharged its combustible contents about a third of the way across the channel. Undoubtedly he had used more gas than was necessary for the distance in the early stages of the balloon's passage as he tried to remedy the consequences of the trespassing wind, the hijacking of the French car and the disappointment of sailing over the white cliffs. The needle of the gauge on the first gas bottle lay dead on the brass pin at the end of the red warning crescent on the calibrated dial that arched from full to empty. Now the needle on the gauge of the other gas bottle had swung inexorably through its calibrated arc into the red zone.

"Look Uncle Frank" shouted Winston pointing ahead "land".

Frank looked at the thin darkening line evolving between the sea and the sky. He disappeared down into the basket to retrieve an antique instrument of navigation.

"What is that?" asked his inquisitive nephew. Betty the guide dog barked.

"This?" shouted Frank O'Flannagan "this is my sextant Winston it was once the possession of Captain Pilkington-Frobisher and it was handed down through the family from Great Uncle Gunner Frank O'Flannagan. I can use it to calculate how far we are from the French coast".

"How does it work?" asked Winston.

"With mirrors and an arc of sixty degrees" replied Frank appearing to take some complicated measurements and then returning it to it's beautifully pock marked ostrich leather case.

"What does it say?" continued Winston.

Frank glanced at the gauge on the remaining gas bottle.

"We are running perilously low on fuel. Winston we need to throw some ballast overboard we have to act."

Winston had an idea what ballast was because his father had a heap of it in the garden at home. He had it delivered one day from the local builder's yard for a job he was planning to do that involved mixing up some cement with the ballast to make concrete. The job was to reposition the poles securing Mrs. Walpole's washing line away from trees that he had planted carefully yet perhaps, in his wife's opinion a little, 'thoughtlessly' a few years before not thinking about their proximity to the flapping laundry. He was to lay a solid raised path between the poles so that in the winter and on wet days she would not get muddy feet from hanging out the washing. The job had never got further than the barrowing of the ballast from the heap, the builders yard lorry driver had tipped up in the street outside the house at 13 Captain Scott Terrace, to the heap that now obstructed the path from the back door to the old and only washing line. Mr Walpole maintained on reflection that there was no need to move his wife's washing line or lay a nice concrete path because it was to his mind 'Illogical to hang washing out in the winter because it just stays wet and stiffens in the frost, damaging the natural fibres, and on wet days, well it is obvious why you don't hang washing out on wet days is it not?' Mrs. Walpole might have agreed with this but for the fact that after five years had passed the heap had gradually been spread across her path to the washing line by wet and winter days and now on the fine days and the spring, summer and autumn days that she did hang out her washing she carted, caked to her 'housework shoes', the abrasive and heavily pigmented orange sand of the ballast and that was now ruining her linoleum as well as the 'mole worked' mounds that appeared occasionally to trip her up sending her sprawling with a full basket of freshly aired linen. The five years had eroded the shine from Winston's mother's floor covering and her temper and left an orange tincture that fades slowly from the back door into the middle of the kitchen and a red mist before her that deepens on wash days. His father had lately trimmed the trees back anyway. Winston thought about his mother, about where she would be and what she would be doing while he was floating towards France with his Uncle Frank in his fabulous birthday treat.

GLORIA, GRAN AND VERONICA WALPOLE

Veronica Walpole caught the 42A bus at 13:14 from the sheltered stop at the end of the street. The 42A bus route included a drop at the main entrance gates of St Audry's hospital. St Audry's was designed by the Victorian architect Henry Currey based on the pavilion principle. It was an architectural development that meant greater segregation of patients and better ventilation so increasing the chances of survival for the suffering Victorians. In its 'middle years' the design had served purposefully first, as an 'idiot asylum' and then as a 'colony for sane epileptics' who lived and worked there undergoing medical experiments involving valerian, daffodils and yew trees. Gradually as society became more enlightened and epileptics humanized the hospital went through a variety of titled applications all loosely associated with mental suffering. Currently it was caring for people on the journey into dementia or Alzheimer's disease and segregated from these, people suffering mild personality disorders or breakdowns. Veronica Walpole was visiting her mother, Winston's Gran and her sister-in-law Gloria O'Flannagan. She visited them regularly. Gran had been a resident of the old people's wing for almost a year coming into the care of the specialists when it became clear that her difficulties with her memory and her temper and her body clock was breaking the heart of her extended family, when love was not enough on its own to meet her unique needs. Gloria had been convalescing in one of the psychiatric wings for almost three months. Her doctors diagnosis had been 'emotional exhaustion culminating in a breakdown of her capacity to cope' he prescribed a quiet confinement in an appropriate environment. Gloria was recovering slowly regaining her foothold in life, not because of the pain numbing, chemically balancing medication or the group therapy sessions or the psychological archaeology of personal questions intent on digging up and dusting down some extreme cruelty. Gloria was recovering because she had her Frank and his sister Veronica; she had Thomas her brother-in-law and her wonderful nephews and niece. Gloria O'Flannagan had the indelible watermark of Michael her dear departed son in the backdrop to everything and she had her own counsel, her soul had a root, sprung in a time of drought that had found God at the very point of pointlessness. Gloria knew her heart was safe with Him even when she could not take herself beyond her own emotions and into the lives of the ones she so dearly loved.

In this age in which we live, where the oceans of information serve up cataclysmic tsunami upon revelation upon news upon what do you want to know, you must know someone who has had a breakdown? Maybe you know it's you or someone you love. Like a pebble dropped in a still pool the moment a soul cannot cope for another moment, the moment the rhythm of life is utterly lost, the familiar landscape is changed forever, despair begins to ripple through the fabric of family and friendship. The impossible becomes the simple truth and an irrefutable 'condition' the sole preserve of the sufferer while the suffering, try to persevere by inventing communities of shared frustration. By not giving us our soul by acknowledgment so much of our ills are misdiagnosed and our healing wrongly prescribed. I know because I broke down. I know because I spent long periods ingesting mind numbing pharmaceuticals, short violent periods punishing the body that contained my troubled soul and I did not find the end until like Gloria I found that the choice was mine, and why. Every day I have to step over inviting chasms as life serves up its emotional challenges but I am completely alive. I appreciate what Gloria found and has begun, painstakingly, to claim as her own.

As Veronica Walpole walked towards these two women whom she regarded with familial love, they sat peacefully in the disquiet of the institution shaded by their own thoughts. In this place the day smeared light on pallid paintwork and faded furnishings, the night was always suffused with incubus. An unremitting and incessant television kept open a window on the world in one corner of Henry Currey's Victorian pavilion where the three women sat together.

Gran O'Flannagan looked at her daughter as she would look at anyone. She was not reminded by familiar features that this was life that began as a scion of her own from within her own human frailty. The old lady's bewildered countenance drew compassion from her daughter.

"Hello mother do you know who I am today?" she asked in a sanguine manner.

"No" Gran replied pointing at a hospital orderly "but if you ask the nurse he will tell you although you should not need to ask such questions."

Winston's mother and his Auntie laughed with each other careful not to stir Gran's ire, concealing their mirth by embracing each other in warm greeting. A greeting sincerely meant nevertheless. They exchanged a whisper that the old lady 'was her usual self today.'

"What part of this emerald isle have you travelled from today my dear?" Gran asked her daughter.

"We are in England mother" she replied "we came over a long time ago to work for Uncle Zechariah?"

"Quinine" mumbled the old lady "bitter white medicine from the Jesuit's bark."

"That's right mother in the Temperance bar"

Veronica and Gloria looked at the old lady in kindness, she often plucked at a strand of memory this was her working to Zechariah Fitzgerald's secret recipes which he called black beer, the black beer before the raisins and health and safety.

"Did Winston like his vest and pants?" Gloria asked Veronica.

"I am not sure but I made him wear them all the same, they'll probably irritate him but they are the last thing she made with purpose all those months ago and I smeared him with calamine although he did his parts, you know what boys are like when they reach his age."

"Almost" replied Gloria.

Veronica Walpole thought for a moment. When his Gran had knitted the unusual underwear for her dear grandson she had been lucid between bouts of forgetfulness that steadily became bitter confusion. She had spoken of coming home and seeing Winston put them on, she had been proud of the bold number twelve stitched across the chest of the vest. Veronica spoke softly to Gloria.

"Mother loves all of them especially Michael. He would have shared with her in this enchantment you know, I mean that's what it is."

"I believe he would" said Gloria "he had a comprehension beyond our world."

"Whatever they call it and whatever it might be to me it's an enchantment and then she has her dignity" said Veronica.

Both ladies sat in a quiet reverie that was suddenly broken into by a television news report. Ranjit Livingstone was standing between two polished steel rail tracks in front of the entrance to a large tunnel. Behind him was the mangled wreckage of a car strewn across a railway line and a dragon's tail of vanishing tunnel lights. There was a wide police cordon around the crash site marked off with blue and white striped tape that fluttered and cracked in the breeze. Groups of police and soldiers were standing inside the cordon. Police were standing in small groups talking. Soldiers were standing in small groups smoking cigarettes. Many of them were armed.

"Today" began Ranjit "has seen an extraordinary and unprecedented protest, it is widely believed to be, against Anglo-French relations in this region on a day when the cross channel race to celebrate the 'entente cordial' was taking place. This car that you can see behind me has been mysteriously dumped across the rail track that links our two countries through the channel tunnel effectively closing that wonderful link. Eurostar has been suspended whilst the crash site is under meticulous investigation. The car has a number of protest stickers exhorting people to 'Buy British' pasted in the windows and a bumper sticker warning fellow motorists to avoid frogs. The car is one of those French cars that at one time was considered to be fashionable amongst people who enjoy public association with various politically contentious causes and Morris dancers. With me I have Jethro Harbinger the 'look out' for the gang of line engineers who were working on the rail track at the time. Mr Harbinger was you able to warn your colleagues of the danger?"

"Hello" said Mr Harbinger looking deeply into the camera lens.

"Mr Harbinger?" Ranjit repeated.

"Not in the normal manner no I wasn't because normally I am looking up and down the track not up and down so to speak" moving his head in a slow nodding motion, "I suppose you could say that I look along rather than up and down normally so anyway I would have needed to be looking up and down to have seen the car what were dropped like a bomb because it was certainly dropped like a bomb so to speak. I thought that the war had started, can I say a quick hello to my wife".

"Right" said Ranjit

Jethro waved at the camera and said "Hello Maud."

"Maud?" said Ranjit and then continued quickly on "Did you warn your colleagues?"

"We all just ran" said Jethro Harbinger "it was hanging off this weird balloon thing and hitting the overhead cables and sparks were flying everywhere and then it smashed into the tunnel and landed on the track we reckon its' them protestors. Is this being recorded only she doesn't have a telly at the mortuary if it's live?"

"Has a body been taken to the mortuary from here?" asked Ranjit aware that he could be breaking a further news story ahead of his rival networks.

"Not that I know of" said Jethro Harbinger "That's news to me, my Maud works at the mortuary you see, lying them out and getting them ready, so when I call her I'll ask her if she's had an extra one in to make sure if you want me to."

"Ah right well thank you" said Ranjit.

Jethro Harbinger continued speaking "They're always anti something those people they've got too much time and too much money if you ask me".

"Thank you" Ranjit repeated "now I am going over here to speak to...."

"They come over here" Jethro could be heard mumbling "taking our jobs and......I've paid my tax all my working life you know."

There was a muffled sound as the camera panned round the scene and back onto Ranjit a faint tension mirrored for a fleeting moment in his face and then he resumed his report after Jethro Harbinger managed to shout "I haven't finished yet, you're not from round here either are you?"

"I have with me now at the scene Sir Cecil Pitt MP and his wife Lady Pitt who have come straight from a garden party with constituents" said Ranjit resuming his broadcast.

"To raise money for Africa" interrupted Lady Pitt "Cess has done wonderful work for charity I am so proud of him."

"Yes" said Ranjit "Sir Cecil what do you think has provoked this attack on our vital transport link with France?"

"Well as you especially will be aware Rancid the world is becoming increasingly sullied by the frictions of colliding cultures and some unfortunate types are beginning to express their frustration at not being able to adequately persuade their own Johnny Foreigners of the supreme merits of their way of seeing things."

"It's Ranjit actually Sir Cecil Ranjit Livingstone."

"Eh? Yes well anyway liberators have become demons and the battlefield a man's soul" continued Sir Cecil "Livingstone did you say?"

"Nobody has claimed responsibility yet according to a Scotland Yard spokesperson" Ranjit added.

"That's part of the problem today." said Sir Cecil.

"I totally agree responsibility is not being taught to our young people and as parents we are powerless to enforce the disciplines of life" Ranjit began to pontificate until he heard his producer hissing through the umbilical earpiece that tethered him to the news studio's ultimate broadcast control.

"Your job is to ask questions not answer them!"

Ranjit's imbroglio prompted him to tap the earpiece deceptively as he listened simultaneously to Sir Cecil Pitt pronouncing and his producer protesting political protocol.

"Not responsibility Ratchet" continued Pitt "terminology my good man, it is spokesman if it's a man and spokeswoman if it's a woman, who have men and women become offensive to for heaven's sake that they need to become androgynous in order not to upset gender sensibilities" Sir Cecil stared through the camera lens and out into hundreds of homes, high streets and St Audrey's the former colony for sane epileptics "the world is going mad" he finished.

"He riddles me with guilt. He's not wrong enough to make me want to disagree with him but he makes me feel like I am standing somewhere behind him as he gazes at us." Gloria said quietly to her sister-in-law as they continued to watch the spectacle on the hospital television.

"It makes you glad Hitler never had television at his disposal doesn't it?" Veronica replied.

"Or Cromwell" added Gloria.

"My family have fought democrats and fascists alike down through our proud history" Lady Pitt began to rail on behalf of her husband "my family takes its name from the place of Richard the third's birth, Mary Queen of Scots execution and for good measure an Anglo-Saxon forebear who planted the ancient apple orchards of our beautiful land"

"Yes" said Ranjit interrupting Lady Pitt as his producer screamed 'get that silly bat off' through the earpiece "finally Sir Cecil do you suspect that this dangerous dumping of the French car has any link with the race today?"

"That channel thingy?" retorted Sir Cecil "Hard to say...difficult to know what fills their macabre minds."

"My younger brother is swimming for his country in that racy thing" Lady Pitt exclaimed.

"She's back" screamed the producer making Ranjit visibly flinch.

"What is his name?" asked Ranjit

"Lieutenant Winston Fotheringay-Hepplethwaite of the Queens Royal Hussars" she replied.

"I see" said Ranjit who then egged on by his producer thanked the local member of parliament and his dutiful wife for their time before continuing "The police are asking for any witnesses to come forward. There are unconfirmed reports that the car was in fact hi-jacked from a nearby busy market town following an aerial swoop through the high street by a hot air balloon which seems to have been confirmed by Mr Harbinger. Latest reports say that some people are being treated at the town's cottage hospital for shock and a pillar box was knocked off its foundation causing many letters blown to be away and a parcel to be looted although this is not confirmed. The Royal Mail's postmaster has asked people to kindly post any letters they might find but obviously not in the damaged pillar box. Police have been unable to approach the wreckage of the car until the forensic branch get to the scene. There is a suspect object wrapped around the foot pedals incorporating three polished spheres that could be some kind of incendiary device or worse a bomb which can be primed for remote control from something like a mobile-phone signal like in James Bond so police and soldiers are combing the area for anyone acting in a suspicious manner." Ranjit's producer chipped in for Ranjit's benefit only "they won't have far to look will they!"

"Ranjit Livingstone the News in your Region sponsored by Willie Wyrtha's Wonderful Workers the best Personnel Agency in the World for all your staffing needs" said Ranjit signing off.

Jethro Harbinger stumbled into shot behind Ranjit with a member of the outside broadcast crew in a head lock and a policeman hanging onto his donkey jacket. The outside broadcast sound engineer Colin 'Herb Sage' was wielding the sound boom trying to prize Jethro and his colleague apart with the large grey fur covered microphone just as Ranjit was signing off.

"Colin that's Rosemary's Colin" shouted Winston's grandmother at the television in a moment of clarity.

"That's right mother" said Veronica "Colin and Rosemary, she has some good news to, you are going to be a great grandmother."

"Oh that's wonderful" said Gloria "that is really wonderful."

"Oi why is Colin hitting that man with a rat on a stick?" the old lady shouted "rat on a stick rat on a stick he's got a rat on a stick."

A nurse hurried over to where the three women were sitting he tried to placate Winston's grandmother.

"Now Mrs. O'Flannagan its okay, just calm down you're alright it's not a rat it's a microphone."

"Eh" she said as if she was just awakening from a dark dream "is that you Frank?"

"It's alright mother" Veronica said "it's alright."

"She does get disorientated quite a bit and that just distresses her." Gloria was never far from the old lady while she herself was convalescing at St Audry's "Did I tell you who I saw in our group therapy a few days ago?

"No" said Veronica.

"Mr Birtwhistle."

"You've got me worried now a talking budgerigar in a group therapy session well if that doesn't colour the proceedings?" said Veronica "nothing can."

"Not my Mr Birtwhistle" Gloria laughed "Barrington Birtwhistle the bank manager."

"In here, was he wearing his bowler hat, I don't think I ever saw him without his bowler hat."

Barrington Birtwhistle or 'BB' to his tight knit circle of friends, who shared his passions for the lighter opera of Gilbert and Sullivan and fine wines, was a consummate chorus baritone and occasional soloist in oratorios usually performed in St Bartholomew's the local Church. Barrington Birtwhistle also collected foreign bank notes the practice of numismatists and had exquisitely catalogued his extensive collection putting to good use another of his passions calligraphy. He had never stepped out with a lady, certainly locally, and as a consequence was the butt of some base humour amongst the banal borrowers of other banks but to his own customers he was above reproach. How he ended up in St Audry's is a sad tale. The central office of his bank had decreed in the name of progress to change the nature of its personal relationship with its customers. The bank employed call centres, large gatherings of the young proselytized proletariat performing the personal relationship through the technology of the telephone conducting colloquially, conversations in the vernacular of youth culture. Addressing gracious grandmothers as 'love' and old soldiers as 'mate' they use a persuasive methodology memorized from the training manual to telephone at 'certain' vulnerable moments in the day to winkle financial commitment out of the confused. It is perfectly legal and politically correct because it helps the exchequer. This new strategy for reducing the bank's operating cost and for 'bringing it into the twenty first century' was further 'improved' a few years after the demise of the position held by Barrington Birtwhistle when the call centres migrated to the continent of Asia to harness the stronger ambition of young Asian people to tear down the barricades of global commerce and capitalize on the post-colonial burgeoning economies.

I am not prejudiced, I am however deaf enough to have to wear hearing aids and occasionally a little impatient perhaps. I admit that this has sometimes affected my interpretation of what some people say but the advent of these call centres being manned by young people from a continent which understandably has its own unique inflexions layered over compressed pronunciation often spiced with the solecisms of the cultural divide has troubled me deeply. I chose the local high street bank because even when I wasn't even slightly deaf and quite carefree I could still understand the drone of the tellers through the sound proofed plate glass screen and look them in the eye when I queried the' bandit country' bank charges. Now when I telephone my bank I have to keep saying 'pardon' and 'I am sorry I didn't quite catch that' only to be told to turn up the volume control on my handset or try to concentrate if I want to understand my personal relationship team assistant. This all complicated by the fact that if I don't remove my hearing aid before I begin the call I get a mild electronic screaming in my ear which increases my frustration not to say confusion over why I wear it. Anyway I cracked; as any sane human being would crack, I could take no more. I said very politely so as not personalize my response to my personal relationship team assistant 'I am not meant to understand you, I am the customer, you are meant to understand me it's my money you have there.' 'Exactly mate' came the response 'now this is what I suggest that I do with it?'

The nature of the personal relationship of the bank's employees evolved from one of responsibility for the best interests of the customer's financial management to one of a responsibility of managing to sell the customer the latest financial 'product' as often as the banks production line could manufacture a new one. This revolution had its martyrs and numbered amongst them is Barrington Birtwhistle. He did not accept the commercial principles of the bank, instead holding firm to his own he refused the lucrative inducements to step aside into comfortable retirement and continued to serve customers he regarded as his family. Old people that had been the upstanding adults of his childhood, his choir mistress, his scout master, teachers, police, librarians, shop keepers, men from the foundry and women from the brush factory, the man who drove the butchers van and the woman who delivered paraffin every Saturday tea time through the winter. Their children had become Barrington's young adult customers graduating from piggy banking to starting married lives, careers, businesses, raising their own children, changing jobs, buying houses, suffering the sadness of divorce and celebrating the achievements of their children as they began banking the wages of paper rounds, car washing and café waiting, birthday gifts and pocket money. The bank prized Barrington out slowly levering his sanity away from his compassion as a string of young trainees arrived addressing him variously as 'Baz', 'Baza', 'Barry' and even 'Bertie' and eventually 'Basra'. And then the faceless call centre began doing his business for him and informing him so in accents his customers had complained bitterly about, rolling the R's in Barrington. One morning he did not go into work at the bank. On that day he did not keep any of his routines that neighbours and shopkeepers had set their clocks to for a generation or two. Eight days into his absence when he was required to sign something 'official' on behalf of the town council for whom he had acted in a voluntary capacity, one of his transitory juniors noticed he wasn't there and called head office, someone from 'Human Resources' telephoned him but he did not answer. Someone from 'Regional' visited him and found, his once distinguished, empty shell rocking in his favourite armchair, unshaven, unkempt, uncommunicative and undernourished. Barrington Birtwhistle's doctor recommended some rest at St Audry's. It turned out to be an indeterminate 'rest'.

"It's very sad" said Gloria "he was such a lovely man and in group therapy you can still feel that all we believed in and appreciated is in there somewhere, deep down, but the stuff he comes out with..."

"You know they never found his cat" said Verinica "Oh its led to all sorts of rumours you can't believe what some people fill the gaps with, gaps between their ears Thomas calls it."

"Frank says that the first thing to go is your mind when you can't make the stabilizing sense you need of something that is a part of you, he always says it especially if we talk about Michael."

"Barrington Birtwhistle was always very good with Michael whenever we met him in the high street" said Veronica "in fact I remember that day when you had that premium bond win and we went together to deposit the cheque at the counter and because he had read about it in the bungling gazelle he invited through to his office."

"That wonderful desk" said Gloria.

"And that great big leather swivel chair."

"Yes, I remember Michael laughing when Barrington spun him round in it. He nearly slid off the shiny leather seat."

"We felt like real ladies didn't we"

"I know and all because of the premium bond."

"Good old Ernie" said Veronica.

ERNIE, first established in 1957, is the acronym for the Electronic Random Number Indicator Equipment that is employed by the NS & I (National Savings and Investments originally Lord Palmerston's Post Office Savings Bank started in 1861) to select the premium bond numbers for a regular prize draw. ERNIE itself is independently verified by GAD the Government Actuary's Department using the four separate methods of Frequency, Serial, Poker and Correlation to ensure the bias of set patterns does not occur to influence selection hence the 'Random' in ERNIE.

FAR, FAR AWAY

Our Lady of Loreto floated ghostly through thickening cloud cocooned in the wet stillness. There was no way of knowing how close they were to the sea its swell was not breaking its silence, just heaving.

"The first thing to go will have to be the empty gas bottle" said Frank O'Flannagan as he weighed up his options for survival "I will lose my deposit but it's for the best".

"But why don't we get rid of the ballast first?" asked Winston

"This is ballast, anything with a decent weight that helps to stabilise the balloon is regarded as ballast. You and me and Betty we all qualify as ballast"

Winston looked a little mournfully at his Uncle.

"We can't throw Betty overboard Uncle Frank".

"Well" said Frank "not yet perhaps but if that land doesn't soon get here we are all going to be in the briny if we don't lose ballast"

"But" said Winston "we could get very near and then we could all swim the last little bit together"

There was a long pause. Frank O'Flannagan seemed to be searching for the right thing to say to his dear nephew.

"Are you alright Uncle Frank?"

"Well You see" he began "it's not quite as straightforward as that I have a responsibility to your mother, my sister, to look after you and your Auntie Gloria what would she say I mean Betty is just a mutt?"

"Auntie Gloria loves animals" said Winston.

"Ah yes indeed she does but if she had to choose you know what she would say now Winston you know how much she loves you."

"Auntie Gloria would not choose Uncle Frank she would say we can all swim."

"No she wouldn't Winston trust me."

"She would Uncle Frank I know she would."

"She wouldn't Winston."

"She would, I don't believe you Uncle Frank."

Winston felt terrible he always believed his Uncle Frank because his Auntie Gloria said that Uncle Frank never told a lie, he could tell a good story but that was different, now it was a different, different, and Betty could be in danger.

"She wouldn't Winston she wouldn't because your Auntie Gloria knows my little secret"

"What secret Uncle Frank?" There was a long silence.

"Winston; I cannot swim" Frank said finally.

"But Uncle Frank what about all the times you have taken me swimming at the seaside you always come in with me and Auntie Gloria"

"I have never been out of my depth Winston"

"What about the big waves they used to knock you right off your feet you made Auntie Gloria laugh so much"

"Big waves can't knock you over when you're out of your depth they are just submerging you briefly. I cannot swim Winston. I am sorry but you have to believe me"

"I can't believe that you would throw Betty overboard" said Winston.

"We will be just above the water and as close to the shore as I can get" replied Frank "but we need to get to the shore and dogs are good swimmers." Frank O'Flannagan began to loosen the connecting nut on the empty gas cylinder it cross threaded on the flange and stuck. Frank belted it with adjustable wrench he was using which did the trick. The clang of solid metal on the hollow steel cylinder rang out like a prison bell. The job almost exhausted him and he stood momentarily holding his chest again.

"Are you alright Uncle Frank?" asked Winston.

"I'm fine Winston, I'm fine a little dishevelled perhaps but we're going to be alright we're in the hands of the Good Lord you can be sure that wherever we are your Auntie will be offering up her prayers and He's not going to argue with her, she's enough sadness." With that Frank O'Flannagan hauled the empty cylinder overboard and let it drop towards the sea. Frank sank back into the balloon basket and leant against the gas cylinder cage. The empty cylinder dropped like a torpedo from the sky above straight through the deck, galley and finally the hull of large French Cabin Cruiser carrying a race umpire and support crew for a number of the cross channel swimmers, all citizens of the République Française. It grazed the ships cook who was preparing Mousse de Saumon et Câpres, Filet mignon aux Oignons with Gratin dauphinois a plateau de fromages et salade verte to be pursued with a delightful Crème caramel, all from the ships rations. A huge column of water gushed up through the breach spilling a glass of Chateau Coutet Grand Cru, St. Emilion 1999 that the chef was enjoying as he worked, upending the umpire and showering the crew. Everyone braced for the expected explosion directly beneath them but after what seemed an age nothing happened. And then the cruiser began to sink. The French captain sent out a mayday call to the French coast guards. There was no time to observe the irony (the 'mayday' SOS call is derived from the French *m'aider* the infinitive form of the reflexive verb 'help me'. Some etymologists claim that what the convention really meant was an abbreviation of the phrase '*Venez m'aider*' or 'come help me'). None of this concerned any of the people on board the Cabin Cruiser certainly at the time. The cruiser's retired boatswain activated the auto-inflating carbon dioxide canister stimulated life-raft and began a 'women and children first' routine there were two women but no children. Everyone was hurried aboard the life-raft as the cruiser sank down as far as its gunwale as its hull flooded. Salt sea cooled French cuisine formed a slick on the brine lapped deck. Bottles of fine wine bobbed in the water. The captain was the last to leave his stricken tub. Lifeboats were being launched from opposing shores to rescue the bombed crew. The Royal Air Force scrambled two Harrier Jets to intercept the source of the bomb. Downing Street was informed of a possible terrorist threat to European stability because of the trail of events unfolding on such an auspicious day. One of the most important clues, apart from the incidents with the car, was the reporting of what some believed to be inaudible threats being shouted from the balloon basket in an Irish accent during the attack on the street and again on the sailing ship under the chalk cliffs. Spokesmen on behalf of the major political parties and analysts from Royal United Services Institute tried to weave reason into the ancient mélange of Gaelic, Gallic and Germanic genesis gathering over the English Channel. All agreed 'the race must go on'.

After a while Winston stared ahead towards the still distant shore. Betty wagged her tail which wagged the rest of her. As Winston lowered his gaze he saw objects in the sea below that his Auntie Gloria would call flotsam and jetsam. There was a remote beach that his Uncle and Aunt used to take him to on some Sunday afternoons in the summer. They would park the O'Flannagan Pantechnivan Mk 1 near an ancient Saxon church. Winston knew it was a Saxon church because Miss Powell his teacher said it was because it had a round tower. Winston liked the Saxons. The beach that Winston walked to with his Uncle and Auntie was at the end of a trek along sandy headlands balding of corn in the dryness of summer. Under a sparse canopy of pigeon stained pines, twisted hawthorns, and eternal yews through a narrow causeway of gorse that finally opened onto coarse dune grass tufted, tide sculptured sand. The beach was always covered in what Auntie Gloria called driftwood, and flotsam and jetsam. Uncle Frank would trail behind them laden with a roll of blanket a picnic hamper and the swimming togs.

"Let's celebrate being beachcombers" Auntie Gloria would say as soon as they arrived and would then produce a paper bag full of toffee bonbons. They would collect all manner of bleached wood and sea frosted glass, sea weed, sea shells, unusual pebbles, tousled tarry rope, odd shoes, pieces of cuttlefish for Birtwhistle and the black brackly spawn pouches of the carnivorous, cartilaginous flat skate fish that live on continental shelves and feed upon crustaceans. Auntie Gloria called the black pouches 'mermaids purses' characteristic of the egg laying of oviparous fishes.

"Look Uncle Frank doesn't that remind you of flotsam and jetsam" said Winston pointing to the sea below. Frank O'Flannagan followed the direction of Winston's pointing.

"To be truthful Winston it reminds me of a swimmer" Winston looked closer.

"It is a swimmer Uncle Frank" Winston said "we are going to be alright it must be safe I could jump in I'm a strong swimmer you know I am then you and Betty could make it to the shore"

Frank knew what, his inanimate sextant could not tell him, that the distance to the shore had yet, serious implications for them. Winston was his nephew and he loved him like a son. Winston was the apple of his dear wife Gloria's eye, a most precious cargo. Winston could swim it was true but he could not land a hot air balloon especially a hot air balloon that his Auntie Gloria had no knowledge of. Frank O'Flannagan began to weigh the odds for survival and the consequences of the various permutations of survival should they be blessed this day by the good Lord. If the dog went overboard then the boy would be devastated. If Frank joined the dog overboard then the boy would be in grave danger and non-swimming Frank would certainly be destined for Davy Jones' locker and Gloria would not recover from the devastation of that. Not only this, but it would leave Winston to tell his own Auntie Gloria of how her beloved husband met his end leaving her bereft of family and she still a patient in St Audry's. However if Frank and the boy went overboard and left the dog to land in the balloon as the only survivor that might garner the greatest sympathy with an increasingly animal conscious 'civilized' world although it still left Frank and Winston dead. The boy's best chance may well be to swim but not this far from the shore. If Frank could drift the balloon down as near as he dare to the sea and as close as he could to the distant approaching shore then perhaps..... Frank O'Flannagan was startled from his troubled mind. A splash of water hit him in the eye several more followed splattering his cheeks. A sound like the sound of marbles being spun in large cardboard box with corners grew louder as the rain drops peppered the envelope of the balloon and stung the willow wickerwork weave of the basket.

"Just a shower" said Frank O'Flannagan hiding concern and praying under his breath.

"Are you praying Uncle Frank?" Winston asked.

"For sunshine Winston I didn't want it to rain on your birthday it's a bit like crying on your birthday isn't it?" continued Frank

Winston looked at his Uncle.

"Well" said Frank "if you cry on your birthday then you remain a baby for another year so I was thinking that if it rained on your birthday then it might rain until your next birthday but then no that's probably not the same is it?"

"No Uncle Frank it isn't" said Winston "that's saint Swithin or something."

The two drifted a little further towards France in quiet contemplation.

"Help, help me, help" a voice began calling from below "SOS".

HAUL OVER AGAIN

Winston and his Uncle Frank and the guide dog Betty peered over three sides of the balloon basket down into the heaving swell of foam flecked grey water in the Channel directly in the flight path of the balloon a short distance ahead they could see a person was swimming and the emphasis being on the word 'was'.

"Help I think I am drowning" came a second cry.

"You had better be sure" shouted Frank O'Flannagan "because I only have a few seconds to save you if you need saving"

"Yes well I think I need saving" came the reply.

"Oh well" mumbled Frank to himself" if they change their mind I can always throw them back"

"Uncle Frank?" exclaimed Winston.

"Well you know what I mean because this is going to be more ballast when I have been considering the consequences of less ballast" Frank shouted down to the sinking swimmer "are you absolutely sure beyond any conceivable doubt that you are drowning because as extra ballast you will probably drown the lot of us"

"I am sure" replied the resurfacing, retching swimmer for the second time by Winston's count.

"Uncle Frank how many times do you go under before you sink do you stay under the third time or what?"

"Well if you think about it Winston who can say, a drowned man cannot tell you which sinking was his last and anyone who has watched and counted instead of helping well that in my book is a serious crime so they are hardly likely to tell anyone are they now?" replied Frank.

"I think I may be guilty of a serious crime Uncle Frank" Winston shouted "please hurry"

Frank O'Flannagan, Winston, and Betty the guide dog could not see the sinking swimmer, the swimmer had sunk.

"This is the third time they have sunk since we've been watching." said a worried Winston.

"Well it's definitely not three times and drowned then is it" replied his Uncle Frank as the swimmer broke the surface spluttering and spewing salt sea water.

"Help you've got to help me, please help me".

Frank grasped the grappling hook gathering several loops of best jute rope behind it and began lowering it over the side of the balloon basket down towards the swimmer as the balloon drifted over them.

"You will have to grab this and hold on" Frank O'Flannagan shouted.

Frank had begun lowering the grappling hook on the best jute rope carefully so as not to hit the swimmer who did not look robust enough to withstand a smart clout from the claws and flukes of the hook. As he had begun this life saving procedure Frank's green fungus bandage had slipped down his forehead obscuring his clear vision and making him squint. Through his screwed up eyes the swimmer appeared to be the right distance ahead for Frank to hit the water with the hook before it reached the swimmer so he was biding his time. When Frank pushed the bandage back off his forehead and opened his eyes the optical illusion of his squint dissolved and the swimmer began to rush towards him and under him and past him. Frank let the hook drop suddenly shouting,

"Grab it grab it now!"

The hook hit the water just behind the swimmer and caught his costume threading a single claw of the four pronged hook up under the left buttock leg which began lifting the swimmer up in the water spinning him round and as he rose feet first out of the swell his legs splayed as the blast of hot air Frank had released simultaneously with the contact of grappling hook and sinking swimmer suddenly lifted the balloon skywards just as a gust of wind drove them on. There was a moment when Winston, thinking of the times that his Auntie Gloria had tried to win him the popular toy 'Slugman gastropod extraordinaire the creature who saves the world' from the lucky dip mechanical grab on the pier, watched in horror as the upended swimmer suspended with his wrong end under the water began to squirm as 'Slugman' always did when the mechanical grab slowly spun him out of its grip and back into the tangled pile of tantalizingly trapped toys.

"He is going to fall off the hook uncle Frank do something save him please" he shouted.

Frank O'Flannagan was helpless as the swimmer turned on the single prong, his torso gripped by the swell of the sea.

"Please Lord save the swimmer" cried Winston with his hands pressed flat together in front of his anguished face as Betty stared up at him and wagged her tail and then joined in with a loud spiritual bark. Then miraculously the end of the prong appeared threading its way out through the right buttock leg of the swimmer's costume the flukes ripping into the hem stitching. Frank O'Flannagan reached up and pulled long and hard on the gas chain and a great ball of fire exploded up into the petticoats of Our Lady of Loreto. Within seconds the balloon began to rise faster, fishing the swimmer out of the waves. The needle in the pressure gauge cast a thin shadow into the red warning crescent on the calibrated dial that arced towards empty at the brass pin. Frank knew that there were about two more blasts of hot air left. The swimmer was hooked through the crotch of his costume which was stretching up towards his feet which were now from Frank and Winston's perspective at the top of his legs. He was being held in by his shoulder straps. Frank was pulling just as he had pulled Betty the guide dog up into the basket stepping back to the cage and then hand over hand on the rope back to the edge of the basket and pull again.

"I paid out about forty feet of rope when I threw the hook overboard this shouldn't take long" Frank said "I hope his costume is made of strong stuff."

Winston was staring down at the soles of two blue wrinkled feet poking out of the distended leg holes that had travelled from the buttocks up the legs to just below the Achilles. The skin on the feet reminded him of an osmosis experiment in science at school. The hook had kept on spinning slowly and Winston could see a tightening tourniquet developing on the single prong just above the swimmers feet. The wet waterlogged costume was being stretched on a torturers rack between two thin collar bones and a swelling knot of costume crotch. The small matter of the the poor swimmers dignity was sailing mighty close to the proverbial wind. Despite being under great strain Frank O'Flannagan gave his nephew a look that cautioned discretion in the young man's exposure to such a sight.

"It's quite natural Winston, we as men are considerably affected by the prevailing environment from a private perspective if you understand what I mean." Frank said.

"He doesn't look very, well, normal that's all I can say." Winston replied.

Frank pulled and the Anchor Bend knot wrapped, eye and shaft, of the grappling hook, wrung taut to the wet material, hove into view at the rim of the balloon basket followed in succession by the blue wrinkled feet and goose greasy limbs of the swimmer who slipped and slithered flailing in and out of Frank O'Flannagan's frantic grip. The swimmer collapsed into the basket gulping down great drafts of air and gasping his deep gratitude. Frank opened the cage and foraged for a couple of retired picnic blankets that had been wedged between the steel torpedo shaped gas bottles to act as wadding to cushion cold steel against clanking at landing. He went to wrap the blankets around the swimmer.

"Wait Uncle Frank" Winston shouted "he's got a sea slug stuck on his neck."

Frank grabbed the brown salt stained sea slug and pulled it off the swimmers neck so firmly it crushed and oozed between his fingers and gave off a faintly familiar and rather disgusting smell." There was a long pause.

"It's a bit of business isn't?" Winston said after a pause.

"Fairly much Winston, pretty raw business it is at that" there was a bit more of a pause and then Frank added thoughtfully "well at least we know now that the fish we eat with our chips is organic if they live down there" shaking his hand out over the side of the basket trying to release the human sewage plastering his fingers.

"Organic?" questioned Winston.

"Oh yes organic" replied Frank "it amazes me how people will pay a lot of money for anything grown organically which is a euphemism for not grown with artificial fertilizer but with the real thing straight out of the backside of a living animal and fermented for good measure, some people would have us believe that we are distinguished from the animals by our intelligence but 'organically' speaking we share several common biological processes including fertilizing the food chain I have often wondered" continued Frank "why the local fish and chip shops don't advertise 'Organic' fish because when you see all that stuff floating in the sea surely fish can't breathe without this passing through their system and becoming fish meat. In fact if you think about it fish and chips are one of the most popular meals eaten locally so the fish and chip shop proprietors could even add a further virtue to their advertising not only are the fish organic but they are also regularly recycled."

Winston offered him his red and white polka-dot handkerchief; Frank eyed it up and then shouted "I am afraid I am going to have to take you up on the offer Winston and then throw it overboard."

"That's alright" Winston said "it's ballast; we don't want more ballast do we?"

Frank wiped and Betty licked the sea slugs slimy trail from the swimmers neck before cleaning its entrails from his hand and casting the smeared polka-dots into the grey beyond. Betty began to lick the goose grease from the swimmers face with her business tainted tongue. The poor exhausted man tried in vain to push the kindly dog away. Frank and Winston waited as the swimmer slowly got to his blue wrinkled feet coughing and spluttering and wiggling a left forefinger in his ear releasing a small gush of water initiating the resumption of life in his head. The swimmers costume was stretched and the thin shoulder straps looked more like the braces of a circus clown. The body of the costume was dragged down so that the distended legs holes hung just above their ankles. To Winston the swimmer looked the Cumberland Blue Indian Runner Duck that belonged to Geraldine Troughton, Osborne's sister. (Blue because it is a chromo type created by the incomplete dominance of a heterozygote, itself an organism that has different alleles at a particular gene locus on homologous chromosomes). To the duck Geraldine had given the name of 'Lot'. The duck was given to her as a birthday present pet on her last birthday. Right in the middle of a birthday game of catch just at the very moment of Winston's lunge to catch Ezra galloping in his callipers, the duck being somewhat surprised at the hearty activity of the children laid an egg right in the middle of the Troughton's lawn. The two boys tumbled into the duck and onto the egg scrambling it into the lawn grass. Geraldine had tried to excuse Winston but her father, who had probably paid a 'poultry dealer' over the odds for the duck, did not and Winston took all the blame for 'smashing the priceless egg, because Ezra Shilling was a cripple boy in callipers. Lot the Cumberland Indian Runner Duck was left with a permanent limp and a fear of boys. Lot never laid another egg and had her name changed to Lottie.

"Hello" said the swimmer at last recovering his equilibrium "I think perhaps I should introduce myself don't you?"

He was wearing the number 12 embroidered into a bib hanging limply off his costume and now protecting his dignity.

"I know about you you're in that race I saw you on the television news this morning you are Winston the Hussar and you're number twelve, I'm Winston and I am twelve to" said Winston laughing and introducing himself first "and this is my Uncle Frank O'Flannagan and he saved you"

"What a coincidence" exclaimed the swimmer "you are Winston and I am Winston to" he said turning to look at Frank O'Flannagan "Winston Fotheringay-Hepplethwaite, Lieutenant Winston Fotheringay-Hepplethwaite of the Queens Own and Royal Irish Hussars at your very grateful service sir"

"And what are you going to do?" asked Frank.

"I don't think I understand quite" replied the Lieutenant.

"At your service you said"

"Ah yes well it is a colloquialism I mean you have really been at my service for which I am eternally grateful I think I feel plucked from the threshold of eternity actually at this moment in time" continued the Lieutenant.

"Auntie Gloria would say thank the Lord" said Winston.

"You have an Auntie Gloria to!" said the Royal Hussar.

"Only at this moment in time we are all heading for the threshold of eternity as you put it" began Frank O'Flannagan exasperated "because I have approximately two more blasts of burning gas to keep us out of the briny from which you have just come and my blasts are no counterbalance for the ballast that I am carrying and you sir are still more ballast and this small boy is my nephew and the apple of my dear wife's eye and she the mother of our own dear Michael who has already passed over the threshold of eternity" Frank drew breath "so God forbid that I should make a watery grave for this young sprite" Frank drifted off into silent despair his fear reigniting the pain in his head.

"I think I see" said Lieutenant Winston Fotheringay-Hepplethwaite of the Queens Royal Hussars "we have a challenge and you dear sir"

"Uncle Frank O'Flannagan" interrupted Winston.

"Thank you Winston, Uncle Frank O'Flannagan" continued the Lieutenant "seem to have suffered some injury along the way like my unfortunate self"

Winston looked quizzically at the Lieutenant but could not see an injury.

"Hamstring, it gave out a mile back and I have been trailing a leg ever since tide might have carried me but I was beginning to ship water and then the race support boat has disappeared so I had to keep swimming."

The effort of hauling first the guide dog and then the drowning Lieutenant with brine soaked best jute rope had blistered Frank's hardworking hands red raw and slowly and agonizingly wrenched the pivot of his shoulders. The green fungus bandage had become like a vice around his swelling, pounding head and his grappling hook battered, bruise blackened, knees throbbed. Through encroaching deafness he had shouted himself hoarse. Pain and exhaustion were obliterating Frank O'Flannagan in mind and body and his soul shied from going on because he could muster barely the life to kindle it. He needed an angel now, for Winston, like he had once longed, during the vigil he had kept with Gloria, for an angel for his son Michael when he had clung in vain to this world. They had waited together on God for an angel but they came to accept that the angel was in fact waiting for Michael. Of all the angels, he thought now in scant consciousness, the gas inflated angel directly above him at that moment, had blessed him least of all.

"Don't wait for" Frank murmured deliriously as he finally drifted from pain into unconscious.

"Uncle Frank" called Winston "Uncle Frank."

"Don't worry young man your uncle will be alright and we are going to have to pilot this thing to France ourselves to get him the help he needs" the Lieutenant said assuring his young charge.

THE NEW PILOT

"I think we are going to be alright" said Lieutenant Winston Fotheringay-Hepplethwaite as he wrapped one of the blankets around Frank making him comfortable against the cage and adjusted the other around his own chilling shoulders "you see this is my passion ballooning I have done it for years, Africa, Asia, Australasia, The Americas and Europe you name it; cavernous canyons, Siberian steppes, swaying savannah, waterfalls and mountains, lochs, lakes and land locked seas, deserts and glaciers I love it"

"Have you crossed the Channel before?" asked Winston.

"Actually no not the Channel strange really, I know that it was first achieved such a long time ago 1785 I believe by Jean Pierre Blanchard and John Jeffries that it probably doesn't seem to be a significant achievement anymore."

"What about the pressure gauge?" Winston asked.

Lieutenant Winston Fotheringay-Hepplethwaite of the Royal Hussars looked at the gauge the needle was over half way through the red section of the crescent on the calibrated dial and approaching the brass pin. The Lieutenant then eyed the distant beach.

"I need to ascertain the height of the balloon where is the altimeter?" he asked.

"There" said Winston pointing to the shattered instrument hanging from the bracket above his Uncle Frank's fungus bound head.

"Oh dear" said the Lieutenant.

"What is an altimeter for?" asked Winston.

"It tells us what our altitude is"

"You mean our height"

"Well actually I mean our flight level"

"How does it work?" asked Winston.

"It measures air pressure. Do you have a barometer at home?" replied the Lieutenant.

"You mean the Glass" said Winston.

'The Glass' is a term that always brought his father marching into Winston's mind. In Winston's smellagination those two words 'The Glass' would transport him home from wherever he might be. The wafting essence of boiling vegetables and the silhouette of his father in the dim hallway, seen or imagined depending on where Winston was each evening just before he heard his mother calling him for his tea, coalesced into a vivid smellagination. Countless were the times when his father would pause before the bare wall where once the heirloom had hung. Winston's mother would call out "Tea time" and he would walk forlornly into the kitchen.

"We had a barometer once but it sort of vanished, why, do we need to know the weather forecast?" asked Winston.

"We don't need to know the weather forecast "began the Lieutenant "the altimeter is like a calibrated barometer it actually measures air pressure relative, in our case, to the sea level and it needs to be recalibrated regularly to local air pressure".

"Well" said Winston "we're not exactly local at the moment we're nearly in France".

"Ah yes well what I mean is the air pressure around us, because air gets heavier the nearer to the sea we get and if we don't recalibrate then the readings could be misleading and we could be higher or lower than we think".

"Can you recalibrate that altimeter?"

"I think not" said the Lieutenant "but I do have another idea and therefore I think I will have to free this encumbrance".

The Lieutenant began an awkward dance over and around the grappling hook entwined in the distended crotch of his costume, unravelling the single prong, sliding the wet costume off the claw and gingerly freeing the flukes step by step until it was liberated. He then began to measure lengths of ten feet of the best jute rope working back from the eye of the grappling hook shaft marking each ten feet of rope by tying a bow of bandage torn from the remnants in the Oxo Beef Stock Cubes tin. There were enough bits of bandage for five bows he asked Winston for both his striped socks, he used Betty's collar and, without question, a Colobus monkey skull that Betty had been chewing on that she had found at the bottom of the basket which the Lieutenant used without flinching. One hundred feet was marked off. The Lieutenant then threw the grappling hook over the side of the basket and paid out the rope letting it through his hands until he came to Betty's collar.

"Right" he said "when the hook enters the water we have one hundred feet to descend so that takes care of our height, we just haul the rope in keeping the hook skimming the swell and count of the ten feet calibrations by monkey skull, striped socks and bandage bows".

The Lieutenant turned his attention to the pressure gauge measuring the precious gas now no more than a copper hammered Maslin pan worth of liquid languishing at the bottom of a steel torpedo that, vaporized, amounted to two more ignited blasts of hot air to fill up the skirts of the angelic envelope of the balloon. Two more gentle ascents, two hopeful hops to the safety of France and Entente Cordial. Sleeping dogs were about to be wakened.

"I think we will be alright" the Lieutenant paused "except for this rain of course".

"I like the rain even if it is my birthday" said Winston "which birthday was the last birthday that you cried on?"

"My last birthday was the first birthday I can ever remember crying on" said the lieutenant "my poor mother passed away."

"Did you keep secrets with her" Winston continued "not bad secrets or big secrets just secrets that your dad and you brother and sister never knew?"

"How did you know that I had a brother and a sister?" the Lieutenant laughed "actually we did keep secrets I had forgotten about that. I think actually that I cried with my Mother because I had never really been allowed to cry by my father."

"Really" said Winston quite astonished "did he give you special permission to cry then?"

"No he died several years before my mother. He was a Brigadier in the Dragoons; I come from what some might call a military family, all that stiff upper lippy stuff, history and heterosexuals, heritage and homophobia a kind of class thing I suppose. I did not know my father very well but I did understand that he would not allow me to cry it was to him and his generation an essential responsibility of manhood you know".

Winston thought of his father who had never bothered, whenever Terry had bothered Winston to tears. His father would say 'boys will be boys' except that Terry is a man. Only when Winston's mother intervened with 'aren't you going to sort them out' did Mr Walpole 'sort them out'.

"My father works in a hardware store" said Winston "and my mother is visiting my Gran and my Auntie Gloria."

Frank O'Flannagan stirred unconsciously at the mention of Gloria.

"My brother Bram broke the mould" continued Lieutenant Winston Fotheringay-Hepplethwaite "he enrolled in the Royal Air Force."

"What does your sister do, mine works in a haberdashery."

"That's interesting" said the lieutenant "my sister is married to a member of parliament and has recently become a lady."

"What twenty one" said Winston?

"Ha!" said the lieutenant checking the rope "no she is titled, my brother was knighted for his political service. Now; we're at ninety feet with two blasts of gas left I'd say, at a guess."

A SWOOPING BIRD

Veronica Walpole and Gloria O'Flannagan were returning from a walk in the grounds of St Audry's hospital where, though buffeted by the stiff breeze, they had enjoyed watching a green woodpecker puncturing the turf for grubs under the lee of a long double hedge of Turkey oak (*Quercus cerris*). This foresight of man's planting formed a penetrable avenue border between sympathetic and suspicious worlds since the time of the colony of epileptics. It had initially hidden and eight feet high red brick wall to 'soften' the promenading Edwardians. I later times the wall had been demolished in a further attempt to de-stigmatize the hospital in the minds of the outside world.

"I want to come home, I will be glad to be back making Frank's tea and threading Cuttlefish through Birtwhistle's bars. I know that my time here is done" Gloria said as the two women walked slowly arm in arm "I have been helped as much as I know they can help me." The last group therapy session had been difficult for Gloria, there was nothing more, that anyone could do in this context. She had found her own peace and was reconciled to that day when heaven would make sense of everything for her and she would see her Michael. A visiting Pastor from a local Community Church had begun engaging Gloria in regular discussions, helping her to a deepening understanding of herself. Gloria was beginning to know why she felt what she did and to know that it was alright. Gloria was ready to explore this escape from the exhausting clutches of her recurrent deep depression and its accelerating frequency.

As part of her hospital therapy it had been the third group session that Gloria had attended. The previous two had been an arduous introduction to 'sharing'. She had only really shared as the resident consultant had put it, 'in spirit'. She sat on a chair in a circle of patients who, with the exception of Everton an Afro-Caribbean man of middle-age and a resident of St Audrey's on account of a 'personality disorder', all sat looking at each other and were guided through the discussion in the absence the resident consultant by Bernard a nurse who introduced the session and would begin the questioning. Everton always faced the opposite direction in group therapy looking out of a window. Gloria looked at the circle of faces broken by the back of Everton's head, she felt like she was trapped in a box of frogs. Did they rehearse their myriad facial expressions in front of a mirror inside their own worlds or was the whole external world a mirror rehearsing in front of them, as they walked lonely through the labyrinth of a troubled soul. Every unprovoked expression, every unnatural sound made Gloria uncomfortable in their company. She did not want to control, she wanted understanding.

"Gloria" said Bernard "I believe that it is your turn to start the sharing of thoughts with everyone today and remember everyone that we share a commitment to each other's care."

Gloria silently acknowledged him and glanced around the circle suffering their sensibilities, she fixed her eyes on Barrington Birtwhistle, appealing to the depth of him for some assurance that her heart would be safe if she was going to say anything at all into such an unpredictable forum.

Barrington Birtwhistle, as is natural for a diagnosed manic depressive more popularly known as a bi-polar sufferer, sensed Gloria's need.

"Hello Mrs. O'Flannagan, how is Mr O'Flannagan does he still drive that wonderful old converted ambulance with such character? Parp Parp!"

"Hello Mr Birtwhistle" Gloria replied "my husband is fine and so, as far as I know, is the old Dodge." She thought of Frank, she knew that he was going to be giving Winston a wonderful day out on his birthday and she longed to be with them both where ever they would be and whatever they were up to.

"Oh jolly good" replied Barrington Birtwhistle.

"I came to this place" she began and then faltered "I am in this place for a rest I think that's what we all need" she paused "a rest, it's not selfish is it?

There was some shaking of heads amongst the other patients.

"May I speak Bernard?" asked Barrington. Bernard looked at Gloria and she did not demur.

"Okay Barrington if you are sure you have something to add?"

Barrington Birtwhistle began "I gave thirty seven years of my life to my customers".

"You are not selfish Barrington" Bernard the nurse assured him "we have all talked with about this now this is Gloria's turn to share." Barrington showed a little disdain at the interruption. Gloria continued knowing that she had to otherwise Barrington would. "It feels like I discovered my soul, only after a part of it had been ripped away. Like I never fully appreciated my life until the only life I had created was taken from me. You remember, suddenly without warning, you see another child on their own looking lost, a tune plays somewhere or you smell a familiar smell that was the smell you were breathing in when he made another significant step in his life, something special that being his mother made it so very special. Like when he walked barefoot onto grass for the first time. And when his father blew all the seed parachutes off a dandelion straight into his face counting the time of day."

"A species of the Taraxacum genus" said one of the other faces around the circle "it's deeply toothed leaves give it its name from the Old French for lion's tooth."

"Okay" interrupted Bernard "thank you but it is Gloria's turn."

Silence returned to the group.

"I kept everything. Like our blessed Mary, the mother of Jesus, I treasured all these things about my son, my Michael, in my heart. I vowed that I would never ever let any of it go but you do in moments, unguarded moments that convince you that you are getting over it. One more day that's all I have asked for, prayed for just one more day. We both prayed. I know, that I would know that it was just one day, but I convinced myself that I could cope with that, I could cope with knowing I could hold him at the end, as the angels collected him I could have said goodbye. You see I wasn't there. I had a feeling I knew he was leaving and I wasn't there not when it happened." Gloria began to weep softly as her emotion spilled into the room.

"Why do you pray to a God that you believe must have taken your boy?" Barrington asked "what is the point of your faith after what has happened?"

"I have always prayed" said Gloria composing herself "and Michael was the greatest answer to prayer I ever had."

"Your cruellest answer to prayer surely?"

Bernard moved to quieten Barrington's questioning of Gloria in her honesty.

"It's alright" she said "Mr Birtwhistle is being honest with me" she paused "with himself, nothing about Michael, about what happened is cruel my pain isn't a cruelty Mr Birtwhistle my pain is that I…." Gloria trailed off into a gently welling reverie.

"Well if I thought that God had let me down I would just stop believing in him" Barrington continued.

"That's you Barrington and anyway you are free to that but he is not free to do the same to you he is bound by his own promise" said someone else in the circle.

"Jesus I want to know where we are going to go with this" said another.

"That's a good prayer" was the reply "a good prayer."

Someone stood up others began to fidget increasingly. Bernard remonstrated with them.

"Calm, please everyone we are not caring for Gloria and that is the shared commitment of this group so, calm, please, everyone" Bernard paused "sit down now please Barrington and can you each identify yourselves before you make a contribution" he said directing his request specifically at the groups resident theologian.

There was a period of uncharacteristic stillness, Barrington Birtwhistle sat down loosened his trouser legs, adjusted his cravat and folded his arms and looked at Gloria. Gloria began again this time to draw her sharing to a close.

"Michael could not think like you or me. His emotions were raw, unsophisticated and true. I knew his soul I cared to look because that is all I had of him, his soul within his empty little body. That is what I got. As a mother I really understood who my son was. I thought he might live for longer but I knew he would never share his life or father his own children. He loved everyone so unaffectedly."

"He was a lovely child" said Barrington Birtwhistle "I have often wondered what the hell you must be feeling, thinking? I know three couples who have lost children Gloria in all my thirty seven years of dealing with people, three couples. One woman died of a heart that broke in grief, after ten long years and she was still so young herself. And then there was, can you remember the Tilsons Mrs. O'Flannagan, they started a self-help thing for bereaved parents after Harriet but then they separated and everyone said it must have been because of Harriet. And then there's you and Mr O'Flannagan still together, incredible, thank you Mrs. O'Flannagan thank you."

"There is nothing to separate us" said Gloria "children that die don't separate parents."

At that moment Gloria just wanted to be back at home. She wanted to be packing a hamper for Winston's birthday treat. At that moment she knew that agreeing to enter St Audry's was much simpler than asking to leave would be but she wanted to leave this was not helping her.

"I have been helped by being here I have had my rest and I am ready to go home now."

"Will you go and talk to Michael do you visit his grave to talk to him" asked Everton suddenly, still looking outward from the circle at trees being shaken by the invisible wind.

"I visit his grave but not to talk to him he is not there we should not hold onto the dead they have gone" said Gloria.

"Like David and Bathsheba" continued the theologian in the circle "their first child the one born from their lust it died and once it was dead David stopped praying for it to everyone's amazement because it was gone to be with God."

"It doesn't matter what the circumstances of birth are" said Gloria "lust, abandonment, scientific experiment even, or a happy home, death leaves a void and I believe that we are not meant to fill it."

"I talk to my dead sister because I miss her so much" said another.

"Does she answer you?" asked Barrington "or are you answering for her with what you want her to say, it's a fair question" he added looking at Bernard the nurse.

"I think we must bring this session to a close" said Bernard.

"I understand like this" said Gloria "without Jesus, for me death is an absolute calamity a terrible mystery that left me raw in my heart but I will see Michael again and then I will never lose him."

"Okay thank you Gloria" said Bernard. Someone tried to start a round of applause but Barrington stopped them.

"I want to go for a walk now on my own please" Gloria said to Bernard "I feel exhausted."

I don't know about you but dredging deeply to express ourselves is exhausting, it is for me and I have seen it in others. I've seen someone find a sorrow they had buried forever somewhere deep in their own soul a long time ago. I have listened to spoken words breaking amidst the plaintive release of truth and watched a body drained by the fathomless exercise of sheer emotion. To realize something in our innermost depths is more exhausting than any other single human endeavour. But when it is met, with understanding, given context and acknowledged as being real, when it is answered, it is like life begins again. Understanding ourselves at the very essence of who we are it is possible to explore this escape from the exhausting clutches of recurrent deep depression and its accelerating frequency. Personally I don't believe that we should label emotional lives that have lost their reference points they are not irretrievable. We should not isolate in mental illness some who simply got in touch with what they really thought about themselves because that is what experience had taught them.

Gloria and Veronica sat down in the comfortable armchairs next to Grandma's and looked up at the ever present television from where Ranjit Livingstone was once more reporting on the world.

"As I said at the top of the programme it has been an eventful day" the studio news programme anchor man said "This is a second report filed by our busy Ranjit just before he boarded the ferry for France to cover the end of the cross channel race. Some viewers may find scenes in this report disturbing these scenes also contain some use of flash lights".

Ranjit appeared on the cliff top overlooking the beach from where he had reported the start of the cross channel race and filed his interview with Lieutenant Winston Fotheringay-Hepplethwaite of the Queens Own Royal Irish Hussars in the morning. He was surrounded by hundreds of people with telescopes and binoculars who had been stomping around in Wellington boots and water proofs looking for something. There was also a small group of Morris dancers huddled together amongst the crowd. Pictures, beamed into the report from a news agency helicopter hovering halfway up the bald white chalk of the perpendicular cliffs, showed the silhouette of a figure strung up helplessly just below the grass fringe upon which stood a solitary police officer, a clergyman, Ranjit and his crew and the large crowd of people with their telescopes and flasks of tea, binoculars and bird books standing around in their Wellington boots and waterproofs watching, open mouthed, the hovering helicopter.

"Viewers you have an advantage over the rest of us gathered here on the cliff top because just below me dangling high up on the cliff face you should be able to see a man trapped by the straps of his rucksack and all we can hear is his rather disturbing cries for help".

With this the helicopter cameraman zoomed in focusing close up on the trapped man's face and his animated mouth. Ranjit continued his dialogue into Colin's microphone 'off camera' as viewers watched the hanging man's tortured expression twist with silent pleas for help. He seemed aware of voices above him but uncertain of his surroundings and as he mouthed his anguished cries Ranjit rambled.

"Unconfirmed reports are suggesting that the person hanging so precariously up here is in fact a local blind man who had his guide dog plucked away from him while he was out walking, in all probability it would appear by a large predatory bird swooping out of the sky. Expert ornithologists around me claim that there can be no disputing that this mysterious bird is in fact the European Eagle Owl, Bubo bubo, absent from this Island country since the eighteenth century. A native of mainland Europe and particularly Scandinavia it is a carnivorous creature capable of taking a small deer. The sighting by the blind fellow just over the cliff from me of the rarest and largest owl in the world is an extraordinary event that has drawn hundreds of avid avian fans winging their way from all points of the compass. Word spread fast amongst the ornithological fraternity and bird spotters have flocked to the area from all over the country today. The local roads are completely congested and this is rendering rescue almost impossible at this stage. The Royal Society for the Protection of Birds known to many of us as the RSPB are working with the local Fire and Rescue Service and the St Johns Ambulance Brigade who are at this point vainly trying to get through to the scene of this bizarre accident. The man has been dangling there for some hours now. There is of course much speculation as to what the bird could be. You may be able to hear people in the background arguing. Opinions were being aggressively aired, ornithologists disagreeing sharply with a 'side' of Morris dancers who claimed that it could just be a migrating stork blown off course, lonely and looking for companionship. The dog's name has been released as Betty and police are concerned for her safety. The man who is a local whose name will not be released until his next of kin have been informed."

"It was not a bird it was an angel" a voice uttered just as Ranjit's cameraman took over the coverage from the helicopter.

"Oh my goodness" said Gloria "its Barrington, the therapy group have gone on an outing today they must have gone to the cliffs."

"To the cliffs!?" exclaimed Veronica "who's crazy idea was that?"

"Barrington's it was his turn to choose the outing" said Gloria "he loves the coast he says that feeling the swell of the sea and the overwhelming sway of the wind in his soul helps him to know that he is alive" Veronica Walpole looked at her sister-in-law quizzically. "He won't be alive for much longer if he tries to feel the swell of the sea from the edge of those cliffs" she said.

"I'm sorry it's just the way he puts it" Gloria answered.

Colin 'Herb' Sage thrust his microphone at Barrington who had pushed through the 'side' of Morris dancers and was standing in front of Ranjit.

There was the sound similar to the crackle of hazel and hornbeam kindled by a sudden gust through a brush fire, as newshound photographers clicked and captured the image of a bowler hatted Barrington Birtwhistle stepping thrusting Morris men aside.

"It was an angel" he repeated "it swung a twirling grapple and grabbed the dog it was our nurse Bernard who called the police and my friend John sent a text to his brother who watches birds

231

because that man down there" Barrington pointed over the cliff edge "kept saying it was a huge bird the biggest bird I have ever heard and John believed him because he was going to the toilet in the gorse when the angel flew over the rest of us."

"Right" said Ranjit turning to the camera with a knowing twinkle in his eye "it was an angel and you heard it first on this station."

"We were over there on that mound watching the Morris dancers practicing out of the wind when the angel appeared from nowhere it breathed loudly kidnapped the dog and tore through the swimming banner and vanished slowly out over the sea" Barrington paused "it was truly an inspiring sight" Barrington looked serene as he told the truth about what had really happened.

Ranjit turned to the Squire and the Foreman of the 'side' of Morris dancers beside him.

"What kind of a dance is 'out of the wind'?" he enquired. This rather took the Squire by surprise who stood and stared at the camera becoming increasingly crimson with embarrassment.

"I think what the gentleman meant was that he and his party were out of the wind." the Squire of the dance offered.

"A party?" said Ranjit "you perform at parties?"

Again I don't know about you but embarrassment is what I feel whenever I watch Morris Dancers. I'm not sure if it's because I regard both of us as English, me and the 'side' of dancers hopping and skipping and hankerchiefing about in pub car parks and village fetes to the sound of fiddle, melodeon and tabor, the rattle of slapping sticks and the ringing of 'brassed' 'Noddy' bells against leather pads. It may be that I haven't travelled far and wide enough to realize that it is not a uniquely English custom. I do not believe that Gallic or Latin Morris practitioners would dance quite as the English do. In fact it quite suits such a phlegmatic tribe as the English. It's a peculiar thing but I think I also have to admit though that I wouldn't want to lose them, they make me feel culturally unique amongst my brethren in our multi-cultural society as long as they don't come too close. I need to add here that in the pubs where I come from the Morris men and women have little respect for the sensibilities of other folk local or visiting. They take up valuable parking space to execute their folk dancing and when they take refreshment in the bar or lounge they insist on loudly singing their ditties and playing instruments that have limited popularity amongst the pub goers of today.

"We don't perform at parties no but we are Offcumduns" said the Squire, the crimson draining from his face as he regained composure "we were practicing the hop hoodening procession for the blessing of the hop harvest."

"I see" said Ranjit "interesting."

"Yes" said the Squire "it is a custom that we uphold in the Cathedral of St Augustine the first Archbishop."

"Ah" said Ranjit "it wouldn't have anything to do with angels would it?"

A small, old and slightly stooped lady stepped forward she was a member of Gloria's therapy group at the hospital. She wanted to speak to Ranjit, the roving reporter. She beckoned to him to incline himself down in her direction.

"It was Our Lady of Loreto" she said referring to the Angel "I know because I saw it when I was a little girl on the day that the diving showman died in the elephant's bottom."

The lady, her name is Matilda, had spent the best part of her life in St Audry's remaining through various National Health Service transmogrification's of the single purpose of protecting society from its more vulnerable members. She had been committed into the care and control of the institution as a child because she had suffered a pathological withdrawal from communication with the world around her. A withdrawal which no-one understood but everyone with even the slightest knowledge of catatonia had diagnosed for her own good. Her rigidity condemned her. Her stockbroker father and her ballet dancing mother suffered her condition for almost a year but they suffered more deeply and more personally the stigma of possessing her, so they gave her away. A decision had to be taken. It was. And everyone agreed that it was the right thing to do for her dear mother and her very important father. You see when Matilda was five years old she witnessed the shocking fate of the old showman at 'A Most Spectacular Show' and the sorry sight of the suffering elephant. She had been standing with her Nanny beside the shallow tank of imported spring water waiting with her brothers and sister to be splashed by the diving showman.

It was the third day running they had attended the show. They knew exactly what to expect except that the freak gust struck and in the ensuing stampede of shocked show-goers Matilda was neglected by her Nanny as her siblings scattered. She wandered slowly between hysterical women and sonorous men in the melee, until she stood in the fearsome, human hemmed clearing beside the twitching torso of the old showman with an elephant for a head. A pause, the length of which would cast the rest of her life, was finally broken when the Nanny dragged her brothers and sisters through the cordon of petrified adults and gathered the child. It was too late she had witnessed the death throes of the showman, the hideous bellowing of his stricken elephant and the incapacity of the capacity crowd to prevent the deepening horror. Following her compassionless, incarcerated childhood Matilda had spent her early adolescence working in the kitchens of St Audrey's and for a time in adulthood had been allowed, by the liberals of the day, out into 'the community' to enjoy 'normal' employment in a local privately owned hotel working as a as a kitchen maid, washing dishes in an outhouse amongst the fusty odour of potato sacks packed with Annabelle, Anya or Apache, Melody or Mozart and every Maris this and Maris that. On occasions during her residency in the staff accommodation provided by the owners of the hotel, she had been taken advantage of by one ignorant kitchen porter and subsequently returned to the hospital without redress, because there was no one to bear witness to a horrible, gynaecological termination. And then to her old job in the deep and drear flagstone floored hospital kitchens with their high window panes. Ranjit did not know, he could not know that he was the first person to hear Matilda speak since that fateful day, more than fifty years ago. This time surely the growing significance of the surrounding events of the day would not allow Matilda to become lost again.

"Why doesn't somebody help Matilda doesn't anybody realize she is speaking?" Gloria said as she watched her fellow inmates especially Matilda telling their truth to an unbelieving world.

"It was an angel" Barrington repeated to Ranjit "escaping to France."

Bernard the nurse stepped forward and spoke gently to Barrington and to Matilda. Bernard put his arm around Matilda and continued to speak to her to coax her, desperate to secure the awakening.

"Cheerio everyone" Barrington said directly into Colin's microphone.

"Now there's a thought" said Ranjit continuing his report "an escaping angel."

"And other matters of national importance" interrupted Sir Cecil Pitt MP as his constituency agent and PR guru ushered him through the amateur ornithologists and Morris dancers and once more in front of the cameras for another media opportunity, courtesy of a private helicopter delivery "today is littered with a series of suspiciously linked incidents don't you think Rastus?"

"Ranjit!" said Ranjit.

"I am deeply concerned for my constituents who find themselves unwittingly in the front line of political criminality."

Sir Cecil began recounting the litany of events that began with the hijacking of the iconic French car when the sirens of the rescue teams in their adequately equipped emergency vehicles, though somewhat delayed by the activities of the ornithologists, finally heralded their arrived.

Gloria turned to her sister-in-law and sighed at the thought of all that they had just witnessed through the miracle of John Logie Baird's invention and then asked,

"Do you think the angel is finally leaving?"

"What angel Gloria?"

"You know the angel old Mrs. Posnerowa used to talk about in Sunday school."

"Thomas has told me about her all those years ago, how before the morning service she used to teach the choir boys the Catechism and the Collect for the day in that lovely Welsh accent and all, but he never mentioned any angel."

"Isabel Quadling she was by her maiden name, she married Gideon Posner the pawnbroker. My mother used to tell me about her how she cared for the wounded in France during the evacuation of the beaches, she received a distinguished medal of honour from the French government a few years ago. She used to talk to us about the war and about the bravery of men and women who sacrificed their lives for us like God's own son. We tried to get to the truth about Gideon her husband and how he had escaped the Nazi death camps but she would never ever whisper anything."

"What did she tell you about this angel then?" quizzed Veronica.

"Well just that she believed God had posted angel to guard over our country to protect its democracy to preserve all our freedoms never more so than at the battle of Britain."

"I suppose it is feasible" said Veronica "seeing as how it all turned out."

"Everyone was praying at that time everyone I ever spoke to about it said it was an answer to the thousands of prayers being prayed that this blessed island was saved by an angel" Gloria continued "and now that very angel is leaving us, the angel God sent to watch over us."

"Leaving for where though?" Veronica pondered.

"France, Israel, Heaven, I don't know" replied a troubled Gloria "we might not be here and this country would not be where it is today without that angel."

"If it was an angel, I mean why would an angel throw cars about and push a blind man over the cliff that's not very angelic is it?" questioned Everton who wasn't on the day trip, wasn't actually watching the television either but was clearly listening to everything.

"Where would this country be without the men and women of our wonderful emergency services?" declared Sir Cecil Pitt MP to his captive television audience as the rescue teams prepared to retrieve the blind man from over the cliff edge. A cliff trimmed by a woven morass of camouflage covered bird watchers and the random floral garlanded Morris man and woman and flecked with the honest faces of St Audry's fascinated few. Once more the audience witnessed the aerial perspective being beamed back by the helicopter. The blind man hung absolutely still, suspended by his rucksack straps.

"I hope that his next of kin are not watching" said Veronica.

"Is that crowd trying to push a foreign man over the cliff" Grandma suddenly shouted startling everyone in one corner of Henry Currey's Victorian pavilion "what is this country coming to?"

It was true Ranjit's dusky complexion did rather stand out from amongst the ornithological caucus and occasional Morris men. No doubt had Everton been in the party from St Audrey's and true to himself he would be facing in the opposite direction to everyone else leaving the dusky Ranjit quite alone in the sea of white complexions.

"They are not trying to push him over the cliff mother" said Veronica "it's Ranjit, Ranjit Livingstone."

The regal round head of Sir Cecil Pitt suddenly appeared to fill the television screen again.

"These brave men and women deserve our full support" he turned gesticulating to the crowd "stand back give them room to operate."

Ranjit moved back with the crowd as Sir Cecil conducted them.

"Angel or terrorist that is the question facing us all tonight" he began "and who is the man dangling on the cliff face, conspirator or casualty of a calamitous catastrophe? This is Ranjit Livingstone for the news in your region sponsored this afternoon by Bang and Cook; Suppliers of Wild Game to the discerning table" said Ranjit expediently executing a broadcasting 'wrap'.

INTO THE SOVEREIGN AIR OF FRANCE

Lieutenant Winston Fotheringay-Hepplethwaite lifted a couple of coils of the jute rope and created a noose. He stepped into the noose and dragging it up his blue wrinkled legs gathered the loose folds of his distorted costume around his waist and fastened them in place. Frank O'Flannagan did not stir from his pain induced stupor as the Lieutenant began searching out any object he did not deem necessary for the remainder of the flight.

"Winston can you see if there is anything below us in the water" said the Lieutenant

"All clear" replied Winston being drowned out by a barking Betty.

"Pardon" said the Lieutenant.

"All clear" shouted Winston with Betty now springing up and down in their corner of the basket to get a glimpse of what was going on. The lieutenant threw some spare rubber gas piping and all of Frank's tools overboard along with the damaged altimeter. There was only one sea soaked bandage bow, two striped socks, and a guide dog's collar visible on the best jute rope alternative altimeter.

"We are about thirty six feet out of the sea allowing for the depth of the basket" the lieutenant announced on inspection of their position "I think that I need twenty feet of grace after a blast of gas so tell me when we are half way between the socks Winston".

Winston watched carefully as the sea came up to meet them.

"What about a high wave?" he asked.

"Good point but not to worry it won't stick to us" replied the Lieutenant "count me down from ten".

Lieutenant Winston Fotheringay-Hepplethwaite was suddenly making the journey even more exciting for Winston on his birthday.

"Ten.....nine.....eight.....seven.....six.....five.....four.....three.....two.....one" each of Winston's counts reverberated with a bark from

Betty. The Lieutenant pulled on the chain simultaneously engaging the remaining gauge in his eye line the needle hovered perilously close to the brass retaining pin at the outer limit of the Red Crescent on the calibrated face of the dial. The balloon dropped the second striped sock towards the heaving surface of the sea before it began to rise. Flecks of sea spray, mixed with the driving rain, stippled the contents of the basket like the first flakes of snow.

"That was close" shouted Winston as the grappling hook leapt from the waves.

"It will not be enough" said the Lieutenant "we must jettison as much ballast as we can find".

Without further ado he began hauling the four hundred feet of best jute rope overboard. The rope snaked at a gathering velocity over the rim of the basket until it tightened against the noose knot that belted the folds of his costume. Lieutenant Winston Fotheringay-Hepplethwaite was towed abruptly into collision with the willow wickerwork weave of the basket.

"You could use Uncle Frank's machete to keep your costume up" Winston suggested.

The Lieutenant looked at Winston.

"It's on his belt" said Winston pointing to his Uncle Frank "you can cut the rope with it".

The Lieutenant tugged on the rope drawing enough slack to bend down to where Frank O'Flannagan lay comatose. He undid Frank's belt and threaded it out from the loops on his waist band the machete fell to the side, the Lieutenant put Frank O'Flannagan's belt around his own waist loosened the jute noose and stepped out of it the rope then continued snaking over the side of the basket. The end of the best jute rope had been dipped in a strong wax to guard against fraying as it flew out of the basket it whipped back flicking the lump of wax which hit Lieutenant Winston Fotheringay-Hepplethwaite squarely in the area of the groin and just below the protection the gathered folds of distorted costume might have afforded him. The Lieutenant let out an excruciating howl and fell on top of Frank O'Flannagan. Frank erupted from his unconscious. Throwing the lieutenant off he stood bolt upright at which point his beltless trousers fell down, on reaching his full stature he passed out, as his head had arrived ahead of the blood and oxygen needed to operate it, collapsing back on top of the hapless Lieutenant.

"Are you okay? Winston called down.

"I think I am" replied the lieutenant his face partially obscured by Frank O'Flannagan's bare hairy thigh "I do have a terrible pain right where it hurts".

Winston remembered his brother Terry telling him about a game of football he had been playing in one Saturday afternoon. His brother was a terrific left winger for the Corinthian Casuals football club. He was known locally as 'Walpole the Whizz'. Terry had got injured when the opposing right fullback in attempting to kick the ball up field with 'Walpole the Whizz' bearing down on him had not got enough lift behind his kick so the football had struck Terry inflicting incredible pain, in his words 'right where it hurts'. Terry had to be stretchered off by the St Johns Ambulance Brigade. Winston had always been a little bewildered by this 'grown up' expression as he was not sure pain could actually be anywhere other, than where it hurts!

"Right" said Winston.

The Lieutenant managed to slip out from under Frank and continue to throw ballast overboard. The Oxo Beef Stock Cube tin and its First Aid contents went next. Winston undressed down to his birthday vest and pants released Betty from the guide dog harness and tossed garments and harness overboard with his tuck box.

"That's awfully brave of you Winston" said Fotheringay-Hepplethwaite.

They both looked down at the approaching sea. They were flying about two hundred feet above the water but were in uncontrollable descent again. The coast was about half a mile ahead. The biting, rain cooled air, pressed down on the lukewarm balloon envelope. Lieutenant Winston Fotheringay-Hepplethwaite looked at Frank O'Flannagan and then towards his nephew Winston Walpole, birthday boy, twelve years old today. He remembered some of Frank's last words before he drifted beyond pain 'this small boy is my nephew and the apple of my dear wife's eye' and 'don't wait'. He weighed the options. They had one more blast of gas enough to lift them a couple of hundred feet and they were little under half a mile out to sea, Frank was unconscious so they could not ditch. The wind had dropped they were now drifting quite slowly. They would probably need the last blast very soon at a quarter mile and inches above the rolling sea. All of a sudden there was the sound of approaching jet engines and two Royal Air Force Harrier aircraft came up from behind the balloon or put another way from where the balloon had come earlier. The Harrier pilots were in radio contact with French air traffic controllers. They were requesting permission to enter French air space in the execution of Ministry of Defence orders to shadow a suspected dangerous terrorist threat that had swept across the channel from England leaving a trail of destruction on a day previously designated to be unique in the history of Anglo-French relations. One of the pilots was Squadron Leader Bramwell Fotheringay-Hepplethwaite known affectionately to his brother Winston as 'Bram'. Winston's brother was the lead pilot. He was approaching the balloon with caution employing the incredible engineering of the imperious Sea Harrier to control his approach whilst talking to the French.

"Squadron Leader Bramwell Fotheringay-Hepplethwaite British Royal Air Force requesting permission to enter French air space"

"What is the purpose of your visit?" the French controller replied.

"It is not a visit" said the squadron leader "it is a military operation."

"A military operation, we know nothing about a military operation" came back the reply "what is the purpose of this 'military operation?"

"To intercept suspected terrorists and to protect the lives of French citizens" the Squadron Leader replied.

"Surely m'sieur that is our job and one of which we are very capable."

"I am not questioning your capability it's just that we were alerted to the threat from our side first and have been scrambled to action. I understand Downing Street is fully aware."

"Downing Street who is this person?" the French air traffic controller queried.

"The British Prime Minister" replied Squadron Leader Bramwell Fotheringay-Hepplethwaite.

"You must think we are stupid if you think we would believe that 'Downing Street' is the British Prime Minister is, even the French know who the British Prime Minister is!"

"It is where the Prime Minister lives not their name, it is a euphemism for the prime minister's office, now for goodness sake I am requesting permission to enter your air space."

"According to my radar screen you are already in our airspace and this euphemism are you saying the prime minister is not really who we think he is?"

"No; he is who we think he is."

"Then he is not who he thinks that he is?"

"I don't know who he thinks he is."

"Is he listening to this conversation?"

The French interrogator was interrupted by the British prime minister "Squadron Leader Fotheringay-Hepplethwaite this is your prime minister speaking please pursue your mission, over."

"Who do you think you are?" came the French controller retorted.

Bramwell Fotheringay-Hepplethwaite barked "Look I haven't got time to sit here chatting with you Kermit are you going to let me in..."

"You are in" interrupted the controller.

"....or do I have to take this to someone in real authority?"

"What is your beef?" the French controller could be heard laughing at their own joke with colleagues.

"That is in very bad taste" said Squadron Leader Bramwell Fotheringay-Hepplethwaite.

"It was not the taste it was the madness of the cow" replied the French controller to more guffaws from his compatriots

"There is a hot air balloon in the shape of an Angel which I am informed is Our Lady of Loreto drifting into France carrying suspected terrorists who have already caused considerable damage in England and sunk a French boat in the channel."

"Then we must inform the Italians."

"Why?"

"Because it is Italian!" said the French.

"Why would the Italians want to scupper an Anglo-French occasion like this with acts of blatant terrorism?" asked Bramwell Fotheringay-Hepplethwaite.

"I don't know I don't understand the Italians but this balloon it is something to do with the house of the Virgin Mary being carried by Angels to Italy to protect it from the Turkish" said the French air traffic controller "I studied this in history class many years ago perhaps it is a protest on the same day to get maximum publicity, the Italians they are showing off, anyway you cannot come in we will deal with it from here."

"What" shouted Squadron Leader Bramwell Fotheringay-Hepplethwaite "what do you mean we can't come in this is a serious threat."

"We do not believe you, it was not the intention of the Joseph-Michael and Jacques-Étienne Montgolfier to use the balloon for aggressive purposes, we think that you are jealous and want to shoot this balloon down over the place of the birth of ballooning and we will not allow this you are the terrorists not the Italians!"

"That's preposterous the Italians are nothing to do with this" exclaimed Bramwell Fotheringay-Hepplethwaite as he looked sideways upon coming up level with the balloon.

"You have crossed the line on our radar screen you must turn back or we will have a diplomatic incident on our hands."

"What the!" began the Squadron Leader looking directly at the visible occupants in the balloon basket "Winston what are you doing Winston."

"It is no good trying to invoke Churchill or Nelson, Wellington or Henry we will not be defeated on this occasion and anyway you are probably a son of William the Conqueror yourself anyway if you are English" interrupted the French controller.

Lieutenant Winston Fotheringay-Hepplethwaite looked at the roaring Sea Harrier beside the balloon basket and recognized through the cloudy cockpit canopy glass his brother who had removed his high altitude breathing apparatus and was mouthing something to his brother.

"Bram" Winston Fotheringay-Hepplethwaite shouted each could see the others mouths moving but, neither of them being lip-readers of any note, could not understand. The balloon was descending towards the sea below for the last time there was one more blast of hot air left.

"That's my brother Bram in his aeroplane" the lieutenant shouted to Winston.

"Nice of him to follow your race" Winston shouted back now that they were having to communicate above the roar of the accompanying Sea Harriers.

"Yes, pity he won't see me win but there we are, nice to see you Bram but we must get on" he mouthed to his brother and then turned to prepare Winston for his jump into the sea. The lieutenant looked at his small charge and considered for the final time the plan he had settled on in his own mind. Lieutenant Fotheringay-Hepplethwaite's plan was to put Winston into the water to save the uncle, the dog and himself providing Winston could swim. The permutations of every other option left him no choice. Ditching short of the beach meant probable drowning for him and the unconscious Frank uncertainty for Winston and for Betty, if she surfaced facing the wrong way, a long swim back to Blighty. Ditching the basket was dangerous anyway if the deflating angel envelope caught a gust of wind it would become a sail and drag the basket onto the rocks dashing it into myriad splinters of piercing seasoned willow, certain death by acupuncture. Lighter he could save the unconscious uncle and the bedraggled Betty by getting it over the shore line.

"How much do you weigh Winston?" the Lieutenant shouted.

"Not quite one hundredweight" replied Winston.

"Can you swim?"

"Yes I can swim half a mile I have got my bronze award for swimming"

"In the sea?" he asked.

"In my pyjamas actually" shouted Winston "I can swim in the sea and our local swimming pool has a wave machine" said Winston proudly "Osborne and I can both swim a mile actually, we did it last week it's all because of Ezra really."

"Do you fancy a short swim in French waters?"

"Okay" shouted Winston "I think I can manage that especially as I am not wearing my pyjamas, will I need a passport."

"They are very bureaucratic, but we'll have to risk it."

THE PARTY GOERS

Veronica Walpole had made her way home on the bus from St Audry's after she had said goodbye to her tearful sister-in-law Gloria who had so wanted to see Winston on his birthday but was not yet allowed out. Veronica had failed to persuade the hospital to let Gloria come home with her even for just one night. Veronica soon busied herself back at thirteen Captain Scott Terrace as she prepared her young son's birthday party treat. She had been met by a rather obsequious Terry only too willing to help in the preparations for his 'baby' brother. Veronica 'smelt a rat' but set him a task and then switched on the oven to cook some cheese scones. There was a knock at the door and Terry answered it.

Osborne and Geraldine Troughton stood on the step with Ezra Shilling hiding behind them.

"Wah!" shouted Ezra and Terry dived between the twins and grabbed him picking him up and swinging him round a few times until they were both dizzy. Ezra loved it.

"Good job the dizzy gothic has got my present or I would have dropped it Terry" he said. Geraldine gave him a 'you crushed my Lottie' look.

"Who's got your present?" said Terry.

"I have" said Geraldine he thinks he's funny.

"Come in then you lot" said Terry.

"Is Winston here?" Geraldine asked hopefully.

"We are expecting him shortly" replied Terry "what's that Oz" he asked Osborne.

"The swimming shield that me and Winston won it's his turn to have it" said Osborne.

"It's not a birthday present then, I was beginning to wonder why anyone would want a shield for a present."

"A Viking would" said Ezra.

"Oh shut up Ezra you've got an answer for everything you have" said Geraldine.

The four of them walked through the hallway towards the kitchen where Veronica Walpole was busying herself until Terry reached the bottom of the stairs at which point the three friends stopped.

"That's interesting" said Osborne pointing to a barometer hanging on the wall "is that a barometer?" Terry pretended not to hear Osborne's question, took a diversion and walked quietly up the stairs.

"It was once" called Veronica from the kitchen "now it's just a birthmark of the wallpaper."

"More like a huge mole" said Ezra.

"The only mole here is in the garden creating little hills out of that creeping ballast heap" replied Veronica.

I have an admission to make here something I have wanted to get off my chest for some years now. Like a lot of young men (and maybe even some young ladies) I did get up to a bit of mischief when I was growing up. No malice was ever intended proof of this I believe is the ease with which misdemeanours faded, seemingly guiltless, from my memory. Until now that is. You see it is possible for someone to permanently borrow something (I prefer this to the term stealing) and many years later to return it as a matter of maturing conscience. I experienced this with a beautifully hand painted effigy of a Moor, a mediaeval Muslim inhabitant of the Iberian Peninsula intricately carved in one piece of wood that used to hang outside the tobacconists in the main street of the town where I grew up. The old tobacconist used to hang this unusual character over the shop door when he opened at the start of the day and take it down when it was time to close. One night I was walking home alone from a party that had been held in a flat over the travel agents just up the street. Quite by chance I looked up as I passed the tobacconists and the Moor looked down on me resplendent in his majestic turban and flowing robes. Ezra Shilling would be interested in the Berbers, as they were known, because they conquered Christian Hispania which was inhabited by the Visigoths. Anyway I reached up to shake him by his proffered hand by way of an introduction and found that he did not let go of mine and the next thing I know is that I am holding the ancient Moor, historic symbol of the Tobacconists trade. Now it may have been the warm balmy air of the summer night, I may have thought of it as an ideal token of love for a girl I remember having a crush on around that time or it could have just been the effect of something I had eaten or drunk at the party but rather uncharacteristically I felt compelled to keep the Moor, to enjoy his companionship. I kept him for several years. To my shame the tobacconist retired and later died. The shop had become a shoe shop mainly because the supermarkets didn't sell shoes in that era and then a photography shop selling cameras, and I forgot about the Muslim Moor. And then, and here's an irony I discovered my Christian moral compass and in an act of genuine repentance I returned the Moor to his perch aloft the camera shop door. I returned a lot of other things I had borrowed but none had such significance as the beautifully carved Berber conqueror of the Visigoths. The following week the local newspaper carried a story about the return of this historic figure which was donated to the local museum by the camera shop owner. The shop was subsequently leased by a charity that sold all sorts of things, donated by the public, back to the public. Which when I think about it is like an indirect charity tax that the government levy by stealth to cover the cost of important agencies of care having already collected the original tax on everything. It works like this the more the government tax the people the poorer they become the more they shop at the charity shops. What the government need to wake up to is the fact that the more this goes on the lower the quality of the items donated thus creating a vicious circle of trade. The first signs are beginning to appear of the results of this with charity shops closing down because they have failed to compete with other charity shops. Sorry I digress.

Osborne Troughton stood admiring the barometer mounted on the Yew wood he stepped forward and tapped the glass. The needle moved upwards slightly in an anti-clockwise motion like one tick of a second hand on a clock going back in time.

"It's going to change" said Osborne "my father has one of those Admiral Fitzroy mercury barometers with all the writing about rising and falling and wet and dry behind the pressure gauge thing and the thermometer." Veronica Walpole had walked into the hallway as she listened to Osborne talking about the 'missing' barometer. She saw for herself the instrument hanging where it had once hung on the day she made number thirteen Captain Scott Terrace her home as a young bride full of hope and joy. It took her breath away. As an ornament it was misplaced. As a piece of wood it was indomitable, almost spiritual and as an instrument it was invaluable, prophetic of the uncontrollable, precautionary in the forecast. The sight of the long lost barometer returned something to her so much so that she did not question why it was there but joined with the children in admiring it. It was a moment of magic in the true sense of it being mysterious and transforming. Terry walked back down the stairs after composing himself in the bathroom.

"Good grief mother" he exclaimed "I remember that thing it's Dad's old barometer didn't it go missing or something, have you found it then, he's going to be like a dog with two tails he is."

"I am not sure if we are looking at a miracle here Terry" she said before returning to the needs of the children "what do you think Geraldine?"

"I think" said Geraldine being, as ever practical, in the company of two of the three boys "that Winston is going to get a fine on his library books if he doesn't soon get home."

"My goodness" said Veronica "you're right, Terry could you run your brothers books to the library please before it closes?"

"Okay" said Terry glad of the distraction.

"I could come with you and choose some more books for Winston" said Geraldine "I know what he likes to read."

"Okay" said Terry "let's go to the library."

As Terry walked along with Geraldine towards the town library he asked her if she had seen the balloon that had caused so much damage in the town or if she had seen the ridiculous broadcast by 'Roving Ranjit' on the breakfast news that morning. She hadn't because along with Ezra, her brother Osborne and her mother she had taken the train up to the city to get a present for Winston and to see her granny. Terry related the whole episode on the way to the library. Geraldine was disappointed that she had missed everything because when she grew up she wanted to be a story writer and she said this would have made a good plot.

WINSTON IN BRINE

There was one last blast of gas left in the remaining steel cylinder. The lieutenant had to employ this single breath of potentially lifesaving hot air with absolute precision.

"Right" shouted the lieutenant to Winston "I think I have a plan so listen carefully this will get us all home safely. I am of course prepared to sacrifice myself you understand I could jump overboard but then there is no guarantee in going down that route for you and your uncle's ultimate safety I mean who would fly the balloon and I am a qualified balloon pilot?"

"Yes" shouted Winston "Auntie Gloria cannot lose Uncle Frank as well".

"When we are within a few feet of the waves I want you to slip over the back of the balloon basket and into the water and swim you will probably reach the shore before us as we will hopefully rise straight up as high as the blast will take us for one last time but don't worry just keep swimming I believe that you will have the tide with you. Now, let's get you ready".

The lieutenant began scraping what grease remained on his arms and legs balling it in his hands and then slapping it into Winston's palms.

"Oh dear" boomed the lieutenant "do you have a skin disease?"

"No it's calamine lotion" Winston replied "my mother made me wear it because of my vest and pants they itch".

"It is most appropriate if you spread this gunk on yourself" shouted the lieutenant "it will help protect you."

"From what?" asked Winston.

"The cold." replied the lieutenant, which was actually not true as it is a pretty ineffective protection as is the alternative lanolin taken from a sheep. More mess than protection.

Winston spread the grease without enquiry further trusting in the Lieutenant's judgement.

"What is a Hussar?" Winston asked after a while.

"It is originally a fifteenth century Hungarian horseman of the light cavalry" the lieutenant responded proudly.

"Are you Hungarian?" Winston continued.

"No it's one of those words we English have borrowed and not returned".

"What like the Elgin Marbles?" Winston replied.

"Well yes I suppose so really" continued the lieutenant "several yards of frieze, a few sculpted panels and seventeen life sized marble figures from the Greek's Parthenon that was around five hundred years before Jesus Christ is as valuable as a word like Hussar" he laughed.

Thinking of the value of words Winston remembered that his library books were due back today. Every third Saturday Winston went to the local library with Osborne, Geraldine and Ezra who loved the history shelves, and today was a third Saturday. Some of his birthday money would be wasted on a fine.

"What?" asked Winston "is a Dragoon, like you father?"

"Well it is not dissimilar to a Hussar in being a horseman except that we Hussars carry a blade into battle and the Dragoon carries ordnance". Winston looked at the lieutenant.

"A gun Winston; I suppose the Hussar is somewhat more elegant and refined and the Dragoon fierce yes, fierce as a dragon. Now have you finished smearing that grease it will keep you water proofed and warm I hope and less nearly one hundredweight of best ballast we shall be safe to the shore your Uncle and I".

"Can Betty stay in the basket?" Winston asked.

"Well she might be a guide dog on dry land but she could swim the wrong way out to sea so we had better let Betty stay".

The balloon drifted along unhurried, the sea once again coming to meet them.

"I will count you down Winston then try to lower yourself into the water using the step holes when I get to three, when you get to the shore line boulders of rock you will have your hardest task climbing ashore but you will be alright, we are nearer to the shore than I could have hoped".

Winston shouted goodbye to Betty telling her that he would see her again soon in France. He climbed out over the rim of the balloon basket and down to last two woven holes in the willow wickerwork weave. He looked into the grey swell, the rain peppered his face and he asked God to make the water warm and safe.

"Ten" began the Lieutenant
"nine…..eight…..seven…..six…..five…..four…..three"

Winston stepped out of the woven holes his feet trailed in the cold water. The hug of the tide pulled him away from the basket and he let go his grip. He sunk and his ears filled with a peculiar whistling and his nose filled with the 'organic' ocean brine. Winston kicked his legs and clawed at the water pulling his body up. His chilled head broke the surface and the sound of little waves breaking on the summits of the swell around him replaced the whistling. The lieutenant shouted down encouragement to him as the sound of the last blast evaporated above. The balloon rose, Winston hoped to safety. The swell lifted him onto a crest to see the shore and then dropped him into a trough to pray. Under his breath he asked God to help him swim and breath, with this he grew in confidence and struck out for the shore. Winston thought about his mother and his father, about Terry and Rosemary and the photograph sitting on the mantelpiece the photograph where they were all together and happy sitting in the back garden in their house in 'Superbia'. Winston wondered what they would all be doing right then, while he was swimming the longest hundred or so yards of his twelve year life, one enormous 'Wale' of a journey.

Winston was finding the swim challenging not least because he was in the French sea which just felt inexplicably peculiar and unpredictable. The tide was definitely a rising tide that would carry him to the shore if he could stay afloat. The waves passed him on their way in lifting and dropping him revealing and then hedging the rock shore. Gulls screeched and wheeled above him Winston had expected them to screech with French accents but they did not appear to. He saw the balloon with the ballast of an unconscious Uncle Frank, excited Betty and the lieutenant drift overhead towards the headland of France still escorted by the noisy Royal Air Force Sea Harriers. Winston's wonderfully knitted woollen underwear weighed heavy in the French water and his Gran and his home seemed a long way away. Wool is not the most appropriate material to use in the construction of a long distance or for that matter short distance swimming costume but swimming in Winceyette had prepared him well. Winston was finding that salt sea soaked wet wool weighed heavier than his fear of not reaching the safety of the rocky outcrops of the Cap Griz Nez. He tried to tread the waves in order to shed the heavy load of his sagging dragging birthday suit but it clung to him. Winston began to swim again drained to the bottom of his body, mind and soul. The sea picked him up and carried him on. The remembrance of his little party with Ezra and Osborne at five thirty reawakened with his desire to see Geraldine and to steal that first perfectly legitimate 'birthday' kiss. On he swam fearless and hopeful. And then joy of overwhelming joys one of his big toes on the end of one of Winston's tired trailing hanging heavy legs stubbed into the stone pudding seabed. Winston swam a few more strokes to be sure and then stood, up to his shoulders, upright in the forward current hard against the sea stained rock. He found a foot hold beneath the waves, grasped at the rocks waited for another surge of the tide to lift him and then scurried like a crab up onto the safety of the rocks rising away from the invisible level S on the Plimsoll line. (*S is the level of summer seawater it comes below TF tropical freshwater F freshwater and T tropical seawater and above W winter seawater and WNA winter North Atlantic*).

In the sky above Winston as he lay exhausted on the rocks there had arrived four Dassault Mirage 2000N airplanes of the Armée del l'Air the French Air Force. These had been on exercise close by and were ordered by the French Ministry of Defence, to intercept and escort Squadron Leader Bramwell Fotheringay-Hepplethwaite and his fellow pilot in their two Sea Harriers to Avord Air Base for an international violation of French sovereignty. Following a meeting with the President of the Republique. The Squadron Leader had radioed back to his base information concerning the occupants of the balloon basket confirming that the threat was under control due to the intervention of a Queens Own and Royal Irish Hussar working undercover although he did not name his brother. He also expressed his considerable pique at being 'advised' to comply with the orders of the French air traffic controller to follow the Armée del l'Air back to base. Winston sat up and watched the balloon carrying his stricken uncle and his new found friends, drift in land. He was so pleased that his Auntie Gloria would see them all again. He gradually stood up and began to clamber over the rocks climbing towards a large banner which he assumed marked the end of the race that the lieutenant had been competing in. Suddenly people appeared over the short horizon of the rocks and grey French sky, official looking men in bowler hats and smart mackintoshes wielding clip boards, waving towels, bearing sheaves of aluminium foil and crates glucose drinks, followed by English policemen in uniforms and helmets and then more smartly dressed men in the uniforms of the Gendarmerie or the customary cap and tricot of the Breton. They surrounded Winston, the English contingent showering him with congratulations wrapping him in towels and tin foil, gathering him up and carrying him shoulder high across the rocks towards a firing squad of camera lenses and Ranjit Livingstone. The French contingent just eyed him with deep suspicion and there was much mumbling amongst them.

BACK AT 13 CAPTAIN SCOTT TERRACE

Terry and Geraldine arrived back at thirteen Captain Scott Terrace just a few minutes ahead of Thomas Walpole and his daughter Rosemary who had kindly been given a lift home in the red Routemaster double-decker bus in the company of Tertius Napoleon Sawadogo, his extended family and Clement Christmas Longfellow Cobb. Geraldine was showing Veronica which books she had hurriedly chosen from the library for Winston. Terry had gone out into the backyard to kick a football with Osborne and the energetic Ezra. Thomas, on seeing a football hit the chimney before bouncing back from where it had been propelled, alighted from the bus thanked Tertius and decided to go through the gate to the backyard to see what other possible damage had been inflicted upon his precious greenhouse windows or his cage of 'Autumn Bliss' raspberry bushes.

"Would you like to come in for a cup of tea?" Rosemary kindly asked everyone on the bus "it's my baby brother Winston's birthday, I'm sure that he would love you all to come in."

Veronica Walpole was not exactly used to seeing the equivalent of a small African tribe file into her kitchen at tea time but being a thoroughly hospitable soul and wise to the vagaries of the world she simply asked her daughter who wanted squash, tea or coffee and put the kettle on. Most of the children in Tertius Napoleon Sawadogo's party quickly collected a beaker of Robinson's flavoured barley water fruit squash and headed for the backyard to join in the football game developing between Terry and the two boys, Osborne and Ezra.

"Wow" said Ezra as the children poured out onto the makeshift 'pitch' "we could have a cup final Oz".

"Let's pick up sides then" replied Osborne "your team can be skins and we'll keep our shirts on."

Terry appointed 'Oz' and 'Ez' to be team captains, organized all the African boys into a long line and then took out a coin and asked Ezra to call 'heads' or 'tails'. Ezra's call was good so he began team selection. Not knowing any of the other boys or how good they were selection became rather 'natural' being based on the phenotype. Ezra motioned to the African boys that he had picked to take their T-shirts off so that they would all be the same except for the goalie a position Ezra was giving to the sturdiest looking boy.

"You'll have to go in goal Ez" said Terry.

"Why" asked Ezra who hated being in goal.

"You're the one with the goalies jumper on" replied Terry slapping Ezra's lily white skin.

"No he's not" exclaimed Long Clem who loved a game of 'footie' "I'm on your side Ezra."

Long Clem pulled a pair of fingerless gloves from his pocket and put them on before steering the sturdiest boy into the 'centre half' position.

The language barrier was no obstacle to a group of boys in possession of the round leather ball and once the young ladies in the party could see what was happening they quickly gravitated to Geraldine and Rosemary who were digging out the old dressing up box that Veronica had 'packed away for posterity' a couple of years before under the stairs. The sisters of the man from Burkina Faso made themselves comfortable in front of the television which Rosemary had switched on to the watch any news reports that Colin may be involved in involving the extraordinary race across the channel. Thomas Walpole still standing in backyard looked on bemused as Terry began refereeing Troughton's Tigers versus Ezra's Academicals in the Captain Scott Terrace Cup Final.

Thomas Walpole finally walked into his overcrowded dressing room cum kitchen and gently kissed his wife on her cheek.

"How is Gloria?" he asked.

"She's much better I think they will soon let her home now, I don't think there's much more they can do to help her, you know Gloria she will work it out for herself and she has been helped a lot by this new Pastor fellow" Veronica replied "where on earth did you find all these people?"

"They came in this afternoon with Gustav and the three

musketeers."

"What is Clement doing with you?" asked Veronica.

"Well" began Thomas "he was with Frank and Winston and so far all he has said is that Frank and Winston should be home in time for the party because he thought Frank would probably be returning in a taxi but I have to say he looked a bit sheepish when he said it."

"From where" Veronica asked her husband "they were only going for a short balloon trip."

"Going for a what?" began Thomas.

"A balloon trip, that was Frank's treat for Winston I didn't mention it to Gloria for obvious reasons."

"I just hope that he wasn't on the balloon trip that I witnessed this afternoon" said Thomas.

"Perhaps I could help" interrupted Tertius "only we followed the balloon for a while and it looked as it was going to land the last time we saw it."

"The last time you saw it!" exclaimed Veronica.

"Mum" screamed Rosemary "look!" she was pointing to the television it was the 'News in your Region'.

"Look out" said Terry summoned from the cup final by his sister's scream "it's roving Ranjit again I wonder if he has swum the channel yet". The studio news anchor man was talking over the picture on the screen.

"And now thanks to those giant Goonhilly dishes we can go live to Ranjit who is close to the shore at Cap Griz Nez awaiting the winner of the Anglo-French Cross Channel Race, Ranjit....Ranjit can you hear me Ranjit?"

Ranjit Livingstone was standing next to Winston who was unwrapping himself from aluminium foil that was bouncing the exploding flash bulbs of the paparazzi back at the camera. He looked bedraggled and bewildered. He was looking beyond the camera being pointed at him to where his sister's 'Herb' was operating a large fluffy microphone wondering if he was going to speak to him instead of just sticking his thumb up, nodding and grinning.

"Good evening" began Ranjit "it is the end of a long and arduous day for Winston the wonderful number twelve who, as our early morning viewers will recall, I interviewed this morning from Shakespeare beach and I think he deserves a loud hurrah for the brave Hussar." Winston just stood staring at Ranjit overawed that he was in the presence of this famous television personality for the second time in his short life.

"Well done Winston you are a national hero today" continued Ranjit "we English are all very proud of you we have triumphed yet again over the French." Winston wasn't really listening he was thinking about what he would be telling Osborne and Ezra and especially Geraldine and then he thought of Geraldine and the kiss he was hoping to elicit in the genuine context of his birthday party.

"I have a party to go to" said Winston.

"You certainly do" shouted Ezra who had abandoned the cup final to stare at the television "hurry up we're hungry."

"I am sure there will be plenty of parties for you to go to" said Ranjit.

"I don't recognize that bit of seaside we don't have rocks like that around here do we" said Winston's mother "have we ever been there Thomas?"

"I don't think Ranjit recognizes it's the wrong Winston" replied Thomas.

"He probably remembers him from the railway bridge incident" added Rosemary. Geraldine just stood watching Winston quietly admiring her friend who was once again featuring in a special news report from the roving Ranjit Livingstone. Suddenly someone in the background of the television picture began shouting in French.

"Oh" said Veronica "that's nice the losers are cheering that's very sporting I like the French very cultured they are."

The studio news anchor interrupted Ranjit as he continued to talk about the sporting English "I am sorry Ranjit but we have to interrupt you there as we are going live to Downing Street where the Prime Minister is just coming out to speak to reporters" and with that the large black door with its consequential polished digits of one and nought loomed up before everyone watching at number thirteen Captain Scott Terrace.

"Nombre dix" shouted one of the members of Ezra's 'skins' football team who was standing at the back.

"Premier Ministre" replied Osborne who quite enjoyed French class at school.

The Prime Minister had momentarily paused before the rich cream coloured interior of possibly the most famous door in the world and was looking up at the light streaming in through the glass of the peacock fan window above. The ornately traced minute hand of the grandfather clock built by John Benson of Whitehaven in the 18th century ticked though the number ten and into the month of March marking the minutes above the hour of two. This is the loudest it gets since Winston Churchill had silenced its music and in that moment before a Prime Minister emerges to face the world it is the sound that goes deepest into the soul, the passing of all time towards the coming of a time. From the First Lord of the Treasury this threshold of Mercy's seat has awed even the 'Iron Duke' the liberator of Europe. Arthur Wellesley, product of Dublin and the Irish peerage, of Eton and of the Royal Academy of Equitation, Angers, France. Even he and how his life somehow shadowed this moment must have felt that common feeling of all who attain such office. The brilliant lacquered Downing Street black door opened and the Prime Minister stepped into the little street and approached the gallery of world press walking across the grey brickwork to a bank of microphones. A thousand light bulbs flashed and cameras clicked.

"It's the Prime Minister" shouted Ezra.

"As many of you will know" began the Prime Minister "there have been reports of an incident in the English Channel earlier today that may be related to other unconfirmed acts of terrorism. There cannot be at this stage any credence given to the allegations that these acts are related to a political cause that has dogged the history of Great Britain and its closest neighbour The Republic of Ireland. As your Prime Minister I can confirm that we are currently working with the French government at the highest diplomatic levels to understand why two Royal Air Force fighter planes have violated French air space and our pilots taken hostage. I will be flying to Paris following this briefing to meet the President of French Republic for discussion which we both hope will produce a solution."

The questions began to fly;

'Was this retaliation for cheating in the swimming race' came through clearly above the cacophony of more politically astute questioning. The Prime Minister looked blankly at the inquisitors.

"I wish they would go back to Ranjit" said Veronica "I want to see where Winston is."

"I understand that the winner of the race may be under some suspicion" said the Prime Minister "but I can confirm from early intelligence reports from one of the captured pilots that the winner of the race or otherwise was in fact also working undercover and was responsible for a single handed act if extreme bravery in securing the safety of the French by disarming the alleged terrorists." The Prime Minister thanked everyone for their patience and support at such a time of international concern before getting into a large black ministerial cavalcade of cars and, escorted by armed outriders, sped forth from Downing Street in the direction of the Palais de l'Elysées on the Rue du Faubourg Saint Honoré.

"Good" said Veronica "perhaps now we'll see Winston again."

SOME CORNER OF A FOREIGN FIELD

Our Lady of Loreto was seen safely into France by the French escorts of the Armée del l'Air, carrying the suffering Frank O'Flannagan and his saviour Lieutenant Winston Fotheringay-Hepplethwaite of the Queens Own and Royal Irish Hussars slowly down into a yellowy brown field of ripe garlic. There had been little need to 'brace', the basket had made an almost perfect landing under the experienced handling of the qualified lieutenant. The deflating angel drifted down enveloping the basket in her voluminous skirts trapping the pungent perfumes of the garlic, anesthetizing the two men into a state of unconsciousness to await their fate at the hands of the gendarmerie just arriving in the field.

Winston stared at the sky above the silhouette of Herb's bobbing head as he walked towards the 'birthday boy'. The sky was ripped, bleeding incandescent pink gold into smoking clouds and offering a glimpse of heavens pure, blue headland.

"Can I go home now" he asked emboldened by adventure "I have a girl to kiss."

To be continued.....

ABOUT THE AUTHOR

Stephen Hall lives in Suffolk and has worked in farming all his life. Born in the early 1950's he has witnessed much social and economic change. In working within the farming community throughout the country and attending a small vibrant local church he has been kept close to the heartbeat of life. His story telling is a translation of the experiences shared and singular that shape life and make it what is, something to be celebrated.